I0823368

HOUSE GLUTTONY

STORM OF SINS

HOUSE SLOTH

HOUSE PRIDE

THE FLAMING TOMBS

HOUSE ENVY

HOUSE GREED

BLOODWOOD FOREST

THE WICKED

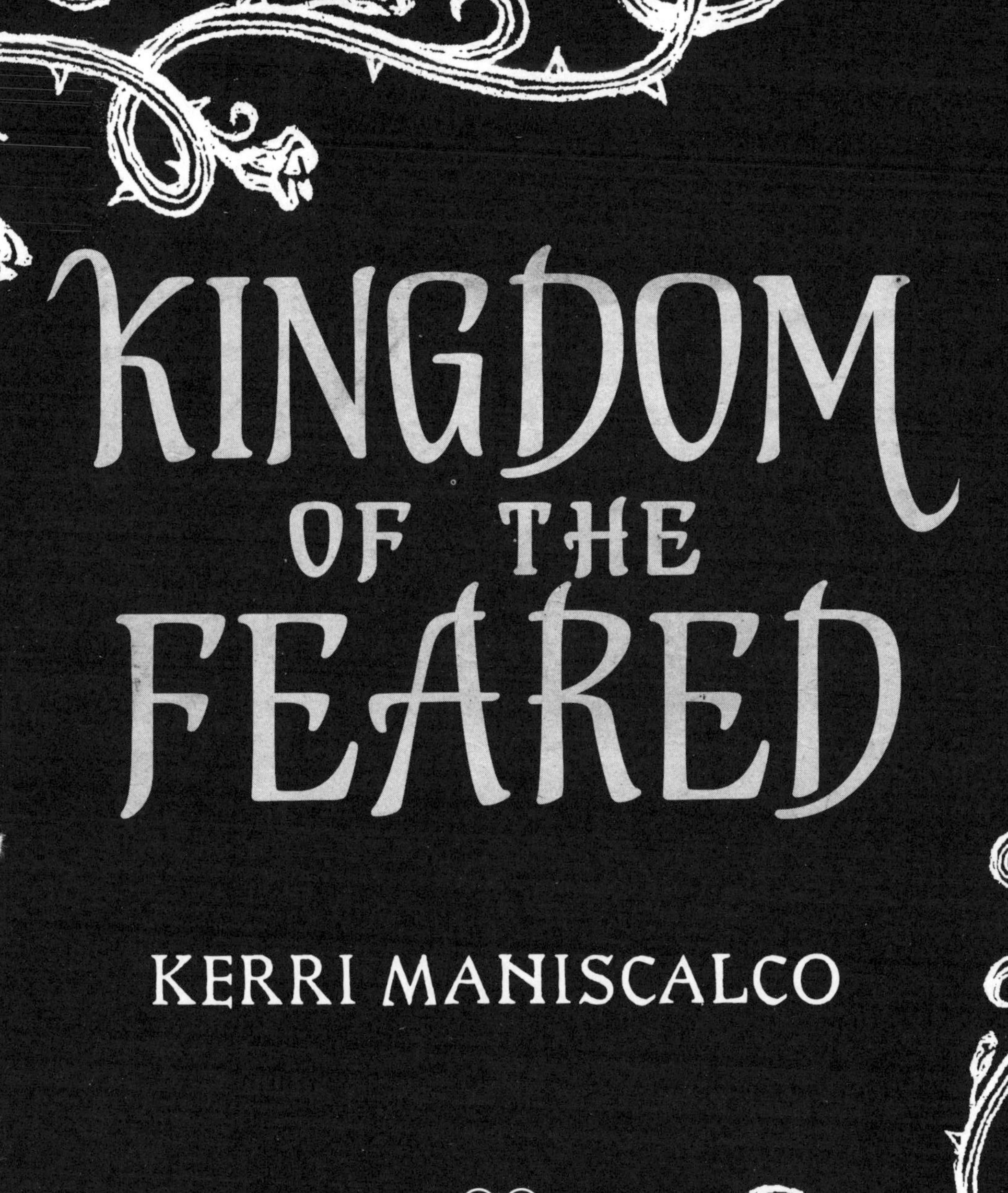

# KINGDOM OF THE FEARED

KERRI MANISCALCO

LB
Little, Brown and Company
NEW YORK BOSTON

Little, Brown and Company
Hachette Book Group
1290 Avenue of the Americas, New York, NY 10104
Visit us at LBYR.com

First Edition: September 2022

Little, Brown and Company is a division of Hachette Book Group, Inc. The Little, Brown name and logo are trademarks of Hachette Book Group, Inc.



Library of Congress Cataloging-in-Publication Data
Names: Maniscalco, Kerri, author.
Title: Kingdom of the Feared / Kerri Maniscalco.
Description: First edition. | New York ; Boston : Little, Brown and Company, 2022. | Series: Kingdom of the wicked ; 3 | Audience: Ages 16+. | Summary: Emilia is determined to clear Vittoria's name when she is implicated in the murder of a high-ranking member of a rival demon court—even when her investigation forces Emilia to face the demons of her own past.
Identifiers: LCCN 2022019884 | ISBN 9780316341882 (hardcover) | ISBN 9780316342087 (ebook)
Subjects: CYAC: Demonology—Fiction. | Blessing and cursing—Fiction. | Supernatural—Fiction. | Sisters—Fiction. | Twins—Fiction. | LCGFT: Paranormal fiction. | Novels.
Classification: LCC PZ7.1.M3648 Kih 2022 | DDC [Fic]—dc23
LC record available at https://lccn.loc.gov/2022019884

ISBNs: 978-0-316-34188-2 (hardcover), 978-0-316-34208-7 (ebook), 978-0-316-52942-6 (international), 978-0-316-48563-0 (Walmart special edition), 978-0-316-47988-2 (B&N special edition), 978-0-316-50826-1 (Bookish Box)

Printed in the United States of America

LSC-C

Printing 2, 2022

*Trust in your heart, dear reader; it will always guide you where you need to go.*

## BY KERRI MANISCALCO

**STALKING JACK THE RIPPER**

*Stalking Jack the Ripper*
*Hunting Prince Dracula*
*Escaping from Houdini*
*Becoming the Dark Prince*
*Capturing the Devil*

**KINGDOM OF THE WICKED**

*Kingdom of the Wicked*
*Kingdom of the Cursed*
*Kingdom of the Feared*

# KINGDOM OF THE FEARED

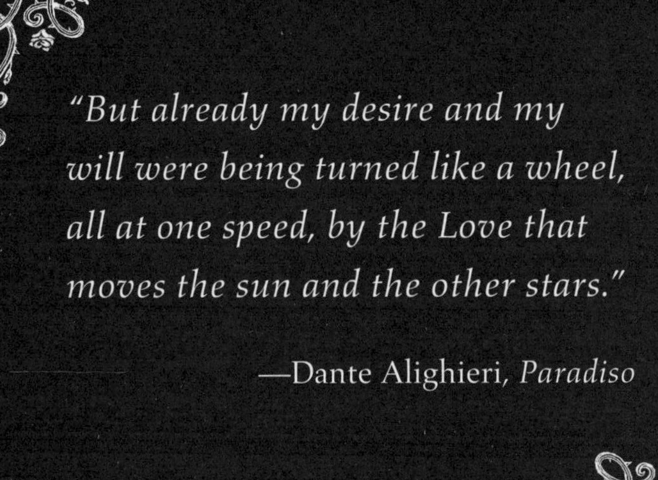

*"But already my desire and my will were being turned like a wheel, all at one speed, by the Love that moves the sun and the other stars."*

—Dante Alighieri, *Paradiso*

*Once, the Prophecy of the Feared was thought a myth, a story of divine vengeance passed down through the centuries. It served as a warning of the chaos and destruction that Death and Fury could bring if unleashed. A tale two enemies should have recalled well before they cursed each other in a fit of rage. On that fateful night, two powerful magics converged, binding each party from uttering—or sometimes even remembering—the full truth. The curses had even greater consequences none had predicted. For years, demons and witches tensely awaited the day when all would finally be revealed. When that midnight hour arrives, it's advised to stock the home with ambrosia and nectar and pray to the goddess for mercy.*

—*Notes from the secret di Carlo grimoire*

# TWENTY YEARS BEFORE

**Coven elders seldom** agreed on anything, save for two matters considered to be their highest of laws: The devil should never be summoned. And, under no circumstance, were black mirrors ever to be used for scrying.

As one of the best seers on the island, Sofia Santorini believed some rules were meant to be broken, especially when her newest visions kept whispering troubling tales in her ear. It was those insistent murmurs about the dangerous prophecy connected to their curse that finally convinced Sofia to steal the first book of spells: the only grimoire that outlined how to scry with dark magic. The fate of the coven might very well depend on her actions, sanctioned or not.

Though, at the last meeting, the council hadn't sounded *quite* so grim. They didn't need to. Sofia had sensed the shift of magic the way birds felt the turning of the season, listening to that innate warning to fly away, to survive. A violent storm was gathering on the horizon. She had no wings, and even if she did, Sofia refused to flee without her family.

Breaking two rules to potentially save dozens of witches seemed like the right thing to do. Any information Sofia could gather about the curse before either the Wicked or the Feared took their revenge would only benefit their coven. Surely the elders would understand.

Placing the black mirror on the floor in Death's temple along with the foil-stamped spell book, she gathered her skirts and knelt before the objects. A shudder went through her that had nothing to do with the cold stone seeping through her thin muslin layers. She stared into the forbidden mirror, its inky surface reminding her of the still waters of a lake she'd once visited to collect freshwater stones for her spells.

Except this surface didn't have any soothing moonlight shining overhead, blessing her path. In fact, it seemed to devour any light that dared to touch it. Any manner of demon might be lurking below the unknown depths, waiting to strike.

She exhaled the fear away. It was time to do what she'd come to do, then go home to her family. Removing the slim dagger from her skirt pocket, she held the point to her fingertip and pressed until a bead of blood welled up, red as the devil's eyes.

Rising back to her feet, Sofia walked to the altar in the center of the room. One didn't perform magic in a goddess's temple without first paying tribute.

On either side of the altar, fire crackled in the offering bowls she'd lit earlier, the tendrils of smoke curling through the air, as if beckoning her to step into the underworld. She swore she felt eyes on her, watching from the shadows, waiting to see if she was bold enough to cross that forbidden boundary. Sofia's gaze swept around the quiet chamber, falling on the two human skulls she'd stolen from the monastery. Dark days called for even darker deeds. She'd not falter now.

Holding her pricked finger over the first of the two offering bowls, she watched blood droplets sizzle then steam as they met the flames. Sofia quickly moved to the other side of the altar and repeated the gesture with the second bowl.

Satisfied she'd paid enough for the goddess to grant protection, she turned and retrieved the skulls, ignoring the bloody fingerprint she left on the bone. Kneeling once again, skulls placed on the north and south points of the mirror, she opened the spell book and began chanting.

For a few tense beats, the mirror remained unchanged. Then smoke started swirling within its surface. Slowly at first, then picking up speed like the hell winds she'd heard gusted through some demon circles, confusing the poor souls unlucky enough to find themselves there.

"Goddess, protect me."

Sofia leaned closer to the mirror, anxious to learn all she could about their enemies. Any information might prove valuable, especially since all their memories were slowly being consumed by the curse with each passing full moon. While she stared at the mirror, a window to the underworld cracked open, giving Sofia her first glimpse of the demon realm.

"Show me how to break our curse."

The mirror pulsed as if the magic acknowledged her request and agreed to grant her wish. In place of the smoke, strange images began flickering over the darkened glass, and Sofia quickly realized she was being shown a story through a series of still pictures. She let out a quiet breath. Thus far, despite the forbidden magic she'd used, it was similar to her usual visions.

The magic propelled the images to leave the mirror and swirl around her as if she were standing there the moment they happened. She saw a dark throne room, a furious demon.

Bits and pieces of the familiar appeared, but the magic must not have been working. Certain images weren't aligning with their history or what Sofia knew of the prophecy. She watched as a witch, who must be the First Witch, cursed that demon. Her vengeance and hate were so powerful Sofia could practically *feel* it through the illusion.

Next she saw a strange well with crystals—memory stones, thousands of them. The scene abruptly shifted again, this time to a small cottage overlooking the sea. A young witch—one she knew well—gripped a memory stone in one hand and a dagger in the other. The First Witch had been there, too, handing the witch the stone that would take away whatever she wished to forget. The images faded, needing more magic to fuel them.

"Wait!" Sofia cried out.

Desperate to learn more, she gripped the skull resting on the south point and whispered a spell that made it shatter, scattering bone shards across the dark surface, hoping the mirror would use them to fuel more images. And it did. Except once more they weren't quite what she'd expected. Sophia saw her island, then flickers of other unfamiliar cities and times bleeding in and taking over. The images had to be wrong.

Yet...if they weren't, then everything the coven elders had told them had been a lie. Including where they were from.

It was so preposterous; there was no way that could be true. Determined to figure out the mystery, she reached for the last skull. This one had rubies in its eyes, an added gift for the goddess who ruled over the dead. Sofia shattered the skull and was immediately thrust into another time, one where that same young witch from earlier appeared to be...a rough hand came down on Sophia's shoulder, shaking her from the vision.

Heart thundering, Sofia blinked until Death's temple came back into focus. Fearful of what—or who—had torn her from the vision, she snatched her dagger and shot to her feet, her attention landing on the person who'd interrupted. The robed figure tossed back the hood on her cloak, revealing a familiar, stern face.

Sofia's shoulders slumped forward as she lowered the blade. For one frightening moment, she thought she'd summoned an enemy. "Thank the goddess it's you. I've learned something incredible about our curse and our city. I know who the First Witch's daughter is, at least I think I do. You'll never believe this discovery."

Sofia was too full of dark magic, too shaken by the truth she'd learned, to notice the dangerous gleam entering the other witch's eyes. "Neither will you."

"I don't understand—"

With a flick of her wrist and a harsh curse, the witch cast a spell that knocked Sofia backward. Her skull cracked against the altar, causing her to see a bright flash of stars that left her momentarily stunned. Before she could gather her wits and utter a protection spell of her own, Sofia's mind fragmented just like the mirror the other witch stomped on, destroying the truth still playing across its dark surface.

Sofia opened her mouth to scream but found herself unable to do more than speak in tongues. Soon all she could see were those strange images the mirror had shown her.

If she'd been about to call for help again, Sofia couldn't remember why.

She stared, not truly seeing, as the other witch retrieved the first book of spells and slowly made her way through the temple, never once glancing back at her friend. All the while Sofia quietly repeated one phrase, a chant, a benediction, a plea.

Or perhaps it was the key to unlocking everything…

"As above, so below."

# ONE

**All at once,** candles flared to life around the Prince of Wrath's bedchamber.

Despite my best efforts to not grin at the demon, my traitorous lips curved upward on their own. Tracking the small action from where he stood on the balcony, the prince's attention moved to my mouth and remained there a beat longer than necessary.

His heated stare coaxed a different kind of warmth to spread over me just as gold-tipped flames erupted in the fireplace, sizzling and crackling like mad.

It was a welcome feeling, especially after the coldness that had swept in earlier and settled in my bones. Seeing my sister in the Triple Moon Mirror broke something vital in me.

Something I refused to examine at the moment.

Lingering near Wrath's bed, tunic now discarded at my feet, I knew it wasn't his namesake sin that had the fires blazing in his private chamber. It was the desire he was struggling to control; the passion I'd ignited when I chose him—knowing *exactly* who he was—and still agreed to become his wicked queen. Since he'd already stolen my soul, I was now offering him my body. Without games or magical bonds urging us together. Without focusing on Vittoria and the way my heart ached each time I thought of my twin's deception.

My eyes prickled with unshed tears just thinking of my sister now, and I tried desperately to rein in my emotions. Wrath would sense my hurt, and it was a conversation I didn't wish to have. That sorrow could wait until I met my twin on the mysterious Shifting Isles tomorrow and heard what she had to say.

Until then, I didn't want to spend another minute wondering why she'd faked her death. Or how she could hurt me so horribly for so long. I'd already given Vittoria months of my tears and fury while on my path to avenge her.

Tonight I simply wanted Wrath. Samael. King of demons. Most feared of the seven immortal princes of Hell. General of War and the literal devil. Temptation and sin made flesh. A nightmare to some, but to me he currently looked like a dream. And if the cursed demon didn't crawl between the sheets with me this instant, I'd unleash a bit of hell myself.

"Are you going to stand out there all night, your majesty?" I arched a brow, but Wrath's solitary response was a slight narrowing of his golden-eyed gaze. Stubborn, untrusting creature. Only he would question why I stood in a state of undress before his bed and not simply unleash his baser, carnal urges like I desired. "If you require further proof of my decision…"

"Emilia."

The way he said only my name made me brace myself for disappointment. His tone indicated we needed to talk, and talking was the absolute worst thing I could imagine right now. Talking would lead to tears, and that would force me to confront just how deeply seeing Vittoria earlier had affected me. I'd much rather lose myself in Wrath's addictive kisses.

"Please don't," I said, quietly. "I'm fine. Truly."

The demon looked apprehensive, unconvinced. He'd once told me to want but never need, but tonight I felt both strongly, and I didn't care if that made me weak. I prayed he wouldn't send me to my own bedroom suite alone. I couldn't bear the solitude. I needed comfort, a connection. Some bit of peace only he could give me right now.

Just then, the sheer curtains separating his bedchamber from the balcony fluttered in the wintry breeze, enticing him to join his half-naked queen. It was as if the realm itself wanted us to finally be united. With softly flickering candles and midnight fabrics, the bedchamber exuded quiet sensuality. It was a room made for all sorts of whispers: the ones where words were spoken tenderly, reverently against lips, and the whispers of clothing sliding slowly over skin.

Two things I wished to experience with this prince at once.

By his own admission, Wrath believed in the power of actions over words. And with that reminder, I made my move. He remained motionless outside, watching me bend over and shuck off my boots. I couldn't tell if he'd picked up on my emotions about Vittoria and misinterpreted them or if he still didn't trust that I wanted to complete the next step in accepting our marriage.

Sleeping together was one of the two final acts needed for us to become husband and wife. We could certainly have sex and not be married, but I *wanted* to complete our bond.

Given how we'd first met—my summoning of him in Palermo, then accidentally binding him to me for eternity—and how we'd both vowed to hate each other and never so much as kiss, I understood if that was the source of his trepidation.

Several months ago, I would have claimed tonight an improbability, too. That was before I acknowledged there was more to our story. That I burned for him as fiercely as the fiery rose-gold flowers I could summon from my fingertips at will. Another thing I would have thought impossible, and one more mystery for me to solve along with the truth of who I actually was. But all that could wait. The only thing I wanted to think of now was claiming my demon king.

Snowflakes started falling around him, lightly dusting his dark hair and broad shoulders, yet he didn't appear to notice. The harsh elements of this winter realm never seemed to bother him, though that was probably because he was a force of nature to be reckoned with himself.

I held his intense gaze as I shimmied the tight breeches over my hips and stepped out of them, tossing them on top of the tunic. Wrath's breathing all but stopped when he noticed I hadn't been wearing undergarments. Fists clenched at his sides, his knuckles went bone white from the strain. Not exactly the reaction I'd hoped for upon disrobing.

Brow furrowed, I silently replayed our exchange, carefully recalling each word. After tricking me into a blood bargain with him—to ensure none of his brothers took advantage of me when I first crossed into the underworld—I'd asked if he still considered me his.

Now, while rigidly standing outside in the snow, not making a move to follow me into his very warm and inviting bedchamber, I worried I'd misunderstood him. He'd said only that he didn't require time to think it over. Which, technically, didn't mean he considered me *his*.

"Have you changed your mind?" I asked.

Wrath scanned my face, his own expression closed off. "You willingly choose me. Knowing who I am. What I'm capable of."

They weren't questions, but I nodded in affirmation. "Yes."

"And this decision has nothing to do with your sister?"

He watched me carefully, and I knew he was trying to sense even the slightest shift in my emotions. Wrath would not take me to his bed if he believed any force aside from my own desire was driving me there. For one of the first times since we'd met, I offered him nothing but truth. If we had any hope of moving forward together, the games between us needed to end.

"I wanted you that night at Gluttony's party. And before that…do you remember when you magically removed the intoxication from me while we trained against his sin? I wanted you to take me then, too. Those times were both well before I saw Vittoria." I forced myself to hold his gaze, to prove to him how serious I was. "And I realized tonight that throughout everything, you've always been there for me. Your methods might not have always been ideal by mortal standards, but everything you've done has been to help me. I want *you*, and it has nothing to do with anyone else."

After a long pause that had me tensing for rejection, he finally prowled from the balcony into his bedchamber, slowly closing the distance between us. His attention meandered from my eyes to my lips before it dipped lower to take in my body.

A knee-clenching savagery entered his gaze while he mentally devoured me inch by brutal inch, pausing on that throbbing place between my thighs that suddenly ached for him. A low growl rumbled in his chest, confirming he sensed my desire.

I sincerely hoped he allowed whatever beast *that* was to break free tonight. I wanted to experience every wicked and deviant thing he'd just dreamed up.

He flashed a grin born of sinful promise, indicating he was more than willing to deliver.

Even with the chill clinging to him from the storm, I felt anything but cold as he neared. Between his scorching stare and the way he silently traced each of my curves as if plotting all the things he was about to do . . . it was almost enough to melt me right then and there.

"Tell me every dark desire, Emilia"—he tilted my face up—"every fantasy you wish to come true." His fingers lightly stroked the pulse point at my throat before he brought his mouth to mine, the kiss a mere brush of his lips that left me breathless and wanting. He pulled back and slowly ran his hands down my silhouette. "And I vow to make every one of them happen."

My focus roved over the expanse of fine clothes and the hard body hidden underneath them. "I have quite a few ideas."

The new look he gave me indicated he had some interesting ideas of his own.

We might argue elsewhere, but in this we were blessedly united. I pulled him in for another kiss, wanting to cherish this moment for eternity. Soon the sweet kiss turned ravenous, neither one of us content with being slow or delicate anymore. We were beings fueled by rage, by passion. And I wanted our first joining to be as explosive as our tempers.

If Wrath wished to give me every dark desire I'd ever had, I hoped he was prepared to keep up. I nipped his lower lip, and with a growl of approval, he responded in kind.

Wrath quickly deemed war on my mouth and battled like the general he was, taking no prisoners. There was ownership in this kiss, possession. And I gave it right back. He was *mine*. Every inch of his wicked soul, every steady thump of his heart, belonged to me.

His hands caressed my body, and a honeyed heat pooled low in my belly, spreading with each glorious pass of his calloused fingers. Of all the times for him to be fully dressed...

I yanked his suit jacket off, then tugged at the edge of his shirt before ripping it apart, needing to see him, *feel* him, skin to skin.

He broke away from our kiss, his mouth lifting in amusement. "Boring as virtues normally are, patience might prove worthwhile right now."

"In this instance, I hoped you were more skilled with sin. If I recall, you once asked if I'd like to see how very wicked you could be." I ran my attention over him, hiding my smile as his eyes flashed. "Is this truly your best?"

"Are you challenging me?"

I lifted a shoulder, knowing exactly what I was doing and enjoying the reaction it sparked in him. Given the bulge in his trousers, he didn't appear to mind, either. Twisted demon. "And if I am, what will you do then?" I asked.

"Get on the bed, my lady."

His voice was soft, but there was nothing meek in the command. I boldly stepped backward until I reached the bed and leaned against it, fingers sinking into the ebony throw placed tastefully on its edge. Once, I'd imagined what the fur would feel like on my bare skin.

I was about to find out.

Wrath jerked his chin, indicating he wanted me *all* the way on the bed, not simply perched against it. Heart thumping in anticipation, I lifted myself up and slid across the oversized mattress, biting back a moan as the soft fur quickly gave way to his cool silk sheets. It felt better than I'd imagined. Luxury and decadence mixed with something a bit wild and untamable.

Much like the master of this House of Sin.

Wrath unbuttoned his trousers, his gaze locked onto mine. A challenge in its own right to see if I was truly ready for what was to come. His pants hit the ground, and his hard length sprang free, intimidating and tantalizing, and just as eager to claim me.

I bit my lower lip, nearly overcome with want as I drank him in. Goddess above he was glorious. My attention slowly moved from his proud arousal and traveled along the rest of his body. Over six feet of pure muscle with bronze skin that seemed to glow with vitality filled my vision. He was a study of masculine power crossed with rugged beauty.

He stepped forward, and my focus shifted from the metallic snake inked onto his arm to the tattoo on his left thigh—a downward-facing dagger with roses etched onto its surface.

I couldn't quite make out the geometric designs on its hilt, and as Wrath took himself in his tattooed hand and slowly pumped his fist, my mind emptied. The demon gave me a smug look, like he knew exactly what his seductive taunting was doing. *Goddess curse him.* I wanted to replace his hand with my own. Better yet, I wanted to use my...

...A violent crack split the air like an angry god's whip, and Wrath's bedchamber—along with the demon who owned it—vanished, replaced by an empty, cold room without any light.

It was such a drastic shift, I didn't immediately grasp that it was real. I blinked rapidly, trying to adjust to the sudden dark. Shadows moved around what I sensed was a small space, almost writhing on top of one another in a frenzy.

Goose bumps rose along my arms as the chill in the air turned biting.

This had to be another strange illusion. I'd had a few before but none so vivid. They seemed to be triggered each time Wrath and I engaged in romantic acts, so that was probably the cause of this one now. I cursed the timing of this unwanted intrusion, loathing that someone else's past had taken me away from my delicious present.

I went to rub my temples but couldn't move my hands. My attention shot up, noticing a pair of manacles clamped tightly around my wrists. I tugged at them, but they were bolted high up in the ceiling. Chains clanked with each movement, the sound antagonizing my swiftly fraying nerves. *Blood and bones.* I glanced down. In this vision, I was just as nude as I was in my current reality. Wonderful. I'd left a dream only to enter a common nightmare.

I released a long sigh, my breath coming out in little white clouds, then tensed. *How odd.* Unlike other illusions, I also seemed to be in control of this one. It wasn't like stepping into a memory or seeing the past from someone else's perspective. My eyes narrowed.

If this wasn't an illusion or a memory...

"What in the seven hells is going on?" The unmistakable sound of a boot scraping over stone had my pulse pounding as a strong pang of fear shot through me. "Wrath?"

Somewhere close by, a match was struck, the hiss preceding the scent of sulfur as it wafted over. A small flame flickered on the far side of the room, though whoever had lit the candle was magically gone. I shook my chains again, yanking as hard as I could, but they didn't give an inch. Unless I ripped my hands off, I wasn't escaping until my abductor set me free.

To stave off rising panic, I squinted through the semidarkness, trying to find some clue of my location or my captor. It was a stone chamber, and I was chained in an alcove of sorts.

In the center of the main room sat an altar carved from the pale stone that made up the walls and floor. Straw and dried herbs littered the ground. It almost reminded me of the monastery back home where my friend Claudia worked on the dead, but not quite.

Thinking of those chambers brought on memories of the invisible mercenary spies who once haunted me there. It felt like forever since I'd encountered an Umbra demon, and I fought a shudder. If I never saw one of those ghastly demons again, I would have lived a good, happy life.

"Whoever's there, show yourself."

I rattled my chains. The echo of metal clanking was the only response I received, though I swore I heard the faint sound of someone breathing nearby. I didn't see any puffs of breath, but I knew that didn't mean I was alone. Wrath would never play this kind of trick on me, especially given what we'd been about to do, which ruled this out as any twisted demon foreplay.

I mustered false bravado. "Even chained you're afraid of speaking with me?"

"Not scared," a deep, accented voice said from the darkness.

My breath caught. I'd heard his voice before but couldn't place where. It wasn't Anir—Wrath's human second-in-command. Nor did it sound like any of the demon prince's brothers. This accent was from my island in the mortal realm. I was certain of that.

"If you're not scared, then you have no reason to hide from me."

"I'm awaiting further orders."

"From whom?" Silence uncomfortably stretched between us.

It was hard to feign authority while nude, chained, and speaking to a phantom kidnapper, but I tried anyway. "Whoever your master is will likely be here soon enough. There's no need for secrecy."

"You don't need to worry about me."

A phrase every murderer and criminal probably uttered to their victims right before they slit their throats, too. I swallowed hard. I needed him to keep talking to figure out who he was, and I'd found that annoying someone made them react, even if they didn't want to. Wrath and I had used that same tactic on each other over the last few months, and I could kiss him now for the practice.

"Did your master order you to remain in the shadows?"

"No."

"Hmm. I see."

"What?"

"You're simply a pervert who enjoys watching your victims, knowing they can't see you in return. Tell me, are you touching yourself now? Imagining what my skin feels like while stroking your own? Why don't you come closer?" *And allow me to knee your groin into your lungs.* The man materialized in front of me with a look of pure aggravation on his face. Definitely not a demon, but that wasn't comforting. I drew in a sharp breath. "Domenico Nucci."

The young man who sold arancini with his family in Palermo stared at me with vehemence. Deadly looking claws shot out of his fingertips, then retracted, reminding me that he was no more human than I was. I'd almost forgotten that the man I'd thought my twin had been secretly courting was a shape-shifter. Werewolf, to be exact. Temperamental creatures at best, and based on what I remember his father telling me, I'd just provoked a newly shifted one. I had no idea how much control he had over his wolf, but I'd wager not much.

Domenico's eyes—normally warm brown—glowed an unearthly pale purple as they narrowed on me, confirming my suspicion. He was close to shifting.

I held my breath, waiting for him to deliver a death blow. He seemed on the verge of stepping closer, his jaw clenched from restraint as anger radiated off him like a furious sun. The wolf took several deep breaths, then rolled his shoulders, breaking the mounting tension. With a wave of his half-clawed hand, a few of the shadows broke away from the frenzy and re-formed around me, creating a dressing gown of sorts.

"Where are we?" I asked, ignoring the strangeness of my robe as it settled over my skin. And the fact that the werewolf had magicked it without so much as a whispered spell.

"The Shadow Realm."

I quietly absorbed the information. Growing up, Nonna Maria taught us about shape-shifters, along with a few other magical creatures. According to my grandmother's stories, the wolves fought supernatural wars between themselves and demons in the spirit realm, which must be what he meant by Shadow Realm.

I'd always pictured the spirit realm with ghosts walking through walls, haunting and ethereal like they were depicted in gothic novels. This was very different from my imagination. Domenico was fully corporeal. And I definitely felt the weight of the icy manacles as they bit into my skin.

I also felt something I hadn't before—the slight buzz of magic in the metal. These were no ordinary shackles; they were spelled to keep my own powers locked away.

I sent a subtle prod to my magic's source and, just as I'd suspected, hit a barrier that prevented me from summoning fire.

I had a terrible feeling I knew who his master was and did not want my magic bound for our encounter. I glanced at my captor. I'd never heard of wolves transporting anyone with them to the spirit realm, and until now, I wouldn't have believed it possible, especially for a newly shifted werewolf. Domenico must be immensely powerful. A future alpha in the making.

"Is my physical body still in the Seven Circles?" I asked.

Domenico ran his attention over me, his eyes losing some of that shifter glow. "Yes."

I wasn't sure how that was possible, and the werewolf's glare indicated he wouldn't answer another question about it. Knowing how dangerous he would be if he fully turned into a wolf, I left well enough alone. He'd given me the important information I needed anyway.

My body was still in Wrath's bedchamber, and the demon would undoubtedly be searching for a way to bring me back now. If I couldn't escape on my own, I simply needed to bide my time until he came for my soul and unleashed his power. Anyone foolish enough to attack his bride-to-be in his royal House deserved to feel his namesake sin. I almost grinned, imagining the carnage he'd wreak as he meted out justice, but caught myself.

"It's freezing here."

"Not for me."

I wanted to rub my hands over my arms, forcing warmth back into my nonbody, but couldn't with the chains. Domenico watched me closely, a menacing gleam entering his eyes. One wrong move would have his jaws clamped around my throat, no matter what his orders were. He was far more volatile than the first time I'd met him, though that was probably from the shift. I'd heard young wolves sometimes took years to fully mature.

Unable to tolerate his silent staring, I cleared my throat. "When I saw you in the monastery after Vittoria's 'murder,' I thought you were praying for her. I later discovered you were there because you'd shifted for the first time. Did you really not suspect what you were before then?"

A muscle in his jaw twitched. "Do you know what you are, Emilia?"

It didn't escape me he'd said *what* not *who*. I had my suspicions, but he didn't need to know what they were.

"I know I'm your prisoner. I know Wrath will hunt you down and rip you limb from limb if any harm comes to me." I smiled, a vicious, wicked curve of my lips. The wolf seemed to realize that he might have chained me and bound my magic, but he wasn't the only predator in the chamber. "And there isn't a single realm you can hide in before he finds you. That is, if I don't get to you first. He is the merciful one. Keep that in mind."

"Well, well, sister."

Even though I'd been half-expecting her, hearing my twin's voice caused my heart to clench painfully. My attention shot to the other end of the chamber, landing on Vittoria at once.

My sister glided around the small room like a ghost of the past, wearing a long white gown that flowed behind her as if caught on a phantom breeze. There was a dreamlike quality to her presence, but she was as real as me and Domenico. I carefully looked her over, searching for any injury, though I knew she was the one commanding the werewolf, not the other way around.

Tears pricked my eyes as it all sank in. Vittoria was truly here. Alive. It was hard to believe it had only been an hour or two since I'd learned she wasn't actually dead. Despite her treachery, I wanted to wrap her in my arms and never let go.

This was a goddess-blessed miracle.

"Vittoria."

It was barely a whisper, but at the sound of my voice, my twin's lips twitched up in a familiar smirk. If I hadn't been chained, I'd have collapsed to my knees. Seeing her in the Triple Moon Mirror earlier was one thing; having her here, in front of me, was overwhelming. Words failed as my twin circled closer, watching me curiously.

"Let's unchain you and see what tricks you've learned." Her lavender eyes glittered, reminding me she had changed entirely. This wasn't the girl with brown eyes that matched mine. The young woman who'd loved to make her own drinks and perfumes. This stranger was something other. Something that made the fine hair along my arms stand on end. "Goddess knows I've got a few of my own to share. Shifter?"

Domenico moved with preternatural speed and fisted my hair, forcing my head to the side. He brought his nose to my neck and drew in a deep lungful of my scent, likely memorizing it to track me if I tried to escape. I cringed from the sudden pain but managed to bite back my yelp.

He snarled, the sound far from human as he brought his mouth to my ear. "Try anything stupid and I'll rip out more than just your mortal heart, Shadow Witch."

"Down, puppy." Vitoria tsked. "Don't play too rough. Yet."

Before I could absorb the hurt of that statement or wonder how much rougher things would get aside from being chained, Domenico shoved me away, and with another lazy wave of his hand, the locks on my manacles clicked open. My restraints clattered to the ground, the sound as foreboding as an executioner's blade coming down on the condemned.

This was it, the moment I'd been dreading, and I felt wholly unprepared.

Heart hammering, I turned my back on the raging werewolf

and faced my undead twin, steeling myself as our gazes met and held.

For months Vittoria had let me believe she was dead. Murdered violently. Allowed me to discover her heartless body, broken and bloody in that tomb. Tearing my world apart and destroying who I was on the most basic level. Vittoria's deceit was a wound that would never properly heal; it would forever leave emotional scars on my soul and in my heart.

Even with her standing before me now, alive and well, there was no hope of ever returning to *before*. Too much had passed between us to simply forget and move on, and that, more than anything else, was something I mourned. No matter how hard I wished otherwise, we'd both changed irrevocably. And I wasn't sure the pieces of our new lives fit together anymore.

To push past the growing ache in my chest, I thought about my betrothed. Of how my twin had ruined this night for me, too. Instead of sorrow, I focused on the fury, *the wrath* that had gotten me through my own personal hell. And all emotions, save one, disappeared.

If I'd been capable of feeling worry instead of pure wrath, perhaps my sister's triumphant grin would have caused a flicker of unease. As it stood, *she* was about to discover that she was not the only one capable of instilling apprehension. It was time Vittoria feared *me*.

I dipped into my source of magic, relieved to feel the enormous well of power that crackled under my skin. If my sister wanted to see what I was capable of, I'd gladly show her.

"You have five minutes to explain yourself." When I spoke, my voice was colder than the air around us, colder than even the most wicked circle of Hell. I swore the shadows paused before skittering into nothingness, hiding from the great reckoning they sensed coming.

"And then?" Vittoria asked.

My smile was a beautiful nightmare. For the first time, Vittoria's brow creased as if she'd just realized there was one fatal flaw in her plan. Monsters could be created but never tamed.

"And then, dear sister, you'll meet the witch you forced me to become."

# TWO

**"Bite your tongue** or I'll remove it." Domenico stepped forward, claws extending and quietly snarling at the threat I posed, but Vittoria raised her hand, stalling him. I was too furious to be surprised at how quickly he backed down from the simple, unspoken command.

"Have you not become more powerful? More...bold?" Vittoria asked, cocking a brow. "You've finally stepped out of the safe little hole you've been hiding in, only to live a life now worthy of a bard's pen. Do they sing ballads of boring *witches*, wiling away their time in hot kitchens, pining after equally boring holy men like Antonio? I would imagine a grand romance with the king of demons is something much more interesting. Especially in the bedchamber. For the sake of the Great Divine above, Emilia. The death of your former life is something you should thank me for. Antonio, Sea & Vine, you and I were always meant for bigger things."

"Boring?" Anger lanced through me. "I *loved* my life and our kitchen. Apologies if what I consider fun, or who I found attractive, is so repulsive to you. And since when do you hate Sea & Vine? You loved our family and our time cooking together, too. Or have you forgotten us? In your quest for…whatever it is you're after. How could you do that to us, to *me*?"

My voice broke on the last question, and I yanked hard on my fury again, centering myself. Vittoria watched me closely. "I did what had to be done *for us*. It might not seem like it, but I swear this has all been for you and me. The curse—"

She bit down on whatever she wished to say but couldn't.

"Oh, yes, the curse." I swatted the air as if the curse were a bothersome housefly. "The bloody, fucking curse that no one can speak of. I'm finished with this fickle magic and every hexed being involved! Why did you fake your murder? How was that in any way helpful to me?"

She seemed to choose her next words carefully. "Even the most volatile fuel requires a spark to cause flames."

Cryptic as always when the curse was at play. "Why could you possibly need so much fire?"

Her gaze turned into a hard, glittering gem of hatred. For a second, it wasn't lavender that flashed from her irises, but a deep ruby red. "To watch our enemies burn. To reclaim what is ours by might and birth. And to break the final chains that bind us once and for all."

"And our family? Are they your enemies? Did they deserve to bury you in that crypt? To believe you were rotting away with our ancestors?"

"Yes. Though I highly doubt they believed I was rotting away. That little lie was something I imagined they fed to you, their favored one. Or should I say, the most feared." Vittoria's admission fell between us, heavy under the weight of the truth she believed it to be. "And they aren't the only ones who will come to fear us. I have adopted one bit of advice from our dear family. Keep your acquaintances close, but your enemies closer."

I looked at the stranger who wore my sister's face. There was hardness in this Vittoria, darkness where light had once shined brightly. My sister had been playful, friendly. Capable of making friends and dancing for hours on end. A quality I'd always admired and wished to possess. This harsh version of her was difficult to reconcile.

"What if I don't want to be feared?" I asked.

Vittoria's smile was a quick flash of teeth, razor-sharp and threatening. "A bird without wings is still a bird, sister mine."

"Have you been speaking to the Prince of Envy?" I heaved a sigh. "I swear you sound exactly like him after he's had too much truth-spelled demonberry wine."

"Envy?" Her gaze flickered inward with a memory. "I rode his pet vampire just to watch those green eyes flame with his favorite sin when he caught us. Vampires make exquisite lovers, being creatures of the night and all. They are masters of mixing pleasure with a bite of pain. Once you finish playing with your demon, you ought to visit the vampire court and give one or two a ride. I recently called upon their prince and was not at all disappointed. The things he could do with those fangs..."

Domenico growled, and my twin shot him a placating look. Clearly he hadn't known his—whatever my sister was to him—had cavorted with some of his mortal enemies. I was unaware there was a vampire court, and for the time being, it wasn't a priority to ask. Unless it suddenly became an issue, it was the least of my concerns now.

"I..." I wanted to purge the thought of my twin bedding that particular vampire from my mind. I'd had the misfortune of meeting him once, and Alexei had been frightening. And not in a forbidden, dark fantasy type of way. He'd looked ready to rip out a heart to drink it dry for sport. "Why are you here now? I thought we were supposed to meet tomorrow on the Shifting Isles."

Vittoria lifted a shoulder, suddenly not meeting my gaze. "I wanted to deliver the message myself in case you didn't get the skull."

I didn't believe her but didn't call her on the obvious lie. My sister was keeping another secret, and it likely had something to do with the Shadow Realm since we were here. Perhaps it had been a test to see if Domenico could bring me here without any issues. Which meant our time was probably limited and I needed answers. "How did you fake removing your heart?"

"I didn't."

"I saw the blood. The gaping hole in your chest. Obviously, it was some magic or illusion, unless you no longer require a heart to live. Don't stand here and keep lying to my face. You've done quite enough of that over the last several months. I deserve to know the truth, Vittoria."

The temperature abruptly dropped, ice crystals snaking up the walls and crackling like frozen flames as they rapidly spread. The candle flickered in the sudden breeze before blowing out, leaving us in the dark. A thin ribbon of smoke curled through the air, the scent of sulfur permeating the coldness; an omen sent from a ferocious hell god. One I knew well.

Domenico stepped forward, wrapping a hand around my twin's upper arm, and tugged her near. "Time to go. He's breached the Shadow's wards."

My heart thrummed. I knew exactly who *he* was. Wrath had

come for my soul, charging across the barrier of the spirit realm, his namesake sin powerful enough to make even the ground here tremble at his approach. I palpably felt his fury, and it did something peculiar to me in this realm. I suddenly wasn't thinking of my twin's betrayal or feeling hurt. Heat crept over me where the cold had previously sunk its teeth. Wrath's sin made me feel alive, buzzing. It also made me want to shed civility and become an elemental force fueled by baser instincts.

Vittoria's lips lifted in a half smirk. "Remember, sister. Enjoy the sausage all you like, but don't purchase the pig. It's the only warning I can offer."

"Why should I listen to you?"

"I'm your blood." Domenico half-dragged her across the chamber, then waved his hand until a glittering portal opened before them. Vittoria paused, glancing back at me. "Some bonds can never be broken, Emilia. And some choices have consequences akin to death. Take it from someone who knows all too well what that's like."

Chills danced down my spine from the first part of her warning. Wrath had said something similar to me on the night I discovered the truth of why he'd given me his royal Mark.

My fingers absently brushed against the nearly invisible *S* on my neck, the magic causing a slight, pleasant tingle that traveled down my nonbody.

"What does that mean?" I demanded. "No more games, Vittoria."

"Choose him and you'll give up part of yourself," she said, offering an answer that only raised more questions. "See you tomorrow. Don't be late."

"Stop! Why must we meet on the Shifting Isles?" I asked. "Why not tell me what you need here?"

"You'll just have to wait and see."

Vittoria blew me a kiss, then stepped through the portal with the werewolf on her heels. Apparently, Domenico, an alpha in his own right, knew a bigger threat had entered his territory. Retreat was the smart option. Or perhaps he'd only choked on his pride to save my twin. I wasn't sure how I felt after our encounter; too many emotions were warring against one another, but I was grateful she had a loyal ally. She needed one.

"Emilia."

Wrath strode into the chamber a moment later, his body humming with the threat of an impending war. A battle he was bringing to our enemies. He glared at the closing portal, then swept his attention over me, sharp as the blade in his fist and promising the same level of violence on anyone who'd hurt me.

I glanced down, noticing the shadow robe had also abandoned its post at his arrival. Once again I stood nude, but not cowed.

"Did they harm you?" His voice was clipped, as if he were saving all his energy for the fight. Domenico might have escaped, but Wrath would hunt him down. The cold, unforgiving look on his face promised nothing but pain and torment.

I shook my head, not trusting myself to speak the partial lie. Harm wasn't always inflicted physically. "It was my sister. She wanted to make sure I received her message about tomorrow. Where are the Shifting Isles?"

"Just outside the mainland." The demon's gaze methodically took in each inch of the chamber before coming to rest on the manacles. In a flash, his blade was gone and he was in front of me, gently bringing my wrists up for closer inspection. Red splotches that would turn into nasty bruises had Wrath's anger flaring impossibly higher. His voice was now laced with deadly promise, and the air turned so frigid my teeth began to chatter. "If *anyone* chains you again, I will become every nightmare mortals have ever had of me and then some."

Ice shot up the walls and coated the ceiling as the temperature continued to plummet. Chunks of stone cracked and fell to the ground. If he didn't rein in his temper soon, we'd both be encapsulated in ice or buried under stone.

"What if I ask *you* to tie me up?"

The harsh expression on Wrath's face faltered as he blinked down at me. He hadn't expected that. Good. Perhaps we'd make it out of this realm before we turned into ice sculptures. I disentangled myself from his light grasp and wrapped my arms around his middle, listening to his heart beat faster from the embrace. Almost immediately, I felt warmer.

"Simply saying 'I love you; I'm pleased you're all right' would have sufficed, too."

A beat of silence passed, and I could practically feel Wrath straining to leash himself. Only his iron will would cage the immense power struggling to break out, to attack. I couldn't imagine the discipline, the absolute control he had over his namesake sin, to finally wrangle his wrath into submission. The air warmed a fraction, though it was still deathly frigid.

He held me a little closer, as if comforting himself that I was safe and secure. "Torturing and disemboweling your enemies would be an *act* of love."

"No one can deny you are a demon of action." I snorted and drew back enough to see mirth entering his eyes in place of the icy rage, though there was still something haunted in his expression that wasn't as quick to disappear. "Take me home, please. It's been a long night. I need a warm bath and an entire bottle of demonberry wine."

And, no matter what had just happened or the warning Vittoria tried imparting, I still wanted to claim my king in the flesh. That, more than anything else, would soothe me, mind, body, and cursed soul.

Wrath magicked us back to his bedchamber, reuniting our souls with our physical forms, and I blinked at a room encapsulated in ice. The ceiling, walls, fireplace—*everything* except the bed—were frozen, the ice so thick it gave off a bluish tint. I thought the Shadow Realm had been bad, but this was extreme.

I gingerly pushed myself up from where I'd been lying and raised a questioning brow. Wrath ran a hand through his hair, the action drawing my attention to cuts on his knuckles I hadn't noticed before.

"Did you have to fight wolves?" I asked, beckoning him to come closer. "Please. Let me see that." Reluctantly he did, offering me his injured hand. "Why isn't this healing?"

"I punched through the realms."

His expression was coolly aristocratic, and if I hadn't come to know him these months, I might have missed the subtle signs that he was still churning with emotion. His sensual mouth was set in a hard line, his chiseled jaw strained. There was a ruthless flicker in his gaze—an unyielding promise to commit terrible acts of violence—that gave away how close he'd just come to ripping the realm apart. A shiver rolled down my spine, and whatever dark place he'd been in disappeared.

"It's all right," he said. "Easily fixable."

"I don't care about the state of the *room*. Are *you* all right?"

The demon prince gave me a tight smile. "I am now."

I'd never seen him lose his temper with such a massive showing of his power and wondered at the severity of his reaction. At what he might not be able to tell me or might not wish to tell me. I sensed he needed time to sort through it all and gave him a small smile in return. "As long as you're certain."

"I am." He magically set the room to rights and had just called for the tub to be filled when there was a knock at the door. If I could have hexed someone right then, I would have.

"Don't answer it," I half-groaned. "I beg you."

Wrath looked torn but heeded my request. After casting a ward to keep everyone away from entering his private quarters, he swept my legs out from under me and walked us into his bathing chamber, kicking the door shut behind us.

I hadn't seen this room before and took in its elegant beauty. Slate-colored floors, black marble walls with gold veining, candles dripping ebony wax, faucets and fixtures in gleaming gold, and a massive claw-foot bathtub that could fit several people in the center of the room.

An oversized black crystal chandelier hung low over the tub, completing the look. The room was dark, sensual, and utterly relaxing. Just what I needed after my stressful evening.

The prince carefully deposited me into the bath, then returned with a chilled glass of demonberry wine, the silver seeds sparkling like miniature stars in the candlelight. For the first time in what felt like hours, I exhaled, feeling peaceful.

Wrath drew a stool over to the tub and sat, watching me sip my drink and submerge myself to my shoulders in the perfectly warmed water. "Do you want to talk about your sister?"

"Not particularly." I sighed. "I still don't understand why she wants to meet on the Shifting Isles. It would be much easier to simply talk here. Is there any reason why that you can think of?"

Wrath didn't respond right away. "Maybe she has something there she wants you to see."

"You're probably right. But she could also simply tell me that. I don't understand all the cloak-and-dagger theatrics. Though I suppose that is very Vittoria in a way. Maybe one of the *only* familiar aspects about her." I took another sip of wine, savoring the bright flavors that burst over my tongue. "How did you punch your way into the Shadow Realm?"

"I'm the king of the underworld. The spirit realm is under my domain. And even if it wasn't, do you really believe a lone werewolf would stop me from getting to you?"

"I'm not sure anything could stop you. What's it like to be invincible?" I teased.

Wrath's expression turned contemplative as he pulled a linen cloth from a tray near the tub and dunked it into the water. He upended a glass bottle of soap over it, then motioned for me to spin around. "Lift your hair."

I happily obliged his request to pamper me. He dragged the soapy linen across my shoulders, gently washing my body before dipping it back into the water. Wrath, the mighty demon of war, was giving me a sponge bath. And it felt positively divine.

For someone who'd just frozen his entire bedchamber in a rage, he certainly could be warm and kind. At least where I was concerned. I doubted anyone else ever saw this side of the demon. Which made me appreciate his actions all the more.

Goose bumps rose along the careful lines he made from my neck, following the curve of my spine down to my bottom. He tenderly lifted one arm at a time, paying special care to my sore wrists. Slight coolness nipped at the air, and I realized he must be exercising an enormous amount of restraint to not have his anger overwhelm the temperature again.

Once he thoroughly saw to my back and arms, he slowly moved to my sides, skimming the underside of my breasts, causing my nipples to harden as he drifted closer to them. I didn't think he was intentionally attempting to seduce me, but that didn't stop my body from reacting to his ministrations. Heat pooled between my thighs, and my thoughts immediately shifted to where he'd drag that cloth next. If my luck had finally turned this evening, perhaps he'd use his fingers instead of the linen. I leaned back, granting him better access to that particular place…

"There is a hexed blade that can kill me."

A chill descended, erasing the pleasant feeling at once. I sat up, twisting around, the sudden movement splashing water onto the pristine floor. "What?"

"Your so-called First Witch created hexed objects. Our records indicate three, but the actual number was never confirmed. Only one was ever found to be truly dangerous to a prince of Hell, the Blade of Ruination."

As if that made it better. "Please tell me you are in possession of it."

Wrath held my gaze, the strength and power of it meant to fortify my nerves. It had the opposite effect. The prince sighed. "None of the objects have been recovered. They disappeared when the witch and her spies did."

"You can be killed."

He offered a slight incline of his head in confirmation. The thought of someone extinguishing his flame had panic irrationally seizing me. All these months we'd spent arguing, fighting each other and our attraction. And it could be gone. Some selfish, hateful creature could take him from me. I thought he was invincible, and this one hexed blade made him too vulnerable for my liking. Made every little thing except cherishing our time together insignificant. With the rival demon House daggers, he could be injured, but not *killed*.

Perhaps it was my sister's reemergence in my life, the fact that she was capable of anything, including faking her own murder, that had me coming undone. Or maybe it was whatever she'd been testing tonight by bringing me to that realm. Maybe they wanted to see how long it would take for Wrath to track me there.

I had no idea if he could be harmed in that realm with his soul detached from his body. One thing I was certain of: I couldn't trust my sister.

If Vittoria got her hands on that blade, she'd probably attack Wrath. She'd warned me not to complete our marriage bond; I could see her ensuring that never happened. I had no idea who her enemies were, but I knew she'd go to impossible lengths to destroy them. If she believed my marriage to Wrath would in any way force me to give up part of myself that she needed for her plans, he would definitely become an enemy in her eyes.

With strength that seemed to catch the demon off guard, I yanked Wrath forward, pulling him off the stool and into the tub, clothes and all. I needed to feel him. Alive and breathing and solid beneath me. I leapt onto his lap and tugged his wet shirt open, buttons flying across the floor and bouncing into the tub as I pressed my hand to his heart, my own beating rapidly.

If anyone took him from me... my magic surged up, ready to incinerate this realm and every other one that possibly existed.

That ancient, rumbling power I'd felt once before cracked an eye deep in my center. Whatever that monster was, it was growing more ravenous the longer it remained awake. It wanted to be set free, to ravage and destroy. And I barely held it at bay.

Buds of rose-gold flame burst into the air above us, the fiery flowers unfurling along with burning roots and stems with thorns. It was a garden made from embers and flames. And I suddenly couldn't tell if my eyes were open or closed; all I saw was a rose-gold haze as my rage took magical form. I breathed in a ragged breath and exhaled, half-convinced flames and smoke would follow. Vines with sharp, oversized thorns twisted up around the tub, crept up the walls; in moments, we'd be overtaken by them...

Strong, powerful hands slid down my body, the sensation grounding me as the maelstrom within calmed a fraction. I swallowed hard, my throat parched, as I inhaled deeply and dragged my attention to the demon. Wrath gave me a bemused look but didn't stop lightly caressing me, like he knew I was still half under the spell of my fury. My attention followed the careful path his hands traveled, my breathing evening out with each long, slow stroke.

My rage simmered, then sputtered out, taking the swell of magic with it. The burning flowers slowly returned to embers, then charred, the ash drifting away on a magical wind Wrath must have summoned. The vines also receded back to wherever I'd wrenched them from. I hadn't even known that was something I could do, but Wrath didn't appear surprised.

I watched in silence as the room returned to normal, though inside my emotions were still churning like the sea after a particularly brutal storm. Wrath's caresses slowed, then stopped, his hands now resting on my waist. We stared at each other, not acknowledging I'd lost control.

"I thought my death would no longer excite you as it once would have." His tone was light and teasing, but I detected an undercurrent of tension. "Should I be worried?"

*Should I be?* I glanced down, noticing that I'd somehow straddled him and that my hands were fisted in his half-torn-off clothing. I very much appeared to be on the verge of savagery.

Maybe he should worry. I could barely contain myself once I entered that dark place filled with rage. It was like all humanity had been stripped away and I was nothing but an elemental force meant to destroy.

Though, upon closer inspection, the rock-hard bulge nestled against my apex said Wrath enjoyed my rough handling. I eased my death grip on his clothing. "I want to find this blade."

The smile that had been tugging at the corners of his lips formed into a wicked grin. "While I admitted to being fond of knife play, I'm afraid this one is off-limits. We can play with my dagger. The magic imbued in it won't hurt me."

"Don't make light of this. If Vittoria gets that hexed blade first..."

"She'll have to get in a very long line of demons searching for it. Envy's spies, for one, are always listening for whispers of it across the realm. If it's in the Seven Circles, he'll find it."

"Because Envy—of all demons—is precisely who I'd trust with a blade that can kill you."

I silently counted to ten. How quickly the princes forgot stabbing and gutting one another. A thousand centuries could pass and I'd never forget the way Wrath's blood had coated my hands after Envy had sunk his House dagger into him.

"My brother is many things, but a murderer he is not." Wrath tucked a damp strand of hair behind my ear. While he could make that claim with certainty, I couldn't. My sister would slay our family if it served her ultimate goal. I seemed to be exempt from her vengeance, which meant she needed me for her plan. For now, at least. "When the blade is close, I can sense its magical imprint. I'm not entirely without defense, my lady. Most would think twice before attacking me."

Unless they were confident the weapon they had could put him down.

"How close?" I caught the slight wince he wasn't quick enough to hide, and dread filled me again. "I see. So it has to be *extremely* close for you to sense it. Wonderful."

I stood up, bathwater running down my body in rivulets as I stepped out of the tub. The idea of relaxing was no longer appealing. I wanted to tear this realm apart, inch by inch, and find this hexed blade. Wrath arched a brow but didn't say a word as I bypassed the towel and strode toward his bedchamber, dripping all over his immaculate tile.

My clean clothes were in the next chamber, and without thinking, I opened the door to the corridor that connected our rooms. The man standing on the other side dropped the fist he'd been about to knock with, his tawny skin going scarlet.

"Devil's blood, Em." Anir cringed. "Warn someone before you march around like"—he waved a hand at me—"that."

I fought the urge to roll my eyes. "Have you ever seen a naked woman before?"

"Well, yes, but—"

"What about men? Have you seen a man bathing or strutting around without a stitch of clothing on? Considering where we live, I imagine you've seen much more than that."

"I have, but—"

"Then kindly step aside and stop blushing like a boy in his small clothes."

Wrath's human second-in-command glanced up at the ceiling, as if requesting divine assistance. When he brought his attention back down, he stared at a point over my shoulder. The prickle of heat indicated Wrath had come up behind me.

"Is there a problem?" he asked, draping a robe around my shoulders.

"Yes, your majesty." Anir was no longer blushing. "House Greed has requested your presence at once."

A terrible feeling skittered across my skin like a horde of spiders as I cinched the robe around my waist. "What's happened?"

"Greed's circle has been breached." Anir glanced between me and the demon at my back, his expression grim. "There's been a murder."

# THREE

**House Greed did** not give the appearance that anything nefarious was afoot.

Well, anything more nefarious than the gambling club's patrons lining up to be admitted to the sin-fueled den of iniquity.

I stood beside Wrath on the main floor we'd entered, waiting for our escorts, my gloved hands tightly gripping the ornate bronze railing as I gazed two stories down into the receiving hall.

On the brief carriage ride across the Black River to this House of Sin, Wrath had asked me to not speak until we'd entered Greed's private quarters. Curious demons would be paying close attention to our rival House and the appearance of the king. It was best, Wrath said, to make them wonder. Greed did not want word spreading of the murder he'd called an "extremely unfortunate incident" in his letter. He wanted his subjects to be focused solely on indulging their greed, ever concerned with adding to his power.

I took the silent moments to inspect House Greed, interested in seeing how the sins shaped each demon court. Four grand, curving staircases converged in the center of the room, spilling patrons in from each corner they'd arrived from, though the circular chamber below was merely a place for members of the House to await gondolas.

Merlot-colored water snaked off in different directions, the signs above each canal indicating a different gaming hall patrons could choose for their entertainment. From where we stood, the water combined with the staircases resembled a beating heart and its chambers. I'd never been to Venice, but something about the flat-bottomed boats and canals reminded me of that famed city.

Except everything here was contained within the enormous castle. And was fitted to the extreme with riches. The gaming hell I'd visited in Palermo was nothing compared with the splendor of this House of Sin. In the mortal realm, Greed's den was a secret, underground establishment that changed locations on a whim, worthy of being deemed a "hell." There, it was easy to imagine innocents like Domenico's father getting fleeced by card sharks and being completely taken over by the demon's greedy influence.

Here, it was an entirely different story. The gleaming fixtures and elegant mosaic tiles were as carefully curated as the patrons' neutral expressions. No one appeared to be in danger of losing their innocence; these were all various kinds of predators circling one another, each more dangerous than the last. Women and men both wore their finest clothes, the silks and brocades and stitches and embroidery all speaking to their wealth. And if their clothing didn't inspire greed, their sparkling jewels did. Half of their adornments could fetch enough coin to feed a village for a year.

I was surprised that some didn't simply wear gemstones—they'd had them fused to their skin. Diamonds and pearls and all manner of gems glinted from lips and noses and brows.

A few women even had gemstones tastefully placed on the side of their hands and forearms in place of gloves, while some more daring demons opted to wear only long, flowing skirts that had slits traveling high up each thigh, their bare breasts also sparkling with jewels.

Not to be outdone, men strode down the stairs toward the lines of gamblers waiting for their gondolas wearing nothing but jewels on their well-endowed members and smirks on their lips. Apparently there was a fine line between inspiring greed, lust, and envy. As I'd been learning held true for most demon circles. Sin and vice overlapped often, though the way they were expressed in each circle was slightly different.

Before I could ask Wrath about the body adornments, two lesser demons entered the balcony and beckoned for us to follow them. One had the pale green skin and eyes of a reptile, and the other was covered in short fur and had the liquid ebony eyes of a deer.

Large antlers curved back from the second one's head, and I swallowed hard, remembering the first time I'd encountered these two particular guards. Except for a chance encounter with Domenico Nucci Senior, I'd been alone the night I'd found Greed in the private office of his traveling gaming hell, these demons standing watch.

They were my introduction to lesser demons. Though after my encounter with the witch-blood-craving Aper demon, they were by far the most civil.

Wrath nodded to them, then motioned for me to walk ahead. We traveled down a secret, winding staircase that deposited us in a private tunnel where a gondola waited at a quiet dock. Torches cast shadows along the stone walls, dark enough to hide a spy.

The reptile demon jerked his chin at the gondola. "This boat is spelled to take you directly to his highness. Do not attempt to get off until it docks."

With that word of warning, the two guards inclined their heads slightly, then disappeared back up the stairs. A slight crease formed between Wrath's brows as he took in our conveyance. It looked the same as the other boats, if perhaps a bit more gilded.

"What is it?" I asked, my own focus drifting back to the unsettling shadows before returning to my prince.

Wrath stared at the canal and the boat a beat longer. "Greed's power propels the boats, and the demon-fueled water boosts—or more accurately, reflects—his sin. It's a system that helps expend as little energy as possible on his end, while still using his magic."

"So it will be like traveling in the Sin Corridor, but only focused on greed?"

"Yes." Wrath held my gaze. "You will need to lock all your emotions down. My training lessons were powerful, but this will be even more so because of the demon water. It will sense your hidden desires and target them just as they were targeted in the Sin Corridor."

The seemingly innocent boat and merlot-stained demon waterway suddenly felt ominous. "I wish I knew this was a potential issue sooner. Perhaps I could have taken a tonic."

"I didn't think my brother would wish to meet in the heart of his club. Greed has a building he uses for meetings outside the castle proper." He held out his hand, helping me into the gondola before following me onto it. "You can fight this, Emilia. You're strong enough and have trained hard. Remember what to feel for—that slight lick of magic, then shut it down."

My foot touched the bottom of the boat the second he said "lick," and the timing couldn't be more unfortunate. Desire raked its claws over my skin before I shook the magic away. Wrath hadn't exaggerated; the demon waterway certainly enhanced this circle's magic. I greedily wanted Wrath's touch—had craved it all night—and the circle knew it.

I quickly sat on the bench opposite Wrath, arranging my clothing to give my hands something to do. I'd chosen a gown with blush-colored tulle skirts and a black velvet bodice that had little gold and pink flowers sewn onto the straps and carefully placed around the sweetheart neckline. It was modest by demon fashion standards, but it was soft and pretty and I liked the way it made me feel. Perhaps a little too much. And so did my prince.

Wrath's attention moved over the corset as the boat pushed itself off the dock and began gliding over the otherwise quiet water. Maybe it was the magic of the realm, or our betrothal bond, or the excess greed pumping through the lone canal, but that slight spark of desire suddenly blazed again the longer my prince admired me. All I could think of was how much I wanted to be in Wrath's bedchamber.

I clenched my knees together, tried counting the waves our gondola made, but that worked against me. Thinking of waves lapping made me think of Wrath's skilled tongue and all the things he'd done to me with it. I squeezed my eyes shut, but that only brought on memories of Wrath between my thighs, a king indulging in a royal feast.

*Blood and bones.* I needed release.

"Emilia." Wrath's voice held a note of warning, but it did

nothing to soothe me or bring my desire under control. If anything, it made me crave him all the more. "Breathe."

I exhaled slowly, thinking of the reason we were invited here. Murder. For the love of the goddess. That ought to be enough to dampen the fires of passion, but one look at Wrath's strained face indicated he was struggling, too. Fantastic. My lack of control was bleeding over to him. If he unleashed himself now, we'd both be in trouble.

I focused on the waterway, on the rippling surface of the merlot waves. There were fewer torches this far into the tunnel, larger stretches of darkness. I'd almost wrangled my emotions back into a tight fist when I saw the bulge form in the demon's trousers. That was all it took for me to submit to the sea of sin and my own wants.

Without breaking his stare, I removed my gloves, then stood, gently rocking the boat with the motion, and went to my knees before him. Power, unlike any magic I'd summoned before, filled me as something dark and dangerous glittered in his eyes.

"What are you doing?"

A coy smile curved my lips as I unfastened his trousers. "Conquering, your majesty."

"Emilia—" Before he could remind me why this wasn't a good idea, as if I weren't already aware of that, I pulled his hard length free and slowly licked him from tip to base. "Demon's blood," he growled as I closed my mouth around him and sucked a little harder, testing the action. His hands fisted at his sides. "You're going to destroy me."

Recalling what I'd seen at Gluttony's House of Sin during the Feast of the Wolf, I gripped him in hand and repeated the motion using my mouth and tongue to work him, moving a little faster and holding him a little tighter with each pump, adoring the rasp of his breath.

Wrath sat still, allowing me to set the pace, but from the way his thighs tensed, I could tell he was holding himself back. And I wanted no part in that. This moment was meant for unleashing ourselves. I glanced up, silently commanding him to give in to his own dark passion. To show me just how wicked he could be. Because I wanted it. And so did he.

When he still didn't move, I grew bolder. "Stand up, your majesty."

Understanding flared in his eyes. With an impressive curse, he obeyed my order, then sank his fingers into my hair, guiding himself deeper. The boat rocked dangerously, but the flat bottom ensured we wouldn't tip over. Perhaps that was why they were used here. I doubted we were the first travelers to give in to the greedy desire pumping through our veins.

I grasped onto Wrath's hips, loving that this mighty demon was finally losing control. I might be the one on my knees, but I owned him in this moment. And he well knew it.

His grip tightened in my hair, possessive and an edge shy of painful, yet it made my knees clench together from the pleasure steadily building in *me*. It did not matter that we were in a rival demon House. That at any moment someone might spy us in a compromising position. Only pleasure mattered. And maybe it was greed fueling me, or maybe I didn't mind the thought of others greedily watching us from the shadows. In fact, that scandalous thought made the honeyed heat in my belly spread, made me grow bolder still, hungrier for as much pleasure as I could get. I tugged him closer, urging him to thrust deeper, to not deny me my greed-fueled desire to taste him. I wanted him to mark me in every way, just as I intended to mark him.

"Fuck." He needed no further encouragement.

Wrath pumped into my mouth as if he were pounding that slick junction of my body, claiming me with the same fervor I'd soon claim him. That very area throbbed at the thought of him being there now, dominating because I wished him to, but only in that one instance.

His awareness of my growing arousal must have finally sent him careening over the edge. With one last thrust and a groan that was more animal than human, he came undone. He gently stroked my hair back, massaging my skull tenderly as if he'd just realized how tightly he'd been holding on.

I swallowed him down, then gave one final, slow lick, grinning as he twitched from the aftershocks of pleasure.

"Godsdamn, Emilia."

"That was . . . incredible." I went to my feet, feeling immensely gratified. "I'm not sure who enjoyed that more."

"I'm curious to test that theory." He reached for me, a sinful twinkle in his eye, when the trance we'd both been in was suddenly broken by the sound of a throat clearing.

I yanked my attention up and froze. The Prince of Lust leaned against a doorway that led down a narrow corridor, arms crossed. I hadn't seen the corridor or the prince. Not that I really cared to look for either; Wrath had held all my greedy attention.

"If you're both quite through," Lust said, managing to sound immensely bored despite what he'd witnessed, "there's a little matter of murder to attend to." Even fully dressed, I still felt the heat of a blush kissing my cheeks at being caught. Lust watched his brother, shaking his head slightly. "Put your cock away and follow me. You'll have plenty of time to pleasure your bride later. Greed sent me to see what was taking so long. He's losing his temper. And you know how irksome that can become when any of us feel another sin."

"Leave us." Wrath's voice was glacial, like his expression. "We'll be there shortly."

"Afraid I can't do that," Lust volleyed back. "Wouldn't want you to get distracted again."

The greedy influence was gone, but the desire wasn't. I was still tempted to ignore Lust and Greed in favor of finishing what Wrath and I had started. I wanted to know what my prince had planned for me. "Did you—"

"See you blow my brother until he questioned his belief in the Divine?" A devious smile curled the edges of his lips. "Let's just say I was impressed, Shadow Witch. And that's saying a lot for the lord of pleasure."

"That's not what I was going to ask." I shot him a nasty look as Wrath assisted me out of the boat. "Did you use your influence on us?"

"Didn't need to. You both greedily went after your pleasure on your own. That little tableau was all you—and our demonic host. If it makes you feel better, I called out several times. I assumed you wanted the attention, so I gave it." Lust cocked his head. "Are you planning on putting that vicious little mouth on me while my brother pleasures you from behind?"

My body flushed crimson. "You're disgusting."

"Your blush sings a different tune," Lust said. "If you're wondering, yes, it would feel twice as good as you imagine. Though I suspect my brother would have my balls for trying. Remind me to send you a gift later from House Lust."

The prince of pleasure stuck his hands into his pockets and turned, walking down the corridor as if he were out for an evening stroll.

"Hurry along," he called over his shoulder. "Some of us have yet to indulge in our baser desires. Murder, unfortunately, seems to be an aphrodisiac only for House Wrath. Surprising to none, actually."

# FOUR

**The Prince of** Greed scowled from behind his gilded desk. "You're late."

We paused just inside the threshold of his private chamber, surveying the occupants. Greed, Lust, and two demon guards. Wrath brushed his knuckles against the back of my hand, then strode into what appeared to be Greed's study, promptly commandeering one of the velvet wingback chairs without uttering a single word. His expression didn't shift, but I felt the iciness in it. The cold, imperious royal had replaced the warm lover from a few minutes before.

Wrath looked every inch the king he was, claiming his throne. Power emanated from him that wasn't purely magical in nature—it was his confidence, his knowledge that he owned every space he walked into, even in a House of Sin that wasn't his. Wrath's words from a card game we once played came back to me suddenly. *"I believe I'm powerful, therefore I am."*

Others believed it, too. Greed watched him, eyes narrowed, but didn't strike out.

I made my way into the room, but stood back, taking in the princes and the aggression that continued to radiate from each of them. As far as pissing contests went, it was subtle but effective. *Stride into a space, act as if you own it, and bow to no one.* I'd need to remember that. Greed was barely leashing his anger, which only fueled Wrath's sin, giving him the upper hand.

Silence ticked by, the tension in the room growing thicker the longer the brothers stared at each other. Wrath's eyes glinted as Greed's grip on his tumbler tightened. He looked half ready to throw the liquor glass at Wrath, but he must have thought better of it when he noticed the demon of war's dangerous grin.

"Were you saying something?" Wrath's tone was conversational, but there was an edge of danger in the casual way he leaned forward, as if he wanted to lure his brother into thinking he was about to share a secret. The promise of violence simmered just below the surface of his elegant veneer—something far too primal to remain hidden beneath the finery any longer.

Greed must have sensed the same danger. He inhaled slowly, then exhaled. "I got word you arrived here forty minutes ago. Keeping your host waiting is rude, especially given the circumstances of our meeting."

From where he now leaned against an oversized mantel sandwiched between floor-to-ceiling paintings, Lust released a low chuckle but didn't comment on either of his brothers' behavior. I was surprised he didn't offer the reason for our tardiness.

After the way Lust had torn all happiness and pleasure from me back in Palermo during the bonfire, he was by far my least favorite of Wrath's brothers. He didn't seem to notice—or care—that leaving someone an empty husk for sport was not the way to win friends. If Wrath hadn't brought me out from that dark place I'd been lost in, I'd likely still be curled up in bed.

"You're lucky we came at all." Wrath finally sat back, ignoring Lust's snort at his choice of words. I released a quiet breath, unaware I'd been holding it for so long, and shook my head. Adolescents, the cursed lot of them. "A midnight murder in your circle is hardly a major concern of House Wrath. This could have waited until morning to deal with."

"I disagree." Greed set his tumbler down. "Theo? Bring the hexed skull."

A blue-skinned demon with brilliant red eyes and vampirelike fangs came in from a secret panel hidden within the wall of books flanking the desk. In his hands was something familiar: a human skull. Unlike the ones I'd received, this one had dark rubies in its eyes, adding to the terror.

I swallowed hard, already fearing what was about to happen. Once the skull was placed on the edge of Greed's desk, it magically came to life, speaking in a voice that raised the hairs along my body. Only this time the voice didn't sound like my twin; it sounded like a true nightmare.

*"Tick tock, goes the clock, counting down your dread. Unless you cede, you'll watch more bleed. To pay you back, the next attack will be the highest head, dearest Prince of Greed."*

Greed settled his attention on Wrath again. "The monstrosity must have found out about our alliance. She no doubt believes I was acting on your behalf all along and, therefore, wanted to teach me a lesson for double-crossing her. This"—he jerked his chin at a second demon with a toad's head, who quickly stepped forward, rolling a cart with a shroud over it—"is what's left of my prized third."

The toad demon yanked the shroud off the body, and the stench hit me at the exact time the horrid sight did. My hand flew to cover my mouth. There was hardly anything recognizable of the demon left. Chunks of bloodied meat, stringy sinew, some bones. Bones that appeared to have been gnawed on by great, serrated teeth. My stomach lurched.

"Goddess above."

Each of the prince's attention shifted to me, but I didn't return any of their gazes. I refused to look away from the body. I was to be queen. And a queen, especially one hailing from House Wrath, didn't shy away from the terrible parts of ruling. She welcomed them.

"What do you think attacked..." From what was left, I could not tell the sex of the victim.

"Vesta." Greed moved to stand over the remains, his voice quiet. It was the first time I'd seen him act in any way human. Out of each of the princes I'd met, I always thought he didn't care to play the role of anything other than a prince of Hell. "She was the commander of my army. Unique. Coveted by many."

"Why was she coveted?" I asked.

Greed motioned for her to be taken away before answering me. "Because of her immense talent at strategy and battle."

I didn't say so aloud, but her immense fighting talent hadn't saved her from her fate.

An unfamiliar demon slipped into the room as what was left of the body was rolled out. He slowly removed a bloodied pair gloves and tossed them into a garbage bin. His hair was a shade caught somewhere between silver and gold, as if it were too lazy to be bothered with choosing one color. I took in the shrewd eyes that were now studying me as closely, a blue so pale they could only be described as ice. He slowly turned his attention to the princes.

"It's as we suspected." His words came out in a quiet drawl. "Werewolf attack."

"You're certain?" Wrath asked, coming to stand beside me.

"It's either that or a hellhound," the blue-eyed demon returned. "Have you set yours loose in other circles lately?" Wrath's only response was an impressive glare. "Didn't think so. There are few other creatures with the strength and power to cause those marks in the bone. Given what we know of our main suspect and who she associates herself with, it's the conclusion that makes the most sense. Especially combined with the rubies. Though I can't rule out any other beast for certain. The lacerations were definitely made by claws, not a blade."

"Father slay me," Lust groaned. "Must you always speak as if you're reciting a medical text?"

My interest shifted away from my own thoughts to regard the demons. The princes rarely spoke to other demons in such a derogatory manner, which meant this blue-eyed one was related to them. There was only one prince I hadn't been formally introduced to, though I'd been curious after catching the briefest glimpse of him at House Gluttony during the Feast of the Wolf.

I studied the blue-eyed demon again.

"You're the Prince of Sloth," I said. He inclined his head but didn't elaborate. "I thought you'd be—"

"Lazier?" Lust supplied. "He is, trust me. All he does is lounge about with his books. His House is one giant, messy library. Not an orgy or sinful tableau to be found in the whole of his circle. I can't tell you the last time he engaged in debauchery. I bet he hasn't even stroked his own cock in a decade. Fucking insulting to demons everywhere."

Sloth gave his brother a slow smile that was anything but pleasant. "There are many texts in my collection that outline adventurous sexual positions. I probably know more ways to make a body shiver from pleasure than you do."

"You may know *how* to," Lust said, "but actually *doing* it is an entirely different thing. You'd need to put the book down and put some effort into it."

"I can still read with someone's mouth on my—"

"That's enough," Wrath interrupted just as a dagger flew through the air, sinking into Lust's shoulder.

"What the fuck, Greed?" Lust yanked the blade free, glaring at Greed as he stepped forward, aggression rolling off him in waves. "You want to brawl, brother?" He shrugged his suit jacket off, eyes flashing as he roughly rolled up his shirtsleeves. "Let's go."

"Lust, stand down." Wrath stepped in front of his brother, checking him with his massive body. "Either stay and be useful or take this trivial nonsense elsewhere."

"Greed threw his House dagger at me; that's not trivial nonsense. I'm here doing him a favor. I could be well into debauchery and drink instead of listening to cursed skulls and Sloth's less-than-scintillating observations."

"You're still standing here. Which means Greed didn't hit anything vital." Wrath turned to Greed, not giving Lust a chance to respond. "Where did you find Vesta's body?"

A beat of silence passed before Greed responded. "In her bathing chamber. She'd finished training and was cleaning up before our dinner meeting. When she didn't arrive, I knew something was wrong. Vesta was never late to anything." He strode over to the tumbler he'd left on his desk and gulped the liquid down. Almost faster than I could process, he threw the glass against the wall, watching it shatter. "Vesta was special. There is never going to be another like her. You *know* who did this. She even placed rubies in the skull's eyes to send a message. On honor of my House, I demand a blood retribution. If you do not grant me this, then House Greed declares you and yours an enemy."

Wrath slowly turned to me. "Emilia."

His quiet tone, the way Lust and Sloth suddenly found the invisible lint on their suits to be interesting, the hard stare coming from Greed. The insistence it was a werewolf. They were laying out the evidence. Against my sister.

I wasn't entirely sure what their blood retribution entailed, but I couldn't let them harm Vittoria without more facts. At the same time, I knew we didn't need Greed to be openly at war with us.

Wrath glanced at me, his expression now the cold mask of a ruling prince of Hell, before turning back to his brother. "Sloth, what is the probability a beast other than a shifter inflicted those wounds?"

"Slim. I don't have exact percentages, but it's highly unlikely another creature breached the walls or wards surrounding the castle without first being noticed. Now, a shifter who can cross realms magically would have a much better chance at transporting themselves into these walls."

"And Envy said the abomination had no trouble getting through his wards," Greed added. "She made it all the way to his private wing, where she put on quite a show, but Envy suspected her taking Alexei so publicly was a ruse to keep him distracted. There's no telling what nasty trick she was up to. He's been searching to see if anything was stolen but hasn't reported anything."

"I doubt Envy would be so forthcoming if he did find something missing," Sloth said.

I shook my head—was that enough evidence to confirm my sister was to blame? I turned to Greed. "Vittoria had an alliance with you. Why would she attack your House? What were the terms of your agreement?"

Greed didn't appear inclined to answer my question, but Wrath gave him a hard look that had him rethinking ignoring his soon-to-be queen. I let the slight roll off me for now, though I wouldn't tolerate such disrespectful behavior a second time.

"Your sister wanted an ally in the Seven Circles for reasons I will not disclose in front of rival demon courts. Part of the terms included a vow to not harm any wolves. Something that seemed fair since she'd already formed an alliance with them and demanded the same from them in return. I was interested in the idea of taming such beasts. Seeing what they might offer. We are normally at odds, so it was an interesting gamble to take."

"It doesn't sound as if Vittoria would have cause to make you an enemy." I looked him over. "Why would she go back on her word? You keep mentioning how special Vesta was, but if you're not inclined to share with us *how* she was special—aside from her battle talents—is that something my sister would have discovered?"

"I do not deign to act as if I understand the way Vittoria's twisted mind works. Your sister likely found out I was acting as a spy for Wrath and took her revenge. I imagine it's that simple."

I glanced at my prince, unable to hide my surprise. "You were having him spy on my twin?"

"I wanted eyes on any potential threat to you." Wrath didn't sound or look sorry.

"You see?" Greed said. "Even your betrothed knows to keep a careful watch on her. She is a vengeful, spiteful wretch." Greed looked ready to exact some vengeance of his own as he leveled his glare at me. "She sent the hexed skull to taunt us. She not only murdered, she *maimed* my third beyond recognition. Your sister needs to meet her maker for her crimes. And if my brother does not sanction her death, then I will come for you and your family, and I will not stop until the last drop of her tainted blood has been wiped from this realm. Vittoria took from me, and now I will return the favor to make us even."

My heart stuttered. Yes, the evidence was damning, but anyone could have made it appear that way. "You cannot—" I moved away from the princes, needing a second to think. "The skull, it didn't sound like my twin."

"And how would you know what her enchanted skulls are supposed to sound like?" Greed challenged. "Has she sent threats to House Wrath, too?"

I spun around, hope filling my veins as I looked to Wrath. Vittoria had admitted to me earlier that she'd sent me at least one enchanted skull. I wasn't sure if Wrath wished to share this House secret, but he didn't offer any indication for me to keep it to myself.

"I recently received enchanted skulls, but they weren't threats. And each skull always sounded eerily like her. This one does not. She also never sent a skull with rubies before." I met Wrath's gaze. "We still have the skulls, correct? We'll fetch them and bring them here, and everyone can listen."

"That doesn't prove a thing," Greed argued. "She could have easily had someone else speak the rhyme in this instance. Maybe she did it to plant a seed of doubt. Besides, the rubies are a stone she's widely known for."

"All the more reason to think someone could have framed her."

"Who?" Greed challenged.

"Is there anyone who would want to harm Vesta?" I shot back. "Anyone who'd wish to harm *you* by attacking her? And how are you so certain the remains belong to your third?" I asked Greed, gaining the attention of each prince again. "There's not much left that's identifiable. Aside from finding the remains in her chamber, how do you know it's Vesta and not one of her attendants? Or how do you know the sex for that matter?"

"I—" Greed paced around his desk. He looked to Sloth. "You tested the blood?"

"I did, but there were a couple of different profiles—demon and werewolf—that made identification difficult, though werewolf was the strongest scent. Not unsurprising given the content of their blood typically reads stronger than that of any other creature. And Lady Emilia is correct; I couldn't determine the sex."

"Which means you cannot know with certainty that Vesta is dead and not simply kidnapped or gone of her own free will." I looked directly at Sloth. "Correct?"

Sloth blew out a slow breath. "Correct, though I believe unlikely."

"And what of the werewolf blood?" I asked Greed. "Why would the commander of your army have anything other than demon blood show up?"

Greed scowled. "I imagine that could be from her attacker. Further proving the werewolves acted on your twin's behalf."

"You cannot know for certain who acted on who's command. That's pure conjecture. If you're to condemn my sister"—I faced Wrath again, speaking directly to him—"I should hope you'd do so based on facts, not simply the likelihood of her guilt. You say the rubies are something she's widely known for, but then anyone with that knowledge could easily frame her. Including Greed."

"You overstep, Shadow Witch." Greed's voice was a low growl.

"If you have nothing to hide, this conjecture shouldn't offend you, your highness. The skulls she sent me recently did not contain any rubies. It's rather odd that yours did. If I were you and seeking the truth, I'd be very curious about Vesta and what she was doing in the hours leading up to her death. Did anyone hear anything unusual or see anything strange outside her chamber?"

"No," Greed said curtly.

"Was Vesta at odds with anyone in court?" I pressed.

The prince of this circle gave me a nasty look. "She was the commander of my army. Talented beyond measure and focused on her duty. She had little interest in pleasing anyone at court. She was meant to be feared, not adored."

"With all due respect, your highness, someone made it past her private defenses and overtook her. If she could be so easily harmed, then who's to say the same couldn't happen to you?" I glanced around the room, but no one—except Wrath—met my stare.

"My brother already determined that the most likely creature to break our wards and enter her rooms undetected was a shifter." Greed motioned toward Sloth, who inclined his head. "Your abysmal sister has taken one such creature as her lover. She clearly wishes to incite an internal war. Why else would she go to the trouble of forming an alliance she had no intention of honoring? You need to come to terms with the truth and stop putting the innocent on trial. Vesta is dead. Your sister is responsible. That's the end of it. Your mortal sentimentality is clearly clouding your ability to see the obvious."

My sister might be guilty of horrible things, but she was my blood. I would fight for her until I knew the full truth. And that was something that ought to be done for anyone accused of such a serious crime. The fact that Greed was content with leading what could only be described as a witch hunt, without any true proof of guilt, was appalling. How his brothers could stand here, entertaining it, was maddening. I felt my betrothed's attention on me and turned to him.

Wrath's gaze was penetrating as it held mine. And wholly unreadable. Something like dread crept into my belly the longer he held my stare. This wasn't my future husband staring deeply into my eyes; it was the demon fearsome enough to rule them all.

Greed moved around his desk, planting his hands on either side of the dagger he'd just retrieved after flinging it at Lust. "What's your decision, brother? Do you declare war on House Greed or the monstrosity your intended calls a sister?"

A flicker of something cold and calculating in Wrath's expression made me want to drop to my knees and beg for mercy, but I forced myself to maintain eye contact with him, keeping my own emotions locked away. He seemed on the verge of making his decision, so I spoke for my twin once more.

"A general and a king must make the tough decisions, even when unpopular. Judgment, in order to be fair, must be based on facts. Not emotions."

A muscle in his jaw clenched.

Wrath didn't look at any of his brothers when he said, "By attacking a member of House Greed, causing severe bodily harm and death, Vittoria Nicoletta di Carlo has openly declared war on the Seven Circles, and as such, she is now considered an enemy of the realm. If she is seen anywhere in any circle, each prince of Hell may act as he deems fit to ensure the safety of his people. House Wrath hereby accepts House Greed's request for blood retribution. If any official member of the seven Houses of Sin is found harboring the condemned without notifying me of her capture, they, too, shall be executed."

I stared at Wrath. I knew I heard him correctly, but I couldn't believe it. I could barely *think* past the sudden ringing in my ears. My betrothed, the demon I'd been about to complete an eternal marriage bond with, just sentenced my twin to death. His brothers murmured their approval, and I glared at them all as rage simmered. They had no facts. No evidence, no proof of guilt.

"I'll have the blood oath written up." Greed nodded to someone I didn't care to look at. "It may take a while since we'll need to use language acceptable to Houses Lust, Sloth, Greed, and Wrath. For now, please accept a guest suite to rest in or enjoy one of our many gaming halls."

Wrath nodded and finally turned to me. His expression wasn't one of sorrow or forgiveness. It looked like duty and cold justice. It looked like triumph.

Fury had my vision going nearly red as I dove into Source—a dozen roses burst into flames around the room. Lust and Sloth moved back, a flash of fear crossing their features. Heat from the raging flames had sweat breaking out across their brows.

It was the first time my magic actually produced fire with the ability to cause damage. And it was fitting, because I wanted to watch them burn. Fire crackled and popped, needing a place to go, to destroy.

I glanced at the painting Lust had been standing by, and my magic responded at once, each rosebud crashing into the canvas, setting it ablaze.

Greed shouted a command, and a demon stepped forward, grabbing a pitcher of water from the sideboard. He needn't bother. I silently bid the flames to retreat, meeting each of their wide gazes as the scent of charred canvas permeated the air. Perhaps my sister had been right. Maybe it was time for the demons to fear us for a change.

"Apologies, my temper got the best of me."

I gripped my skirts and spun on my heels, following the trembling attendant out of the room. I had just gotten my sister back, and it would be the coldest day Hell had ever known before I allowed any harm to befall her. Deceitful, conniving wretch that she was, she was *my* blood, and I'd protect her with each drop of mine whether she deserved my loyalty or not.

# FIVE

**"I won't ask** you to not scheme," Wrath said once we were tucked into our guest chamber and he'd thrown a ward up to keep our conversation private. "Only to use caution."

"How could you—*what*?"

I immediately stopped pacing and spun around, staring. I could hardly believe he was telling me to disregard his royal command. He looked at me intently, and it was then I knew; he'd been scheming himself. I thought back to his careful wording: *If any official member of the seven Houses of Sin is found harboring the condemned without notifying me of her capture, they, too, shall be executed.* Wrath was well aware that, without our marriage completed, I was not yet officially a member of any House of Sin, and his royal decree didn't apply to me at all.

My eyes burned with unshed tears. For better or worse, he was my partner and had been guarding my interests. Except this decree did complicate one aspect: he'd not be able to directly assist in my investigation himself, or he'd break his oath. All my ire drained away.

"Your brothers will want your head if they discover your treacherous negotiation."

"It wouldn't be the first time." His smile was predatory. "Nor will it be the last. You forget, their anger will only fuel my power more. I welcome their attempts at war."

I strode over and hugged him tight. His arms automatically went around me, embracing me back, and I sighed happily. "You are one cunning, magnificent demon. And I'm pleased you're mine. Even if I did just wish to strangle you."

"Or incinerate me?" Wrath sounded pleased instead of worried by my show of power.

"I'm sorry if that lapse of control will cause a complication for you."

"It won't. And even if it did, I rather like your anger."

Now that my fury was under control, I focused on what we'd just learned about the murder. Pieces of the story didn't sit well with me, but I couldn't quite determine why. "Do you know anything of Vesta's background?"

"Only that Greed had been searching for her specifically for a few years before she came to his House. We don't often share secrets regarding our closest counsel, so I don't know much else."

"Does Envy?"

Wrath expelled a slow breath, considering. "He might with his spies. But I have my own spies, and they have never uncovered why Greed wanted Vesta to command his armies."

"That's odd, isn't it?"

"Depending on any hidden talents or magic she possessed,

it would make sense that he'd covet that. His sin pushes him to acquire things that inspire greed, demons included."

And yet Sloth had mentioned there were a couple of different types of blood.

"*Was* she a demon?"

"I have no reason to believe otherwise." Wrath rested his chin against my head before pressing a kiss to it. "What are you thinking?"

"That perhaps she was something other than a full demon. Why else wouldn't Greed expand on why she was so special and couldn't be replaced? And why was there so much werewolf blood?"

"During a fight that brutal, blood would have been left by the assailants as well as the victim."

"I understand that. But Vesta was ripped to shreds. Even if she harmed a wolf severely, she would have lost the most blood—*demon* blood..."

"It's a valid point. But the potency of werewolf blood overwhelms our senses. Similar to the scent of a strong astringent. If you smell ammonia, then try to pick out any notes underneath it, the ammonia will always dominate."

"Blood and bones. All one has to do to get away with murder is splash some werewolf blood around the scene."

"Which is part of the reason werewolves want nothing to do with demons and vampires. They used to be hunted for that very reason."

My lip curled in disgust. No wonder the wolves despised vampires and demons.

Putting that gruesome piece of history aside, I thought of other viable options for the case at hand. "If we spoke with Vesta's family, perhaps we might learn information about who might want to harm her. Who she might have spent time with away from Greed, when she wasn't training his army. If we know what she did outside of her duties, we might have a solid thread to follow."

"I'll see what I can find out when I sign the oath." He ran a hand down my spine in slow, loving strokes. "Speaking of that. We'll need to find an excuse for you to miss the blood oath later. If you sign that document, even my scheming won't matter."

I rested my head against his chest, thinking. "Well, they certainly know I was furious with you when we left. What if we go down to one of the gaming halls and I happen to drink one too many demonberry wines? I won't get truly intoxicated, and if I do, you can magic it away like you did when you tested me for gluttony. I'll make a terrible scene, and you can encourage me to go back to our rooms and sleep it off. We'll simply have to convincingly playact in front of one of your brothers so they can vouch for us."

Wrath drew back to look me in the eye. "If you make a scene, it will have to be debauched enough to draw attention in a gaming hall in a House of Sin. It will truly have to cause a scandal worthy of notice, and that will be extremely difficult here. Short of destroying part of the castle, or unleashing another sin, I'm not sure it's possible. Are you up for that challenge?"

He was asking *me* the question, but I had the sense *he* was also wondering the same thing about himself. But maybe *that* was the key. I thought back to Greed's receiving hall while we waited for our escorts, and a wicked idea sprang to mind. I was fairly confident I could create quite the stir. And my betrothed's legendary temper would help to ensure that.

I didn't have to cause a scandal; I only needed to light Wrath's fuse.

"Go find Lust or Sloth in a gaming hall and send word to me of where you are. You can plant the seeds of giving me space to cool off, and I'll make my grand entrance."

"I don't—"

"You need to trust me, Samael." Whispering his true name made him go perfectly still. I trusted him, knowing his truth. It was time for him to return the favor. "You need to be just as affected by my performance as everyone else. If you know my plan ahead of time, it will not only ruin the surprise, but it will also make it impossible for you to lie about it. Now go." I rolled up onto my toes and kissed him quickly before pushing him toward the door. "And please have a lady's maid sent up at once."

I strode into the darkened gaming hall, swaying my hips a bit more than necessary as I snatched a glass of demonberry wine from a passing tray. I took a slow sip, my painted lips curving seductively, as I scanned the room. Felt-covered card tables lined the perimeter and were packed with lords and ladies of this circle. All the wood furnishings were dark, elegantly carved, and plush enough to entice gamblers to sit and stay awhile. Alcohol and food also made frequent rounds, ensuring demons didn't have to leave their seats for any refreshments.

The carpet was ornate if one took the time to admire it, but it also blended into the dark, enchanting feeling of the gaming hall. Torches flickered softly from each corner, creating a comfortable ambience. Greed clearly wanted patrons to forget the world outside of this House of Sin. Near the center of the chamber was a prominent stage with a few demons slowly stripping off clothing. Several small tables were placed in front of it, offering patrons an opportunity to sit and watch the sultry show. It was mostly empty, save for a few demons drinking alone at the foot of the stage. If my first idea didn't pan out, that stage might be a perfect second option.

Toward the right was a long, gleaming bar that featured towers of liquor bottles and wines, all ready for consumption. Just as I'd suspected, I felt the first licks of Greed's power bolster my actions. I desired attention, and therefore, those who were happy to oblige were drawn to me. Instead of shrugging off the magic, I welcomed it, used it as fuel for my secret mission.

Wrath had walked into Greed's study with confidence, so I adopted his demeanor and behaved the same way, even if my heart was racing.

I spied my mark at a serious-looking table where they were throwing dice, and I paused to survey the occupants before they spotted me. The demons seated around him all seemed particularly refined, and I hoped that meant they were upper nobility. Aside from creating a scene, I needed to inquire after someone who knew Vesta. It wasn't simply enough to eliminate my twin as a suspect, I wanted to know the truth. Greed seemed to have made up his mind about Vittoria awfully quickly, which I found suspicious even if the other princes didn't.

I made my way over to Lust, enjoying the feeling of the pearl tassels swinging against the back of my thighs. As far as skirts went, this was barely considered that. There was no fabric, only hundreds of strands of pearls that barely reached midthigh. I had nothing on underneath, so each step and extra flounce of my hips ensured patrons got quite the show. My top was equally daring. Featuring a choker that had strings of pearls connected to the straps and cups, it was really no more than a half corset made up entirely of gemstones that left very little to the imagination when I moved.

Nudity wasn't scandalous here, but Wrath's reaction to what I had planned should get demons in this circle talking. I knew the moment Wrath spotted me across the crowd of gamblers—his attention was scorching, palpable. I ignored him completely and sidled up to Lust. The temperature around us chilled a degree or two, but I still didn't spare my betrothed a glance. He had his part to play, and I had mine. My sister's life might very well depend on whether I could avoid signing that blood oath and gather information to clear her from guilt.

"Having any luck, your highness?" I leaned over the felt table next to Lust, knowing anyone standing close would get a clear view of my backside and a glimpse of my breasts as they moved against the pearls. Predictably, Lust allowed his attention to linger everywhere it shouldn't.

I sensed the slightest bit of his sin, though it felt as if he were keeping it at bay. He truly did fear his brother. I supposed a House dagger to the chest left quite the impression. An inconvenience I'd have to overcome. Wrath and I both needed Lust's sin for this scene to work.

"Seems it just turned." He flashed a smile, then looked back at the table. Next to him, a male demon with an exceptional amount of gold stole a glance at me. On his right hand was what appeared to be a signet ring. He had to be upper nobility, which made him perfect for this game.

I gave him a coy smile as I leaned into Lust. "Who's your friend?"

Lust drew back from his roll and followed my gaze. "The Duke of Devon. One of Greed's top advisers."

My smile grew. "Pleasure to meet you, your grace. I'm—"

"There's not a demon in here that doesn't know who you are, Lady Emilia." Devon grinned. Too bad for him it actually seemed sincere. "Have you ever played Dead Man's Pride?"

I watched another demon blow on the dice and toss them down the table. "I'm not much for playing games of chance."

His attention flicked over my top, his look indicating he might be intrigued to know if I preferred a different sort of game instead. "Would you care to indulge me?"

I would rather gouge my eyes out. "I'll just watch for now. Perhaps, if you're talented enough, your grace can persuade me otherwise."

Wrath's annoyance caused the air to chill slightly again.

I squeezed between Lust and the duke, purposely brushing my hip against the latter's arm. I turned to Lust and whispered loud enough for Devon to overhear. "Earlier you said something about a present from House Lust." I sipped my wine, then discarded it before grabbing another full glass. No one seemed to notice I hadn't completely finished the previous one. I leaned closer to Lust and dropped my voice. "You've piqued my curiosity. Is it like your last gift, or will I actually enjoy it?"

"Oh, it's *much* better." Lust fully turned to me, his game forgotten as he took my measure. Whatever he saw in my face must have been convincing enough for him to decide to play. "I can give pleasure without taking. Would you like a little taste?"

"Here?" I glanced toward the duke. He was pretending not to listen, but as he leaned forward in his seat, he seemed quite eager to hear the response.

The Prince of Lust nodded to the stage where several demons danced in various states of undress. One male—who wore nothing but the gems on his member—slowly stroked himself, seeming to enjoy the greedy gazes on him. Another male beside him whispered something in his ear, then bent to take his hard arousal in his mouth, pleasuring the other demon for all to see.

Lust watched me closely. "You could join them up there, experience the power of two sins at once. Those body adornments they wear enhance every sensation. Imagine how those pearls would feel as they slid over sensitive flesh, hitting areas of pleasure inside you never dreamed of."

I tore my attention back to Lust and flicked it over the Duke of Devon. "I'd prefer to stay here, actually. Could you still give me a taste, or will that distract from the game?"

The mighty chill of Wrath's anger hit me like a storm a second before he reached my side, and judging from the way several gamblers at the table staggered away and abandoned their game and stack of coins, I wasn't the only one who'd felt it.

Warm fingers brushed along my wrist. "Emilia."

"Don't." Even though my body screamed otherwise, I shrugged him off. "I'm in the middle of a *pleasurable* conversation with people who didn't condemn my twin." I turned my attention to the duke and gave him a polite smile. "Prince Wrath, please say hello to the Duke of Devon."

Wrath flashed his teeth. "Fuck off, Devon."

"Easy now." Lust grinned at his brother. "Keep that up and Lady Emilia will experience three sins at once."

"Not if I cut off your goddamn head and serve it to my hounds." Wrath managed to scare off another gambler. Thankfully, the duke wasn't to be deterred. The goddess must have been watching over me, because Devon's preferred form of this court's sin was attention, and our little show was feeding his form of greed expertly.

I finally met Wrath's furious stare. Goddess above he was something magnificent to behold when he let his magic out of its cage. He was playing his role expertly. Soon he'd go feral, and I couldn't wait for that beastly part of him to finally be unleashed.

"If you'll excuse me. I've experienced enough of *some* sins for one evening. Please go back to your own table." I caught myself before I lied, knowing Lust would sense it as easily as Wrath. I faced Lust, but purposely looked at Devon when I said, "Will you give me a taste now? Or must I wait?"

Lust slid his attention from where Wrath still hovered behind me, then leaned in. "It looks like if you get your gift now," he murmured close to my ear, "you may incite a riot."

"A risk I'm willing to take." I stumbled into the duke and allowed him to steady me with one hand splayed a bit too low on my back. The moment he touched me, Lust's sin enveloped me. I'd been ready for it, though, so I drew the power to me, used it as an extension of what I wanted instead of allowing it to overrun me.

The Duke of Devon quickly dropped his hand, but the sensation of being touched didn't abate. Lust's sin felt as it did the first time I'd experienced it—like invisible hands were on me, dancing up along my body. Only this time the invisible hands were bolder, likely the result of being in Greed's House of Sin and openly desiring attention.

Music I hadn't noticed before grew louder, the drumbeats urgent and primal. Carnal. It was time to put my plan into motion. I dropped onto Devon's lap, earning a surprised huff from him, though the duke was only too pleased to have me perched there like a prize he'd done nothing to win but was more than happy to show off.

His chest brushed against my back as he leaned in, "Your companion won't murder me, will he?"

"Unlikely, your grace. Not when we were asked here to investigate a murder."

The magical hands Lust had gifted me with wasted no time with seduction; they slid over the front of my body and inched downward. With that magical sensation moving all over me, it was going to be wildly hard to concentrate on gathering information, but it would be rather easy for the second part of my scheme.

I leaned against the duke as those wicked invisible hands continued their slow, tantalizing path across the swath of bare skin that ranged from just under my breasts to my navel then stroked upward again. The magic was like a drop of liquid heat rolling up and down my neck, between my breasts, circling their peaks as it continued languidly stroking me.

I slowly slid down the duke's thigh, my attention split between the action and reaction I sensed coming from a different point in the room.

"It's a shame what happened to her, isn't it?" I asked.

"You mean Vesta?" Devon's breath caught with the next shift of my body.

"Yes," I whispered breathlessly, eyes still closed. Goddess curse Lust's power. It was too good. "Did you know her?"

Another lick of heat that had nothing to do with Lust's magic-fueled desire had me cracking an eye. Wrath had commandeered a seat on the opposite side of the gaming table, his hard, burning gaze fixed on me and the duke, whose knee I was grinding against.

I gave my betrothed a secret smile. Having Wrath there, watching, made it feel as if he were the only one in the room with me. It was *his* attention I desired above all, *his* greedy hunger I wanted to ignite. His fury. I longed for him so desperately, so deeply, I ached. What we'd shared in the gondola wasn't nearly enough, and the greedy desire I'd felt for him came rushing back, mixing dangerously with Lust's gift.

"I knew Vesta a little," Devon said, answering a question I nearly forgotten I'd asked. If I had any hopes of keeping my wits, I needed to stop looking at Wrath while Lust's sin worked me. "She seemed distracted as of late."

"How so?"

Lust's soft chuckle sounded to my left, followed by a stronger wave of his magic. The demon bastard was going to kill me with pleasure or help to incite the riot he'd warned me against. A soft, breathy moan escaped my lips. Goddess above, everything felt *so* good. The pearls of my skirt hit interesting places as I rolled my hips again, searching for more of that glorious feeling. The duke swore roundly when he noticed what I was doing, but he kept his hands on the card table where Wrath could see them.

My attention locked onto the demon prince again as euphoria swept through me. I wanted to be on *his* lap, riding him until we were both sated. Wrath gripped the arms of his chair as if he were holding himself back. I wasn't sure if it was anger or desire that had his attention riveted to my show. I didn't care. This game we were playing just turned more interesting.

"Your grace?" I managed to ask between invisible strokes. "You mentioned Vesta seeming distracted. Do you recall how?"

"She'd—" The duke shifted in his seat beneath me. "She lost several games. It was unusual enough for the court to start talking. Vesta never lost focus. I even heard she'd been asking odd questions lately, about scenting blood and the intricacies of it."

"I was under the impression all demons could detect information in blood."

"That's precisely why some were growing curious about her.

She'd assign a guard to test any blood disputes during skirmishes. An odd amount of werewolf blood kept tainting the scenes."

Which would certainly enrage any werewolves whose blood had been taken, giving possible credence to Greed's suspicion of them being responsible for the attack. "Did anyone ever mention this to Greed?"

"His highness punished anyone who brought up Vesta in any negative light. Everything I've heard has all been the result of court gossip."

I inadvertently slid down the Duke of Devon's lap as he adjusted himself again, immediately feeling what he'd been hiding. His arousal. I quickly moved away from it, but not before a low growl sounded from across the table. Wrath looked close to launching himself at the duke, every muscle in his body appeared strained, and his stubborn will was probably the only thing keeping him in check. Goddess above he was incredible. Thanks to the heady combination of greed and lust mixing with Wrath's sinful allure, I wanted him to lay me down on the gaming table, spread my legs, and own me right here and now.

My king swallowed hard, his gaze darkening, and I realized he sensed *my* arousal. At first, I wasn't certain if he could tell the difference between who had turned me on—it certainly wasn't the duke. I only desired my favorite sin, but with the amount of anger radiating off him, I realized he'd misjudged. It seemed our performance was very close to finally causing a scene. It was time to gather any other information I could before Wrath lost control.

"Was anything else unusual about Vesta before her death?" I asked. "How are her family members taking it?"

"No...no family." The Duke of Devon's breathing turned erratic when my hands skimmed along the front of my top. "Vesta wasn't originally from this circle. Prince Greed kept that a secret that only he and Vesta were supposed to know, but word travels in court. For the right price. Vesta wasn't her given name, according to gossips."

*Interesting.* "Do you know what her name was?"

"No. She never spoke of it."

"And she was alone at court?"

The duke flicked his tongue over his lips. "Vesta had dalliances over the years, nothing that took her away from her duty. Some believed Greed wanted to make her his consort, but he's always denied that and so has she."

"Did they ever"—I ran my fingertips along my outer thighs—"have relations?"

Wrath's hands flexed. And the sudden thought of him pleasuring himself while watching me do the same made me forget this was supposed to be a scheme. All I wanted was him. And greed took over. The Duke of Devon began stroking my outer arms, and I wondered if Lust had sent him a little encouragement or if it was simply greed driving him to participate in my show.

"Vesta typically preferred the company of females. Though she was known to sleep with the occasional male if she desired him."

"Have you heard anything else that would be interesting?"

"I'd rather not think of anything else at the moment, Lady Emilia." The duke leaned over my shoulder, his attention locked on my fingers as they traveled under my skirt and I—

The temperature plummeted. Startled cries sounded from the stage. I glanced over in time to see what had happened. Ice shot across the stage, and gyrating couples slipped but didn't fall. We were getting very close to creating a scene now, but it still wasn't enough to make an impression on this court. Wrath needed to lose control. Embrace the devil he was.

I pushed myself up from the duke's lap and perched against the gaming table, my back to Wrath as I slowly kicked one leg up and over to the other, crossing my legs primly and effectively drawing Devon's hungry stare. My wineglass rattled then cracked, spilling wine over the table.

The Duke of Devon didn't notice. His greedy attention had finally been captured in its entirety. He undid the stays on his trousers and yanked himself free, then stroked his length as the remaining players at our table turned to him, indulging in his sin. My attention remained fixed on his, though I was truly focused on the massive presence behind us.

A low rumble rolled through the gaming hall, not disturbing enough to stop the gambling or the greed-fueled tableaus, but enough to have drinks splashing onto the card tables. I sent a silent prayer to the goddess, hoping Wrath would act soon. I'd already heard more than enough from Devon. The duke stood and stroked himself harder, groaning as if he was getting close to his release. Lords and ladies at our table hungrily leaned in, feeding into his desire to be watched.

"Lady Emilia," Devon groaned. "Touch your—"

*"Enough."*

Wrath's voice was barely more than a whisper, yet the hair along my arms stood on end. Power pulsed in the air around us like a storm was about to hit. That was the only warning anyone received. And then it happened; a thunderous crack rent the air, silencing the drumbeats. The duke standing before me froze, a look of confusion quickly turning to fear as he dropped his cock and jumped back, narrowly missing a chunk of ceiling that crashed before him. Bits of plaster rained down, falling in a circle around me, protecting me from the impending chaos.

I drew my attention up—lines spiderwebbed across the ceiling, the cracks growing until it crumbled. Wood splintered, crystal chandeliers rattled, the stage started caving in on itself as if the ground was swallowing it whole. Demons shouted and abandoned their sex shows as they rushed for safety. I sat in the center of my impenetrable ring, watching as gaming table after gaming table was suddenly coated in ice, heavy and thick enough to break and shatter the ornate wood.

"Blood and bones." Our game had worked. Maybe too well.

A table nearby disintegrated. Another quickly following. All around the gaming hall, furniture exploded into dust or was coated in ice that was so heavy it broke all it touched into shards. My table remained undamaged, the one speck of calm in the storm of wrath.

Wrath's fury was demolishing the entire room, piece by piece. My breath came out in white clouds, the temperature now dangerously below freezing. It was as if we'd crossed into a world made entirely of ice; it was cruel and harsh and lethal. Just like the look on my prince's face when he turned that wrathful gaze on the duke. I shuddered. And Devon promptly pissed himself.

Then Wrath was truly there, tossing me over his shoulder like a barbarian, his large hand covering my backside as he carried me from the destroyed chamber.

He was practically vibrating from the pressure of holding back his power. I couldn't imagine what else he could do, what else he could destroy, if this was only a taste of his magic.

My attention landed on Lust, who was chuckling in the chaos. Recalling our game, I began pounding on Wrath's back. "Put me down!"

The demon prince didn't respond, not that I expected him to. Wrath was focused only on his sin as he swiftly removed us from the gaming hall, where shouts were still ringing out and the violent, unnatural blizzard swirled within that chamber. Snowflakes kissed my bare skin, so cold they felt like little nips. Wrath truly was a force of nature.

Using supernatural speed, he had us back in our room before I knew it.

He gently set me on my feet and paced away, his fury lashing out. I hid my grin. Our plan worked beautifully. Wrath's sin had ruined one of Greed's gaming rooms, and we got information on Vesta. Overall, it was a wild success. Though the poor duke would claim otherwise.

"Well?" I asked. "Do you think it was a believable scene?"

It had to be—Vittoria's life depended on it.

Wrath slowly turned from where he'd magicked the room to conceal our voices, his attention raking over me. He did, indeed, look like a feral animal whose leash just snapped and was testing for any new cage. My heartbeat quickened, and not in fear. I'd wished to provoke him into action. And he certainly looked primed and ready to act. His arousal strained against his trousers, and the way he was staring at me, like he'd devote himself to wringing pleasure from my body for hours on end, made me ache for him all over again.

"Did you enjoy the show, your majesty?" Holding his gaze, I pivoted in place, making sure the pearl tassels swished against my backside. "You could have at least allowed the poor duke to finish. The nobility at the table was enjoying his performance."

"Emilia." It didn't sound like a warning as much as a plea. One more step, and he'd be as gone as I was.

"Was I wicked enough to fool a prince of Hell?" I ran my hands over my barely there top, allowing one strap to fall down. "Better yet...was I wicked enough to entice the devil?"

Wrath cursed gods I'd never heard of as I sauntered closer. He looked like he was a breath away from pouncing. I practically felt the tension snapping between us, and I leaned into it.

Wrath took a small step toward me, his gaze locked onto mine. The hunter had come out to play. "Tell me you want this."

My attention ran over him, slowly and thoroughly. I hadn't forgotten that anger acted as an aphrodisiac to him. Hadn't forgotten how it also made me feel.

"Right now, I want the demon, not the prince. Show me why they call you the Wicked." I grabbed his shirt and tugged him to me, my lips hovering above his. "And don't you dare hold back."

# SIX

**Wrath had me** against the wall before I drew my next breath. He fingered the pearls of my top, his breath hot against the back of my neck as he roughly ground his hips against me. "If you change your mind—"

I spun around and cut him off with a violent kiss. "Stop again, even for a *second*, and I promise we'll test your fondness for knife play, demon."

Wrath's answering smile promised deviance. He gently stroked my breasts over the pearl top until they grew heavy and ached for more.

"This top." His fingers curled around a strand, his warm, bare skin *almost* brushing mine. I never hated a piece of clothing more. "Needs to go."

The prince's grip tightened on the strand, and he yanked, the pearls bouncing across the floor as my top broke apart. He allowed his gaze to slowly peruse my eyes, my lips, and every inch of my body until he'd reached the floor and dragged it back up. I loved when he looked at me like that. Like I was the beginning and end of each of his fantasies. He certainly was mine.

"You are absolutely devastating."

He dipped his head, kissing his way down my neck, not stopping until he'd cupped one of my breasts and sucked it into his mouth, his teeth scraping ever so lightly. I leaned against the wall, my hands traveling down his powerful arms, holding him close as he lathed his tongue over the sensitive peak.

"Wrath." I writhed against him, unable to stand the slow, expert flicking of his tongue. My body was drenched and ready. "I want you. So bad I can't think straight."

He pressed openmouthed kisses to my other breast, laughing quietly as I gripped his hair and held on. "When I saw you on that idiot's lap, soaking wet and nearly coming, I wanted to fuck you right there. In front of the whole damned court."

The way he growled, low and rough like his very un-princelike words, set my blood on fire. I pressed against him, needing to feel him as I went up on my toes and whispered, "I would have let you."

Wrath's lips crashed against mine, the kiss neither sweet nor tender. It was animalistic and wild. A claiming and battle for domination. Tonight, we'd complete the physical part of our marriage bond, and Wrath did not want a submissive queen. He longed for an equal. Just as I did.

I broke away from our kiss, then licked up the column of his throat, pleased when he released a string of curses and roughly ground his hips against mine again, his length as hard as granite. He buried his face in my neck, kissing and sucking until a breath hissed out of me.

He drew back and brushed a loose strand of hair away from

my face, like he was checking to make sure this was real. "I spent that whole time thinking about what I'd like to do." One large, calloused hand traveled along my left side, slowly sliding over my hip, down my thigh, until he reached the back of my knee and hoisted me up against him. "Imagining how you'd feel. The sounds you'd make. When I murdered that bastard, spread your legs, and pounded into you. Right there on that fucking table."

His tantalizing words, the heat and desire in his eyes. It was too much.

"Please. I need you inside me. Now." I ripped at the stays of his trousers, slipped my hand inside the material, and began to play.

"Emilia."

My name on his lips, the reverence of his tone—it awakened something in me. A feeling so strong I could only express it with action. I sucked his bottom lip between my teeth, biting down gently, and stroked him faster. His skin was as soft as silk, but his arousal was stronger than steel.

This magnificent, deadly creature was *mine*. I would commit ugly, savage acts if anyone interrupted me from claiming him right here, right now.

"Emilia, demon's blood." He thrusted a few times into my grip before tearing his pants off, his shirt following in rapid succession. Wrath spun me around, placing my hands against the wall. "Keep your legs close together and lean forward."

"Yes, General." I did as he commanded, my body already slick and ready.

"Smart ass."

I grinned at him over my shoulder as he grabbed a handful of my bottom, the move pure possession as he playfully squeezed it. "Perhaps you should punish me."

"Is that a request?" His eyes flared with desire as I nodded. "Tell me when you've had enough, my lady."

He parted the strands of pearls and gripped my hips, angling me up. He pressed himself against my entrance, and my body went hot and tight from the erotic feel of it. He teased me, sliding his length back and forth across my slickness.

I arched against him, silently pleading. He rubbed against me harder, pressed a little deeper, but only nudged the tip in. I swore roundly and went to push myself onto him, but he pulled back, sliding across my core again. And again. And again. Until I was practically panting and crawling up the wall with need.

"Wrath. Please. Fuck me."

"As my queen commands." With a single, fierce thrust, the demon was fully seated inside me. He gave me a moment to adjust to the feeling of him, my body stretching not unpleasantly. He leaned his weight against me, kissing the back of my neck, nipping at my earlobe as he slid out, then in, going deeper. And deeper. "Tell me now."

"What?" The breathless, sultry voice barely sounded like mine.

Wrath repeated the motion, no longer for me to adjust to his size, but to slowly torture me to death from the pleasure.

On his next deliciously slow thrust, he hit a bundle of nerves that drew a moan from me. He brushed his lips against my ear. "That I am your favorite sin."

He pulled my backside toward him, pushing me down a little more, finding the perfect angles to elicit the most ecstasy. It was a little rough, a bit wild, and intensely primal. I couldn't imagine a more perfect joining.

"Tell me you're mine." Wrath's passion burned hotter than his sin, and I burned for him. My body tightened around his, my core throbbing, and fire seared my veins. I was his. Forever.

Just as he was mine.

"You are my favorite everything." I leaned against the wall, pressing back against him, working my hips in time with his deep thrusts. To give as good as I was getting. "You're *mine*."

"Fuck, Emilia." Wrath groaned, one hand now locked on to my hip so he could tug me against him, while the other hand found the front of my body, his fingers playing me like an instrument he was proficient in. It was almost too much, and yet I never wanted the feeling to stop. "You feel like heaven."

"Goddess curse me. Harder."

Wrath obliged. He unleashed all of himself, pounding against me so hard the light fixtures began to shake. The painting I'd barely noticed crashed to the floor.

And then it happened, the past slammed into the present, and a vision overtook me.

*In a different demon House, Wrath pressed me against the wall in a darkened corridor, wringing pleasure from my body as he thrusted into me. We'd both torn my clothing entirely off but kept his trousers on. And the idea of him half-clothed drove me wild. My attention was riveted to the hand with the serpent tattoo as it worked my body, bringing me to the brink of climax then slowing down until I was mad with want. He liked to tease, to draw out my pleasure until I took it on my own.*

*I could hear the sounds of others just outside our secret corridor. At any moment, someone might come upon us. Neither one of us wanted an audience, but balancing on that knife's edge of discovery, the slight bite of fear that came with it, suddenly heightened the experience.*

*As I came closer to the edge, I noticed a faint glow coming from my hand; a tattoo was beginning to appear along my left ring finger. Wrath thrusted again, deeper and faster—my mind and body were both on the brink of giving in to the pleasure he was demanding.*

*He bent me over. "Keep your legs together. Closer."*

*His command and the friction the new position created had me calling his name despite our need for silence.*

*I arched my back, and the demon hit a spot deep within that had me seeing stars. I breathed hard, my attention fixed on the large hand that held my hip. A tattoo had appeared there, too, on Wrath's same ring finger. I smiled, thinking of the words he'd spoken earlier.*

*The eternal vow.*

*I covered his hand with mine, braiding our fingers as he slammed our bodies together one last time, shuddering and cursing as we both came.*

The vision abruptly disappeared, and I was once again in the present. It must not have lasted for long, or else my prince would have noticed. Wrath pulled out, then pushed in, his breathing ragged against my neck. We were both close, our skin damp and hot. I was nearing my release . . . but I still swore I felt the aftershocks from the climax in my vision, which only heightened my experience now.

"Goddess above. Don't stop."

"Never."

His words were spoken with the promise of a vow. Wrath rubbed my clit in wicked circles, right where he still thrusted into me, and I came violently. A moment later, he joined me with a harsh curse. My legs trembled as he leaned forward and gently kissed my neck.

As I caught my breath, I stared at the tattoos that had now appeared on our fingers in the present, finally making out the words as the light faded into our skin.

The letters were written vertically in rose-gold, from just under my nail to where my finger met my hand.

S

E

M

P

E

R

T

V

V

S

The words were spelled like Roman inscriptions. It took a moment for me to piece together what the Latin said. *Forever yours.*

Wrath reached around and placed his left hand on mine, revealing the rose-gold ink that now also ran along the entire length of his ring finger. *SEMPER TVVS.*

Past and present collided and, for a moment, I couldn't tell which was which.

"Emilia." His voice was soft, measured. I couldn't stop staring at the tattoo. I gently tugged my hand from under his and sucked in a breath. This was no illusion or past memory; the same phrase really was inked onto my skin in the here and now.

I held up my hand, twisting it around. "Is this because of the marriage bond?"

Wrath pulled free of my body and turned me until I faced him. "Yes. And no. Did you remember something?"

"I... I'm not sure. I saw us. In the past. Just now." I moved to the bed and sat, my gaze locked onto the ink. "We were in a dark corridor, making love. And these same words appeared."

"Do you recall anything else? Anything at all?"

"I had the impression you'd said the words earlier that evening." I rubbed my temples, suddenly feeling unwell. "Dear goddess above. It was *me*. Wasn't it? Not the First Witch. Not Pride's missing wife. Not some reincarnation. *Me*. But... how?"

Wrath crouched before me, his hands resting gently on my knees. His touch was not simply meant to soothe and comfort, but to reinforce. As if he could somehow help break the hold the curse had on me. The curse. Heart hammering, I squeezed my eyes shut. The curse...

There was something else *there*, something niggling around the edges of my memory. Fuzzy and out of focus. Like opening your eyes while under water. A memory was straining to break free, to fight its way back to me. I opened my eyes and focused on the new ink on my finger.

"Has this always been here? Hidden by a glamour?"

"I have a theory, but..." Wrath's voice trailed off, likely the curse's fault.

"Who am I?" I demanded. The room was spinning. "*What* am I? Do *you* remember?"

It took so long for Wrath to respond that I almost jumped when he spoke.

"For a long time, I didn't. And if I did, the memory would warp."

"And now?" My voice was quiet, tense. "Do you remember who I am?"

Wrath's gold gaze latched on to mine as he slowly nodded. My whole body tensed as I waited. "You are the one she tried to make me hate for eternity. But she failed." His grip on me tightened slightly, but not painfully, like he was never going to give me up. Unless I wished to leave. *"Remember."*

The single word—spoken with authority and pure dominance—kept playing and replaying in my mind, almost spinning wildly like a top out of control. There was something there, in the way he'd commanded me to remember... magic. He'd commanded me through magic.

Wrath was feeding me his power, likely a result of our marriage bond. I sensed the slight trace of Wrath's magic in the air, deep inside me, and gripped onto it, wanting—more than anything—to understand how I could be both enemy and lover. How I could have ever forgotten.

My heart thundered in my chest, too strong, too powerfully. Something was wrestling and fighting within me, something that was snarling and feral—something that wanted to break free.

Our power seemed to merge, to braid together, creating new magic. Strong magic. A well of power too enormous to be contained. It was fire and ice and full of rage and passion. Whatever spell or curse or lock that was on my mind cracked. I cried out as magic flooded my system, lighting me up from within.

"Samael." I reached for Wrath, but he was already there, holding me. Offering his strength. He must have sensed the slight fracture in whatever held my memories at bay, and he seized upon it, turning his power into a spear and aiming it for that one opening.

"Tell me who you are." His voice was filled with that same magical command. *"Remember."*

It felt as if I were now submerged, struggling to breathe, to think, to fight for air. I gasped, choking. Panic descended, and I was suddenly convinced I was on the edge of death. A warning rang in my head.

Death was not for me. Not yet.

I closed my eyes and stopped fighting, knowing innately I needed to let go, to give myself over to the force rattling its cage. The second I imagined myself floating instead of sinking, the frantic feeling subsided. The sunken memory skyrocketed to the surface, then broke free.

I opened my eyes, and Wrath drew in a sharp breath. A reaction so small it would be deemed unremarkable coming from anyone other than him, yet I knew this was the beginning of the end. The truth I'd fought so hard to find was no longer hidden by magic.

"I remember." My voice was scratchy as if I'd been screaming for hours. Maybe I had been. Time felt strange. My prince looked weary, but hopeful. "I know who I am."

Wrath's dagger was now in his hand. He stood and motioned for me to do the same. We walked to a mirror hanging near the bathing chamber, and the demon nodded to the glass. "Tell me what you see. Who you see."

Glittering rose-gold irises steadily gazed back at me. A mark of my true power. Though part of me wasn't as surprised as I ought to be. Maybe deep down, where the curse couldn't sink its claws in, I'd always known. There was a reason I was aligned best with my sin of choice.

Celestia's words drifted back to me from the night I'd met her in Bloodwood Forest; the Crone had said Wrath was my mirror. I'd suspected then but couldn't reconcile the truth of *how.*

Now the truth was staring back at me, waiting. "I see fury."

"And?"

My fire. My anger. That ancient, terrible power I'd only barely scratched the surface of. They all belonged to me. "I see the goddess who rules it."

"I see my equal. My queen."

Wrath handed me his blade, his lips curving seductively. He seemed lighter, slightly less weighed down, like a nightmare was finally over. I wasn't as sure but held my tongue. There were still plenty of things I couldn't yet remember, which meant even with some of Wrath's power inside me, the curse wasn't fully broken.

My memories were only just starting to slip out through the crack we'd made, and I had a terrible suspicion that many more unsettling truths were waiting to be revealed.

Wrath pulled me against him, and tucked within the safety of his arms, I hoped perhaps he was right. That even if the curse wasn't completely broken, maybe things would be better now.

He angled his mouth close to me and whispered, "Welcome back, your majesty."

# SEVEN

**"I need to** sign the blood oath." Wrath pressed a kiss to my forehead, then pulled his trousers on. It was so normal, mundane, after the cataclysmic realization of who I was. After what we'd just done, not to mention the scene we'd created and the potential consequences of Wrath's destroying part of his brother's castle. And terrorizing the duke. Goddess above. The duke. After his fear had worn off, I imagined he'd be embarrassed to have soiled himself in front of other members of the nobility. The last few hours felt like a wild, years-long fever dream. "We can discuss everything in detail once we're home. Will you be all right?"

I kept staring at my reflection in the mirror. I was not a witch. I was the goddess of fury. If I didn't just witness the truth, I'd still not believe it. My irises slowly returned to the warm brown I'd been used to for so long, another reminder I was not fully free from the curse yet. "Yes."

Wrath watched me, noting the moment I *really* looked at the dagger. It wasn't his House dagger as I'd thought it was. Up close it was slightly smaller than his. Lighter.

The snake also didn't have lavender eyes; the gemstones in this dagger were dark pink. Vines twined around the hilt, winding delicately around the serpent, much like the vines I'd summoned earlier in his bathtub.

"It's yours," he said, answering my unspoken question as he shrugged on a crisp, new shirt. I searched for a memory of the dagger but didn't recognize it at all. Wrath moved before me, tilting my chin up until I met his steady gaze. "I never had the chance to give it to you before. But it is yours. I designed it myself."

My attention dropped back to the dagger. I liked the feel of it. The weight. It was perfect for me. Just like the clothes he'd had waiting in my wardrobe when I'd first entered this world. Because Wrath knew me. For goddess knew how long. I was no eighteen-year-old witch; I was an ageless being. Unable to handle the full scope of what that meant, I shook those thoughts away, concentrating on the weapon in my hand. I had my own House dagger.

Worry gnawed at me.

"Now that we completed the physical part of our marriage bond, will the decree you made earlier about Vittoria apply to me?" I asked.

"You're not officially a member of my House until you swear a blood oath." He buttoned his shirt, seeming to choose his next words with care. "And the decree gives each House the authority to do as it sees fit. Technically, that allows me to do just that without breaking the oath. We will find Vittoria before my brothers can. You won't have to swear a blood oath unless it's what you want. In fact, I might see how we can arrange for us to swear an oath together."

If I didn't already know I loved him, that would have sealed his fate. I looked at my dagger again, a new realization forming. "Vittoria is the goddess of death, isn't she?"

"Yes."

Hysterical laughter bubbled up my throat, but I choked it down, refusing to start crying instead. I'd prayed to the goddess of death and fury countless times after Vittoria's "death." She was the deity I connected with most during my quest for vengeance. Now I knew why.

Except it was all much more complicated than I'd ever imagined. Instead of one deity, there were two goddesses: Death and Fury.

Even now, seeing my eyes change color from my power, I had a difficult time accepting it. I'd grown up. Had a mortal family. Lived a fairly unremarkable life in Palermo before my sister "died" and I'd accidentally summoned the king of Hell.

Or maybe not so accidentally? It could not have been a coincidence that Vittoria had left the incantation needed to summon Wrath where I'd find it. I just needed to know why.

Did she think he was the key to freeing the rest of my memories? And if she believed that, then why would she tell me to not marry him now? Was it really only because she believed that in order to join his House, I'd have to give up something of me in return? There was clearly much more to the story, considering some of her actions didn't quite line up with her words.

For now, I couldn't imagine how our lives as goddesses had been covered up. Magic was the likely source, but I'd never heard of such a spell. Every memory I had of our life seemed real. If it was a glamour, it had been cast by someone with immense power. Someone like La Prima Strega.

I thought of Nonna Maria, of the secrets she'd kept from us. The stories she'd twisted about the Wicked and the First Witch and the devil's bride. Nonna told us that when it came to the Wicked, *nothing* was ever as it seemed. But maybe the true villain had been much closer all along.

To even *think* that made my stomach clench. A betrayal that large was unfathomable, though nothing would surprise me now. The people I'd loved unconditionally were turning out to be morally questionable, and the creatures I'd been conditioned to hate were not so terrible after all. My world was collapsing around me, from the ground up. It seemed as if a giant chasm split open and was swallowing me whole. Wrath reached over and stroked my arm.

"I can't... I can't remember much else." I glanced back up at Wrath. "Will I regain all my memories? Or will the past always be fuzzy?"

Instead of answering, Wrath summoned clothing—a velvet gown, gloves with buttons running up the side, and a traveling cloak—from the ethers and laid them on the bed. Little vines and flowers were embroidered along the edges. Rose-gold and black.

A blend of his colors and mine, apparently.

I forced myself to focus instead on what had driven us here and the new consequences of failure. "The duke mentioned several interesting things about Vesta. Did you hear any of it?"

"Most of it," Wrath admitted. "Vesta wasn't from here originally. My brother Greed supposedly wanted to wed her. And she was distracted lately. Couldn't scent blood, but inquired about it in detail. A curious amount of werewolf blood would be present at any scenes she'd attended. All, unfortunately, is court gossip without fact. Though I'm particularly intrigued by the blood. It's unusual enough for the commander of an army to be unable to trace information one can easily and effectively glean from scenting the scene, but on top of that, wolf blood frequently appearing is perplexing."

"If she was unhappy here, those inquiries might indicate she was trying to find a way to fake her own murder. If it were me and I couldn't scent the same information a demon could, I'd want to know every last detail to craft a believable ruse. Perhaps those instances of werewolf blood before were for practice. Maybe she was seeing how much was needed to overwhelm a demon's senses."

My sister had certainly proved that feigning a murder was possible. Until I found irrefutable proof otherwise, I'd remain suspicious that Vesta might not be truly dead. A new thought occurred to me, but it was another complex riddle, one that needed time to sort out.

"What is it?" Wrath asked.

"Things aren't quite making sense. Vittoria chose to strike an alliance with Greed. It was supposedly to unite his court and the werewolves, but it's peculiar that his commander should be 'murdered' under such mysterious circumstances. Especially when Vittoria is an expert at crafting a believable death. If Vesta is truly as talented as Greed had claimed, I find it hard to believe she was easily overtaken. No one hearing the attack can be explained away by a ward, but—for the sake of argument, let's remove werewolves from the equation—who would have had access to her private suite? Your brother didn't mention anything amiss outside her chamber. No scratches or forced entry. Which means she must have known whoever she'd allowed in. There has to be more to his story. Will you question your brother and see what he says?"

"Of course. But we might have a better chance of learning the details from your sister. Greed will not likely cooperate with a rival House, even if he'd sought our assistance." Wrath pulled on a pair of leather gloves, hiding our new marital tattoos. "After you dress, the carriage will be waiting for you out front. I'll meet you there shortly. Wife."

Despite everything chaotic and wrong, a smile tugged at my lips. "Husband."

It felt right. More than right. It felt like coming home.

The demon prince drew me close, kissing me fiercely enough that I melted against him, then left. Our game of deception wasn't yet over. He had one more part to play. Hopefully, Greed would be annoyed enough by the destruction of one of his gaming halls and wouldn't press for my signature or appearance. He'd want me as far away from Wrath as possible, lest I set off his brother's temper again and ruin the rest of his castle. I'm sure the duke was already in his ear, too. Nobility didn't care to be made fools of.

Which made me wonder if that could potentially be motive for someone to murder Vesta. At this stage, I wasn't ruling out any possibility. Greed's behavior was certainly odder than usual, continuing to cast him into question for me.

I pulled myself together, quickly dressed, and had just stepped outside into the softly falling snow, reaching for the coach door, when Wrath appeared. It should be disconcerting that someone so large could move so silently, but my husband was a predator who only pretended to be civil.

Wrath helped me into the carriage—the driverless black-and-gold beauty pulled by the four horsemen of the apocalypse, Wrath's pet demon horses—and pounded his fist against the roof, signaling for the red-eyed, ebony horses with metal teeth to take off.

He flicked the velvet draperies aside, regarding the passing landscape with a growing scowl. To our left, the Black River churned, the dark-capped waves bubbling like a cauldron.

An uneasy feeling crawled along my spine. The water had been much calmer when we'd first arrived, and if Nonna Maria imparted anything, it was to look for signs of trouble.

Unrest was certainly brewing.

I wondered if it had anything to do with the blood oath the princes just signed. Perhaps the Seven Circles were already preparing for my sister's demise. And, despite Wrath's promise that we would find her first, maybe danger was already pounding at her door.

Wrath met my inquisitive gaze and gave a slight shake of his head. We hadn't traveled far enough from the rival House, and Greed probably had spies stationed near the edge of his castle's immaculate, snow-covered lawn. Like all magic, there were limits to the spells Wrath used to keep our rooms private. Since this was a moving conveyance, it was likely too complex for the magic to keep up. I nodded my understanding and turned my attention on the window. I was desperate to ask if he'd gathered any more information on Vesta from Greed, but we'd be home soon enough and could discuss everything freely there. My burning curiosity would need to wait.

We sat in tense silence as the carriage rolled down the long drive that led over a small tributary. After what felt like an hour, but had probably been only half that time or less, we finally ascended the steep hill that would take us to a bridge connecting the land between House Pride and House Wrath.

At the top of the hill, Wrath went on full alert. I wanted to know if he could sense Vittoria or if there was some other cause for alarm, but he flashed me another look that indicated it wasn't safe to speak yet. I racked my mind for any other known threats but couldn't think of one. He removed his gloves and withdrew his House dagger, pressing the tip into his palm, hard enough to feed the blade a bit of his blood. Both the metal and jeweled eyes glowed as if pleased and fortified by his offering. His cut healed within seconds. A fine perk of immortality. I wondered, if I was a goddess, how I could be mortal. Wrath finally broke the silence.

"If anyone approaches the carriage and anything goes badly, for whatever reason, activate your cloak and run for our fortress. Anir will command the army while I hold them off."

"Activate my cloak? It's magic?"

He nodded. "Feed it a bit of your power and it will reflect the world around you, essentially making you invisible. It won't mask your scent but should give you time to escape."

"You expect me to abandon you if we're attacked?"

"Yes. Right now, I'm the general and you're a soldier. You'll do as ordered."

"Is that so?" I raised my brows. "I don't recall swearing an oath or making any vows."

My tone had been measured, but my king was no fool. Wrath's answering look would probably send his demonic soldiers running to the latrine with loose bowels.

I was not his solider. I was his wife. And if the arrogant ass thought I'd leave him, to whatever enemy might be lurking, he was sorely mistaken.

As was just evident by my power-fueled rose-gold irises, and my ability to produce fire that now burned physical objects, I was not without frightening magic of my own. And I would stand beside him, fighting with my last breath if it came down to it.

"I'm immortal, Emilia."

"And what am I?" If I was a goddess, and we'd had years together in the past, then there was something else he wasn't telling me. Something I'd get to the bottom of once we were home.

Wrath's gaze battled mine, all golden fire and icy fury. It was a skirmish he wouldn't win; my mind was entirely made up. No point he could argue would dissuade me from staying with him. After another long moment, he finally surrendered.

"If anything goes wrong, I'll try to *transvenio* us onto our grounds. Stay close and get your blade out. Strike first and fast. If anyone is brazen enough to attack us during the afternoon near my House, they won't hesitate to harm you."

"Do you believe it's V—"

A howl rent the air, the sound reverberating through the coach. A second howl went up. Followed quickly by a third and fourth. Soon, a whole chorus of mournful howls filled the air, bouncing back against the mountains in the distance and echoing softly.

Fine hair all over my body raised.

Wolves. From the sound of them, they were large, otherworldly werewolves. That answered my question about *who* was out there, but it left the *why* up for contemplation. The horses whinnied and growled, the sound unlike any mortal horse I'd ever encountered.

At first glance, Wrath seemed calm, focused. Until I saw the flicker of excitement in his eyes. He was made for war, for battles. Where others would shut down from fear, something shook him awake. He gave me a slow, cocky grin. "The shifters are angry."

And that blessed emotion was fueling the demon's already incredible store of magical power. I returned his smile, feeling relief sink into my bones. We'd be fine. Wrath let the curtains fall back, hiding us from view. Apparently, he wasn't concerned with seeing his enemies.

Another howl went up, closer this time, louder and filled with what was probably alpha command. Domenico was here. I couldn't imagine why the wolves were in the Seven Circles, and after Greed's insistence that they'd attacked his commander, fear gnawed at me despite my husband's excitement. Given the way Domenico had been with my sister, how easily and quickly he'd heeded her command to stand down with me, I couldn't picture him acting against her.

Wrath hit the roof of the coach with a closed fist, startling me, and our carriage rolled to a sudden stop. This was it. Nervous energy hummed through me.

If the werewolves were here and so was Domenico, I prayed that meant my sister wasn't far behind. If she was, and if they weren't planning an attack on their own, then all we had to do was neutralize the shifters, grab Vittoria, and take her to House Wrath. None of the other princes would even know we'd found her and stowed her away.

Wrath jerked his chin toward the door, indicating he was about to open it. I clutched the hilt of my dagger, my palms damp and heart pumping. If I could find my sister and speak with her, perhaps we could avoid bloodshed altogether. Surely when she saw me, she'd stand down. Then we could discuss Vesta, and I'd have my answer one way or another about her guilt.

"Remember, stay close. Strike fast." The prince paused with his hand on the knob, then shook his head. He grabbed me around the waist and kissed me hard and fast. "If you die on me now, I'll hunt you down and drag you back."

"Sounds rather threatening."

"It's a fucking promise, my lady."

"I love you, too." I cupped his face. "If you're quite through, let's kill some werewolves."

His gaze darkened. "Bloodshed turns me on almost as much as your little performance did. I'm going to take you directly to bed after the fight." Wrath flashed a devastating grin. "And we're not going to reemerge for a long, long time. I hope you packed the pearl skirt."

Any nervousness or trepidation I was feeling vanished. I suspected Wrath's speech was meant to get my mind on what would happen *after* the battle, to give me something to focus on. He was a good general; I'd tear through a thousand wolves just to get him back into bed.

His smile was filled with male arrogance. Deservedly so after our earth-shattering lovemaking, so I couldn't fault him there. Sensing I was ready, Wrath palmed his dagger and shoved the door open. He burst through it in a flash of violent movement. I jumped out directly after him, my blade ready.

The elation I'd just felt disappeared as I took in the sight before us.

Wolves, nearly a hundred of them, oversized and monstrous, stood on the bridge, shoulder to shoulder, blocking our path to House Wrath. But that wasn't what had my heart thudding in my chest. It was the dozens of wolves that floated in a semicircle around us, their paws ten feet above ground. They were spirit walkers. And they were waiting in the wings to pounce if any of their brethren went down.

*Blood and bones.* I had little doubt Wrath would take a huge portion of them down alone, but there were so many. Too many.

My sister had amassed an army. As if my thoughts summoned her, Vittoria appeared behind a row of particularly vicious werewolves. Gone was her signature smirk, the mischievous light dancing in her eyes. The being that stared at us was cold, devoid of humanity. Immortal. She was what I truly was, and it chilled me to the core.

"We had an appointment to speak today, sister. I got tired of waiting, so I brought some friends to escort you to the Shifting Isles." Vittoria's focus moved to Wrath. "I suggest you let her go quietly."

The ground rumbled, as if Wrath's fury had shaken the very core of the realm. "Surrender yourself to House Wrath, willingly and peacefully, and I'll allow your puppies to live."

"How very magnanimous of you." Vittoria's mouth curved into a slow, vicious smile. "And foolish. It seems you've not heard what I can do. Allow me to demonstrate."

"Vittoria," I said, forcing calmness into my voice. "Come with us."

"Why should I?"

"Because you're suspected of murder, and there's a price on your head."

"Is that so?"

"Yes." I held her amused stare. "And I believe there's much more to the story. Please. Stand down and come talk to me. I want to hear your side of things. Let me help clear your name of any wrongdoing."

"Why should I care if a prince of Hell thinks I'm a murderer? None of them can be trusted. They trick and manipulate and pride themselves on it. And I've tolerated playing by their rules long enough."

My sister held her right arm up and bent her elbow as if she were holding a ball. She was too far away for me to make out the words she was whispering, but I watched in growing fear as she softly chanted. Glittering lavender light swirled around her bent elbow, slowly circling her forearm and wrist, before settling around her hand.

Wrath cursed and stepped in front of me, shielding me with his body. I peered around him, horrified as my sister's fingers lengthened. Claws emerged from her too-long fingers, ebony as the night and sharper than daggers. Her arm looked charred, as if she'd stuck it into some hellfire and yanked out magic that wished to be left alone. Dark veins crept past her elbow, seeming to mix with her blood. The swirling lavender light winked out.

She held up her clawed hand, proudly showing off the demonic-looking appendage. I could do nothing but stare as she turned to a shifter. "Domenico, my love. Come."

The grayish-blue wolf to her right—the size of a bear with glowing pale purple eyes—padded toward my twin, whining softly as it crouched before her.

Without warning, Vittoria's magically altered hand punched through the wolf's chest, the sound of bone crunching and muscle tearing sickening in the eerie silence. I could hardly believe what had happened. Vittoria ripped her arm back, clutching a still-beating heart and pivoted, holding it up for all to see. Domenico collapsed in an unmoving heap of bloody fur, dead.

"What have you done?" I whispered. My stomach lurched at the brutality. The gore. I'd seen wounds like that before. On witches. Wrath and I hadn't quite known what had removed their hearts. He'd guessed animal, unable to identify any trace of a demon. I'd been convinced it was a prince of Hell. I slowly shook my head, unable to process that my twin was capable of an act so violent, so merciless. She'd murdered her own lover. *She'd* murdered the witches on our island. The why was still a mystery, but I now knew who. And it sickened me. "You killed those girls."

Not Antonio, or an angel of death. My sister. My blood.

And at this moment, it was hard to believe she hadn't also killed Vesta.

Vittoria looked me over, her gaze calculating. "Anyone can kill, dear sister. Would you like to see the true reason they fear me? Why they wish to see me caged?"

"Please." My voice came out pleading, but I didn't care. "Please. Don't. Just come with us."

"Begging is for mortals."

Vittoria shifted, her attention dropping to the lifeless wolf at her feet. With her free hand, she bent two fingers in a "come here" motion, and Domenico's lifeless wolf body levitated. She cocked her head, looking at the heart that still beat slowly in her hand, then shoved it back into his chest. When she ripped her demonic hand back out, the wound healed immediately.

His matted fur disappeared, replaced by a shiny, nonbloodied wolf coat. All signs of death were gone. Domenico's glowing eyes opened, and he snarled, baring his teeth.

Not at the creature who'd slain him, but at us. All I could do was stare, unable to process that my sister had not only murdered someone but also brought them *back*.

"We are hell gods, Emilia. *We* are the Feared." My twin looked at me again. "Neither witches, nor shifters, nor even princes of Hell can stand against us when we're united. Your power is awakening. It's time to take back what is ours. It's time to come home."

My home was House Wrath. By choice. Something dark rose up inside me, protective.

"Is this why you cautioned me away from Wrath? Because you want me to join you?"

"Of course. You don't belong with the demons. You belong with your blood."

"And if I refuse to go with you?" I tested my grip on my dagger. "What then?"

My sister allowed a few beats of silence to pass, just long enough for it to be uncomfortable.

"We'll find another way to free your power from its magical cage." Vittoria ran her attention over Wrath, amusement lighting in her eyes as the ground rolled beneath her feet. "You are kerosene. Volatile. Noxious." She pulled a dagger from the ethers. Its blade glowed with strange magic symbols. Wrath went preternaturally still. "And I am the spark you need to ignite."

My husband didn't wait for her to strike.

In a whirl of movement and fury, he unleashed the full might of his power.

And the wolves attacked.

# EIGHT

**Wrath fought with** brutal grace, moving like a living, breathing nightmare as he cut a bloody swath through our enemies. He killed without mercy or pause. Something leapt, he destroyed, already on to the next kill before the former hit the ground.

His body wasn't simply made for war; it was built for it through hard work, a weapon he'd honed to perfection for this very purpose. For a moment that just lasted from one heartbeat to the next, I could only stare at the warrior.

He struck; wolves went down and didn't get up. Blood splattered across the snowy ground. The metallic tang thickening the air along with the gamy scent of adrenaline. In the matter of mere seconds, the demon of war had already taken down a dozen werewolves. A dozen more froze solid, their bodies suddenly encapsulated in ice, midattack.

Here the infernal truth of his power was on full display.

Wrath sent out a pulse of magic that traveled like lightning across the land. A signal, no doubt. The demon horses broke free of their carriage gear and bridles, charging through wolves, their metal teeth gnashing, tearing through flesh and bone with ease.

I snapped into action, fighting my way through the horde, trying to close ranks around us. Body memory guided my actions, as if I'd always known how to kill with the same sort of cold violence. As the goddess of fury, I'm sure I'd had plenty of practice, even if I couldn't remember.

I smashed the hilt of my dagger into the frozen wolves, ignoring the chunks of bodies and bloodied meat that shattered with the ice. My body sung with power, with fury. But there was a limit—it felt like the wall that had been erected when Envy stole my magic.

The curse was still holding me back. For the first time, my anger at being purposefully kept in the dark overwhelmed my fear of learning the full truth. If we made it out of this fight, I silently vowed I would do everything I could to return to my true self.

Never again would I feel powerless or caged.

Snow started falling heavily, the already gray sky growing darker, more foreboding. If Wrath commanded snow and ice to do his bidding, it made sense that the underworld was a frozen tundra. His power could not be contained, so much that the very land bent to his will. I hoped it terrified our enemies. I wanted the realm itself to swallow them whole.

Wrath pushed forward, reaching the edge of the bridge right as more wolves dropped down from the Shadow Realm. The demon threw his powers behind him, freezing anything that moved other than me and his demon horses. Through the chaos of battle, I searched for my twin.

Vittoria had disappeared, but I felt her presence on the periphery. She was waiting. Whatever she had planned wouldn't be good. I needed to get to her, convince her to stop, or incapacitate her myself. A wolf leapt, jaws snapping, and froze, crashing to the ground a foot from me. Blood splattered across my face. I didn't stop to wipe it.

Behind me a whisper of movement drew my attention. I twisted, striking hard and fast at a wolf that went for Wrath's back. It had come close. Too close. My fury bubbled deep within, threatening to boil over. I stayed close to my king, my rage a war beat that pounded in time with my heart.

Wolves attempted to strike the demon, but either he took them down or I did. His horses growled to my right—biting and kicking their way through wolves.

On and on, it felt as if we fought for hours. Blood saturated the ground, my cloak soaking it up like an offering. I reveled in it, thanked it. I welcomed more.

More death. More rage. More *vengeance.*

My blade glowed rose-gold under the blood staining it, drinking up the offerings I served it. We'd almost reached the center of the bridge when I heard a sound more terrifying than the werewolves and horses combined. It snarled and barked like a rabid dog. Several of them, actually.

Footsteps pounded, shaking the ground. At the edge of the bridge, coming from House Wrath, four mighty hellhounds paused. I swore under my breath. Wrath hadn't been kidding when he'd called the hound I'd encountered in the Sin Corridor a puppy. It had been the size of a pony. These three-headed beasts were the size of elephants. Their ice-blue eyes flashed—and the wolves nearest them raised their hackles, their attention now split between Wrath and his attack dogs. The fight just got harder for the wolves and my twin. Thank the powers that be.

Without wasting another moment, the snow-colored hellhounds entered the fray. I watched long enough to see their pale fur splattered red with their kills, then resumed my own bloodbath. I focused on the blade in my hand, turning and striking like it was all some well-choreographed dance. The battle was the music, and death my skilled partner. All the while, vengeance pounded against my soul.

Wrath fought with the same fervor as when he'd begun, not looking close to being tired. The wolves couldn't say the same. Some of them stumbled out of the way, thick white foam coating their muzzles, their chests heaving from exertion.

Between the hellhounds, demon horses, and Wrath, victory seemed close. Imminent. I ducked as a wolf leapt over me, then slit its throat, its blood spraying my face and dampening my hair as it crashed to the ground.

"EMILIA!"

I turned at the sound of my sister's bloodcurdling shout, unable to stop my first instinct to seek her out and protect. It was a mistake. The world went to hell from that one act of familial affection and humanity. A werewolf knocked me to the ground, its jaws snapping at my throat. Claws tore at my cloak, ripping the flesh of my chest, and I screamed.

Then the wolf was gone, yanked from me and tossed against the bridge so hard its neck and back cracked, loud enough to be heard over the fray of hell horses and hellhounds battling on.

The wolf trembled once violently, then stilled. I exhaled and bit down on another yelp. The wound on my chest throbbed with each accelerated beat of my heart. The full pain hadn't exactly hit yet—a result of adrenaline, no doubt. Though I did feel oddly light-headed.

Wrath's eyes were twin flames of gold as he stood over me, surveying the damage done to my body. The temperature dropped impossibly colder. His anger had reached its limit.

My twin, the werewolves, they'd better retreat before he obliterated them. He reached for me, then dropped to his knees. Blood blossomed across the front of his shirt. He looked down, brows tugged close, as if he couldn't believe it, either. A glowing blade protruded from his chest.

"Wrath!" I scrambled up, ignoring the tearing sensation as my wound split further and I gripped him, wrapping my body protectively around his. "It's all right." My hand fluttered over his wound. "I'll take it out. You'll heal."

"You know." Vittoria stood behind Wrath, yanking the dagger from his back without remorse. "So many people are searching for the Blade of Ruination..."

I looked from the wound that was still furiously bleeding to my twin. Wrath said the hexed blade could kill him, and my sister stabbed him through the heart with a blade that clearly did damage. Wrath usually healed within an instant. He'd also said he could sense it when it was near, but he'd been distracted. Because of me.

His bronze skin was rapidly going pale, but his fury was unmatched as he held my gaze. "Your cloak."

I gave him a look indicating the dagger had clearly affected his common sense. There was no chance in this realm or any other that I'd leave him like this.

"Fix him." I glanced up at my sister. "Fix him now!"

Vittoria appeared to consider my demand. She shrugged. "No."

"Vittoria." My breathing became faster, erratic. "You would deny me this?"

She signaled to the wolf that must be Domenico, and he sank his teeth around my shoulder, hitting the wound on my chest as he yanked me backward. Pain overtook my senses. And the werewolves used the distraction to form a barrier between me and my husband.

I shoved past the agony and stepped to the snarling wolves. "Stop this. Vittoria, just *stop*. I'll do whatever you want."

"Maybe I want to watch him bleed. How does that make you feel, Emilia? Mad?"

Vittoria kicked Wrath's back, right where the blade had struck, and he coughed up blood.

"Angry?" She hit him in the temple with the hilt of the dagger, hard enough that it would have killed a mortal, based on the loud crack alone. He winced as blood poured down his face but didn't cower. Something was definitely wrong or else he would fight back. "Or furious?"

"Stop!" I screamed.

"What will it take to wake your magic?" Vittoria grabbed him by his hair and yanked his head back, exposing his throat as she pressed the blade there. "This?"

Whatever that dagger was, it had done extreme damage to him. If she cut his throat, if I lost him . . . I detonated. That ancient power, that slumbering beast—it woke with a vengeance at the sight of Wrath's blood. I didn't bother holding it back. I didn't grasp for control.

I let go.

And fury overwhelmed my senses entirely. I became a pillar of rose-gold flame. The air turned scorching hot, though a protective ring flared up around me, Wrath, Vittoria, and Domenico. Everything else except for Wrath's hounds and horses . . . burned.

Wolves yelped, and the ones not fast enough to leave caught fire. The stench of burnt fur wafted through my barrier, the sickly sweet scent of charred flesh following. Vittoria watched with great interest but said nothing as my power raged even hotter.

The snow and ice turned to puddles, the river water boiled beneath us, wolves farther away blinked out of existence, returning to the Shadow Realm. The stones on the bridge began to melt. In seconds, we'd fall into the steaming water, our flesh boiled from our bones.

I didn't care. I'd take my sister with me. My need for vengeance was an unquenchable thirst I couldn't satiate. I'd take them all and then—

Sleet pelted me suddenly, the icy sting of hundreds of frozen drops briefly snapping me out of my trance. Wrath's fingers clasped mine, squeezing once before his grip went limp. I dropped my power, then I went to my knees, cradling him against me.

"Of course the Blade of Ruination has been impossible to find," Vittoria finished, tossing the blade aside. "Which is why I had to resort to poison instead. Being the goddess of death has its perks. It took some time to get the potion correct, but I made something strong enough to take down an immortal."

It took a second for my brain to catch up from my emotions and piece together what she'd been saying. I jerked my attention to my sister. "You didn't find the Blade of Ruination?"

"Not yet." Vittoria sighed dismally. "Though lying about it worked just as well, all things considered." That was why Wrath hadn't sensed it. It was all a fucking ruse. My fury took hold of me again, but before I could unleash myself, my twin raised her arm and made a squeezing motion with her hand. "Sleep."

My heart slowed. Panic seized me as I realized there was no

way I could help Wrath or myself now. My head hit the ground with a crack. I stared unblinking at my husband, who seemed to have rallied and was shouting my name.

His face was the last thing I saw before the world went dark.

I awoke to the sound of fire crackling, though cool dampness permeated the air instead of warmth. It smelled of turned earth. Like a grave. The very ones Nonna used to take us to each full moon so we could collect dirt to bless our amulets and ward off the devil. My husband.

I blinked up at a ceiling covered in roots and sat up with a start. It was dark, underground dark, and the thick roots crisscrossing the ceiling indicated that wherever I was, a giant tree was above me. I glanced around the empty room...cell. Bars made up one entire wall, too close together to slip through—the other walls were packed dirt, the floor impenetrable stone.

Lines of painful fire ran down my chest and turned agonizing.

The battle. Wrath. Wolves.

Everything came crashing back at once. Despite the burning wound, I shot off the straw mattress I'd been placed on and gripped the bars, hoping to rattle one loose.

Sharp pain lanced up my arms, and I quickly let go. The bars were spelled; hopefully it was only a complication, not a complete hindrance. I dove into Source and summoned my fire, aiming for the metal; the flaming rosebuds sank in, the metal angrily glowed crimson, then...nothing. The cursed bars absorbed the magic.

I tested them again and was knocked backward from the surge of power.

Perfect. My magic fed the spell; the more I fought to get free, the more trapped I'd become. It was a nasty little trick, but effective. Goddess curse her. "Vittoria!"

"Do you recall the night you eavesdropped on me talking about the Stars of Seven, Shadow Witch?"

I jolted at the sound of another voice and focused on what I'd thought was a darker shadow pressed into the far corner of my cell. "Envy?"

The prince of that sin sat forward, just enough for the light from the lone torch in the corridor to show his cool, handsome features. "You're not the only one disappointed, pet. I'd rather my brother was here instead, too."

"How *are* you here?"

Envy gave me an annoyed look. "Your sister couldn't keep her demonic hand off me." He absently rubbed at his chest, right where his heart should be. His shirt was torn like Vittoria had, indeed, wrenched out his heart. He caught my horrified expression and gave me a slow, wicked smile. "Not to worry. It grew back. Shriveled and just as black. But it's there."

"I don't want to know."

"Immortality." He shrugged. "Wounds heal, hearts regenerate. Life goes on. And on."

When stated like that and muttered in a bland tone, it sounded dreadful.

"If Vittoria didn't want you dead, why would she rip your heart out and lock you in a cell?"

"In case you haven't noticed, your sister is both a sadist and a psychopath. Though judging from that nasty wound on your chest, that's not surprising news." Envy rose to his feet and brushed the dust from his trousers, then he scowled at his dirty hands. "She also happens to be obsessed with me, though I suppose I can't fault her for that. I'm unbearably handsome. My refusal of her advances, as well as her offer of an alliance, drives her mad."

"You're unbearable, perhaps, but the rest remains to be seen." It was interesting that my sister had also sought out Envy when she'd had an alliance with Greed. Unless it happened the other way around. "Were you her first or second choice for an alliance?"

"Second. Though I'm sure she wishes she came to me first. My coffers are bigger than Greed's."

"I doubt that, your highness."

He really grinned at me this time, showing off his boyish dimples. I'd only seen them once before, and it softened me to him.

"Looks like your sister isn't the only one with sharp claws. Believe what you like, pet, but remember I can't lie." He glanced at the marks on my chest. If I didn't know better, I'd think concern creased his brow. "You need to get that taken care of. It already looks infected, and the rot will stink up the cell to high hell."

"Duly noted." My eyes narrowed. "Why do you keep calling me a shadow witch?" I asked. There was no healer, no bandages, no point in dwelling on something I couldn't tend to. If the wound got that badly infected, the stink would be the last thing to worry about. "I know what I am. Who I am."

"Do you now?" He sounded unconvinced as he sat on the floor again.

I drew in a deep breath, focused on the last image I had of Wrath to fuel my sin. To allow it to temporarily break free from its cage, then I let go. "You tell me."

"Your eyes..." Envy raised his brows, looking almost impressed. "Mortal no more. Seems like immorality has won out. No surprise there. Though you're not healing, which is rather curious."

I released my fury and exhaled. Envy scrutinized my features but didn't comment on what I imagined was the return of my warm brown irises. I lifted a shoulder, then motioned to my eyes. "Not quite immortal."

"You may not have your full powers, but mortality submits to immortality in the end. It's the strongest force of the two. A drop of immortality is more powerful than a bucket of mortality."

That made sense. Almost. Except for the fact that Wrath had fought very hard, more than once, to keep me from "dying." I would get to the bottom of why soon enough. "Let's not get off track. I asked about shadow witches. Tell me what that really means. Please."

Envy cocked his head, considering.

" 'Shadow' because you possess a mere shade or shadow of your true power. 'Witch' because with so much dilution of your magic, that is what you are. What all witches are—descendants of goddesses."

"Why couldn't you tell me that before?"

"The curse wouldn't allow me to. Seems like more than your eye color is changing."

I thought about the magic bond between me and Wrath. The one that had allowed him to spear into my mind and crack whatever had been holding my memories at bay. "Do you believe my marrying Wrath has anything to do with that?"

Envy regarded me as if I was suddenly very intriguing. "You both accepted the bond?"

"This appeared on both of our fingers." I held up my hand, showing the new tattoo. "After we..."

A smile flickered at the edges of his lips. "You consummated your bond at Greed's House of Sin. I'm surprised Wrath lost control at a rival court. It's something he's vowed to never do again."

I glanced away, thinking of the events that had led up to our impromptu lovemaking. "Part of Greed's castle collapsed; Wrath's emotions were running a little high."

Envy's bark of laughter drew my attention back to him. "I imagine my dear brother and his temper had something to do with that. It would certainly explain why he'd claim you right then and there. Well played, little Shadow Witch."

"I hadn't intended for that to happen."

"Once something is put in motion, we rarely have control over the outcome, no matter what our initial intentions are."

Envy leaned back, elbows propped on his knees, hands clasped casually in front of him. His shirtsleeves were rolled to his elbows, showing off surprisingly corded muscle. There was a warrior lurking under the practiced sneer and air of disdain he wore like armor. His dark hair was tousled and out of place, but it only made him seem more indolent. More regal.

It wasn't the first time he reminded me of what he truly was: a fallen angel. Before I knew that, I used to think he looked like the sort that had a broken halo, which was fitting enough, but now I recognized it as a broken heart.

His emerald gaze flicked to mine, a warning flashing deep within them. "Do not mistake boredom for friendship or charity."

"I wouldn't call it friendship or charity." I smiled a bit sadly. "I'd say kindness, but you'd bite my head off."

Annoyance radiated off him. "I'm many things, but kind isn't one of them. Selfish? Definitely. Anything I say benefits my true goal in the end. Never forget that."

"You know," Vittoria said as she strolled into the corridor outside our dungeon, "what's truly pathetic is, I think you actually believe that."

# NINE

**My sister stood** outside the cell, looking cold and ruthless in her frost-blue gown. Her humanity was gone, but I struggled to believe there was nothing of it left. Even if it was buried deep, deep within her miserable immortal soul. Her gaze shot to me. "You reek of hope. It doesn't suit you, sister."

"Where is Wrath?"

She scanned me from head to toe, barely sparing my injury more than a cursory glance as her attention paused on my forearm. On the serpent, crescent moons, and flowers that permanently marked my skin past my elbow now. The very same tattoo Wrath had as well.

Her lip curled back in disgust. "Do you find it odd that he can sense your general whereabouts through those hideous matching tattoos, and you cannot?" She tsked when I pressed my lips together, refusing to answer. "I'd wish to know why the magic only travels one way."

I wasn't quite sure that was the truth any longer, but I didn't reveal something had shifted when we'd completed the physical aspect of our bond.

"Well, I'd wish to know why you're so brutally annoying, but none of us are getting what we want tonight." Envy had moved supernaturally fast and now stood beside me. His mouth twisted into a cruel smirk when Vittoria snarled at him, baring her teeth. "Get to the point of your visit so we can continue plotting your demise in peace."

"My sister would never harm me."

"Oh, this *is* amusing." Envy tossed his head back and laughed. "Let me see if I've got this right—you maimed her love, injured her with your overgrown lapdogs, set her in a cage, and believe she's not plotting to find her way back to him and destroy you if you stand in her way?"

"She would *never.*" Vittoria bristled. Though the look she cut in my direction seemed less certain. "We're blood."

"And he is her *fate*. As she is his. 'As above, so below.' *They* are the balance. Light and dark. One fallen from above, and one created in the underworld below." Envy's spine straightened, and all his amusement vanished. Something inside me clicked into place. His words *felt* right—like a key sliding into a lock. "Did you not listen to a word I said when you'd invaded my House and fucked my second? You cannot win against love. It is a force more powerful, more terrifying, than any magic you possess or fear you inspire. Even now."

I stilled. His words brought on a recollection that seemed important. Nonna had said love was the most powerful magic, that it would always guide me where I needed to go. I'd been convinced she meant the love of my family, but knowing what I did now, I wasn't as sure. Especially since she'd said that right after pointing out I'd been Marked by a prince of Hell.

"Fate is an unfaithful bitch. Just like love." Vittoria seethed. "With the right prompting, her head can be turned. Just like Pride's was."

"Was his head really turned?" Envy countered. "I wouldn't be as sure."

"I will not permit my sister to be bound by such foolish constraints as fate or love."

Envy flicked his gaze to me. "I'd love to see you try to stop her."

I was through with being spoken about as if I weren't present. And I was not without power, no matter if I'd been taken against my will. I would bend this meeting to my advantage. Before my sister could retort, I quietly cast a truth spell. I was still a witch, but my magic was closer to that of a goddess now. The spell lashed out and gripped my twin, squeezing her tightly.

When I spoke, my voice was laced with pure dominance. With the surge of power, I sounded more demonic than any of the princes ever did. "Where is Wrath?"

Vittoria's eyes nearly bulged as she tried to fight off the magical command. I fed the spell more power, watching coldly as blood trickled from her nose, dripped onto her pretty gown.

Her teeth ground together; sweat dotted her brow. It was all happening so quickly, but I'd crush her skull and break her mind to get what I wanted. Envy chuckled at my side, likely sensing my growing savagery. Her attention shot to him, glaring. "My temple."

"WHERE?"

Vittoria's nostrils flared. She was strong, but I was fueled by rage. "The Shifting Isles."

"Did you murder Greed's commander?"

"No."

"Did you hire someone to murder her?"

Vittoria bared her teeth again but managed to keep her answer to herself.

The magic had already been receding, so I wasn't sure if she lied about murdering Greed's commander or not, but it gave me a sliver of hope that she hadn't. "Thank you, sister. That wasn't too painful, was it?"

She staggered away from the bars of my cell, her expression murderous as she swiped the blood from her nose. "You'll regret that."

I made sure to mimic her cold look from earlier, my voice full of malice. "Like you'll soon regret locking me in here, keeping me from Wrath."

"I warned you." Envy practically bounced on the balls of his feet. "You struck the match; I hope you meant it when you said you enjoyed the burn."

I ignored their side argument and stared at my twin. "Did you send the enchanted skull to Greed?"

"Anyone with the correct spell can enchant a skull. Even a prince of Hell."

It wasn't a direct answer, but it did make me wonder again if Greed had been behind the skull. Thus far, I hadn't found anything to prove he *didn't* send it to himself.

"Yes," Envy drawled, "even lowly demon princes can do parlor tricks. Just like a goddess."

"Have any of your wolves been attacked by demons or gone missing?" I asked. "Aside from the coup you just pulled with me and Wrath."

"If a demon harmed a wolf under my care, that demon would no longer breathe."

"Even if that demon were a high-ranking official of a court you'd aligned yourself with?"

"Especially then." Vittoria's attention slid to Envy. "If you continue smirking at me, I'll tear your heart out a second time, demon."

"Vittoria," I said sternly. "Have any of your wolves been slain or stolen in the last week or so?"

"Why do you need to know that?" she asked. I gritted my teeth. It was a familiar deflection tactic that Wrath used when he was avoiding a question.

"I found out werewolf blood can overwhelm demon senses. There was quite a lot of it found around Greed's commander's remains. You remember Vesta, don't you? I'm sure you must have met when you'd made that alliance with House Greed."

"I didn't pay much attention to Greed's lapdog."

"You sound bitter," Envy remarked. "Did she refuse your advances, too?"

I wanted to press the issue, but my sister obviously wouldn't speak in front of a demon. "Why am I here, Vittoria?"

She wrenched her attention from Envy and took my measure. "I want you to accept your full power. It's time to shed your mortality, punish our enemies, and reclaim our House."

"How in the world am I supposed to shed—"

I halted what I'd been about to say. A memory was rattling around, trying to slip free.

Our House...I flicked my attention to Envy, who seemed very interested in my internal struggle. At his House of Sin, I'd said seven hells, and he'd corrected me to *eight*. I'd been focused on the truth-spelled wine and had let it go, not wanting to waste an opportunity to gather information I'd been after then.

I closed my eyes briefly, allowing the memory to materialize.

"House Vengeance." I snapped my attention to my twin as its name came rushing back. An eighth House. "I can't remember anything else about it."

"That's a story for another time," Vittoria said evasively.

Envy chuckled. "Please, feel free to share your House secrets. I've certainly been curious about it. My brothers, too."

"Have you never been?" I asked Envy, drawing my brows together. "Or Wrath?"

"No. And none of my spies or any other prince of Hell's spies has succeeded in entering that circle, either."

"Is it not here?" I asked, looking to my twin again. A flash of mountains crossed my mind. Snowcapped and treacherous. Isolated. "That's what you meant by taking back what is ours by birth," I said. Vittoria nodded but didn't elaborate. Of which I was grateful. I couldn't remember anything specific of our House and needed to absorb one life-altering event at a time. I was also fairly certain that was why she didn't want me to join House Wrath. She wanted me to rule over our House of Sin. And I would likely have to give that up for our rival court. "You mentioned something about shedding my mortality. How am I supposed to accomplish that?"

"All you have to do is let me remove that mortal heart they gave you."

Time seemed to abruptly halt. *"What?"*

Vittoria drifted closer to the cell. "I'll make sure it's quick, near painless." She nodded to my chest, to the claw marks that still burned. "Those will heal instantly. No infection. No scars."

I clutched a hand against my chest, stepping backward. She was serious. My twin wanted to take my heart. "I don't . . . what do you mean that someone *gave* me a mortal heart?"

"I mean, you were shackled from accessing your truth. You were given something mortal in hopes that humanity would bleed into the fabric of your soul. They wanted you tamed. Who do you think would have done such a thing?" Vittoria leaned against the bars again, the magic sizzling against her skin. She didn't seem to notice any pain. Or care if she did. "You know. Suspect. And yet you still don't want to accept what they did to us. What *she* did. They took our power because that's how much they feared us. Feared the vengeance we'd reap."

"No." I shook my head, the denial sitting uncomfortably. Because I knew I was lying to myself. I knew my sister was telling the truth. And yet I couldn't—wouldn't—allow myself to admit it. Out loud or even silently. "Nonna wouldn't. She couldn't have done that. Why would she?"

"It's a spell-lock. Meant to bind. Cast by the darkest sort of magic. Human sacrifice."

"Nonna hates dark magic. Almost as much as the Wicked." I glanced to Envy, who was uncharacteristically quiet. Sadness. That's what flashed in his eyes before he looked away. He believed it to be true. Bile seared up the back of my throat; I felt close to retching. "She would never kill a human. We weren't even allowed to use bones or dark spells."

*Because we probably would have discovered the truth much faster,* a little voice whispered in the back of my mind. Vittoria didn't say another word, instead granting me the space to come to terms with how much our grandmother kept from us.

My stolen mortal heart broke. Knowing it had come from a human... part of me wanted to have my twin rip it from me at once.

"Don't." Envy was suddenly in front of me, shaking his head. "Don't even consider it. You're not ready. Trust me."

"Why?"

He looked like he didn't wish to answer, probably because he wasn't used to sharing information so freely, but he relented. "There's a small chance you may not survive the transformation."

"You just said immortality always wins."

"I say a lot of things I *believe* to be true. That doesn't make it fact."

"And yet here I stand," Vittoria interjected, "fully restored."

"You rule over death," he snapped. "Of course you'd survive."

I held Envy's stare. Six months ago, if someone told me I'd be considering taking the word of a prince of Hell over that of my twin, I would have thought them mad. I thought of Wrath's conviction about his brother—how he was no murderer. If my husband trusted him, then so would I.

Plus, I wasn't sure what *he* meant by my not being "ready," but I knew *I* certainly wasn't ready to make that decision. Spell-lock or not, I liked my heart where it was.

"If my heart is the only thing standing in your way," I asked Vittoria, "why not just take it?"

"She can't," Envy said. "You must choose to let it go."

"Or?" I asked, searching my twin's face. "What's the consequence?"

Vittoria exhaled. "You'll die. Just as they'd always intended. We were never supposed to remember what we are. The night we took our amulets off? It made a fissure in our curse. That's why she warned us against switching them. They weren't going to alert the devil. They were going to begin a chain reaction that would set us free, another one of their prophecies. No one wants to free vengeance goddesses, especially when they'd wronged them."

"How did you learn of this?" I asked.

"A spell book whispered its secrets to me. Soon after I'd taken my amulet off and had given it to you, my latent ability was unlocked, and it grew stronger over time, the whispers becoming louder and more insistent that I act. One day the whispers led me to the first book of spells. That's how I learned the way to remove my own spell-lock."

It was true. I'd read the entry in her journal that mentioned the whispers and Vittoria's desire to understand. I moved away from the cell bars and collapsed onto the mattress, dust motes puffing up from it in a blast.

Nonna knew this whole time. She'd not only known, but she'd also been the one to bind us into our mortal forms. Knowing we'd eventually die—trapped as mortals—if we didn't willingly choose to break the spell-lock. Our lack of education in offensive spells made sense now. All of it did. And I hated it. I wanted to keep fighting against it, but it all fit.

"But we were children. We grew up. *How* is that possible?"

"Do you remember traveling to that cabin in the woods? The one with Nonna's friend?" Vittoria suddenly asked. I nodded, my unease growing. "How did we arrive there? How did we get home? Why was it so brutally cold and covered in snow? It felt a lot like here, didn't it?"

Recently I had wondered the same thing. Had questioned the true purpose for that visit and how I couldn't remember little details like traveling there and returning home. All I could remember were the cashmere gloves, the bubbling cauldron…

I felt the first prickle of tears forming and locked my jaw together. Our memories, our whole lives, nothing was real. It was all magic and lies and betrayal. And yet it still *felt* real.

"What about our parents?" I asked. "Did they know?"

Something like pity entered Vittoria's eyes. "I'll be back later to see what you decide. I don't suggest waiting too long to make up your mind. Wrath won't fight the poison off forever. He's immensely powerful, but not against a magical poison crafted by Death." She looked to my wound again. "And that needs to heal, or your choice will be made for you."

"How?"

"If you die naturally, I'll just bring you back. Without your mortal heart."

"You could bring me bandages and supplies."

"You're right. I could." Vittoria cocked her head. "But I won't."

I'd been lying on the mattress for only a few minutes, staring at nothing while trying to process everything I'd learned, when Envy appeared above me. His glare was impressive. A little haughty, a little vexed, and as brutally intent as I'd ever seen.

"Do you recall the Stars of Seven?" he asked.

"You asked me that before."

"And you didn't deign to respond."

"In case you failed to notice," I said, a bite in my tone, "we were interrupted."

"Are you going to lie there and sulk all evening? Or focus on the task at hand?" His voice was crisp with annoyance. How dare I not immediately heed his royal demands.

Aside from a murder I wasn't certain was truly a murder, there was the blood retribution on Vittoria, Wrath's poisoning, and everything I'd just learned of my family to contend with in a short amount of time. My world was crashing down faster than

Greed's gaming hall, and Envy ought to crawl back to his corner and leave me to think for a few minutes. I needed to set an achievable list of goals, and at the moment, I was struggling to string together a single thought.

"Allow me to refresh your memory," he said. "You went searching for the Seven Sisters. You found them and the Triple Moon Mirror I was after. Do you recall where?"

"Why does that—" I sat up, wincing at the resurgence of pain. My skin was beginning to burn up, like a fever was overtaking me. I looked at the roots on the ceiling, piecing together what Envy was getting at. And my stomach sank. "There was a tree in the Sin Corridor. I had to feed it blood to open the secret door in its trunk."

"Do you know why I sent you after the mirror?" Envy pressed, his tone taking on a bit of urgency. I shook my head. "Because the key to unlock the magic on the tree requires hell god blood. Goddess blood. No one else can get that doorway to open. And I mean *no* one, no matter how powerful."

"Blood and bones." My head ached. "If Wrath even managed to somehow break free, he can't find me. The Sin Corridor blocks our bond. And even if he found the tree, he can't access it."

"The tree has roots, but it often moves around, making it nearly impossible for any demon to track. Which means we need to devise an escape plan." He glanced at my wound with disgust. "And we need to do so quickly before you're of no use to me at all."

"Your concern for my welfare is truly touching." I sighed when Envy nodded in agreement, clearly missing the sarcasm in my tone. "I can't melt the bars. I doubt I can burn our way out. I can tell my sister I'll agree to giving her my mortal heart, but if she gets to my heart before we can subdue her, I imagine my acceptance will be enough for her to act. What do you suggest?"

Envy paced around the small cell, running a hand through his hair. He worked his jaw as if he'd come up with an idea but was silently arguing with himself. Finally, he stopped and turned to me. His expression was cold. His eyes twin pits of fathomless hatred. "Your sister wants me."

I blinked as his meaning sank in. "You're going to what? Offer to sleep with her?"

"We are on the brink of war, Emilia. I'll fuck her senseless if I must. I'll use my sin and make it so good she'll envy any other lover I take after her. It might buy you time to slip out of the cell."

"What about you?" I asked, hating that I'd even consider going along with something that clearly made him look on the verge of experiencing my husband's sin. "If I slip away, you'll still be trapped. With her. There's no telling if she *did* murder Greed's commander. And I'd hate to see what she'd do to you if you betray her."

"Your concern for my welfare is truly touching," he quoted back to me, earning himself an offensive hand gesture. "I'll move so I'm near the cell door. Then I'll shove her toward the mattress, be as rough as she likes, and slam the door before she knows what we're doing. If we're lucky, I won't have to touch her more than the prodding toward the bed."

"I don't like it. There's—" A low, rattling cough startled us both. I shot the prince an accusatory look, and he shrugged. "How did you fail to mention there was another person here?"

"Regenerating a heart is no small task. I awoke shortly before you did." Envy strode over to the bars, peering into the semidarkness. "Who's there?"

Another cough. It didn't sound good.

"Hello?" I asked, coming up beside Envy. "Wrath?"

"Emilia?"

My heart clenched painfully. It wasn't my husband. I couldn't tell if I was relieved or more worried for his welfare. But still, I recognized that voice.

"Antonio?" He coughed again, the sound closer. As if he were in a cell beside ours. "Are you imprisoned, too?"

His quiet laugh turned into racking coughs. "She promised I'd see my mother again. If I did everything she said. She wanted me to pretend I killed those girls. If I played my part, she swore she'd bring my mother back. Just like she did to the wolf. Angel of Death. That's what I'd thought. Who else but an angel could bring back the dead? I thought maybe she'd bring the witches back, too. I didn't know...I didn't know she wanted vengeance against their families."

I closed my eyes. His actions made sense. He'd never been the same after his mother's death. Had abruptly joined the holy brotherhood, withdrew. Grief wasn't simply a shadow that followed people around; it was the worst sort of companion. It was an emotion that could either encourage someone to wither away through sorrow and tears or turn them into a monster. Craving vengeance like blood. Justice. Retribution. As if spilling blood would bring that one person back. I would know. It was the very same spark that ignited my current path.

It was cruel of Vittoria to dangle that sort of impossible hope in front of his face. Inhuman. I grasped onto the belief that some noble side of her was still left. *Something* redeemable. A bond between us that could never be broken. If there wasn't, then perhaps Greed had been correct. Maybe she was not meant to be saved.

"She deceived us all, Antonio. Even me."

Envy flashed a look that stated *he* hadn't been deceived, and I motioned for him to keep his troublesome mouth shut. He held up his hands in mock surrender and went back to his corner to lurk and plot. *Goddess, grant me strength to deal with superior, arrogant demon princes.*

"Would you want to go back home now?" I asked when my old friend hadn't said anything else. "It's not too late, you know."

"Home." He said the word as if testing it out and finding the taste a bit too bitter for his liking. "It's all another deception, isn't it?" Before I could think of a response to comfort him, he said, "Domenico never leaves her. Even when she comes down here, he stands at the end of the corridor, guarding. And he's not alone. It's hard to make out, but there are usually several others. They brought a new one here. She doesn't come near the cell, but I see her watching. She seems wilder than the others. Like a feral dog that can't stand being caged. Domenico seems on edge whenever she's near. Which is all the time lately."

"How do you know she's new?"

"I heard them whispering the night she arrived. Something about her being unable to travel between realms. Domenico and another wolf had to retrieve her."

I glanced at Envy. His expression was strained. Even if our plan to lock Vittoria in our cell worked, we'd have the wolves to contend with. Which wouldn't be too troubling if it wasn't for my festering injury and lack of a weapon. I also wasn't sure what Envy's power did, but I wondered if being in a place locked by goddess magic tampered with his abilities at all.

Judging by his bleak reaction, it wasn't good. And if there was a new wolf who put the others on edge because of her inability to travel to the Shadow Realm, I didn't want to come face-to-face with her. I strained to see around the bars again.

"Do you know if the new wolf is still here?" I asked.

A terrible sound—bone crunching, followed by a squelching noise—broke the silence. Vittoria stepped into view, holding a dripping, severed heart. Horror turned my blood to ice.

She couldn't have...

"There. Now we don't have to hear him prattle on and he can see his mother again. It *is* what he wanted." I dropped to my knees and retched. My sister slowly knelt, meeting my gaze, Antonio's heart still beating in her hand. "Did you wish to fuck him first? I can bring him back. I forgot you had that crush. He'll be as good as new if I act now. I'm certain it won't hinder his performance, though he is mortal, so he's probably not that impressive on his best day. Though, given how much he liked to talk, perhaps his mouth might be pleasing enough."

"What is wrong with you?" I cried.

"I am doing exactly what I was created to do, Emilia. When will you do the same?"

While battling the wolves, I'd made a vow to myself to do everything I could to unlock my full power, but there had to be some other way for me to achieve that. When I returned to House Wrath, I'd search every damn grimoire I could for a solution.

Vittoria tsked at me and stood, summoned a glass jar from the ethers, stuffed the heart inside, and twisted the cap to keep it secure. It vanished in a wisp of smoke. Gone with the rest of her morbid collection. It made me think of a dream I once had—the night I'd gotten hypothermia and Wrath nursed me back to health. I'd seen images of hearts in jars.

Now I knew where they'd come from. Memories of a different time and place. Her temple perhaps. Or wherever she kept her collection. Perhaps there was a ghastly chamber in our House of Sin that held her trophies.

"I rule over death," she continued. "You're the one who's confused about who you are and what your purpose is, *Fury*. Did you think House Vengeance was not vicious?"

"You told him you'd bring his mother back."

"Our little friend misunderstood," Vittoria said. "I told him he'd *see* his mother again. Then Domenico and I showed him my little heart trick. Antonio filled in the rest. It's not my fault he didn't ask for clarification. I kept my promise. I imagine his soul is reuniting with his mother now. If you don't wish to fuck him, what is your issue? He was nothing but a mortal tool. He certainly had no trouble stepping over you when it suited his needs. Do you know how easy it was to get him to agree to my plan? Even knowing he would hurt you in the process?"

I stared at my twin, at the stranger she'd become. Seeing her this cold and emotionless, so easily able to murder—maybe she did kill Vesta. I could see this version of my sister standing idly by as her wolves tore the demon apart, leaving the scent of their blood everywhere. Perhaps the new wolf Antonio mentioned had done the honors. Antonio... I retched again, unable to look at his blood coating my sister's hand.

"Bring him back," I begged, wiping the sickness from my lips as I stood. "I swear on my blood, if you do not, I will never help you get our House back."

Vittoria's eyes flashed with something that looked like victory. "His heart for yours?"

I paused. I didn't want to give up my mortal heart, but I

couldn't let my old friend die. Vittoria had me backed into a corner, and she knew it. I took a deep breath. "I—"

Envy—who'd been silent up until now—spoke. "You know, I'm curious. How does it feel, knowing your mother favors Emilia? I don't have a mother, but I imagine it's a nasty feeling. One that would inspire my namesake sin."

I felt the slight pulse of Envy's sin, so subtle my sister might not have realized he'd used magic at all. Her eyes narrowed. "For that to be true, our mother would need to show an interest in our existence. She created us, then moved on to the next passing fancy. Do you see her here?" Vittoria didn't even bother to make a show of looking around. Though her use of the term *create* did make me cringe. Apparently, we hadn't been birthed. It was another oddity I had to get used to, though my sister didn't appear disturbed at all. "The Crone is not here because she has more important things to do, souls to torment, and whatever else she indulges in."

Envy's smile was feline—a large, predatory cat who was about to pounce. "My spies have whispered interesting stories. Ones Emilia can verify."

Another soft flicker of his sin. I remained where I was, unmoving, not wanting to break the spell. Though internally I was screaming for him to hurry. Antonio needed his heart back.

"Would you like to know where your mother has been these last years," Envy continued, his tone taunting, "what she's been doing?"

And then I saw it. The slight movement of a shadow on the wall. Someone was standing just out of sight. I tensed, hoping Envy had sensed something my dulled mortal senses had not and that was why he'd started distracting my twin. Vittoria hadn't taken her focus from the prince, making me wonder if she was already aware of who was slowly approaching and was unworried. Or if they'd cast a glamour, hiding themselves from her. I prayed the latter was true.

"I don't care," Vittoria finally said. "She hasn't been trying to break our spell-locks. Hasn't bothered to come to our aid. She created us to watch over the underworld, then left. She's wonderful at disappearing, traveling to whichever realm or universe that strikes her fancy. It could be a thousand years before we see her again."

"House Wrath is a peculiar choice of residence for someone who is uninterested in her daughters. Well," Envy amended, "at least one of them." He looked to me then. "I believe her title was the Matron of Curses and Poisons."

"Celestia." My voice came out in a shocked whisper. I wasn't answering Envy. I was speaking to the woman with silver and lavender hair that had come up behind my twin.

Her dark eyes met mine before dropping to the claw marks on my chest. Something like anger flashed in her ancient gaze, something I recognized in myself.

From one blink to the next, she'd summoned the roots from above us, wrenching them from the ceiling, and wrapped them around Vittoria, chaining her arms, legs, and body. My sister thrashed, completely caught off guard, then stilled as the Crone stepped in front of her.

Celestia's smile was the thing that made monsters afraid. Here stood not simply a goddess of the underworld, but its creator. "Hello, daughter."

# TEN

**"Mother." Vittoria's shock** dissolved almost as immediately as it had appeared. She thrashed against the roots binding her, shouting curses and hexes. Celestia watched, unconcerned. My sister was a powerful goddess, but Celestia was the Crone. A titan. Seeming to realize that, Vittoria stilled, breathing hard, her gaze even harder. "You proved your point. Let me go."

The bars on my cell flared with lavender brilliance, then sank into the earth. I gingerly stepped over the barrier, relieved when I exited the cell without pain or difficulty.

I rushed to the cell beside mine, gripping the bars tightly. Antonio's broken body was slumped on the floor, a pool of ruby-red blood catching the torchlight. My twin lying on an altar, a similar pool of blood surrounding her, flashed across my mind. Unlike my sister, Antonio wasn't immortal. He wouldn't rise again. He would rot, his bones eventually turning to dust. And he would cease forever. No matter what he'd done to me, he didn't deserve this.

"Help him," I turned to the Crone, "please. Give him his heart back."

Celestia's attention moved to the body. There was nothing in her expression to indicate her thoughts. She looked back at me. "He's gone, child. To bring him back now…it is not natural. *He* would not be natural."

I looked from the Crone to my twin, desperate. "Vittoria brought a werewolf back. And Antonio didn't die a natural death. There must be *some* way to fix him."

Celestia pulled the jar with his heart from the ether and held it up for me to see. I wanted to be sick but forced my gaze to not waver. Celestia tapped the glass. "It no longer beats. There is nothing to be done. He's beyond our reach now. You must let him go, Daughter of the Moon."

"I can't."

The tears I'd been holding back broke free and spilled down my cheeks. It was too much. All of it. Wrath was missing and poisoned; he could be suffering at the moment, and I felt powerless to help him. My childhood crush was brutally murdered before we could find true closure and forgiveness. And my twin—who I literally traveled to Hell to avenge because I loved her that much and was desperately trying to save—was the source of all the heartache.

A sob racked through me. The more I tried to suck it back in, the more I broke down. It wasn't just Antonio's senseless death. It was *everything*. My whole world was crumbling. My family. My life. Nothing was as it seemed. Not even my understanding of my own life, of who I was as a person, as a goddess. The weight of it all, it crushed me.

I went to my knees and submitted to the waves of grief tugging me under. I didn't know how to go on. To get back up. I didn't know if I *wanted* to get up. I was tired of fighting so many battles, both emotionally and physically. Maybe the world would be better off without goddesses and their cruel, inhuman power and wicked games.

Everyone I loved, everyone who had the misfortune to meet me, was suffering.

Envy's gleaming boots came into view as he stepped beside me. I half-expected him to offer a cutting remark, to provoke me into feeling something other than the crushing sorrow weighing me down. Or perhaps to call me the pathetic creature I was.

Instead, he extended a hand. Tears streamed down my face as I stared at it, my sobs nearly choking me now.

"Rise," he said softly. "Just as they always feared you would."

His words, the very same he'd spoken to me weeks ago while I'd visited his House of Sin, drew my attention to his face. He wasn't looking at me like I was pathetic. He looked like someone who understood, intimately, what it was like to lose everything. To be forced to stand when you wished to fall. To get up on your own and defy the hand of fate that brought so much pain by smacking you down time and again. To choose to live and flourish despite the bad. And most important, to dare to dream of better days while your current world was a living nightmare.

"Rise, Emilia," he repeated, his hand a lifeline. "Remind them all."

My tears slowed as my fingers clasped his. He tugged gently but firmly, helping me to my feet. I took a deep, ragged breath and held on tighter, the last of my tears drying. "Thank you."

He squeezed my hand once before letting go. "Naturally, this benefits me. Don't be too grateful. I still don't like you all that much."

I knew it wasn't the complete truth, but I didn't question how he'd managed to partially lie. Instead, I looked at Celestia and Vittoria. My family by blood. My twin still struggled in her magical root chains, and my mother's face was impossible to read. There would be time to talk, to see what could be done about my mortality and memories, but right now I had to get to Wrath.

I addressed my mother. "The wolves?"

"Are locked in the Shadow Realm for the next hour," she said. "Go. And don't forget, you owe me my book of spells. I'll come for it soon. Have it ready."

"I will." I held the Crone's stare and nodded once. Like any god, I imagined she was mercurial. Her moods shifting with her next whim. I did not need another enemy to look over my shoulder for and was grateful I'd remembered to stick her book into my satchel the night I'd discovered Vittoria was alive.

Envy started down the earthen corridor, not bothering to see if I followed. As promised, when we emerged in the room where I'd first found the Triple Moon Mirror, no werewolves lay in wait.

Envy glanced around the space, his attention landing on everything as if mentally filing the information away for later use. "Not very goddesslike, but I suppose there is a certain amount of rustic charm. If one overlooks the stone and dirt."

Smiling at his commentary, I shook my head and moved toward the pedestal in the center of the room. Last time I was here, it contained the Triple Moon Mirror. Now my dagger gleamed from where it hovered, point down, in its center. I wrapped my fingers around it, feeling a surge of determination fill me. And perhaps hope. I would find my king, then I'd find a way to break my spell-lock. Somehow during that time, I'd also figure out the truth behind Vesta's murder or disappearance and clear my sister from wrongdoing. Or see her pay for her crimes.

I let loose a breath. It wasn't going to be easy, but I'd find a way to accomplish it all. First, I needed to find my partner. My husband.

I faced Envy, remembering what my sister said about Wrath's location. If she could be believed. I wasn't fully a goddess again, so I couldn't be certain, but so far *I* didn't have any issues lying. Unlike the demon princes.

"Do you know where Vittoria's temple is?" I asked. He nodded, his attention fixed on the dagger. "Then let's go."

We stood outside the gates of Hell, right at the beginning of the Sin Corridor, looking at the fierce magic that crackled over the bones. Wrath had cast a spell to lock the gates when we'd first arrived in the Seven Circles, and the magic twisted around it like demonic vines.

This magic seemed slightly off in color and the way it felt, but I couldn't exactly trust my memories. The curse was still hard at work, though it wasn't quite as powerful now that I'd allowed a bit of Wrath's magic into my soul.

The winter storm that always seemed to be present in some capacity was in a full rage. Wherever he was, my husband was furious. His temper and the way it impacted the realm gave me hope, though. Wrath must be unharmed to cause such turbulent weather.

I blinked snowflakes from my lashes, shivering as Envy placed his hand to the gate as Wrath had done. He spoke in an unfamiliar language, and green-colored magic lit up his hand and sank into the gates. He kept his hand there, waiting for that click to sound.

And nothing happened.

Envy swore roundly and tried again. With the same results. He turned away from the gates, shoving his hands through his hair as he paced, muttering to himself. He yanked his House dagger from inside his hunter green suit jacket and pricked his finger. Like Wrath, his wound healed instantly, but he managed to smear blood on the gates. They didn't open.

Any hope I'd been feeling was slowly receding back to fear and uncertainty. Even though I was fairly positive he was all right, I needed to get to Wrath. "Will my blood open them?"

Envy stopped pacing in a circle, narrowing his eyes. "You can try, but I suspect the magic binding the gates was placed here to prevent your kind from returning as much as mine."

He hadn't said "your kind" with any venom, and yet I still flinched. To someone outside this realm, I was akin to a demon. That was going to take some time to get used to. I stepped closer to the elk antlers that acted as the handles.

"Wrath locked them. Why would he bind me or any other prince from leaving?"

"The magic isn't demonic." Envy sighed, his breath fogging in front of him. "The Star Witches have been up to their old tricks again."

Star Witches like Nonna. She'd told me they were the guardians between realms. They acted as the wardens to the prison of damnation. Which I assumed was their name for the Seven Circles. She'd also claimed I was one of the guardians, but I now knew that for the lie it was.

Imagining my grandmother traveling here to lock me in was one more dagger to the heart. She'd promised to come find me after she told me to run and hide from the princes of Hell; she swore we'd reunite. I hadn't told her I'd decided to come to the Seven Circles, and part of me wanted to believe that if she knew, she wouldn't have locked me here.

"I'll try anyway," I said, still hopeful, though I had doubts.

I pressed my blade to my fingertip, wincing as the blood beaded up, and smeared the antler as Envy had done. I pictured the gates creaking open. Or even blasting open. I hoped that if I believed hard enough, the desired result would manifest. Nothing happened.

I studied the magic, a troubling thought entering my mind. Wrath was trapped outside this realm. Which meant either my sister transported him to the Shifting Isles *before* the Star Witches worked their hex or they somehow had worked in conjunction with each other.

If that was the case, then Nonna must know I was here.

Fire erupted in the air around us, vines crept up the gates, crushing and burning and yanking as if I could incinerate any barrier they tried putting between me and my husband. Blast after blast hit the gates, my fury growing with each failed attempt.

Envy cursed and stepped back, the flames rising higher and higher as if damning the heavens. Whatever spell the witches used, it didn't so much as crack. I let my magic go, my shoulders slumping in defeat. My grandmother had really locked me in Hell.

"Nonna can't be the villain."

"Well, that's the curious thing about perspective," Envy said. "In her version of this tale, you're evil. The prophesied dark one she must protect the mortal world from."

"But I would never hurt anyone. Regardless of a prophecy."

Even as I said it, I knew it was a lie. If someone hurt Wrath or anyone else I loved, I wouldn't hesitate to bring them pain in return. To strike back brutally and viciously.

Envy pressed his lips together, likely already knowing what I'd just realized, and kept his commentary to himself.

There were so many layers to peel back. The curse. The prophecy. I'd barely remembered there was one at all, though the details of it had always been murky. Something I'd been told was a result of the curse, how it twisted with each retelling of the tale.

My friend Claudia had been the one to tell me the hazy memories were a result of the curse, that it was what stopped all of us from remembering. Until then, I hadn't even known there was a curse or a prophecy, only a blood debt owed to the devil. Or so Nonna claimed. My grandmother finally told me about the prophecy the night we said our good-byes. She hadn't given many details, only hinted that Vittoria and I somehow signaled the end of the devil's curse.

"It's like you said the night I met you," I said, smiling sadly at Envy. "It is a tangled web."

"And we have only begun to snip the threads."

We were both quiet for a moment. "If you were going to kill someone here and didn't want anyone detecting details, would you use werewolf blood to cover your tracks?"

If Envy was surprised by my subject change, he didn't let it show.

"If I wished to incite a war, perhaps. The wolves' senses are superior. They'd eventually track down the truth and strike hard and fast. It's one of the reasons demons stopped kidnapping wolves years ago. Using wolf blood wasn't worth the price they'd end up paying."

"Do you think Vittoria killed Greed's commander?"

"I think it doesn't actually matter one way or another. Whether it was her or witches or shifters. Whether Vesta was kidnapped or feigned her death," Envy said, "Vittoria is the catalyst.

She could have apologized, told the truth. Called a truce, anything. Instead, she gathered an army of wolves. She tried to entice Greed into an alliance, knowing it would pit him against us, to use him for whatever game she'd planned. She toyed with me, broke into my House, slept with my second. She went to the vampire court, stirred discord there. She mocked Pride."

"She did?"

"Vittoria clearly enjoys chaos." Envy surveyed the gates one last time. "I know of a secret portal—one the witches don't have access to that will take us to the Shifting Isles." He glanced at my dagger. "Keep that ready. I imagine we'll need it."

Before I could ask where it was or why I'd need a weapon, he grabbed my hand and we *transvenioed* to the secret portal. As the smoke cleared from our demonic travel, I realized why I needed the weapon. Several Umbra demons stood shoulder to shoulder, not so invisible, as they blocked our path. Behind them was a massive pearl-and-gold castle. Ornate to the point of excess, and yet it wasn't Greed's or Gluttony's House of Sin. It was Pride's.

I flashed Envy an incredulous look. "Let me guess, you don't have an invitation."

Wrath had told me a prince showing up to another demon circle uninvited was an act of aggression. Envy lifted his shoulder, undisturbed. "I didn't exactly grab a quill and bottle of ink when your sister ambushed me. Pride will be reasonable. An access tunnel to the portal sits at the eastern edge of his circle, right before the Flaming Tombs begin. I doubt he'll cause trouble."

I slanted a look at the normally incorporeal demons. They didn't seem like a welcoming party. The Umbra demons pulled their half-rotted lips back, their pointy teeth and dark gums clacking as if they were already imagining our blood wetting their tongues.

"Prince Pride will not see you," the Umbra demon closest to us hissed. "Best to turn back. Hide in your castle until your prince rescues you, little princess."

There was something especially infuriating about a sneering, miserable, mercenary spy spitting the words *little princess* that made my blood boil.

Envy's low chuckle drew their attention. "Looks like my brother's spies have been slacking. You really shouldn't have flung that match." He glanced at me, nodding. It was time to unleash my simmering rage. "Now you'll feel her burn."

The Umbra demons struck fast, but my magic was quicker. Flaming roses and flowers exploded between us, landing on the usually invisible demons. Before they could activate whatever power turned them incorporeal, my thorn-covered vines erupted from the earth.

With just a thought, the vines crawled up their legs, binding them to the ground, and I shoved them down their throats, preventing anyone from casting any spell or shouting for help. Oversized thorns tore through their throats, choking them with their own blood.

I released my fire magic and let the vines do the hard work of maiming and slaughtering. I used to love wearing flowers in my hair, now I loved watching them turn into pretty weapons and destroy my enemies.

One demon sneaked up behind me, but Envy shouted a warning. I turned just as its blade arced down, slicing my already tattered gown. I danced back with only a small scratch. Then I pounced on the demon, my dagger at its throat. It spat in my face and laughed.

"Your prince must not have been interested in teaching you

how to fight." It raked its oily gaze down my body. "I suppose he has other ideas for you. Too bad he's about to be replaced. That never was a problem before, though, was it?"

I hauled the demon to its feet, shaking it a little with strength I didn't know I had. "What do you know about Wrath?"

"Only that your beloved will soon be dead. And you will be nothing but the divine whore you are. Poetic justice if you ask me."

Before I thought about what I was doing, I dragged my blade from ear to ear across its throat. Hard enough to tear its head from its body. I coolly stared down at the dead demon, unfazed by what I'd just done. It struck me then what I was slowly becoming. The more the curse lost its grip on me, the more I remembered what it was to be a goddess. To feel no remorse. To be fueled by vengeance and openly welcome the vice of my House.

I bent down and retrieved the head.

Envy whistled and stuck his hands into his pockets, rocking back on his heels. "Remind me not to call you any nasty names. At least not without donning armor and casting a protective spell or twelve first."

"It wasn't what it said about me." I smiled, though it was tinged with sadness, not happiness or pride, at what I'd done. At the prince's questioning look, I added, "Its mistake was saying Wrath would die. Imagining a world without him... I couldn't bear it."

Envy carefully studied me, his expression inscrutable. "If Wrath can't ever give you his heart, would you still fight for him?"

I surveyed the bodies around us. Some still twitching from where they choked on the vines. If only I'd been able to do this during the battle with the werewolves, perhaps my husband might not have gotten stabbed or poisoned at all.

"I can only hope one day you won't have to ask me such a question," I said. "That my actions will speak louder than my words."

I thought of Wrath with that last statement, understanding exactly why he preferred actions over words. They held more value. More meaning than words that could just be pretty lies.

With my prize in hand, I faced the castle and started walking for the doors. It was time to pay the prince of this circle a visit. One way or another, Pride would let me use that portal so I could get to my husband.

Envy fell into step beside me, stealing glances I pretended not to notice. If he was about to question why I took a souvenir of our bloody battle, he decided against it.

And that made the mortal part of me wonder if I'd actually frightened a prince of Hell.

# ELEVEN

**After much arguing**—mostly due to my less-than-palace-worthy clothes—and helped largely in part by a little display of my fire magic, we were announced to Pride's court. His throne room was a testament to his sin. The first time I'd been detained in his House after wandering through his fields of slumber root, I'd seen only one room. It had been ornate, gilded, like something the Sun King would have adored. Perhaps Louis XIV was inspired by this prince.

The floor was white marble with delicate gold veins. Cathedral ceilings with colorful frescoes painted on them were also gilded where the wall met the ceiling. Oversized crystal chandeliers hung the entire length of the room in even intervals, giving off a warm, sun-kissed glow.

Ornamental molding was used as trim on both the floor and upper wall. Arched mirrors hung along the walls on the left and right, creating a mirrored pathway to the prince. Of course someone as prideful as he was would require so many opportunities to gaze upon his glorious self.

At the end of the very long hall of mirrors, Pride lounged on his throne, wearing a deep navy-and-gold brocade waistcoat, slim trousers in charcoal, and dark brown boots that gleamed. He looked every inch the prince he was, styled in the highest of fashion. With my battle-worn and blood-flecked clothing and lack of a bathing chamber visit, I knew I looked wildly out of place. I didn't care. Only one thing was on my mind at the moment: the portal.

Envy and I walked through the parted crowd of sneering courtiers, all dressed impeccably, like each demon court I'd visited. Each of these demons had nearly perfect features, making me wonder if their eerie perfection was the result of magical enhancements, not a result of nature. It also made me think of the scar their prince had on his lips; how he probably had the option to conceal it but chose not to. Which made me wonder how he'd gotten it once more.

"Some of us take pride in our appearance," the prince of this circle said, almost answering my thoughts. I schooled my features into an unreadable mask. Pride looked down his nose at me, his lip curling from either the blood or—more likely—the shredded material of my gown. "Not all of us, clearly. Though I suppose as an unofficial member of Wrath's court, you don't count."

"It's lovely to see you again, too. Thank you for the warm welcome." I dropped the severed head on the floor, enjoying the hiss of disapproval coming from the courtiers as it rolled to the base of his throne and crashed to a stop. "And some of us spend our time doing more than sitting in fancy chairs, pretending to be drunk and looking pretty."

"I don't simply *look* pretty. I am dashing," he said arrogantly.

I fought the urge to roll my eyes at his vanity. "To what do I owe the honor of this unannounced visit?"

"I need access to a portal on the outskirts of your land."

"For what purpose?"

"To bring my husband back to his House of Sin."

Pride glanced at my hand; if he noticed the *SEMPER TVVS* tattoo on my finger or recognized what it was, he didn't let it show. "Perhaps it's for the best that he remain where he is."

My fury started rising, erasing all other emotions. Like diplomacy and civility. Envy cleared his throat, but I did not heed his warning. I was tired, the claw wound burned miserably, and I was a breath away from either crying or screaming or some mad combination of the two.

"If you do not allow me to pass, I will return. And when I come back, I'll have the might of House Wrath's army. No one will keep me from him. Not you. Not my sister. Not any other cursed creature in this realm or any other. If I come back, I will unleash my power. I will burn all you hold dear. That, I can promise, is no threat." I dragged my blade across my palm, letting blood drop all over his beautiful floors. He watched, his brows rising slightly. "It's a vow."

"Making a blood vow is serious in this realm."

"I am well aware."

"I don't think you—"

Pride's head whipped toward the throne room door, and a second later, I heard it. The sound of an impending storm. Footsteps echoed like thunder. The temperature plummeted. Heeled shoes clattered over the marble floor as several courtiers rushed to the exit, their steps echoing as the sound of sleet suddenly smashed against the windows.

I glanced at the arched window behind Pride, noting the sky

was now an ink black. Wind howled, more menacing than any werewolf could hope to be. The very walls shook with the next gust outside. A mirror cracked from the sudden coating of ice.

My heartbeat ticked faster, and I slowly turned, hope igniting deep within. Unlike the rest of this court, it wasn't fear pounding furiously in my chest. A courtier ran toward the dais, a golden crown nestled on a crushed velvet pillow. He placed it on Pride, then backed away, nearly tripping over his feet as the doors crashed open, shattering against the wall.

Smoke and snow swirled into the room. And then Wrath was there. Striding into the chamber with an expression of murder on his handsome face. His attention shot to me, softening for the briefest moment, before he noticed the claw marks down my chest, looking just as bad—if not worse—as the last time he'd seen them. He turned that frigid gaze back on his brothers, and another icy blast circled the room. I wanted to rush over to him, yank him close, and kiss him senseless. I settled for remaining as controlled as he was. Though inside I was battling the desire to make sure he was as unharmed as he appeared to be.

"Explain." Wrath's voice promised violence. "Now."

An explanation for how my prince made it here was exactly what I desired, too, but our conversation would have to wait until we could speak privately. What had been left of Pride's court fled the room, not bothering to stay and witness what promised to be quite the show. The prince of this circle watched as the last one rushed off and left me and the three demon princes to our private battle. Pride gave his brother a haughty look.

"You didn't think I'd simply welcome a queen without first testing her loyalty, did you?" Pride said, ignoring the anger rolling off Wrath in waves. "Your judgment hasn't always been the best where she's concerned. We all have a right to know her true motives this time."

*This time? Testing my loyalty?* I still didn't know what transpired before my spell-lock, but the more I gathered, the more I knew Vittoria and I had schemed against Pride and Wrath in the past.

"This was a test?" I asked, looking between Pride and Envy. "All of it?"

"Not quite *all*. I told you I choose myself over all else. And this benefited me." Envy shrugged. "It was his idea. Except it didn't quite go as we'd planned. Still, a test was necessary, given what happened... before."

"How comforting." I pressed my lips together, furious that the curse wouldn't allow for more details and that my memories were still under siege. "What was your original 'test'? Have *you* been working with Vittoria? Did she even kidnap you, or was that a fabrication as well?"

Envy didn't bother looking to Pride or Wrath but instead met my hurt stare. "Once your carriage left Greed's, we were going to send the Umbra demons after Wrath again. Our plan was to see how far you'd go to rescue him. You may say that you love him now, but your motivations haven't historically been so... noble. The Umbra demons worked quite nicely last time. I'd been leaving here to gather my forces, but then your sister showed up and ripped out my heart. I ended up in that cage, and here we are. Reunited."

I glanced at Pride. "And you didn't bother to help him?"

"Envy being removed from my circle suited me well enough. Plus, there was little time to act. She'd grabbed him and immediately had a wolf take him to the Shadow Realm."

"Vittoria could have hurt him."

Pride's gaze darkened. "Your sister does have an impressive record of hurting others."

Wrath slowly took the steps leading up to his brother's gilded throne. I hadn't noticed before, but the chair was fashioned like a lion. The great beast's legs and claws were the arms of the chair, and his head and mane were the back. The lion's mouth was open as if roaring.

My prince towered over Pride, who still managed to sit indolently. "I don't give a shit about your test. Vittoria brought wolves onto our land; you should have stopped her."

"It's not as if I asked her to do so, and it ultimately served my needs." Pride's voice turned hard. "Just like how Envy was aware she'd traveled to the vampire court in the south, doing the devil knows what, and didn't bother telling anyone except Greed. You know how prickly they've gotten. Rumor has it they are plotting. And our dear brother here didn't share any of that, did you?" he flung at Envy. "So why am I being raked over the coals for serving my best interests?"

Envy smiled. "Are you jealous Vittoria went to the vampire prince instead of seeing you?"

"*Stop,*" Wrath said. "Our land was breeched by wolves. Vittoria is stirring up discord with vampires none of us need. She ripped out Envy's heart, potentially killed Greed's commander or aided her in escaping, poisoned me, and kidnapped my wife. And this little test of yours seemed justified? All while we are trying to solve a murder to avoid an internal war?" Wrath looked ready to strike his brother off the throne. I was surprised when he didn't. "You not only gambled with my wife's safety, but with the peace of our land."

"And I'd do it again. Now we know for certain Emilia isn't scheming against us. Or you. The end justified the means, whether or not you like it. Tell me," Pride went on, rising to his feet, "there wasn't a seed of doubt in your mind. Not *one*." Wrath's jaw tightened, but he didn't deny the accusation. "Now you know."

My husband glanced at me, and I straightened my spine. I had doubted him. For months. I could not fault him for any doubts he might harbor for me in return. What mattered now was building our new future. Together. The foundation was there, and with some work, we could make it in the end. The longer Wrath held my gaze, the more uncertainty started to creep in. *It would be all right, wouldn't it?* Surely this was a temporary hurdle we'd overcome. It had to be. My husband's forbidding expression eased. But Pride's voice broke the moment.

"Besides, I refuse to believe we're all going to allow one miserable goddess to succeed in sowing discord among us. Let her try with the wolves and vampires. If Greed is irked that my test might have inadvertently taken you away for *one* night from his boring investigation, he will simply need to get over it. Everyone knows Vesta was unhappy there. He's just angry he lost something valuable. You know how pissy he gets when a gamble goes wrong for him."

Despite my anger at being deceived by these princes of Hell, I recognized this as an opportunity to potentially gain valuable information. "How do you know Vesta was unhappy?" I asked. "Do you have spies at other courts?"

Pride's expression turned as wicked as the gleam in his eye. "Pillow talk, darling. People tell me all sorts of interesting things after I grace their sheets."

"Who told you about her?" I pressed.

"She did, naturally."

I drew up short. That was quite an unexpected answer. The princes couldn't lie, so he had to be telling the truth. "When?"

Pride lifted a shoulder. "Maybe a week or so ago? I can't recall."

Envy pinched the bridge of his nose. "You fucked Greed's commander. Are you that daft?"

"She sought *me* out, for your information," Pride snapped. "She couldn't keep her eyes off me, and I returned the favor, lest I damage her ego."

"And then she was murdered," I said, my tone hard. "Do you think Greed would harm her if he believed she gave you private House information?"

"Of course not." Pride didn't sound as sure.

Wrath studied his brother intently. "How did you end up in the same place together?"

"She came here. To one of my gatherings." Pride glared at us. "What? I received an official request from House Greed for her to attend. Didn't he tell you?"

Wrath and I looked at each other. Greed had not mentioned anything at all about sending his commander to a rival demon court. "You said she sought you out," I started, mind spinning. "What did she wish to talk about?"

Pride shrugged. "Mundane things. The ball. The wine. The portal. My bedroom."

"What was her interest in the portal?" I asked, sensing we were close to unearthing a clue.

"The same as anyone's," Pride snapped. "She wanted to know if it was secure and if it only went to the Shifting Isles. As if I'd leave something like that unattended."

"Was there anything she said, anything at all, that might have been peculiar or out of place?"

"We didn't do much talking after that." Pride gave me a hard look. "If you're through interrogating me, I'd really like a bottle of wine. This evening has turned rather dark."

My chest suddenly ached again, reminding me of my injury. I wanted to interrogate the idiotic prince more but needed to tend to my wound. And Pride seemed to need a break—his anger was growing, and it was never a good thing to push a prince to feeling another sin.

Wrath strode down the steps toward me, not missing anything. "Let's go home, my lady."

Without looking at Envy or Pride, I accepted Wrath's arm and held on as he magicked us away. With this new information, it was becoming harder to convince myself that Vesta was truly dead. Was it possible she had betrayed Greed and taken up with my sister and the wolves?

I couldn't be sure now, but I would certainly find out. If I asked enough questions, I'd eventually get answers to this growing mystery. And if I made a few enemies, it would be a small price to pay.

# TWELVE

**Wrath didn't take** us to his bedchamber or mine. He didn't even take us to a bathing chamber to remove the dirt and blood. When we emerged from the smoke of his demon magic, we were standing on the glittering shore of the Crescent Shallows.

Steam rose from the ice-blue surface, inviting us to dive into its deceptively peaceful-looking waters. Nothing "made" could enter the magical water or else it would kill. Plenty of bones jutted out of the shallows like the hulls of broken ships to prove death was no old wives' tale. Despite its gruesome appetite, there was something serene about the underground lagoon.

The prince turned me until I faced him, then gingerly reached for the front of my gown, peeling it back to get a better look at my wound.

I hissed through my teeth as the material suctioned to my cut gave way to Wrath's gentle prompting, taking some skin with it and causing it to reopen. It oozed and bled.

Wrath winced as if my pain were his own. "This is infected."

"Where were you?" I asked, unable to wait another second to know. I ran my hands over him, relieved to find him whole and healthy. Not that I'd see any indication he'd been hurt with his ability to heal quickly. "How did you escape? And what about the poison?"

Wrath looked like the poisoning and stabbing he'd just been through were the least of our concerns at the moment, but it was greatly important to *me*.

He sighed and withdrew a small vial from his pocket, holding it up. The liquid shimmered like a morning sky on my island, a crystal clear blue.

"Celestia is very talented at creating tonics and tinctures." He pocketed the tiny vial. "I always carry something as a precaution. I took it as soon as I could, then left your sister's temple when the wolves shifted back to human form. The gates were spelled shut, so it took some time for me to get to the portal that leads to Pride's circle."

"Couldn't you *transvenio* there?"

Wrath shook his head. "Magic cannot be used to travel there, so I had to go on foot."

I thought about Envy and Pride's test and the jab the Umbra demon uttered before I'd killed it. I had well and truly made enemies here. "What did I do to you... before?"

"Nothing." Wrath's face went perfectly blank. "Don't worry about Envy or Pride's foolishness. They shouldn't have tested you or your loyalty."

"If I betrayed you, that's not nothing."

He glared down at the claw marks as if they personally offended him, promptly avoiding the subject. Which made me think perhaps his brothers *did* have cause to test me. "I should have ripped that wolf's spine out and shoved it down its throat. Made it suffer for every ounce of pain it inflicted upon you."

He certainly didn't lack imagination. To mitigate the anger I saw rising in him, I nodded toward the sparkling water. "I thought this was off-limits for me, given what happened last time."

Last time, I'd felt as if my heart were about to stop; the pain had been so acute, so terrible, he'd taken me directly to the Matron of Curses and Poisons, my mother unbeknownst to me at that time. She'd crafted a tonic for me, and all had been well. As far as I knew, she was still holding Vittoria underground for the time being, and I wasn't thrilled by the prospect of having a similar reaction without her nearby.

Wrath drew me closer so he could inspect my wound again, his gaze icy and hard.

"It wasn't you; it was my wings. The magic that binds them reacted against the spell-lock that obscures your memories. When combined, there were too many magics at play, and the waters acted as if both were threats." He took in the uncertainty in my face. "I had Celestia research more about it. She doesn't think you'll have an issue if you reenter the water. The healing properties should work now, as they were always meant to. If I thought otherwise, I'd not chance it."

A story came back to me. One Celestia had mentioned that night. About the water belonging to the goddesses and trying to take back what was theirs. Wrath had called it a folktale and told her to stop spreading lies. I looked from the water to him, trying to puzzle it out. Something didn't quite make sense... something—

"Strip." Wrath stepped back and nodded to my gown. He shrugged out of his shirt and undid the button on his trousers. His devious lips curled at the edges, like he knew exactly where my thoughts had traveled with that one word. "Let's get into the water and heal that wound before it gets worse."

"I *am* immortal, aren't I?"

"Not fully. At least not yet." He held out his hand, encouraging me to step into the water I remembered being as warm as a bath. "Come join me, my lady. Please."

I recalled he'd once said there were truth properties to the shallows. Right now, I wanted some truth from him as much as I wanted to heal. I stepped to the edge of the glittering dark sand and let the ice-blue water lap at my toes. The lagoon was magical, enchanting. It called to me.

Wrath moved back, going a little deeper, to make room. I followed him in and took his hand, relishing the tiny bubbles that fizzled pleasantly across my skin.

We waded out until my chest was fully submerged and the magic of the water began tending to my wounds. It felt incredible. And a little odd as the magic cleansed my cuts, then knit my skin together. Even the wound I'd made when I'd sworn a blood vow in Pride's throne room healed. Any momentary discomfort vanished almost as quickly as it appeared.

Wrath watched the magical water work, concern present in his normally stoic features. He looked ready to jump in and attack at the first sign of trouble. "Better?"

I glanced down, pleased to see the wound had healed. Faint silver lines remained, but the scar didn't trouble me. Not half as much as the secret I feared Wrath was still keeping. "Much."

My husband tentatively reached over and dragged a finger over my flesh, checking to make sure it was well and truly healed. I looked over his shoulder, admiring the moon phases painted along the cavern's walls while he continued his thorough inspection. I had wondered before if he'd painted the celestial scene but couldn't picture him spending hours with a paintbrush or bucket of paint. Though he often surprised me. Perhaps he had.

"Is there a reason you keep saving my life when it's not exactly in danger?" I looked at him again, waiting. "I imagine there must be something that worries you."

Wrath circled me, the waves from his movements gently breaking against the shore. I wasn't sure if the curse made it difficult for him to speak or if he was purposely picking and choosing what he'd share with me. "As far as I know, if your heart stops now, while you're not entirely immortal, it could kill you. Until I know for certain, it's a risk I refuse to take."

"Envy said a drop of immortality wins out against mortality every time." Though I left out the part where Envy had also been concerned if that were entirely true.

"Are you that willing to give up your heart to find out?" he asked.

I wrapped my arms around his neck, needing the physical contact. His arms went around my waist automatically, anchoring me against him, solid and comforting. We'd been through hell, and I wanted a reminder that we were here, together. Safe. He dipped his face and captured my mouth with his, the kiss hungry and filled with raw, powerful emotion.

When we finally broke apart, breathing hard, our lips pleasantly swollen, I grinned. "For you? I'd give my heart up."

He looked at me, his expression hard to read. And I wondered if maybe he wasn't quite ready to give me his heart in return, that even though we were now mostly married, perhaps all the demons from our past hadn't yet been banished. Maybe that's why he hadn't mentioned anything about us completing the ceremony that would seal our marriage for good.

Granted, there hadn't been much time to discuss it before we were attacked by wolves and separated, but still. Before I could worry over it, Wrath's mouth slanted over mine again, like his very life depended on the connection.

His tongue demanded entry, and I parted my lips for him, welcoming his taste. Wrath's kisses were certainly intoxicating. Each expert flick or tease of his tongue against mine had my body craving other unspeakable things he could do with that wicked mouth.

Heat pooled low in my belly, stirring my desires as it slowly spread. Soon all I could focus on were his hands as they lazily moved from my waist to my ribs, his thumbs brushing the underside of my breasts. He palmed one as he moved his mouth to my throat, the sensation causing the little bud to harden as a shiver of pleasure went through me.

Roughened hands glided up and down my spine, his caress light and gentle and maddening in the best of ways. He was touching me like I was precious, like each embrace was a moment to cherish, to indulge in and savor. And it was. For him, he knew what it was like to have this end, to have me wrenched away. It had been a mercy that I couldn't recall that.

I touched him back as languidly, exploring every inch of his warrior's body like it was uncharted territory that belonged only to me. I would never allow someone to rip us apart again. And I'd fight with everything I had to remember him and what we'd shared.

He broke away from the kiss, his gaze darkening as he dragged it from my eyes downward, watching as I touched his sides and powerful back, my inquisitive hands searching for a way to evoke ecstasy for him. They dipped beneath the water again, skirting over his sex to play with the toned muscle of his thighs before I curled my hand around his thick length and pumped.

Wrath's breathing turned sharp as I stroked him, his mouth parting on a groan.

I tightened my grip, feeling his sex respond enthusiastically as it twitched against my palm. When I slowly ran my hands back up to his chest, he drew me against him and began kissing and biting along my neck with ravenous hunger.

"I want to be inside you." His hands drifted down, cupping the swell of my bottom and squeezing. I melted into the feeling of the fizzing water and his sizzling touches. His rock-hard length pressed between us, causing my own flesh to pulse with need. "I missed you."

"I missed you, too." I sank my fingers into his hair as Wrath brought his mouth to my breasts, licking and suckling the peaks in a rhythm that had me arching against him, seeking the feeling of him between my thighs. "I was about to destroy the realm to find you," I admitted. Wrath suddenly dipped below the water, then wrapped his arms around my waist, standing up with me perched on his shoulders. "Samael!"

I grabbed onto his head from the swift movement, earning a deep chuckle from the prince. With me secured in his strong grip, he waded over to a cave wall that had a group of stalactites hanging close to it. I braced my back against the smooth stone wall, still holding on to Wrath.

"Grab onto them." His voice was husky, low. Desire rolled through me.

With my thighs wrapped around his shoulders and his mouth

tantalizingly close to my apex, I did as he commanded. I'd just grabbed the stalactites and anchored myself when he hooked his arms around me and spread my legs a little wider. My breath caught from being on display, and a flash of lingering mortal modesty had my legs automatically trying to close.

Wrath flashed a sly grin, then licked my core with long, soft strokes. It was so delicate, so intimate, I had to bite my lip to keep from moaning while he worshipped me. I forgot all about any embarrassment; Wrath made me feel wholly comfortable.

Our last joining had been explosive; the first time he'd tasted me had been fueled by unbridled passion. This... *this* was a true religious experience.

Wrath devoted himself to my pleasure, and I fully surrendered to him. I tilted my head back, breathing hard as he continued his slow, tantalizing tasting. He didn't rush, didn't roughly suck or tease. He made love to me with his warm, wet tongue, allowing it to say everything he couldn't or wouldn't as it dipped inside me.

When I got close to falling over the edge of pleasure, he pressed openmouthed kisses along my inner thighs, and it was the best sort of torture as I waited for him to return to that aching spot, to the swollen bundle of nerves that would soon have me calling his true name.

"Touch yourself, my lady." His voice was an erotic purr, and his request...

Without breaking his stare, I trailed one hand down my own body, teasing him before slipping a finger inside. Wrath's mouth was on me again in an instant, licking my sex and my fingers while I continued to touch myself, and in seconds I was calling out his name again.

I repeated it like a whispered prayer, and he continued his own faithful worshipping until the last of my climax rolled through me, leaving my legs shaking and my chest heaving.

And craving more. Goddess curse me. I couldn't get enough of him. Wrath kissed his way up my body as he slowly lowered me back down, our slick skin sliding against each other its own euphoric experience. Wrath ran a finger over his lips, then he lifted my hand as if he were about to press a gentlemanly kiss to it. His gaze turned molten as he brought my finger to his mouth and sucked. I cursed, and he flashed a grin that was all masculine smugness. The mighty hunter just conquered his prey, and I hadn't even put up a fight.

"You're about to start whispering all sorts of filthy curses, my lady." He moved until he'd caged my body between him and the smooth stone at my back. Impossibly, my desire for the demon grew. "This time, Emilia, I'm going to go slow."

Wrath kissed me lightly, then moved his mouth across my jaw in another whisper-soft caress. He pressed the blunt end of his arousal against my swollen entrance and slid it back and forth until I whimpered from pleasure. "Oh, goddess above."

My seductive prince ran one calloused hand down my side, slowly hoisting my leg up. With his other hand, he continued his delightful torture, driving us both wild. What started as a way to get me closer to that glorious edge now seemed to have the same effect on him. Wrath sheathed himself with one magnificent thrust. He drew back to look me in the eye as he pulled out, then slid in. Each movement and joining of our bodies was slow, languid.

The damned demon was right; I started cursing, the filthy words encouraging him to continue. His hand cupped my jaw as he covered my mouth with his and deepened our kiss. My fingers dug into his shoulders as I clenched around him.

Wrath brought those wicked lips to my ear. "You're close?"

"Yes."

"Thank fuck."

His hand slid between our bodies, and he placed his thumb against my sex, increasing the timing on his thrusts, adding more pressure to that spot that sent a hot ripple through me.

I climaxed again, his true name flying from my tongue. He withdrew and thrust in deeper, a little faster this time, my own name slipping from his lips. Before I had time to come down from the soaring heights of my last release, Wrath had me climbing that same pleasure peak again. Soon we were both panting, our lips and breath mingling.

"You're *mine*." His voice was rough, deep.

"Just as you are mine. Forever." Wrath hitched my leg a little higher, and I gripped his shoulders, a moan escaping me. My responses had him working even harder. He thrusted again and again, pleasure steadily building until I thought I'd combust. My body throbbed, and I could no longer hold myself back from the tidal wave of pleasure that broke. "Samael!"

He rode me through my orgasm, then joined me, my name shouted into the cave, bouncing back at us. We caught our breath, hearts pounding as he kissed me gently and lowered my leg. It prickled a little; I'd been so caught up in pleasure I hadn't noticed it had gone numb.

My husband rubbed my aching calf muscle, searching my eyes. "Are you still here with me?"

The warmth of the water, the feeling of Wrath against me, cradling me. I hadn't once drifted into another time or place. "I am."

Relief flashed in the demon's eyes, and I wondered if he'd

always seemed so tense when we'd kissed or had been physical. "Let's go to bed, my lady."

Instead of swimming to the shore, Wrath scooped me into his arms, splashing me playfully in the process. It felt so good to just laugh, to not feel the weight of the world for once. Down here, with my prince, I didn't have to think of betrayal or murder. Fear and darkness. Down here, within the magical lagoon under House Wrath, only love existed.

I wriggled out of his arms and dove under the water, exploding near him and earning a surprised chuckle when I succeeded in my return fire.

Afterward, we fell onto the glittering dark sand, and I pounced on my husband, who didn't seem to mind one bit as I guided his length into me. Once we were tired from laughing and making love on the shore, Wrath magicked us back to his bedchamber.

A beautiful pale lavender slip was folded on a pillow, and when I pulled it over my head and shimmied it down my body, I noticed the tiny gold stars across the top. It was soft and feminine, and I adored it.

Wrath gave me an appreciative look. The slip hit at midthigh, showing off my bronze skin. If I wasn't so exhausted from our ordeal, I'd have been tempted to take him once more. He patted the bed, a debauched twinkle in his eye. "Save your energy for morning. You'll certainly need it."

With the promise of waking up and making wild, untamed love, I climbed onto the massive bed. Wrath tucked me against his body, and within moments, his breathing turned deep and even. I relaxed into his embrace and closed my eyes. Peace. I couldn't recall the last time I felt so settled on the inside. There was still much chaos in the world, but in here, in this bedchamber and moment, I knew the true meaning of the word. Perhaps it was that sense of security that was my undoing. I'd forgotten, for a brief moment, what it meant to be cursed.

From one second to the next, I was magically wrenched from Wrath's bedchamber. And the next nightmare began.

# THIRTEEN

**"Welcome back, princess."** Domenico bared his teeth in what no one would mistake as a smile. A quick survey of my surroundings confirmed my fears. Once again, I was in the Shadow Realm, chained. It was the same small stone chamber, the same alcove with manacles.

This time, at least, I had a slip on and wouldn't need a shadow robe. It was the only positive bit of luck. They'd struck while Wrath was asleep, and it would likely be hours before he woke up and found my soul gone. Given his extreme reaction before, they better hope he remained sleeping. I didn't bother testing the chains. I already felt that same bite of magic, locking my powers away. I glanced at my captor, hating the smug look on his face.

"I assume this means my sister would like to talk."

"Maybe I just wanted to see if you still bore my mark." The werewolf raked his gaze over me, pausing on my chest. It wasn't sexual in nature, but I didn't like it, either. "Did you know, a wound from an alpha can sometimes cause a feeling similar to what animals experience when they go into heat? Especially if that alpha infused his bite with a bit of magic and intent."

"I wasn't wounded by you, I was clawed."

"And who sank his teeth into that wound? Not your demon," he said, his tone mocking. "Have any animallike urges, lately? Perhaps you wished to get on all fours."

"No. And you're disgusting."

He laughed, and it raised the hair along my arms. "Don't worry. I didn't actually infuse you with an alpha mark. And I have no desire to touch anything tainted by demon cock."

I refrained from pointing out that my twin had also slept with demons. And vampires. And whoever else ignited her desires, as was perfectly customary here. "Where is Vittoria?"

"She's bringing a guest. You would have known sooner, before we were interrupted by your mother." He casually leaned against the wall in the alcove, entirely too close for my liking. "This promises to be quite the evening. Maybe if you're very nice, I'll unchain you."

"How did Vittoria escape our mother?"

Domenico's smile was all teeth again. "You didn't really think the Crone would hold her for long, did you? She had other tasks to accomplish, and once you were safely away, she left."

I was spared from further conversation by the sound of approaching footsteps. Two sets. One pair was measured, unhurried; the other sounded as if they were being dragged. Trepidation rolled down my spine. Whoever else was coming was also doing so against their will.

Vittoria strode into the chamber and shoved her "guest" forward.

The older woman stumbled into the candlelight, and fear became an arrow that was shot straight into my heart.

"Nonna!" I struggled against my chains. My grandmother—who wasn't truly my grandmother—was bruised and badly beaten. Her bottom lip was swollen as if she'd been hit with either a fist or hard object. Dried blood caked her temple. No matter what she might have done, seeing her hurt made something violent wake up inside me. "Let her go, Vittoria."

My sister flung her onto the floor, then glanced at me. "There. I let her go. Happy now?"

I turned my attention on Nonna, and she finally looked at me in return. Sadness and... worry... marred her features. She took in my night clothing, the *SEMPER TVVS* tattoo on my finger and the other tattoo on my forearm, my chains, and still, she cringed back.

As if *I* were the monster in the room and my sister hadn't either beaten her or had her beaten and dragged to the Shadow Realm.

I swallowed the rising lump in my throat. "Nonna. It's all right. It's *me*."

Vittoria watched my reaction with a detached look. Then she kicked our grandmother in the side, forcing her to curl in on herself, to gasp for breath. I shouted for mercy, but no one seemed to notice. Nonna's lips started moving, and I realized it wasn't a spell she was whispering, she was praying. Her words washed over me; she was begging the ultimate divine goddess above for protection. From us. Something twisted in my center, painful and unpleasant.

"You didn't want to believe me earlier"—Vitoria thrust her arm out in accusation—"so here is your proof. She's not rushing to your aid. Nor is she praying *for* you, though you're the one in chains. She is only out for herself. Tigers don't change their stripes, and she is not the little house cat she pretends to be. Have you tried leaving this realm lately? Run into any difficulty, dear sister? I imagine you did, because I found her hexing the gates."

I released a shaky breath. Nonna stopped praying and met my gaze again. This time a spark lit her dark eyes. Defiance. Vittoria was correct. My grandmother wasn't sorry, nor would she deign to apologize to an enemy. And that's exactly what she thought of us. Of *me*.

What had been left of my stolen heart broke.

"Why?" I asked, my voice quiet, brittle. "Was anything of our childhood real?"

For the briefest moment, Nonna's expression softened. The grandmother I'd known emerged, kind yet fierce. Protective and loving. Here was the woman who'd comforted me when my twin "died." Here was the rock in my world, the steady force anchoring me during the worst storm I'd been through. Or so I'd thought. Here was one of the people who'd betrayed me. And yet I couldn't find it in my soul to hate her. Even now. Which meant their spell-lock had succeeded. I might still be a goddess underneath the curse, but I now felt as mortals did.

"I'm sorry, bambina." Nonna's voice warbled. "We did what needed to be done."

Tears I'd managed to hold back burst out in a torrent. They streamed down my face, the salt coating my lips. It was true. Every wicked, dark thing Vittoria claimed.

I drew in a ragged breath, trying desperately to get myself under control. I needed to understand how someone who'd loved me as their own grandchild could betray me. I needed to hear her admit she'd murdered others for their hearts. Goddess above.

I couldn't begin to process that part. "You used the darkest of magic to bind us. How could you resort to human sacrifice?"

My grandmother, who now felt like a ruthless stranger to me, thought it over for a moment.

"Wartime is rife with sacrifice. Humans understand that just like witches." Nonna said it without emotion, as if she were reciting ingredients for a spell or recipe. "Two lives for the whole coven... it's what the elders agreed upon."

My stomach twisted in knots. I felt gutted. There was no remorse, no sadness, only cold justification for evil. "Who did the coven murder for their hearts?"

Vittoria stepped in, her lavender eyes alight with dark glee. "She's jumping to the *end* of the tale when, truly, you must hear it from the beginning." She glared down at Nonna. "Set the stage properly. Or your use to me this evening has run its course. Tell her about Sofia. Your friend."

"Sofia Santorini?" I asked, already dreading what I was about to discover. "What did you do to her?"

Nonna pushed herself to a sitting position, her breathing labored. I wondered if Vittoria bruised or broke one of her ribs. My sister yanked her up and thrust her into a chair that materialized from nowhere. In mere seconds, Vittoria had her chained, too.

Despite everything Nonna had done, I tried breaking free to help her, but there was no escaping my own restraints.

"Go on, tell her," Vittoria demanded, bending down to whisper in her ear. "Or I'll force you."

"I caught her scrying in Death's temple. So I made sure the information she learned never left that chamber. There were certain... truths, only me and one other council member were trusted with. We were told to keep the secret at all costs."

"So you trapped her mind for nearly two decades?" I asked, disbelief apparent in my tone.

"If she hadn't gone against the council, if she hadn't unearthed our secrets, she would have never been subjected to that punishment."

She spoke as if discovering the truth justified her and the council's actions. Horrified was only a fraction of the emotion I now felt.

Nonna drew herself up, a stubborn tilt to her chin as she held my gaze. Her look said she was telling me because she wanted to, not because my twin was forcing her hand. It was difficult to imagine the tears in Nonna's eyes the night I'd discovered Vittoria's body. Where there once was love, hatred burned between them now, bright and all-consuming. I couldn't believe she was capable of cursing her own friend, then using her as a cautionary tale all our lives.

"Now tell her about her prince," Vittoria said. "Don't leave anything out."

"In the beginning, the Prince of Wrath was cursed to forget all but his hate," Nonna said, her voice clipped. Not from anger, but pain. Her breath rasped with each inhale and exhale. "The First Witch told him whatever he loved would be taken from him. At that time, he didn't care for anything, save his wings. That was before he met you." Nonna sucked in another ragged breath. "He cursed her right back, promising to take something she loved in return if she didn't return his wings. So La Prima Strega made a bargain with the devil. No one knows the exact terms. She'd set her spell using her blood, made a sacrifice to the goddess, and was overly confident in her abilities. She forgot whom she'd been dealing with."

She let that sink in and settle. It was a tangled web with many threads winding and twining together until they were so knotted it felt impossible to cut through. Two curses converged, and our lives were caught in between.

"Our curse...part of it was because of the First Witch?" I asked.

Nonna nodded. "You know the first part of the story—that Pride once had a wife who was the daughter of the First Witch. La Prima wanted her daughter back, free from the demon prince, so she came up with a plan to pit Wrath and Pride against each other. She made a bargain with House Vengeance."

"For a price, naturally," Vittoria added, her tone cold.

A memory was rising to the surface. I still couldn't remember who the First Witch was, but I had a strong sense of *what* she'd wanted. "We were pretending to be one person." Vittoria nodded, encouraging me to push forward. To fight to reclaim memories that belonged to me. The magic binding me, it was struggling. I felt for the thread of power that belonged to Wrath and tugged it hard, allowing it to break a little more of the curse. It was stubborn, resisted, but my husband's power was too strong. Another crack split open, freeing a memory. "I was sent to Wrath; my mission was to seduce him."

Something like relief crossed my twin's features.

"And I was sent to Pride with the same mission," Vittoria confirmed. "At the Feast of the Wolf, Wrath was meant to walk in on me and Pride, thinking it was you. The First Witch wanted a war to break out. She wanted her daughter to see that Pride wasn't serious about her, had never been, if he publicly fought his brother over someone else."

"She wanted to break her daughter's heart." I felt sick. It was a cruel game. A scheme that had destroyed so many lives. All because the First Witch didn't want to lose her daughter to a demon. And I'd played a part in it. I'd never hated myself more. "And Wrath? What happened?"

"He gave you *his* heart. He'd caught on to the scheme and didn't care. The night you were meant to leave and let me finish our mission at the Feast, from what my spies have gathered, you sneaked back to him. You pulled him aside at the party, dragged him off for a tryst. When I was trying to seduce Pride, you were in the garden with him, where he confessed his love."

Wrath had...Goddess above. Chills erupted over my body. Wrath, the fearsome general of war, had made himself vulnerable. Likely for the first time in his long existence. And then all hell had broken loose. I exhaled a shaky breath. All these years, he'd been cursed to hate me. Yet he'd fought against it. Tried to latch on to the good. No wonder he was hesitant to give me his heart now. The one time he'd given himself wholly, he'd been punished.

"Before he told me he loved me, I confessed everything that night," I said, suddenly recalling the midnight garden. The night-blooming flowers, the crescent moon. I remembered thinking it was smiling down on us. Now I wonder if it was in mockery. "Somehow, during our game, my feelings changed. I couldn't go through with the plan. I loved him. So I dragged him away before he could see you and Pride."

"I'm not sure what happened between you two then," Vittoria continued. "My spies weren't close enough. All I know is that within the next moment or two, you were gone. There was blood. Some torn-out hair. But nothing else. Wrath went ballistic. He stormed into the castle and nearly destroyed his brothers, convinced one of them had been behind the attack. At that time, no one knew what struck you. Umbra demons were blamed, hired by someone. Envy was the prime suspect, though I know for certain he'd left the party well before the bloodbath began. Then Wrath focused on Greed, and finally Pride."

Vittoria closed her eyes, as if reliving the memory of that night. I wasn't there, but it was easy to imagine Wrath detonating. The chaos, the fear. The raw, unchecked power of his sin seeking to destroy as he unsuccessfully searched for me.

My sister looked at me, and maybe it was the memory of that night, or some mortal piece of her finally slipping through, but she signaled to Domenico—who I'd forgotten was still leaning against the wall—and he magicked my restraints away. They fell to the floor in a heap of metal. It was only through sheer force of will that I didn't follow them down to the ground.

"While the bloodbath between princes continued to rage, I went to find you. Wrath had revealed to everyone that we were twins, so our scheme was over, and even if it wasn't, I wouldn't abandon you," Vittoria said, her voice softening. "It didn't take long to find you, but I'd been too late. Once the witches had you, they moved quickly. The twin witches who had been born? They sacrificed them immediately. Kept their hearts pumping through magic."

"What?" Chills raced along my spine. Another realization clicked into place. I glanced at Nonna, who finally looked regretful. "The prophecy of the twin witches wasn't about us."

Vittoria shook her head. "It never was. The prophecy of the twin witches simply says that they would be sacrificed—we are not those witches. Yes, twin witches—babies—were born that night, and the Star Witches sacrificed them and took their hearts. They put those hearts inside of us and created our spell-locks. We were infused with *their* mortality."

"Nonna raised them, raised us," I said, still reeling. I gave my grandmother a horrified look. "You were in our earliest memories. You taught us to bless our amulets. You taught us to cook." I rubbed my hands over my arms. The chill had turned bone-deep. Our grandmother had brutally killed two innocent witches. Witches she went on to raise. It was unfathomable. Looking at her now, I was unable to process the mixture of emotions swirling through me. She'd been the ultimate force of good in my life. Had hated everything to do with the dark arts. And all along she'd been the ultimate evil. "How could you? How could you do that to those girls?"

Nonna's fists curled at her sides. "Duty. We all knew a day would come when we'd be forced to sacrifice. They gave up their lives, and we gave up our hearts that day, too. It is our destiny to watch the prison of damnation. To ensure the Wicked and the Feared don't get out. Once the curse had gone into effect, you posed a great threat to our world. You are a vengeance goddess. We did not want to risk your fury once you'd discovered that a witch had taken something so precious from you. The First Witch wouldn't—and couldn't—break her curse, and we acted accordingly."

"All to bind us? Because of hate and fear?" I saw the truth of that in Nonna's eyes, but I also saw something else. Something more complicated. Like perhaps Nonna started to question her duty. Perhaps she'd grown to love us, her enemies. And maybe that was why she filled our heads with lies of the Wicked. With telling us who to fear. One of the warnings she'd told us repeated itself in my mind.

*Whatever you do, you must never speak to the Wicked. If you see them, hide. Once you've caught a demon prince's attention, he'll stop at nothing to claim you. They are midnight creatures, born of darkness and moonlight. And they seek only to destroy....*

Knowing what I did now, I understood the true warning. They'd been hiding me from Wrath. They knew he would stop at nothing to claim me, to destroy what the witches had done. He'd bided his time; he'd searched. And even through his hate, he never let that ember of love die.

The story and warning weren't lies. They just weren't *my* truth. Those warnings only belonged to the witches. They did everything in their power to keep us apart. To break our bond. And they failed. I refused to meet my grandmother's pleading stare another moment. I looked at my sister. She might be a monster now, but she wasn't pretending to be anything else.

"I still don't understand one part... how was this scheme to trick Wrath and Pride supposed to work? I know Envy said no spies ever made it to our circle. But didn't the demons know *of* us, even if they'd never been to our House?"

Vittoria uttered a spell, then drew a map in the space between us. It glowed a soft lavender as it hovered before me. My twin pointed to the almost familiar continent. "The underworld bears many similarities to the mortal land of Italy. The upper region, corresponding to Piemonte, is where lesser demons and ice dragons roam." She moved her hand, and a different area, roughly the location of Tuscany, glowed. "This region is where the princes of Hell reside." She swept the magic along the southern border, approximately in the same location as the region of Campania. "And this is where House Vengeance is. There is a treacherous mountain range here that serves as a nearly impassable barrier to our domain—even for immortals. Within the mountains is a veil of sorts, one that erases memories. Except for ours, our mother's, and anyone we choose to gift with true Sight." My twin pointed out another section. "The vampire court is near the very tip, where

Calabria is for humans. And the island of Sicily is nearly identical to the location of the Shifting Isles."

The map faded into the shadows. At least I now understood how the princes—who seemed to know much about everything—were in the dark about us. "I don't understand why we kept ourselves mysterious. For what, centuries? Is there a reason we didn't comingle with the princes?"

Vittoria's expression shifted. It wasn't quite hatred, but there was a coldness about her features that surfaced each time I brought up the princes of Hell. "Demons—especially princes of Hell—cannot be trusted. And are beneath us. We had enough to occupy us in the southern region and had no cause to get involved in their squabbles."

"We were here shortly after the underworld was created," I recalled suddenly.

"And the princes came centuries later, when they were cast from their own realm."

I sensed there was much more to that particular part of our history but left it be for now. Above all else, I needed to understand our current predicament—the curse and how it came to be—if I had any hope of breaking it.

My twin was in a rather giving mood, freely offering information without any magical restraints. I might not have many other opportunities to gather this much information, so I took advantage. "If I was torn away from Wrath, how did you get cursed?"

"Like I said, I came for you." My sister's gaze turned darker than the shadows that slunk into the chamber. She flung a hex at our grandmother, knocking her unconscious. "I hunted you down, and the Star Witches were ready. They set a trap. You were lying on an altar, blood dripping from your chest."

She allowed that punch to land squarely in my gut. It was the exact way I'd found her body in the monastery in Sicily. Now I knew her pose had been by design. It hadn't been a message to me, it had been a warning to Nonna and the witches.

The goddess of death remembered.

"I rushed to you, not noticing the circle of salt and herbs," she went on. "Uncaring about the spell candles or the arcane symbols glowing all over the walls. Once I crossed the circle, their magic locked me in. It overtook my power, essentially making me mortal for brief moments. Which was all the time they needed to perform their ritual. They chained me down and gave me my own spell-locked heart."

We stared at each other for a few tense beats. Despite her betrayal, despite the months of anger and torment I felt, I needed my twin. In this moment. I needed our connection. But Vittoria wasn't mortal. She didn't fold me in her arms. There were no words of comfort or shared tears. There was only one promise shining in her eyes. *Vengeance.* A vow to set right a terrible wrong.

"That's when they made us wear the Horn of Hades, further blocking our memories," I guessed. "And I imagine also hiding us from any of our mother's tracking spells."

"Precisely. The spell-lock and amulets both prevented the Crone from locating us. Something the witches also feared."

Which was why they took extra pains to hide us. Having the Crone, one of the three original goddesses, as an enemy would have posed an even greater threat to their world. I exhaled. Wrath and I hadn't been sure if that was true about the amulets, but it had been a theory we'd batted around. We wore those amulets to not hide ourselves from the devil, but to hide from our true selves. "And when we'd taken them off, that night... our magic struggled to rise."

"So you see." Vittoria walked over to where our grandmother was slumped and unconscious in her chair. "These witches do not deserve your sympathy. They deserve to die. Which is why I went through and started taking their daughters. Let them feel what it was like to lose it all." Vittoria spun on her heels and met my eyes. "No one binds Death or Fury and lives to tell the tale. They wanted to avoid a war? Well, that's precisely what they'll get. I won't stop until each family responsible has paid. The princes of Hell are no better and ought to have paid a long time ago for their sins. You need to be by my side, taking your rightful revenge. It is the only way House Vengeance can rise again."

"You're going to start a war between supernaturals."

"Start?" Vittoria asked, looking around. "War's already begun. It started the moment they cursed us and held us captive for nearly twenty years in that realm. It began when that witch cursed the demon you call husband now and dragged us into their issues. All of them have forgotten who we are. What we are capable of. Some battles are not fought with weapons in fields, sister. Some are much more effective when subtle moves are made over time. I don't ultimately care if other supernaturals fight; I care only for vengeance for us." She looked down at the woman who'd been our grandmother, her expression going impossibly colder. "Wrath will never give you his heart. He cannot. The curse has not been lifted for him. He will always keep part of himself locked safely away. Once you figure that out, come back to me. We have much to accomplish together. Just as we always did."

"I need you to tell me one thing. Did you kill Greed's commander or help her escape? Pride said she'd been asking about his portal."

"Pride has proved to still care *only* for himself. Just as he always has. And there is much you still don't understand—and will not understand—until you remove your spell-lock."

Vittoria ignored my questions and nodded to Domenico. The werewolf stepped forward and made a glittering portal. It was clear my sister wasn't going to talk about the magical skulls or any potential demon murder or escape. And I needed to get back to Wrath before he did something reckless.

I looked at Nonna, and a sliver of worry crept in. "What are you going to do with her?"

"Send her back to the coven with a message." I wasn't sure if her bruises *were* the message. Part of me wanted to beg for her life. To show mercy. To prove to everyone I wasn't the monster they feared me to be. But maybe I was. Before I stepped through the portal, my sister said, "If I come to find you again, you will regret it. I expect your assistance soon."

I paused on the magical threshold and leveled a cold look at my twin. "Do not threaten me. And do not ever take me here against my will again. If I want to find you, I'll do so. I have tolerated this because of what I've gained. You have many enemies here; you don't need another."

# FOURTEEN

**A steely, murderous** rage flickered in Wrath's eyes as I jolted up in bed, my soul thrust back into my body. His expression promised unending pain and torment.

Dragging me to the Shadow Realm a second time was a line Vittoria and Domenico clearly shouldn't have crossed. And now the demon of war looked ready to collect his due. Like the vampire court to the south, Wrath was out for blood. Goddess, werewolf, demon, it didn't appear to matter who received the brunt of his sin as long as his enemies paid.

"I'm unharmed," I said, curling onto my side to face him. "Just drained."

Wrath pulled the blankets up over me, then laid a heavy arm around my waist. His silence filled the room, louder and more tense than any words could. Knowing what I did now, about how I'd been wrenched from him in the past, wrenched from *us* just as we'd truly fallen for each other, I could only imagine that what he was feeling now wasn't good. Vittoria was tearing into wounds from the past, and Wrath seemed ready to strike back, to inflict some pain in return.

"I'm here." I rested my hand over his arm, squeezing the hard muscle gently. He was coiled tight enough to snap. I traced the gold serpent tattoo, hoping to soothe him. A quick inspection of the bedchamber proved he hadn't iced it over, which was a good sign. "I'm all right. Truly. I also warned my sister there would be ramifications if she took me again."

He was quiet for another long moment, drawing in a few measured breaths. The room chilled a fraction before he forced himself under control. He ran a gentle hand over my arm, lightly rubbing warmth back into me while making sure I was, indeed, unharmed.

"Your skin is tinged blue, Emilia. Had you not kicked me awake while showing signs of returning, I would have come for you and obliterated every creature in that realm. I'd have taken you from there, then wiped the entire *realm* from existence."

"Oh." I pulled an arm out from under the covers and glanced at my skin, cringing.

No wonder he was so angry. I looked half dead. I would have been terrified if I had awoken to him looking like a corpse beside me, too. Given the circumstances, his reaction was fairly mild. If any harm came to him, I would have attacked first.

"Your sister is playing a very dangerous game." Wrath's tone was filled with malice.

"I know." I traced small circles on his upper arm. "She's not thinking clearly. Vengeance and retribution are her gods, and she's honoring them regularly."

"What has been so critical for her to share that she cannot wait until you seek her out?"

"I think she senses some of my curse is breaking, and there are cracks where my memories are coming back. She's trying to help me remember so I—"

Wrath turned all his attention on me. "So you what?"

"Vittoria wants to reestablish House Vengeance. She says she means to start a war between witches, demons, and other supernaturals, but I don't necessarily believe that. She certainly hates witches and has a strong dislike for demons, yet her main focus seems to be on restoring our House."

Silence crept into the space between us.

"Is that something you want?" Wrath asked, his tone carefully neutral. "Reestablishing your House?"

"Until I know the full story and regain my memories, I don't want to make that decision." I bit my lower lip. "Is that something that would cause a complication for us? My sister seems to think it would."

"No. I would never stop you from doing anything you wanted. And as long as Vittoria leaves you to your own choices and respects your wishes, I don't give a shit what she does or who she prays to or starts a war with. There's already a price on her head. Greed wants her dead. So do Envy and Pride. Lust and Gluttony can both be swayed easily if it came to war. And Sloth will not go against the majority. I am the only one standing in the way of her total annihilation. And if she takes you against your will again, I will hunt her down. I will hurt her. Slowly. And painfully. Her death will be so brutal, so vile, it will serve as a warning for anyone who dares to touch my wife. Once I'm through, there will be nothing left for my hounds."

A tremor went through his body. I'd been wrong. Wrath's reaction wasn't mild at all. He was desperately trying to keep himself under control for *my* benefit. I thought of what I'd learned tonight, about how Wrath reacted once the curse began. How he'd nearly killed his brothers in his mad search for me. All he'd found was some blood and torn-out hair. Of course he would have thought his brothers had schemed. A curse would have been the last thing on his mind.

I couldn't help but wonder if there hadn't been any strife between the princes before then. As much as they fought and tried to outmaneuver one another now, there still seemed to be some familial affection. Some loyalty. Maybe one day those wounds could heal, too.

I nestled against my prince, laying my head on his chest. His heart beat like a war drum. Mine marched along to the same haunted rhythm.

If Wrath decided my sister was a true threat to me, he would not hesitate to remove her. I had little doubt that, even as an immortal goddess, he would succeed.

As terrible as things seemed with Vittoria, I was still clutching at hope that there was *some* redeemable part in her. Some way for me to reach what had once been warm and kind when we were mortals. I wanted to believe that Vittoria's goals of breaking my spell-lock and granting me my full power were solely because she wanted what was best for me, but I worried it had more to do with her current plan.

If she wanted a powerful ally and hadn't gotten one with the demon princes, maybe she wanted to unlock my power for her gain. And if Wrath was correct—if there was a chance I might not survive the removal of my heart—I understood why Vittoria's insistence would push him to remove her as a threat. He'd had someone take me against my will before.

I was still fighting my way back to my true self. If our roles were reversed, I would destroy anyone who threatened our happiness, too. I would murder without regret or remorse. Just as I'd done to that Umbra demon. But this was my twin, and it wasn't so simple or black and white.

"I can sense your emotions," he spoke quietly, "but can't read your thoughts."

"I'm thinking about my sister. Vittoria is..." I sighed and glanced up at him. "She's no longer human. I'd like to believe I'd retain my morals, but I'm not sure that's possible. Especially now. Our House was *Vengeance*. It seems to fuel us both. Even before I knew what we were, my initial response to Vittoria's 'death' was simple: revenge. Deep down I know that my sister is hurt and that this is the sole way for her to express it."

Wrath regarded me closely, a deep crease forming in his brow. "Everyone has choices they make. Your sister is using her immortality as an excuse to do unforgivable things. She could alter her path, forge a new one easily. She doesn't *want* to. And therein lies the issue. She is a monster by choice, not birth." He bared his teeth in a smile that promised untamed violence. "As we all are. But she's not the only one who can discard moral code to accomplish a task."

I held his gaze for a few beats. Nothing but pure determination and icy promise shone out of his eyes. Once he set his mind to it, he'd move the entire underworld to accomplish his goals. Vittoria was very close to becoming his number one task to eliminate. Nothing I could do or say would dissuade him. I knew that for certain because that would be the path I'd take. And no one would stop me. We truly were a match made in Hell.

"Regardless of the methods used to accomplish it, I learned a great many things this evening." I rolled onto my back and stared up at the ceiling. "I don't believe Vesta is dead. It's the one question my sister refuses to answer—she goes out of her way to avoid it, actually. If she were guilty, I don't see why she'd have any trouble rubbing it in Greed's face. She hates demons, princes of Hell especially. If she truly wishes to start a war, why not admit such a large triumph as slaying someone as important as one of their commanders? Especially if Vesta was as special as Greed claimed. Vittoria hasn't been shy in boasting about any of her other conquests. Why maintain silence now?"

Wrath exhaled. "I also questioned why Vesta had sought out Pride. He's hiding something, but I don't believe it has anything to do with her potential disappearance."

"What do you believe, then?" I rolled onto my side again, facing him.

"I think he'd been after information and thought he was using Vesta." His mouth almost lifted in a smile. "Once he realized he'd been outmaneuvered, I think his pride took another hit. Which was why he seemed surprised and annoyed. He thought he'd been the hunter, and he discovered he'd fallen into another trap. He's been overly sensitive about that sort of thing since your sister trampled all over his carefully crafted image."

"Did he care for her?"

"Your sister?" Wrath's attention slid over me as I nodded. "I'm not sure. But he certainly puts an enormous amount of effort into seeing her destroyed. Though that could simply be because he hates himself for letting his pride get in the way of telling his wife the truth."

"Which was?"

"As far as I know, Pride and Vittoria never did more than kiss. He had his reputation of a debauched prince to uphold, which was why he'd allowed everyone to think he was bedding her."

"You're certain he never bedded Vittoria?"

Wrath considered my question carefully. "I don't think anyone except Pride and Vittoria know the full truth. He's certainly not shared any details from that night."

And if Vittoria had grown feelings for him and they were unrequited, that certainly could have added fuel to her current "destroy demons and witches" mission. I mulled over another theory. "Do you think Greed sent himself the skull?"

"I wouldn't rule it out as a possibility. If he is convinced your sister is to blame, it would give him a clear motive to attempt to create evidence to prove his theory."

It was precisely what I'd been thinking, too. "Without having complete access to Greed's lands, there isn't any way for us to prove where the skull originated from, correct?" My prince shook his head. I turned over a few more thoughts. "The Duke of Devon mentioned that Vesta's family wasn't from here..."

"Are you considering the blood left at the scene?"

I nodded. "We obviously don't know the circumstances that brought Vesta here, but we know that she'd been inquiring about Pride's portal and the blood scenting. If her family was from somewhere outside of Greed's domain, even outside of the Seven Circles, perhaps she used the portal to return home. With the mixture of blood we found, perhaps she even sneaked some other type of demon here to help her?"

And if that were true, then perhaps she hadn't been the victim at all, but the actual murderer. If she was as unhappy in Greed's court as the duke had claimed, perhaps she had killed someone who stood in her way, leaving the mutilated body behind before making a great escape?

"It's certainly an area to look into and either rule out or prove correct." Wrath kissed my forehead, then got out of bed and pulled on a pair of pressed trousers. Something outside caught his attention, and he quietly swore as he strode onto the balcony.

Whatever exhaustion I'd felt vanished. I pushed the covers back and snagged a robe before joining him, stopping dead in my tracks. Glittering red stars were scattered across the sky, red as a blood-drenched omen. While we stood there silently watching them, they slowly formed a shape.

An anatomical heart, struck through the center with a dagger that had a skull at the top of its hilt. Blood dripped from the tip of the blade, or at least it appeared that way as crimson stars winked and spilled down the now pulsing symbol. *Thump-thump. Thump-thump.* It was beating, the pulse waves slowly raising the hair along my arms as they traveled across the realm.

It was a celestial heart. And it was clearly not a naturally occurring constellation.

"What is that?" I asked, my voice hushed.

"The immortal heart." Wrath's expression turned grim. The stars continued to pulse from their position in the sky, the red appearing like a gash in the universe. My own heart sped up. "It's the symbol of the vampire court."

Wrath dropped his attention to the courtyard below, scanning the moonlit grounds. I followed the path his attention traveled, looking for any sign of movement. A fresh blanket of snow had fallen, the crimson stars reflecting off it like drops of blood on the ground. The red splatters made it seem like a battle had already raged and soldiers had fallen.

I rubbed my arms. The night was quiet, but in no way was it peaceful. It felt like the shadows were watching, waiting. Trouble was near.

"An emissary will arrive soon."

From the tone of Wrath's voice and the way he kept surveying the castle grounds, it was not going to be a welcome visit.

In the weeks I'd been staying at House Wrath, I'd seen many impressive chambers—the libraries, guest suites, the training room, the garden, the Crescent Shallows, the dining hall, the circular tower where Celestia had brewed her potions and tonics, my bedroom suite and Wrath's, among many other formal and informal rooms, terraces, and balconies—but I'd never stepped into Wrath's throne room. It was a study of ferocious, gothic elegance.

Part of me wanted to drop to my knees, confess my sins like a devotee, or better yet, claim my favorite sin in front of the court forever. Though an audience would have to wait, the cathedral-like room with vaulted ceilings was empty for the moment, save for me and Wrath.

"It's stunning," I said, voice echoing lightly. We stood just inside the carved double doors, looking at the place where the devil ruled his kingdom. It suited Wrath. It was refined yet still contained an edge of wickedness. I waited for a spark of memory, but none came.

Black marble floors with pale gold veining, soaring arched

ceilings with matching columns in a deep gray stone, and massive chandeliers with ebony gemstones glinted in the candlelight. Muted tones in floral designs were featured in stained glass windows. Which were placed at least twenty feet off the ground on either side of the room, allowing light to trickle in and break up the darkness. Torches set into serpent sconces were evenly spaced along the lower walls, the fire crackling as if to remind those who entered here that they were in the underworld.

Blasphemous though it may be, it reminded me of a church. Except in this house of worship, the demon of war was the only "heavenly" being who was prayed to.

Gleaming gold weapons decorated the walls, similar to Wrath's training room. Shields, coats of armor, swords and daggers. Bows and arrows and curved blades that made me shiver from their wickedness. At the very back of the room, the widest arched window sat proudly above the throne. Taking up almost the entire wall, the stained glass design featured an unmistakable pair of outstretched black wings. I swallowed hard, realizing they must symbolize the wings that were stolen from Wrath. It must be torturous to have them memorialized like that.

I dropped my attention back to the first level. Just below the enormous window with black wings was a roaring fireplace. I'd never seen one quite so large—like the window, it took up almost the entire wall. A deep burgundy runner ran the length of the room, ending at the base of an ebony dais. The opaque gemstone looked like frozen smoke, forbidding yet beautiful. It was similar to, if not the very same, stone that I'd seen when we first entered this realm.

Atop the dais were two matching thrones. As the king of the underworld, I'd imagined his seat would be larger. Champagne bronze serpents curved around black leather, looking very much like the tattoo Wrath had inked onto his right arm. My heart skipped a beat when I spied vines with thorns that were elegantly twined around the serpent's bodies.

Wrath slanted a look in my direction, his mouth curving in a hint of a smile despite the circumstances that brought us to this chamber so late at night. "You're surprised."

"You really mean for me to be queen. Not just your consort."

He faced me fully, and I was struck by the power of his presence. The magnificence of his magic and the regal way he carried himself. With his ruby-tipped crown, flashing gold eyes, and his black suit tailored expertly to his frame, he was the dark king of many dreams and fantasies. Mine included. The devil grinned like he knew it, too. "You are my match in every way. Anything that's mine belongs to you. Never forget that."

The earnest way he said it, the way he reached for my hands and gripped them in his, it felt as if he were communicating so much more. I leaned toward him. "I—"

The double doors behind us burst open. Several demon maids rushed in, holding giant urns of black calla lilies and deep burgundy ranunculus. The soft, chiffonlike petals were some of my favorites. The maids rushed to the dais and artfully placed the urns, allowing the trumpet-shaped blossoms of the calla lilies and the burgundy ranunculus to cascade down the steps. Several more plants were brought in, though I couldn't immediately place the small red berries of one.

"Oleander is an interesting choice, especially if you're sending a message," I said, then nodded toward the plant I hadn't identified yet. "But what are those? I assume they're also poisonous or lethal in some way."

*"Abrus precatorius."* Wrath's tone hinted at amusement. "Rosary Pea. Vampires hate them. Not simply for their pious names, but because they can actually kill them. Some mortals figured it out, which is why you'll often find them beaded onto rosaries. Though the jeweler must be extremely careful—one prick of the berry can cause death."

"I thought vampires could only be killed with a stake?"

"A stake through the heart is lethal for most creatures, current company excluded." Wrath gave me a sardonic look, knowing full well I was intimately aware a blade in the chest wouldn't harm him. "Garlic is a nuisance, holy water does nothing from what I've gathered, but these berries?" He plucked one from a passing servant and pinched it between his thumb and forefinger. "These are one of the vampire's most closely guarded secrets."

"Your majesty!"

I turned at the familiar voice, pleased to see my friend Fauna hurrying into the throne room, looking resplendent in a deep copper gown with jewels sewn across the bodice. It felt like ages since I'd last seen her, though it had been only a couple of days.

Fauna had been my first friend in Wrath's court, and while others seemed content to gossip about my arrival, she'd done her best to make me feel welcome. I don't know how I would have gotten through those first few weeks without her friendship.

"Lady Emilia." She offered a polite curtsy to me and dipped low for Wrath. "I've secured the necklace."

She winked at me as she handed Wrath a rather large jewelry box. He lifted the lid to glance inside before closing it again. "Did you get something for yourself?"

"Yes, your majesty." Fauna brushed her curly jet-black hair aside, showing off a choker that featured little red berries. The color looked lovely against her warm brown skin. "I offered one to Anir, but he declined." Her sepia eyes twinkled. "But he did accept the necktie beaded with them. He's dressing now and should arrive shortly."

Wrath jerked his head in approval. "Make sure he looks like a courtier."

"Of course." Fauna curtsied again, then rushed from the room, her copper skirts swishing across the marble like whispering waves on the shore.

I nodded at the box. "May I see it?"

Wrath popped the lid open and lifted the necklace.

"Oh." My breath caught from its beauty. And its true purpose. This was no simple adornment. It was a weapon. Strands of Rosary Pea berries alternated with rubies. The gemstones the deep red of blood. It was meant to entice. To draw the eye. And then to warn. The vampire emissary could look but not touch. Unless he wished to die. "Subtlety isn't your strong suit."

"Subtlety is for cowards, my lady."

Wrath motioned for me to turn around, and he quickly fastened the jewelry around my neck. I faced him again, running my hands over the exquisite statement piece. The demon prince followed the path my hands traveled with his gaze, then continued lower as if he were seeing me for the first time and drinking in the full sight. A carnal look crossed his features. So primal and intense, I was tempted to see what sort of trouble we could get into on the throne.

"Do you like it?" I asked, knowing he more than liked it. I could almost see him calculating whether we had time to make my newest fantasy come true as he looked me over again.

My rose-gold gown hugged my curves, the color so pale and

soft someone might forget the terrible magic sizzling under my skin. Might be lured in by the pale pink charred roses covering the top portion of my bodice that plunged a bit too low, might mistake the pale vines with thorns that accentuated my hips before fading into the fuller tulle skirts for pretty adornments, and not understand the warning they were. My gown was my magic in wearable form. I quite loved it.

Wrath looked like he wanted to shred if off and show his appreciation for it in a purely animalistic way. Thoughts of him sliding my skirts up to bury himself deep inside had my cheeks going rosy. Not in embarrassment, but want. I needed a fan. Or an ice bath.

"This gown might be one of the hexed objects we haven't located yet." His mouth kicked up at the edges. "It's certainly got me spellbound. Though I think it's just you, my lady."

I glanced at my dress, fighting a grin. I adored when Wrath flirted with me. It was a welcome distraction, a bit of light to balance the dark.

A sharp knock drew our attention. Any hint of sensuality or lightheartedness vanished from Wrath's face. In its place was the hard, unforgiving mask of the strongest prince of Hell. Here was the demon whose power was so overwhelming it altered the entire realm. "Enter."

An older demon hurried in and bowed respectfully low. He wore a suit that reminded me of butlers in my favorite romance novels. "The emissary's party just left the stables, your majesty."

"Alert Anir and the others. I want them here now." Wrath held his arm out to me, so formal and full of manners. "Come, my lady. Let's prepare ourselves for our guests."

"Unwelcome though they may be."

"Indeed." Wrath's grin was wolfish.

I placed my hand in the crook of his arm, and we made our way to the thrones. Even feeling safe in our own House of Sin, nerves still had my pulse pounding. An unfortunate thing considering who we were about to entertain.

Wrath helped me up the stairs, then brought his lips to the shell of my ear, his warm breath causing a delightful shiver to dance along my spine. "Breathe. Or the emissary will walk in on me doing everything in my power to get your heart pounding for more pleasant reasons."

To follow his seductive statement with action, he kissed the pulse point at my throat, his tongue flicking over it lightly as he scraped his teeth against my skin. His hands…those cursed, incredible things, drifted along the swell of my breasts, down my silhouette until he playfully squeezed my bottom, promising to do exactly what he'd said.

I abruptly sat on my throne, earning a deep chuckle from Wrath. I was well and truly distracted as I fought the temptation to have him kneel before me, his head between my thighs, as the vampire entered our domain and the demon's tongue entered me.

Wrath's eyes flared—he'd sensed my arousal and likely felt the emotions I was struggling with. Goddess curse him for being so impossible to resist; this was *not* the time to be thinking of a tryst. Or submitting to desire.

I gave him a slight shake of my head. "Behave. The emissary will arrive soon."

"I have no idea what you mean, my lady." The look he gave me was a mixture of pure male smugness and feigned innocence. "I'm simply admiring my fierce wife."

He sat on his throne and once again adopted that icy demeanor.

I wouldn't wish to be on the receiving end of that look. It promised unending cruelty. Anir and Fauna entered the chamber, followed by several other demons I didn't recognize, all wearing their finery.

Most demons—both male and female—often stood with confidence, but something about the way these courtiers moved made me think they weren't simply lords and ladies of House Wrath. I'd wager anything these were soldiers.

I gave my husband a sideways look. He was prepared to fight. I was unsure if it was simply a precaution or if it was an offensive move. There hadn't been much time for us to get ready, and he'd left the bedchamber to meet with Anir and his top soldiers before I'd finished getting dressed. I had no clue what his scheme was, but I was certain he had one.

Wrath caught my eye and flashed a quick, devious grin. "Always have an arrow nocked and ready to fire if you invite an enemy in."

"Perhaps I can help with the fire portion." I summoned burning flowers and allowed them to hover over the dais. The heat from the fire quickly turned sweltering.

A few of the soldiers tensed but held their ground. Unbidden, I recalled what Fauna said when I'd first met her—about how some soldiers had laughed when one high-ranking officer wished to remove my still-beating heart and serve it to them. My fury slowly burned away other emotions as I turned my attention on the demons in the room. It was not a conscious choice to submit to my wrath, but I didn't fight it immediately, either. Were any of those demons who wished to harm me present now?

One thought and I could destroy them all. Send them screaming as their flesh melted from their bones. I could exact vengeance on them all and—

A soft, feminine laugh broke the spell. I let my magic go and blinked at our guests. I hadn't heard them announced, and I struggled to catch my breath without being obvious.

"Blade." Wrath seemed unimpressed as he addressed the emissary, purchasing me precious seconds to regain my senses. I wished I could lean over and kiss him, but I settled my attention on the two figures approaching us, adopting a look of cool boredom I'd seen Envy use.

Blade, a striking vampire—with chiseled features and tousled chestnut hair—quickly raked his gaze over me, pausing on the necklace with lethal berries, before turning his attention on Wrath, his expression impossible to decipher. His eyes were a deep crimson bordering on black framed with a thick fringe of lashes. He looked like trouble. But more in a defiant rebel way, not the subtle danger Wrath possessed when he chose to become someone's problem.

I barely spared Blade a second glance as I took in his companion, the female who'd laughed. She looked like a warrior queen, though I didn't see any weapons strapped to her. Which meant *she* was a weapon more deadly than any steel blade she could carry.

Dark hair cascaded down her back, her ebony gown looking more like leather armor than the high fashion popular in the demon courts. It was her eyes, though, that made my skin crawl. I'd seen them before. In a nightmare. They were star-flecked and fathomless. Ancient and filled with hate. And they were trained on me as she neared the dais with the vampire.

Wrath leaned forward, his voice dropping to a growl. "Sursea."

The woman hadn't yet taken her attention from me, her mouth twitching in what appeared to be dark amusement. I found myself wanting to throttle the look from her face.

"Isn't this intriguing." Her tone indicated she meant anything *but* intriguing. She took another step toward us, her gaze narrowing. "Do you know who I am?"

She wasn't a vampire. Nor was she a demon. There wasn't anything mortal about her, either, and yet I didn't think she was a goddess. I had a terrible suspicion, and the tense way Wrath sat, as if he were about to spring out of his throne and strangle her, confirmed my fears.

"You're the First Witch," I said. "La Prima Strega."

# FIFTEEN

**The First Witch,** Sursea, eyed me the way predators survey potential threats or prey.

Instinct took over, and I bared my teeth, the vicious smile indicating I might not be fully restored to my former glory, but I was not prey, either. I stared the witch down, my fury growing the longer I held her hateful gaze. *She'd* taken Wrath from me. She'd used me and Vittoria in her twisted game. And I would make her pay in blood and tears for her sins. Not now, but one day soon my face would be the one in her nightmares.

Her attention flicked to Wrath, her expression turning mocking. "Six years and six months have certainly flown by, haven't they, your majesty? Time may move differently here, but it still moves. How many days was it, again? I seem to have forgotten."

Wrath's gaze shot to mine for a brief flash before turning back to our enemy, but it was enough to amuse the witch once more. Her laughter filled the quiet chamber again. Only this time it sounded as if she knew a secret. One she shared with my husband.

And I detonated.

"Bow down to the king." My voice was cold. Imperious. I felt Wrath's attention shift to me, felt the whole room glance in my direction, but I did not break my stare with the witch. She must have sensed the fire burning in my soul. Sursea arched a brow but slowly went to her knees, the leather of her gown creaking in the silence.

I turned my focus to the vampire, who drew back almost imperceptibly. I had little doubt my eyes were now rose-gold and burning with my barely leashed power. If he hadn't cared who or what I was before, he did now.

"Do not make me repeat myself. Bow or you'll burn." I summoned a fiery rose and sent it hovering above Blade.

He clenched his teeth but went to his knees, inclining his head in Wrath's direction. "Your majesty."

I stared at their prone forms, not releasing them from their positions of forced acquiescence. Wrath didn't utter a word, sensing my emotions and giving me the time I needed to regain control. Or maybe he was simply pleased and wanted to see what I'd do next; discover how else our sins aligned in unholy matrimony. He'd said he wanted an equal. Wrath might command ice, but I was all fire. And the First Witch really shouldn't have stoked my fury. Had it been only Blade speaking for the vampires, I doubted I'd have reacted the way I did.

It was Sursea's presence, her foul demeanor, the implication that she had a secret my husband knew, along with her sneer at Wrath, that drove me mad with rage. For hurting him, I wanted to hurt her tenfold. It was irrational. Absolute. A consuming need for pure vengeance. I suddenly understood my sister all too well. I wanted our enemies to suffer. For every year, every month, day, hour, and *second* of pain they inflicted on my loved ones, I wanted to return the favor until they begged for mercy or death. And then I'd deny them that, too.

Twisted though it may be, that was the power of love. It could usher in warmth and light, and it could also turn a single ember into a raging inferno, destroying those who threatened it. Love might be the worst sin of them all, with its two sides.

Or perhaps that was simply the way of House Vengeance.

Torches around the chamber flared higher, the flames flickering wildly in a phantom breeze. I glanced around the mostly empty court, at the soldiers in their finery, Anir and Fauna among them. Respect, not fear, flared in each of their eyes. I might have scared them a little before, but they'd expect the princess of House Wrath to inspire some fear just as their prince did. That I was now using that power on our enemies…I inclined my head in their direction, acknowledging them. My attention returned to the unwanted guests still groveling at our feet.

That ancient, terrible power in my core stirred. The First Witch tensed. Her curse had locked it away, and the magic keeping it confined was deteriorating. One way or another, my spell-lock would break. And then that monster would be free. Sursea sensed that. She had to.

It was that thought, that promise to let my beast go wild one day, that soothed me. Still, it took every ounce of restraint I could muster to not unleash my magic now and watch them burn.

Tendrils of smoke curled into the air, and the acrid scent of leather burning wafted over to where we sat. The First Witch flinched but didn't move to put out the glowing ember in her skirts. Wrath ran a finger along the top of my hand, his caress a cool balm to my fury. I exhaled slowly, quietly. And I drew my magic back to its source. I waited another beat to be certain I'd found my center. One wrong move and I'd become the monster I was feared to be.

"Rise." My expression was now as tightly guarded as my emotions.

Wrath leaned back in his throne, a cruel tilt to his lips. Here sat an amused devil, delighting in his equally wicked queen. He regarded the vampire coolly, ignoring the witch as if she weren't standing there at all. "Why are you here?"

"To discuss a potential alliance between us."

"Strange timing for your prince. He hasn't bothered with the northern regions for centuries."

"Not quite so odd. After a recent visit from the goddess of death and her unique demon-werewolf companion, it made my prince consider the potential for having such unusual allies." To his credit, Blade held my husband's intense stare.

My eyes narrowed. Aside from her claim of wanting to spark unease and potentially start a war between supernaturals, Vittoria was up to something. Perhaps the companion Blade mentioned was simply Domenico somehow throwing off his scent, but another theory rose in my mind, and I chanced following it. "Was the demon-werewolf's name Vesta?"

"No. Marcella." Blade's attention never left Wrath's as he answered. "She hailed from the Shifting Isles."

"You're certain she wasn't from here?" I asked.

"She didn't say anything else. And we were mostly concerned with the goddess."

Suspicion coiled around me, but Blade clearly had no other information on my sister's companion. At least nothing he was willing to share if we refused an alliance.

Given the blood left at the murder scene, it made sense for Vesta to be genetically unique. Which might be why Greed coveted her. And was the first aspect I'd wondered about when both demon and werewolf blood had been found. This information made me now question if Vesta's interest in the portal on Pride's land had something to do with a potential inability for her to travel to the Shadow Realm. If my theory was correct and she was genetically unique, perhaps her demon side made that impossible. Much like the new wolf Antonio had mentioned.

While Blade and Wrath silently battled, I studied the vampire more closely.

Strong brows framed those piercing crimson eyes, his lashes thick enough to make anyone envious. His hair was a bit too long to be fully tamed and looked like he'd carelessly combed it before arriving here. Full lips curved in a half smirk as if he'd just recalled a particularly humorous joke he hadn't bothered to share.

Perhaps the amusement was due to the cunning glint in his eyes—the one that hinted that plenty of victims had fallen for that roguish charm.

His black suit jacket was fitted to his well-proportioned frame, and his white linen shirt and matching cravat were a surprise. Given his appetite for blood, I would have imagined he'd choose to wear all black. Dark trousers hugged muscular legs and were tucked fashionably into freshly buffed riding boots. There was an air about him that said he could dedicate himself to being either your truest protector or your worst enemy based on a whim.

Even standing there, spine straight under the weight of Wrath's scrutiny, he gave the impression that his jacket was seconds away from being discarded. His collar and cravat seemed to chafe, not because they were uncomfortable or lacking finery, but because the vampire did not appear to want to play pretend. He looked ready to shed all civility and embrace the cruel being he was underneath the refinement. Or perhaps he was simply thirsty and wished for a drink after his travels. If he was the emissary, I wondered what the less diplomatic vampires were like.

Wrath didn't move, but there was no mistaking the threat *he* posed while he let the silence stretch uncomfortably. My husband, unlike my impression of Blade, did not act on whims. He was cold calculation and brutal efficiency. Once he decided to make a move, others could either retreat or die. If they grew angry in the process, all the better. Their emotions would feed his sin.

My prince finally allowed his focus to briefly drift over to the witch before he responded to the vampire's earlier proclamation. "You thought bringing her was the best path to peace?"

"I—"

The demon prince raised a hand. With the way Blade cut his answer off, you'd think Wrath had held up a dagger. "Or was she merely a secondary distraction?"

Blade hesitated for less than a beat, but it was enough to notice that Wrath had caught him off guard. "We thought—"

"You thought to come here, to my House, under the false pretense of peace so you could take what you'd been after all along." Wrath cocked his head. "Are you truly that dumb? Or desperate? You know who I am. What I'm capable of. So perhaps it's arrogance and stupidity." My husband stood, his displeasure forcing the air to frost. Ice coated the stairs on the dais. "And you dared to stand here, lying to my face, and believed you'd get away with it."

Sursea stepped forward, reaching for something she'd hidden up her sleeve. A weapon, no doubt. She seethed as she yanked a blade free. "Your wife will—"

Wrath barely glanced in her direction as he froze her in place just as he'd done to the werewolves who'd attacked us.

It was one thing to see a wolf frozen solid, and another thing entirely to see a person encased in a thick block of ice. She'd been caught midscream, her expression twisted in pain or fury. We weren't lucky enough for her to be dead—she was immortal, according to Nonna's stories—but at least she would be tamed for a while, frozen in misery.

I didn't feel sorry for Sursea in the least. She never should have attempted to threaten me. Least of all after she'd been the one to curse Wrath and take us from each other in the first place.

As if he'd been thinking the same thing, remembering the night I'd been stolen by the curse, the temperature plummeted again, the room taking on a blue hue as if the walls themselves were chilled to the bone. All the torches and oversized fireplace made sense now, the air was so frigid, so brutal, that death lurked like a dog scenting scraps outside a butcher's shop. The fires gave a slight bit of respite from an otherwise unforgiving atmosphere.

Wrath had been well and truly pushed beyond his sin.

And the vampire recognized that. He held his hands up in surrender. "I don't want war."

"Considering my elite forces just took out several vampires camped along the outskirts of my circle, and a few within castle grounds, I think otherwise."

I kept my expression neutral, not wanting to let my surprise show. Logically, I understood there had been no time for Wrath to share what he'd learned, but I wished he'd mentioned *something* before they arrived.

Not hindered by the ice that now coated the floor, Wrath

slowly descended the steps, the apex predator on the prowl. "Is there anything you'd like to confess? Now is the time."

Calculation flickered in Blade's otherwise emotionless eyes. "I brought protection. Everyone knows traveling across the realm is dangerous. Lesser demons, errant souls."

The Prince of Wrath now stood within arm's reach of the vampire. Tension filled the throne room, and I fought the urge to stand beside my husband. This was his battle, his move.

The demon soldiers seemed to feel the same compulsion—perhaps it was the sin they all aligned with. Their need to unleash their anger and pummel anyone brazen enough to lie to their king. Given the way Wrath cocked his head, I imagined that was exactly what Blade had done.

Stupid. It was a move he'd no doubt regret. Though I was hardly sorry for him, either.

"You were accompanied by one of the most vicious creatures in the land. How many vampires did you truly need to protect you?" His gaze flicked to the frozen witch. "Anir?"

Wrath's second-in-command allowed a slow, nasty smile to spread across his face at his king's summons. The demon nodded, indicating it was time to reveal whatever they'd previously discussed. As a former fighter, Anir had likely been waiting for this moment, hoping it would come to this. The human bowed, then left the chamber, the soles of his fine boots slapping against the marble. My husband turned his attention back to the vampire.

"Last chance, Blade. Tell me the true purpose of your visit and you'll walk away unscathed. Lie and you'll suffer for it."

Defiance fell over the vampire like a royal mantle. "I told you. I'm here to form an alliance with you for my prince. Unlike the goddess of death, we do not want to tear this realm apart."

"Very well."

Wrath's tone was deceptively calm, crisp. No more threatening than a few snowflakes falling lazily from the sky on an otherwise cloudless day. I saw the truth of what it meant and fought a shudder. It was not the soothing sort of calm that indicated peace or serenity; it was the kind of charged tranquility that made the hair on my arms stand on end. Wrath's cool demeanor was meant to lure his adversary into a false sense of security as the true threat approached.

We were in the eye of the storm now, teetering on the precipice of what promised to be the worst of what was to come. And the vampire had no idea he'd started an avalanche that would soon bury him.

A few moments later, the double doors burst open, and Anir strode in ahead of a chained prisoner. Guards flanked the young blonde woman, swords at the ready.

My features remained impassive as they approached the dais, but I watched Blade out of the corner of my eye. He'd flinched the second he saw the girl. Wrath caught the action, too; he allowed the barest hint of a smile to curve his lips.

"The prisoner, your majesty." Anir stepped to the side and allowed the chained woman to approach. Before she smiled wide enough to show fangs, her red eyes gave her away as a vampire. Despite the rough spun dress she wore, the haughty tilt of her chin indicated a high standing member in their court. She ignored Blade and moved her narrowed gaze to me. Something like alarm crossed her features before she'd adopted that indolent expression again.

Wrath did not bother with introductions or pleasantries. "This was one of the vampires my forces found on the grounds of House Wrath. Are you certain there isn't anything you'd like to tell me now, Blade?" The vampire clenched his teeth together, slowly shaking his head. Wrath looked at the prisoner with deadly fire in his eyes. "Put the charm on."

Anir held up a strange necklace. A teardrop ruby the size of a robin's egg hung from a gold chain that looked to be woven with some organic material. An uncomfortable feeling had me sitting back, not wanting to get near whatever magic sparked from the charm.

"No." The woman was either fearless or stupid. Or perhaps she knew a worse fate awaited her at home if she betrayed her prince.

Blade remained stoic as the guards took hold of her, forcing her to her knees. Anir looped the necklace over her head and quickly stepped back. A shimmering, almost clear veil appeared, draping over her entire body. It melted into her skin, and I watched in horror as her hair changed from golden wheat to dark brown. Her pale skin shifted to bronze, and her features slowly took on a familiar heart-shaped form. I stood, shaking my head. "How is that possible?"

The vampire looked up at me, her eyes flashing from warm brown to rose-gold. The face that stared back at me was my own. A perfect replica.

Goose bumps rose over my body. It was like looking in a mirror. Not in the familiar or comforting way of being a twin, but an invasive foreign way that made me feel vulnerable. Every detail, from my newest *SEMPER TVVS* marriage tattoo that Wrath shared to our bond tattoo, was also on the vampire.

I pressed a hand to my chest, and she mimicked the movement. It was eerie, having someone mime your actions less than a second after you'd moved. My gaze cut to the charm, and I suddenly knew what the organic material was: my hair.

Somehow, some way, she'd gotten a lock and had performed dark magic. It was something Nonna Maria always warned us about and why she'd insisted we burn our nail and hair clippings. I'd thought she was overly cautious and superstitious. And yet she'd been correct. An enemy *had* used them against me. If Nonna feared us, then why protect us?

I didn't have time to sort out any theories. Wrath glanced to me, his expression inscrutable. "Ask her what her mission was."

Understanding what he truly meant, I inclined my head. I whispered the Latin that would force the truth from her. She had just enough time to shoot Blade a worried look—still wearing my face—before the spell lashed out and gripped her. "Why were you sent here?"

Unlike my twin, her will wasn't nearly as strong; she broke easily. "To seduce the king."

Fury fueled my magic, and I speared into her mind, demanding more truth. "For what purpose?"

A tear rolled down her cheek. *My* cheek. "To distract him."

"From what?" My voice was low, nightmarish with power. "Tell me details of your mission."

She swallowed hard, the words burning in her throat to be set free. "To distract him while Sursea incapacitated you and took you to the vampire court."

"WHY?" I was shaking with fury now. They'd dared to come here, to separate us again.

"I don't know! I was only told to entertain the king until you'd been secured."

In a move so swift that no mortal could ever hope to achieve, Wrath was suddenly behind the vampire who wore my face. His expression was the coldest I'd ever seen.

Here was justice in its purest form. It was not kind or merciful. Good or evil. It was just, harsh. Like nature. Wrath gripped her head and twisted, the sickening pop indicating she would not live to cast another illusion. Wrath wasn't done yet. Instead of letting her body drop to the floor, he twisted harder, tearing her head clean from her shoulders with his bare hands.

I swallowed hard as my face slowly melted back into her own. There was no blood, given that she was already dead. No gore. But the sudden end…the finality of her true death…caused me to shudder. Blade stared coldly at the scene, though I noticed one hand had curled at his side.

Wrath said he had the opportunity to leave this circle unscathed. And while the vampire would be set free, he certainly wasn't leaving without suffering a loss. It just hadn't come in the form he'd expected. Fool that he was to attempt to trick the devil.

My husband handed the severed head to Blade. "Take this back to your prince. If he ever attempts to steal my wife using parlor tricks or any other means again, my queen and I will eliminate every last vampire from this realm."

Blade took the head, his jaw clenched tight. "That was his betrothed."

"Then he should have taken more care to protect her from his enemies." Wrath stepped over the body, placing himself closer to the vampire emissary. It was a subtle maneuver that also blocked me from any attempted retribution. "Instead, he sent her here to fuck me while you used the witch to kidnap my wife. Did you truly think that illusion would work? That I would be so easily manipulated by subpar magic? That I would for one second mistake her for my wife?" The demon leaned in. "You saw a small *taste* of what my queen is capable of. If I don't kill you first, she will. Now get the fuck out of my circle. And don't come back unless you mean to start a war."

# SIXTEEN

**"I didn't want** to think Vittoria was serious about the vampires," I said as Wrath entered the kitchen on silent feet. Daybreak was fast approaching, but I couldn't sleep. "Or that they would use her information to scheme up another problem on their own."

I went back to chopping herbs while he headed for the icebox. Fragrant parsley and dill filled the air, the scent fresh and welcome after the last few horrendous hours.

My sister and Nonna Maria in the Shadow Realm. The vampires.

It had been another emotionally taxing night, and no matter how exhausted my body was, sleeping felt like an impossible task. Too many thoughts and worries were racing through my mind. Each time I thought I knew where to start detangling this mess, a new thread knotted itself together. There was still the murder or fabrication of Vesta's murder to figure out, the rest of my curse to break, and our marriage ceremony to perform to seal our vows.

A ceremony Wrath hadn't mentioned or pushed for, even after the vampires had tried to wrench us apart. If we completed the bond, I imagined any future kidnapping attempts would end. Something Wrath had undoubtedly considered, and yet no arrangements were being made. I wanted to believe it was so I could continue investigating Vesta's murder without officially becoming a member of House Wrath, but doubt crept in.

I thought of what my sister had said about Wrath being unable to give me his heart. If his curse was to lose everything he loved and I was still here…

I swallowed hard and chopped the herbs with more vigor than needed. I had to prioritize my goals, and being upset over Wrath ought to be last. What I needed to focus on first was finding proof that Vesta was alive. Then I could figure out a way to save Vittoria from the blood retribution, and then remove my spell-lock.

"Are you all right?" the demon asked, watching with a quirked brow as my knife attacked the cutting board. "Is this because of the First Witch?"

I lifted a shoulder noncommittally. After Blade was escorted from the castle, Wrath had Sursea taken to an underground chamber that would keep her frozen and I'd sneaked away to the kitchen. I needed to create. To do something familiar and calming, something that reminded me I was more than a spell-locked goddess whose twin was potentially murdering members of rival demon courts or setting them free, whose family might be the true villains of a very complicated, nightmarish fairy tale, whose husband might not truly ever love me freely, and whose list of enemies and complications seemed to grow with each passing day.

I hated to think anything could get worse from here.

"What do you think their prince wanted with me?"

"Drink?"

I jerked my attention to his. At first I thought he'd meant the vampire wished to drink me. Wrath held up a bottle of sparkling demonberry wine, smiling. I nodded, and he poured me a glass before grabbing a bottle of the pale purple liquor he preferred and serving himself a generous amount.

He sipped it, then leaned against the counter, watching me rinse cannellini beans with quiet fascination, intrigued when I started to mash them in a bowl until they were smooth enough to spread. I wasn't sure what I was making yet, either, but I had an idea of what I'd like it to taste like. Hopefully, it would be good.

"To answer your question," he said, "I suspect he wants you for your power, given the tumultuous state of his court. Royal vampires have the ability to place someone under their thrall. All the prince would have to do is give you a bit of his blood, and you'd essentially do anything to please him, hoping for more."

I minced two large cloves of garlic, then zested a lemon before cutting it into quarters to squeeze over the mashed beans.

"They could have accepted Vittoria's alliance. Your brother did mention that she'd sought them out, too. She's also fully restored. I'm still only a shadow witch. They knew it would anger you, so it was a rather large, desperate risk. I don't see the value in what they tried to accomplish when they had someone willing to stand beside them."

"Your sister rules over death. They are undead. On a whim, she could decide she no longer wants to play nicely with them and they would cease. Choosing to steal you was the best option. Despite the risk, if they'd succeeded, it would have solved many of their problems. You're also not in possession of your full power, which would have made you easier for their prince to manipulate. The plan was decent enough. But they didn't plan on one thing."

"Which is?"

"You cannot be replicated."

I gave him a sardonic look. "I have a twin."

"Doesn't matter." Wrath lifted a shoulder. "I always knew you. And always will. Your soul calls to mine. It's a feeling of coming home. Of peace. No magic can duplicate it." For a second, I forgot how to breathe. We held each other's gazes, and after a moment, Wrath's lips curved in a troublesome grin. "Plus, no one manages to look at me with such fury and desire like you do."

"Mmm." I smiled and slightly shook my head. "The truth will out, I see."

When Wrath spoke like that, it was hard to believe he didn't love me.

"How am I still here?" I asked, setting my knife down. "Your curse..."

He took another sip of his drink, then wrapped an arm around me, drawing me to his side. "If you don't mind, I'd rather not talk about that tonight." The prince pressed his lips to my temple in a chaste kiss. "I promise we will. Soon. Just not now."

I studied his features. The strain in his jaw, the fierceness in his eyes. The demon looked like he needed a respite from our nightmarish few hours, so our conversation could wait.

"All right." I gave him a tight smile and focused on the food again. He moved to the other side of the island, giving me plenty of space to work. "What do you think of what Blade said regarding Vittoria's unusual companion?"

"Marcella?"

"Mmh-hmm." I scooped the lemon zest up and sprinkled it over the beans, quickly adding the herbs next. I drizzled olive oil, two tablespoons of warm water, then added salt and fresh ground pepper. Wrath's cooks had red pepper flakes in the pantry, so I added a generous pinch of them, too. I stirred everything until it was well mixed, then topped it off with the remaining fresh herbs, pepper flakes, and a drizzle more of olive oil. "I can't help but wonder if Vesta assumed a new identity or reclaimed her true name. If *she's* the demon-werewolf companion he spoke of."

"It would explain the blood."

"It might also explain why Vesta didn't simply escape to the Shadow Realm. If she's both demon and werewolf, she probably can't travel there alone like the other wolves. Correct?"

"I would imagine so. I can travel there because I'm the king. Lesser demons cannot, though. If Vesta is half demon, I think that would certainly hinder her ability to travel there on her own," Wrath said. "Who has been with your sister when you enter the Shadow Realm?"

"Only Domenico."

"The alpha." Wrath removed toast points from the oven and slid them onto a waiting dish. Without needing instruction, he spread the herbed white bean dip over a piece of toast and handed it to me before serving himself one, too. He took a bite and briefly closed his eyes. "This is delicious."

I sampled my own piece and sighed happily. It had been an experiment and turned out exactly as I'd hoped it would. It was creamy and flavorful and felt nurturing after a hellish evening. I adored how simple it was, how each ingredient complemented the other.

I took another bite, allowing my mind to wander with possibilities. "It's good as a dip, but I'd also like to try it with grilled chicken, dressed salad greens, and perhaps roasted red peppers. Or maybe cherry peppers. Make a true meal out of it."

"Mmh."

Wrath sipped his drink, then finished his toast before fixing another, the silence comfortable between us. With each bite, he seemed to relax more, lose some of the tension he'd been carrying since I'd awoken from the Shadow Realm and the vampires arrived.

"I think your theory about Vesta not being dead is correct," he said. "What I haven't quite worked out yet is whether Greed realizes that. I'm inclined to believe that he did fall for the ruse and that's why he might have sent himself the skull. Or, more likely, asked one of his closest guards to provide evidence to condemn your twin. That way he wouldn't lie about the skull."

"So we need to find Vesta or get my sister to confess any role she played in Vesta's escape."

"If your sister did, indeed, assist with her escape, she needs to tell me directly. I can sense if she lies and take the proof to Greed."

Which would then remove the blood retribution he'd been granted and save my twin from any of the other princes. It wasn't going to be easy to get my sister to talk, but I had to try.

Once we'd eaten our fill, we stood quietly with our drinks. Wrath swirled his, staring into his glass, seeming lost in thought. "The cooking is new."

His admission caught me by surprise. I nearly choked on my next sip of wine. "What?"

"Before the spell-lock, you weren't interested in cooking," he said, bringing his attention to mine. "You seem relaxed when you're creating, peaceful. Your mortal family did a lot wrong, but I feel like murdering them a little less when I see you looking at roasted garlic like it's the most wondrous thing in our universe."

"Aside from you, naturally."

"That goes without saying." Somehow, Wrath had managed to slowly close in on where I stood. My heart thumped with each measured step he took, his focus dropping to my lips with unchecked desire. "How am I looking at *you*, my lady?"

Hunger, raw and untamed, flashed in his face. There was little doubt that *I* was about to be his main course. I set my wineglass aside. My breathing quickening in charged anticipation as he stalked closer; his cunning eyes, not missing the reaction I had to his proximity, twinkled.

"You certainly don't look like you hate me, demon."

"Hatred is the last thing I feel when I look at you."

I wanted him to confess his love. He seemed like he wanted to. I was almost sure he was on the verge of saying those most precious words, when the prince pushed me against the countertop, his mouth crashing down on mine instead.

One hand tangled in my unbound hair, angling my head up to run his tongue along the seam of my lips, and my mouth parted on instinct, granting him access to taste and tease. His other arm hooked around my waist, anchoring me against his hard body. Each stroke of his tongue sent a streak of sensation through me, causing me to arch into him, seeking more.

Wrath possessed my mouth with the confidence of a partner who knew *exactly* how to seduce a lover properly and thoroughly. How to kiss with such passion, such vigor to both steal breath and give it. I swore he could tell how hard my heart was pounding and my knees were wobbling and that I never wanted the feeling to end, because he kissed me harder, demanding my body to give in to the pleasure he was offering, to surrender wholly and completely while he took me to heaven.

"I'm going to devour you right here on the counter, my lady."

Wrath trailed openmouthed kisses along the neckline of my bodice, slowly pulling the material down to expose the top of my chest. His warm tongue darted out, teasing my aching flesh as his other hand slid up and cupped my other breast. He suckled over the material and squeezed, each pull of his mouth causing the heat in my belly to dip lower.

I dragged his mouth back up to mine, wanting to devour *him*. He ground his hips against me, and then the devious prince swallowed my moan, pushing his silken tongue back into my mouth. One hand fell to the hem of my skirts, his fingers curling into the material as he slowly dragged the hemline up.

"You're so incredibly beautiful, Emilia."

Wrath pulled back, allowing our lips to hover against each other, our breath mingling in a barely there kiss before he sealed his mouth over mine again. This kiss was probing, consuming. It made me crave him terribly. His fingers finally found that pulsing area between my legs, but just as he was about to bring my torment to an end, there was a knock at the door. Wrath withdrew his hand and pressed his forehead to mine, cursing.

"I am going to murder and maim my entire court. This whole fucking realm if someone interrupts us again. I hope you won't mind ruling over a kingdom of nothing."

"Maybe they'll go away," I offered, glancing down at Wrath's trousers. Goddess above, I wanted *that* inside me now.

He grinned and tilted my chin up, running his thumb over my bottom lip until it parted. "Maybe." He kissed me again, long and lingering. Another sharp knock sounded, breaking us apart. Wrath stepped back and glanced up at the ceiling, and I wondered if he hadn't exactly been teasing about murdering his whole court. "I'll get rid of them."

The demon was across the kitchen a beat later and cracked the door. Lust barged in, grinning as he took in my rumpled appearance, then Wrath's impressive bulge. "Really? The kitchens?" He slapped his brother on the back. "You might end up in my House of Sin yet, you lusty delinquent."

Wrath let loose a deep, rumbling sound of annoyance that I found wildly endearing. "Why are you here without an invitation, and why shouldn't I stab you?" he ground out.

"You're cock dumb." Lust found a pear in a large serving bowl and tossed it in the air before rubbing it on his lapel. He checked the buffed fruit over. "*You* asked us to the Pit at dawn. Everyone's there, and the first fight's ready to begin. They're waiting on you."

"The Pit?" I asked, looking between them. "Is it a boxing ring?"

"Legendary and exclusive. It's *the* best fighting ring in the Seven Circles. This bastard hardly lets us come and watch." Lust took a bite of his pear, his charcoal eyes gleaming at my inquisitive look. "Your husband provides his court a way to unleash their sin of choice. While also allowing mortal souls a chance at redemption. Boring as that part is."

"And there's a fight soon?"

Lust nodded. "From dawn until dusk."

The idea of going anywhere for that long after the night we'd had made my knees go weak. Wrath didn't miss a thing. He was by my side again in an instant, brushing his lips over mine. "I'll return as soon as I can. Get some rest."

Lust snorted and finished his pear. "Judging by *that* look, you'll need it."

Sleep still evaded me after Wrath and Lust left, so I decided to do some research. Until I saw my sister again, little could be done to learn anything else regarding Vesta's disappearance, so I tackled the next biggest item on my list of goals. Breaking my spell-lock.

Thanks to Domenico's snide comment about my mother having

more important matters to attend to, I knew she wouldn't be there, but I went to Celestia's tower anyway. If anyone had any texts or notes on spell-locks, it would be the Matron of Curses and Poisons.

There *had* to be a way to remove the spell without sacrificing my heart. I refused to believe having Vittoria rip it out was my only option. If I could break the spell on my own, it would be one less thing to worry over. One less reason for people to try to keep tearing me and Wrath apart.

"Hello? Celestia?" I gently rapped my knuckles against the wooden door, waiting a few beats before trying the handle. It twisted easily, and the door swung open, revealing an empty, darkened chamber. Wane light trickled in from the windows set high in the tower, muted from the overcast skies and latest wintry storm.

I went in and found some candles and lanterns to light. I set them on the table piled with bundles of herbs and baskets of dried botanicals, then glanced around the circular chamber.

It looked like it had the last time I'd visited. There was a skull with arcane symbols etched onto it sitting on the mantel, various glass jars filled with items that tapped the sides, figurines, herbs, spices, dried petals, liquids in a wide array of colors, cauldrons and steaming vials of unknown origins. But the stack of grimoires and books—*those* were what I set about gathering. Once I had a decent pile, I pulled one of the wooden stools out and sat.

My mother, strange as it still was to think of Celestia that way, had meticulous notes on different remedies. I flipped through one grimoire that had sketches of plants along with quantities needed to blend the perfect tonic. Poisons and potions for love, for heartache, for upset stomachs and aching heads, for cursing an enemy with warts or pox or a flesh-eating rash.

I paused to read one; a spell for forgetting.

# SPELL TO FORGET

* Beeswax candle, three
* Wooden bowl—made from a sapling in Bloodwood Forest
* River water collected during the new moon, one cup
* Grave dirt, one handful
* Black moonstone, one
* Hawthorn flowers, one pinch
* Lemon balm, one teaspoon dried
* Rosemary, one sprig
* Cloth from the person you wish to forget

*Mix lemon balm, rosemary, and hawthorn flowers together with half the river water. Bring to a slow boil and steep. Add remaining river water to the wooden bowl, light the candles, and place black moonstone in the bowl to the north. Sprinkle dirt over stone. Using the cloth of the one you wish to forget, cleanse the stone and repeat:*

*Earth, to send memories to the grave.*
*Fire, to burn times three.*
*Water, to cleanse the emotions enslaved.*
*I drink this tea and command you to*
*forever leave me.*

*Drink tea in one pass then sleep with the stone under your pillow until the next full moon.*

Goddess above. For a second, I'd been worried it was a spell Nonna had used on us, but we'd only collected grave dirt to bless our amulets. We'd never cleansed a stone and slept with it under our pillows. Though I remember teasing my friend Claudia about it once when she'd admitted to doing something similar after her crush rejected her.

That was one of the simpler spells. I flipped page after page of notes that progressively used stronger magic. Celestia had a remedy for any malady or hex.

It was truly astounding what she'd created. I was startled to realize both Vittoria and I had taken after her in some way once we were "mortal"—my sister loved to tinker with perfumes and cocktails, and I loved to create in the kitchen. Putting that unsettling realization aside, I pulled another journal out and flipped through more of the same.

There were no notes on spell-locks. No magic elixirs to cure what troubled me. It had been something I'd hoped to find but hadn't expected to.

If spell-locks were that simple to remove, they wouldn't be very effective. Plus, Wrath knew I had a spell-lock, and he'd likely have had Celestia working on a cure if she hadn't already been trying herself. No matter what Vittoria had said about our mother being distracted by other whims, I didn't think she'd sit back and allow witches to potentially kill her daughters without attempting to save us. I'd just gone through another grimoire when I came to a curious tincture with a ghastly name. The Bleeding Heart.

I ran a finger over an illustrated vial of pale purple liquid the matron had drawn into the margin, my pulse pounding at the familiar tincture. Wrath had an entire decanter filled with a similar liquid. I'd even sampled it when I'd sneaked into his personal library that first time.

Surely it couldn't be the same one, and yet I held my breath. It felt like I was reading a secret, one he'd certainly like to keep, but I *had* to know if this was what he was drinking and why. My attention fell upon the description—unlike the memory spell, this was just a simple list of ingredients along with its use. I read aloud to myself.

*To prevent the ill effects of love or other strong emotions from taking root.*

I reread the handwritten note, clearly depicting its sole purpose. I had to be mistaken.

Bleeding heart plants were toxic to mortals, but Wrath wasn't mortal. I read over the list of ingredients, my stomach twisting into knots. Bleeding Heart petals. Vanilla bean. A drop of lavender oil. Brandy. Orange peels, dried with purple dragonfire and set to distill under a full moon. Almost all the flavors I'd identified in that lavender liquor. The very drink Wrath poured himself tonight. A night filled with high emotion.

"Goddess above."

*That's* how the curse hadn't attacked again. Wrath was magically dulling his emotions, unwilling to fall in love again and have our world torn apart.

A strange mixture of understanding and horror washed over me. I recalled the night I'd first seen him drink it—we'd just come back from the matron's after our dip in the Crescent Shallows.

He'd been pacing and showing far too much emotion. Something I'd pointed out when I'd asked him to sit and stop making me nervous. Then he'd tossed back a single drink, offered me some that I refused. And he'd regained that cold efficiency again shortly thereafter.

Tonight, he'd been wound tightly, furious and likely close to the edge after I'd wrenched the truth of the vampires' mission. And he'd relaxed shortly after his drink. I'd mistaken it for the food nurturing him, now I knew it wasn't the alcohol or snack, it was the tonic. At least in part.

"What have you done?" I whispered to the empty room.

My shoulders slumped forward as I continued to stare at the ingredients. If Wrath hadn't discovered a way to lock his feelings up tightly, I'd be wrenched away again. I knew that, logically, he'd done this for us, and yet my own heart ached at the realization that my husband could not allow himself to love me. He'd even gone so far as to magically bind himself.

"Lady Emilia?" Fauna burst in, her scarlet nightgown reminding me of a torn-out heart, then stopped short when she took in my expression. "What's wrong?"

I glanced at the spell one more time, allowing my fury to replace the sadness. I was not upset with Wrath; I was furious at our circumstances. At the people who were so wrapped up in hate they dampened the fire of our love. I looked at Fauna, my hands curling into fists.

"I want to end this curse once and for all. I want to break the spell-lock. And I want to fully claim my king."

My friend's face split into a lovely, fierce grin. "Let's get to work then."

# SEVENTEEN

**"We should start** with one curse at a time." I slid some journals over to where Fauna had taken a seat beside me. I briefly caught her up on what I'd discovered, and grim determination filled her features. "The spell-lock isn't technically a curse, but I'd like to see what we can find about that, too. Options on how to break it. If it's even breakable aside from removing the heart. Any potential consequences."

"Right," Fauna said, looking over a hefty grimoire. "And what of his majesty's curse?"

"A priority. What do we know about it?"

"Sursea cast it after she made a blood sacrifice to a goddess."

That drew my attention. "Do you know which one?"

My friend shook her head. "His majesty has been trying to figure that out, but only recalls her casting a spell with spilled blood."

Dark magic required sacrifice. Blood. Bones. All the things Nonna Maria warned us away from. And yet something there didn't quite make sense... "Why would a goddess require a blood offering?"

Fauna blinked, seeming taken aback. "Because that's what the witches always do."

And the lesson I'd been taught thus far was that witches could not be trusted.

"Would you be willing to test a theory out?" I asked, hatching a plan.

Excitement flashed in her eyes. "Does it require blood?" I nodded, and her grin widened as she removed a slim dagger she'd hidden under her skirts. Sometimes I forgot that her sin aligned with wrath and that bloodshed made her soul sing. "Who am I making an offering to?"

"The goddess of fury."

Bless her willingness to help, Fauna didn't hesitate, she pricked her finger and squeezed a few drops of blood over a candle, the sacrifice steaming in the flickering flame. "I bid the goddess of fury to come forth."

We sat there silently, both tensed as I waited to feel any indication that magic was at hand. Any magical tug or pull to heed someone's call. Fauna's brow creased as she looked me over. "Anything?"

I closed my eyes for a second and tried to manifest *something*. "No."

She added another drop of blood and repeated her prayer. I closed my eyes, concentrating hard for another minute. Then two. There was still no inner urge to go to her, to do her bidding. I felt as I always did. Just as I'd suspected.

I thought of my mother, the Crone, being summoned by any creature or being who spilled blood and commanded her to their side. It was laughable. Blood was used to summon a demon, but only in conjunction with several other items. Most of which were specific to each demon prince along with a specific spell.

"Maybe it's because you're not fully restored." Fauna sounded unsure. "Or maybe the sacrifice wasn't large enough."

I shook my head. "Before you start sacrificing anything larger, I'd like to test it out on my sister. She is fully restored and should heed the call if the magic of a blood sacrifice does, indeed, work for a goddess."

Fauna's brows raised nearly to her hairline. "If his majesty finds out—"

"I'll take full responsibility. Please," I added when she hesitated, "try."

"I hope we both don't live to regret this." She inhaled deeply and pressed her blade into another fingertip. "I pray to the goddess of death to come forth."

Tension crept into the chamber, making the air feel suddenly colder. The shadows cast by the candles and lanterns even seemed to flicker more menacingly. Death could be lurking, but it could simply be my imagination willing it. We both waited, breath held, for something to happen. A strained moment passed, followed by another. There was no Vittoria. And thankfully no Wrath coming to break up our goddess-summoning test.

I exhaled. "I'll try with my blood."

With my own dagger, I pricked my finger. Instead of allowing a drop to fall into the flames, I stood and held my hand over the skull. "I bid the goddess of death to come forth."

Part of me believed the wind gusted outside a bit harder, that the elements reacted in some monumental way to the magical request, but I knew deep down nothing had changed. Even with my half-goddess blood, it wasn't enough to summon a full deity. Which meant the witches either knew that and had purposely misled their enemies, or they'd been misled themselves.

"I need to get to the Shadow Realm." I turned back to where Fauna still perched on the edge of her stool. "I'm going to ask my sister what she knows about spells cast with blood."

And then I'd find a way to cast another truth spell on her and see what other secrets she'd been keeping. Mainly, if she happened to know where a certain commander had gone.

It took more time than I'd like to have spent searching through grimoires—and Fauna even managed to persuade me to take a break to visit the Pit to see one of the fights—but eventually we came across an incantation to summon a werewolf.

We gathered all the ingredients, then Fauna watched quietly as I set it up and began the summoning.

Within the salt circle, I sprinkled wolfsbane on the north, south, east, and west points before whispering the spell. Unlike when I'd summoned Wrath, the results of this circle were nearly instant.

Domenico appeared in a snarling blast of magic that almost knocked me backward. He whipped around, eyes blazing as he took in the tower chamber. The salt circle. My demon friend who gave him a taunting finger wave. And then he turned to me. His claws shot out.

"You're going to regret this, Shadow Witch."

"If I received a coin every time I heard that, Greed would have cause for alarm."

"He already has plenty of cause to fear *me*."

My cold gaze traveled over the shifter, similar to the way he'd looked me over earlier last night. It was hard to believe only a few short hours had passed since I'd last seen him. His shirt was missing, and his trousers were half-untied. Fine hair trailed into his pants, between sculpted abdominal muscles. Some scars that looked like claw marks marred otherwise unblemished olive-toned skin. His dark hair was rumpled either from sleep or some other bedtime activity he'd been engaged in. The idea of ruining his tryst gave me far too much petty enjoyment.

"I wish to speak with Vittoria."

Domenico opened his mouth—likely to argue—then abruptly snapped it shut. He didn't want to say yes, but he couldn't refuse. Vittoria had clearly stated she wanted me to call on her.

"Fine." His attention cut to Fauna. "She stays here."

That suited me well enough. Fauna and I had already decided that she'd stand guard over my body while my spirit traveled to the Shadow Realm. I lifted a shoulder and dropped it, as if I'd considered his request. "Very well. Are you ready?"

"I don't have much of a choice, do I?" he snapped, then motioned for me to come closer. I took a halting step forward, then paused, surveying him again. Domenico gave me a nasty look. "I need to attach our bodies." At my expression of horror, he snarled, "My claws will do. Stand in front of me."

Against my inner warning to not allow the werewolf's instruments of death anywhere near my body, I did as he requested.

Domenico turned me until my back was pressed to his chest. He hooked his arms under mine, sinking his claws into each shoulder. My teeth clenched from the pain, but I refused to let the shifter feel me flinch.

"My lady. Wait." Fauna took a step toward us, her expression one of concern when the werewolf's claws dug in further. I'd only ever been summoned to the Shadow Realm before, I'd never been the one to initiate, so I hadn't known what to expect in terms of magical payment.

Yet something didn't quite make sense.

My teeth gritted together as his claws lengthened, nearly hitting the bone. "Why do our bodies need to be attached to enter the spirit realm?"

Domenico brought his mouth to my ear, "Who said anything about the Shadow Realm?"

In a glittering whirl of power, a portal appeared. Before I could twist to Fauna, Domenico hoisted me up and jumped through. Magic sucked and pulled at me—it felt as if we'd stepped into the heart of a hurricane and the only thing tethering me to my body was the shifter's claws. Almost as quickly as it had begun, we stepped out of the portal and into a room I knew well. Any disorientation I'd felt from the portal disappeared almost instantaneously.

Domenico released me and moved away, watching as my attention darted around the space. Limestone walls and floors. A little cabinet set into a corner that I knew contained cooking supplies, two cutting boards, knives, bowls. I was in the monastery. In the very room Antonio and I had last made bruschetta together. Right before my world upended. A wave of sadness hit me when I thought of my old friend and how brutally he'd been killed.

"Blood and bones." I pressed a hand to my shoulder and glanced sharply at the werewolf. "Why are we here?"

"You wanted to speak with your sister. This is where she is."

"Nearly all the princes of Hell are searching for her, and she came to the most obvious place."

"One, the demons cannot leave the Seven Circles at the moment. And two, your mortal home is likely the last place they'd expect to find her, given your very reaction."

My heart beat entirely too fast. Vittoria had come home. To the mortal world. Part of me wanted to push past the shifter and run for the door. Instead, I remained frozen.

I longed to rush to my home and have Nonna make sweetened ricotta and smooth my hair back while telling me everything would be all right. That the last few months were only a nightmare, a strange fever dream brought on by her superstitious tales.

And maybe a bit too much wine. It very well could be an illusion. Maybe I *was* still in our trattoria, and Nonna's warnings about the sea being stirred by the devil was true. Maybe it *had* all been make-believe, the result of an imagination well tended by reading books. Maybe Claudia and I had drunk ourselves into a stupor and had crafted this unbelievable tale about the devil being cursed.

Nervous laughter bubbled up my throat. In a strange way, being part of a story made sense. Especially when faced with my current reality.

I could go home now. I knew in my bones that Nonna would hex me if I asked her to. I imagined she'd be all too willing to play along in my denial fantasy—to make me hate and fear the seven princes of Hell once more. She'd steal my memories, and I'd live a normal mortal life, dying at a respectable age surrounded by grandchildren and a wrinkled husband.

Perhaps every once in a while I'd dream of a handsome devil with alluring gold eyes, thinking he was just a character in a romance novel I'd once read. No matter how tempting it was to forget my heartache and the betrayal, losing Wrath again was a price I was unwilling to pay.

"How did you manage to bring us here? We didn't use the gates." I met Domenico's hard stare as I sorted it all out on my own. Then I understood. "The witches' magic only locked those from the outside, they didn't prevent you from bringing anyone out through other means."

And Envy couldn't *transvenio* us to this realm before we'd gone to House Pride because as far as I remembered, that could be done only during the days before and after a full moon.

"Shifters don't deal with witches," Domenico said. "They are one step up from demons. And we do not need to travel through the gates to access other realms like others do."

But a goddess, even one from Hell, was clearly immune from that hostility. I recalled the way wolves worshipped higher powers, perhaps it was the strength of magic they respected. Or maybe in his own way, the wolf cared for my twin, though the feelings didn't seem to be returned. My twin was rather indifferent to her latest lover, which made me wonder if she cared for someone else—if she was even capable of that sort of feeling—and was using the wolf in more ways than one.

"Do the portals work for the princes?" I asked.

"No. My—a wolf saw to it that no demon can use a portal for now."

I studied him. Domenico clearly was going to say something aside from "wolf." Which made me think of the mysterious Marcella Blade had mentioned.

"I heard a rumor from a vampire recently." A phrase my mortal self would never once imagine uttering. "He mentioned meeting a half-demon half-werewolf companion with Vittoria."

Domenico snorted. "Vampires are liars. You cannot trust a word that comes out of their fanged mouths. No werewolf would ever sink so low as to bed a demon. At least not if he wished to retain any sort of respectable standing in the pack."

"Pretend as if it were possible. Would a werewolf with demon blood be able to travel to the Shadow Realm?"

"I told you," Domenico gritted out between clenched teeth, "vampires lie."

Wrath hadn't mentioned anything about Blade lying. And he certainly would have since it would prove our theory about Vesta being alive correct. Domenico was hiding something, and no amount of badgering would get him to talk. It also didn't escape my notice that he'd been very quick to point out a "he" as the culprit who'd bedded a demon. I could use a truth spell, but I needed to stay in his good graces so that he would take me back home. "Where is Vittoria?"

Domenico headed for the door. "I'll escort you to her now."

We didn't speak as we moved through the quiet monastery. Mummies lined up on either side of us, their silent, lifeless eyes cast in our direction, watching but not truly seeing our passage.

Above us in the rafters a bird flapped its wings—everything was so similar to when I'd been here last it made me swallow my rising discomfort. I wondered where the holy brotherhood was, if they were lying in wait. And they weren't the only foes to be concerned about.

I still felt that same sense of an otherworldly presence, as if the Umbra demons were lurking in the shadows, watching my every move to report back to whichever prince of Hell had hired their services. Only this time, I wished they'd go fetch their master.

If the ghostlike demons were really there, then perhaps Envy would know where I was and would leave the fight at the Pit and show up as he often did. His meddling wouldn't be unwelcome this time, a sign things had well and truly changed in my world.

Though none of that mattered since the portals and gates were all locked and the princes couldn't leave if they tried.

"Do you—"

"Quiet. We don't need the brotherhood interfering." Domenico pushed the back door open, its hinges creaking loudly, as he stuck his head out and listened. It had been late afternoon when we'd left the Seven Circles, but it was fully evening here.

We stepped into the balmy night, and I inhaled the familiar air scented with orange blossoms and plumeria. Stars twinkled overhead like they knew a secret and were excited at the prospect of its discovery. Instead of feeling like I'd finally come home, the warmth almost felt unnatural now, stifling and oppressive. It made me crave the snow and ice and the demon who commanded it.

As we crossed the silent courtyard, I looked to the street that would take me to Sea & Vine. It was dark, but people were walking around. Our trattoria would still be open, serving the last of its guests for the evening. Nonna and my mother would be in the kitchen, humming as they prepared food. Uncle Nino and my father would be in the dining room, chatting with guests as they poured limoncello and laughed. I could go there now. Join them.

Despite its many terrible flaws that had been exposed, it had been a good life. Regardless of what Vittoria said, I knew she'd been happy, too. We'd been surrounded by love and light. We had a family who cared for us and a community. We'd had each other.

As far as curses went, ours wasn't hateful. Unlike Wrath, who'd had his heart proverbially torn from him and was then forced to feel hate in place of love, we'd forgotten everything of our past. All our schemes. Our thirst for vengeance. We had been given a new set of memories that might have been filled with fear of the devil and his wicked brothers, but it wasn't all bad.

Domenico cut a look my way. "You don't have to be quiet now. We're far enough away."

"It's a lot to sort through."

For the first time since we'd met in the Shadow Realm, the werewolf seemed to understand and sympathize. Which, I supposed he did. His world had altered as irrevocably not too long before. He'd adjusted, though he still seemed hostile about it. Perhaps that was the alpha magic still wreaking havoc on him until he matured. Or maybe he resented being a shifter.

"Eventually, you'll learn to focus on the present and let the past go." He guided us down a side street I knew well. "Reliving what could have been but never will be is pointless. It'll only hold you back from what you are. One of the hardest things anyone can do is live in the here and now. Not worry about the future, not rehash the past. Be present, that's the secret to changing your future. To finding true happiness."

I mulled that over. "Are you happy?"

"Sometimes." Domenico lifted a shoulder. "It's better than when I first found out...everything."

"How is your father? He seemed worried but proud last time I spoke to him."

The shifter stiffened for a beat, then kept walking, his long strides eating up the cobbled path. Almost as if he wished to run away from the question. "Dead."

My own steps faltered. I didn't want to press on a wound that was clearly fresh, but I needed to know. "Did my sister—"

"Of course not." Domenico spun on his heel, his eyes flashing pale purple. He immediately glanced around, making sure no humans had seen, then visibly strained to rein his emotions in. "Your sister had nothing to do with it."

"What about demons?"

"What about them?" Domenico asked.

"Did this have to do with Greed?"

At the mention of Greed's name, the wolf's claws shot out. "It was pack business. Leave it at that."

I held my hands up in a gesture of peace, and the werewolf resumed his forward trek through the neighborhood bordering ours. Unwittingly, Domenico had given me two answers I'd been looking for. If Vittoria was really hell-bent on creating a larger rift between wolves and demons, killing a pack member would have been a prime opportunity. And the alpha had a large emotional reaction to Greed's name.

My focus shifted from my twin and the wolf issues and latched onto the road we'd just turned down. I stopped walking, unable to pick one foot up and place it in front of the other again. Near the end of the street sat our family home.

Vines curled up and around the trellis, the pale stone gleaming in the moonlight. It was beautiful. Untouched. It had continued on as if nothing had changed at all. My mouth was suddenly parched. Of all the places Vittoria could go, this carved deep.

"My sister is in our house."

Domenico shook his head. "Look closer."

"I don't—" The corner of our house *shimmered,* lifting slightly at the edges. Like an invisible page had been placed over the whole structure and had come loose in a breeze. My pulse pounded, and I stepped back, shaking my head. "No. No, no. Not this, too. Please."

Vittoria was suddenly in front of me, her hair blowing from that same magical wind that was now tearing pieces of our house away. "Demand to see its truth, Emilia."

"I cannot—"

"Yes. You can and you will," Vittoria said. "Look at the truth."

My eyes burned as tears prickled behind my lids. This was the final blow, and I refused to allow one single tear to fall. *Enough.* Something inside me snapped. I was tired of sadness and devastation. I was over all the endless lies and manipulations and days and nights spent crying. My twin was right. I deserved to know the truth, to see it once and for all.

My spine straightened as I set my attention back on our unassuming home. I called forth my magic's source and aimed it straight at the shimmering part. "Show me the truth."

My voice echoed with power just like when I'd cast a truth spell. Magic whipped out and sank into the exterior walls like claws, shredding and ripping apart the illusion. I watched impassively as the facade was stripped away, revealing a stone temple.

Our home was glamoured. And I'd never known, never sensed the magic that had been used. Because Nonna kept us ignorant. The truth didn't break my heart this time; it made me furious. There was no coming back from this deception. A line of demarcation had been drawn—the Emilia before her entire world shattered, and the goddess of fury after all had been revealed.

"What else?" I demanded, gaze fixed on our so-called home. "What else has been an elaborate illusion? A fucking lie."

"I'll leave you two." Domenico quietly entered the temple, not sparing either me or Vittoria a second glance. I braced myself for the final betrayal I sensed was coming.

"This is not truly Sicily." Vittoria exhaled. My attention finally left the house that wasn't our home to settle on my twin. For once, she seemed pained. "Welcome to the Shifting Isles."

# EIGHTEEN

**I flinched as** if I'd received a physical blow.

I'd thought I'd felt the worst sting of betrayal when I'd learned my grandmother used dark magic to murder innocent witches to bind us. *This* was agony. Unrelenting, torturous, emotional agony. Vittoria said nothing as the initial shock slowly began to wear off.

"The Shifting Isles." *This* was why she told me to meet her here, that night in the spirit realm. I glanced down the street, stomach twisting. It was all a lie. Every last part of it. Down to the very world I thought I knew. No wonder Wrath hadn't wanted to say more when I'd asked about the isles. It was something I had to discover on my own. I was grateful no princes could travel here now. I needed time and space to reconcile just how much had been kept from me without the demons around.

I'd once asked Wrath where mortal souls were sent, and he'd vaguely spoken of an island off the western shore of the Seven Circles. Given the map lesson my sister had shown me the last time I saw her, this location definitely fit that description.

"This is where mortal souls are sent." I didn't ask, but Vittoria nodded. "The prison of damnation."

"Yes." My sister's voice was quiet, soft. As if she sensed my power was searching for anyone to latch onto. To punish. Or maybe there was some human part of her left after all. A part that understood how deeply this particular wound went. "Some would consider this to be the worst of the circles. The island shifts time and place. Becomes the reality you choose it to be. Or the reality someone else chooses. For a time."

"And do the mortals here know? That this is..."

"No," Vittoria said softly. "Most mortals are entirely unaware that this isn't truly the city or country they believe it to be. Only select supernaturals know the truth. And some souls that escaped to the demon realm and fight for a chance to return here."

"I see." Hell. That's what it felt like. Not the Seven Circles where the demons ruled. Not the devil's elegant castle. Or in any of the Houses of Sin where vice and debauchery reigned above all. Here. In the place I'd once called home. This isle was where hell truly existed. "We've never been part of the mortal world."

"No, we haven't." My twin's attention dropped to the ground as if she couldn't bear to look at me. "The Star Witches would never allow that risk. They sent us here, to this time and place, where witches had to remain in hiding. We could step through to another reality now if you'd like. It helps. To see the truth play out."

"*No.*" My tone was harsher than I'd intended. "I cannot... I just—I'm not ready."

Seeing another reality, another time or dimension, would snip the last thread of sanity I'd been clutching. Vittoria offered a small smile. "All right."

"Have the witches somehow been alerted to our presence here?" I asked. My sister shook her head. That was positive at least. "Are they able to summon us through a blood sacrifice?"

"We are not like demons or other supernaturals. No one can summon gods."

My mind spun onto the next question. "How often does the isle shift?"

"From what I know, it's multiple underworld dimensions folded on top of one another. It's hard to explain, but there are infinite realities happening at once. Though it's not always a perfect system. At times there will be slight inconsistencies only noticeable to those who are native to whichever time or place is the current reality. Many will simply overlook any oddities they might notice; the truth is much harder for them to digest, and therefore they avoid it. Magic and science are both hard at work, ensuring none of the timelines fully bleed together."

Which was why it had taken Wrath so long to find us. He'd had to search a place that could be anytime, anywhere. It was an incredible feat that he'd managed to locate us at all...

"You." My gaze snapped to my twin. "You summoned a demon, which alerted Wrath to where we were." I thought back to the note I'd found on Wrath's desk. "Greed. You'd summoned Greed under the guise of forming an alliance. Then you left those summoning spells for me to find, just in case." Hope blossomed in my chest. My sister couldn't be all bad. "Why?"

Vittoria grabbed my hand and squeezed it gently before letting go. "Because one of us deserves a storybook ending."

I wrapped my arms around my twin and hugged her tight. "That doesn't sound very House Vengeance of you."

Vittoria held me back, her sudden laughter tinged with

sadness. "If you tell anyone, I'll murder your firstborn. Plus, I would hardly say binding House Greed to my cause was altruistic."

My lips curved upward, knowing full well the goddess of death would never murder my firstborn. I wished to halt time and just stay in this moment with my twin. But wishes didn't exist in this place, only pain and heartbreak. I held Vittoria a little closer, then finally let go. For a brief moment, her eyes had returned to that warm brown.

"You didn't really kill Greed's commander, did you?"

She heaved a sigh. "No, but I would have loved to. Not because I dislike her, but just to twist the dagger for Greed a little more."

"Perhaps you ought to keep that opinion to yourself next time you see Greed or any of the other princes." I exhaled. Despite learning the very foundation of my world had been a lie, a heavy weight was lifted from my shoulders. I knew deep down my twin couldn't be the ice queen she'd been pretending to be. She'd been too warm, too full of life to lose it all when she'd become immortal again. "Vesta wasn't stabbed. She was . . . eaten."

Vittoria's brows raised, looking half-impressed, half-aghast. "Gruesome way to go."

"I have cause to believe *she's* not dead. And I think you are intimately aware of that. I also believe you know who did die in that chamber." I watched my twin, whose expression turned unreadable. "You need to tell me the whole story. Why Vesta wanted to leave. Who took her place. Where she is now. Greed called for a blood retribution. And Wrath granted it. If you don't confess your innocence in front of Wrath soon and bring him proof, the other princes will eventually hunt you down."

"Life would be rather dull if no one ever threatened to obliterate a rival House." My sister grinned, avoiding giving me any more answers about Vesta's disappearance and whose body was found. She did give me some information, which would need to be good enough for now. "I'm pleased to have caused such strong emotions in Greed. He must well and truly be put off that I'd do such a thing after forming an alliance." She playfully nudged my side. We both knew she hated that prince for reasons she still hadn't shared. "Perhaps it's true love."

"And what of Pride? Did it remain only a game to you or did you become attached?"

Vittoria's spine straightened, and darkness fell across her features. "That demon ought to count his curses that I haven't paid him a visit."

I studied my sister out of the corner of my eye. I'd once felt as strongly about my wish to stab Wrath, and now I couldn't stop myself from thinking of his troublesome mouth and all the wickedly delightful things he could do with it. Vittoria slanted a look in my direction.

"Don't. I see what you're thinking, and I swear I'll slow your heart until you lose consciousness."

"You know"—I looped my arm through Vittoria's and started walking down the cobbled road that was nothing more than an illusion—"someone once told me hate is rooted in passion. Perhaps you ought to visit Pride and work out your issues."

"I'd rather bathe in pig's shit."

"Mmh-hmm. Speaking of pigs, if you wish for me to find my storybook ending, why do you keep warning me away from Wrath?"

Vittoria stared off at a point in the distance, though I had the impression she was actually looking inward. "If you become part of his House, you cannot corule over ours. So many things have changed, and I don't want to lose one more familiar thing. Regardless, I wanted you to discover the whole truth before you bound yourself fully to him, so you could make a true choice, with all the facts, between love and your House."

There was the sister with a mortal soul. "Change is terrifying, but we *are* the Feared. Or so you keep insisting."

Vittoria snorted. "Are you telling me to have some dignity?"

"You said it, dear sister. Not me." I smiled as she rolled her eyes. "You know, Wrath said there would be no issue if I wished to reestablish our House."

Vittoria's head snapped in my direction. "Did he now?"

I nodded. "If you stop your campaign to stir up trouble and create inner conflict, it might be something I'm interested in. But I won't help you if you keep pitting everyone against one another. That's not the sort of life I want anymore."

We strolled to the end of what had been our street; the silence was comfortable, but my thoughts had shifted to more pressing matters again. Ones that needed to be addressed before we left this fantasy and returned to the Seven Circles. My sister was wanted in that realm, and we needed to ensure her safety.

We paused at the next street, and I lifted my face toward the heavens. The air was balmy, the salty sea breeze pleasant. Yet chills raked down my body.

I dropped Vittoria's arm and faced her. "If you are harboring Vesta, or Marcella, or whoever she's calling herself, you need to tell Wrath. He will sense the truth of it, and you'll be cleared of any wrongdoing. Please. I cannot lose you, too. Not after all of this." I motioned to the world around us. "Please, Vittoria. Just tell me she's alive and well and you have a damn good reason for making a powerful enemy."

Vittoria pressed her lips together and glanced away. If I was correct and Vesta was alive—which I fully believed to be the truth—my sister was not going to confess anything to me. I had to trust she had a reason, something more powerful than vengeance that drove her.

"Who is the actual villain in this sordid tale?" I asked instead. "Us? The demons? Witches?"

Vittoria thought carefully. "Depending on whose side you're on, I suppose it could be all of us. Though I find the most fault with witches and demons. Their dislike of each other has gone on forever, and they never should have dragged us into their issues."

I blew out a long breath.

"No wonder it hasn't been a simple path to unraveling the mystery. You and I schemed against Pride and Wrath. Pride was careless with his consort's heart. Which enraged the First Witch. Sursea cursed Wrath when he wouldn't whisk away her daughter from Pride, Wrath responded in kind, and the Star Witches upheld their duty to keep the Feared and the Wicked locked away, even if it meant sacrificing their own."

"And on and on the blame goes," Vittoria finished. "I don't think it matters who the first villain is or was—we've all done terrible things."

"But someone did help Vesta escape Greed's court. And someone is truly dead."

Vittoria stared off into the distance for another moment. "I was told the vampires came to steal you away. Perhaps there is a new threat emerging, one that's slipping in while chaos breaks loose."

"You were the one who sparked that particular fire."

"I didn't think they'd come for you. I thought they'd set their sights on House Greed."

"Why? What is it about Greed that's making you do such horrid things?"

"I haven't done *horrid* things," she countered. "I've only done to him what he's done to others. Maybe the vampires have their own war goals, and I accidentally gave them hope of winning."

Frustration built in my chest. If my sister would just trust me with the truth, this could all be remedied. "While I don't doubt the vampires would love to start an internal war to distract from their own schemes, I don't think they're responsible."

"Mmh." Vittoria's gaze took on that faraway look again. "Perhaps it's the witches then. They probably heard of my alliance with Greed and targeted his House to start strife. I'm sure they're hoping the demons will remove us from the playing board once and for all."

"Vittoria," I warned. "Stop. I know it's not the witches or demons or wolves. Just tell me the truth. Why keep so many secrets?"

"Perhaps you'll just have to trust me."

"After all you've done? All the lies and half-truths and games?"

Anger crossed my twin's face.

"I have been trying to work around the curse, break your magic free, reestablish connections to this world, and have done the best I can. If it's coming across as lies and manipulation, I am truly sorry, Emilia. But I have my reasons. And you'll simply need to honor that or continue battling me. If the witches didn't do what they did to us, then none of this would have happened. And if you believe they'll sit back and allow us to regain our full power without attempting to bind it again, you're mad." Vittoria turned to me, her expression calculating. "There is one way for us to ensure they don't succeed."

I held a hand to my chest, my heart pounding faster the longer my sister held my gaze. "Is there no other way to break the spell-lock?"

"Not that I've discovered. Believe me, I looked before I had mine torn out."

"Who did tear your heart out?" I asked. "Domenico?"

"Many creatures in the underworld were only too happy to be considered for the task. Leave it at that for now." Vittoria's gaze iced over before it softened again. "You won't have to worry about that, though. I'll be with you."

I paced away, and my sister just watched without comment as I walked back and forth, my mind and heart racing. The witches bound us. And yet I couldn't stop thinking about Envy's reaction to when Vittoria first wished to remove my spell-lock. He'd been so opposed.

And Wrath didn't really speak about it much at all. I knew he was uncertain, yet my sister had survived. She'd returned to her full goddess self. Which made me wonder once again if there was another reason Wrath didn't say more. I thought of the Viperidae attack—how after the snakelike demon had bitten me, Wrath used magic that took the venom into his own body.

I also recalled something saccharine sweet he'd made me drink...

"Goddess above. He gave me nectar."

Ambrosia. The food of the gods.

I stopped pacing and stared at nothing. He'd also given me something sweet to drink when I'd had the mild case of hypothermia. More nectar. More goddess-healing fuel. Wrath couldn't be worried about my dying. So what else would motivate him to use such caution? I resumed my pacing, letting my mind run over different theories and scenarios until one separated itself from the rest.

Envy was fearful that day in our cell. So were Lust and Sloth and even Greed when I'd lost my temper and set that painting ablaze. And Wrath...he might not be afraid of me, but all the princes of Hell had called us the Feared. My husband didn't fear for *my* life, he feared for his realm. He feared setting me free, fully. Wrath didn't actively stop me, but he certainly wasn't helping, either. This choice was mine and mine alone.

I spun around and met my sister's patient gaze.

"I'm ready," I said, meaning it.

Over these last few weeks, Wrath had been showing me how to control my emotions. To see past my fury. *That* was the lesson he'd taught me the night he'd forced me to stab him, the night he'd said was about sensing other sins and combating them. Yes, learning to steel myself against pride, greed, and lust had been important. But all along, Wrath knew what House of Sin I ruled over, knew how potently my desire for vengeance could grow.

Until I'd stabbed him that night, I would have continued down a path in which I craved blood. And he'd been right—I didn't wish to admit it then, but I *hated* hurting him in that moment. Hated that loss of control, that overwhelming feeling of only being driven by my rage. I ruled over that emotion, and I would not allow it to rule over me.

In the throne room with the vampire emissary and Sursea, my rage had nearly taken over then, too. But it didn't. I could not rely on Wrath or anyone else to pull me from that dark place again. It *had* to come from me. Stalling myself from unleashing my full power any longer would only ensure one thing: I'd fail by not trying.

Fear would hold me back. But faith in myself would set me free.

"Would you be able to...if I—" I drew in a deep breath. "I don't wish to lose control."

"Understandable." Vittoria nodded. "I'll be here. You have nothing to fear about the change. It's disorienting at first, but it feels like taking a large breath of fresh air after being submerged in the sea."

I exhaled and nodded. "All right. I'm ready to break the spell-lock now."

Vittoria led us back toward our childhood home. The flap of illusion that had peeled back was securely in place again, making the building look as it had my whole life. We walked up the stairs and entered through the front door, and what had once been a small living space now had cathedral ceilings and decadent furnishings. It smelled of honey and wildflowers.

On the far wall in the first chamber were shelves of books; another nook had a wall of jars with hearts. I averted my gaze and walked toward an altar set off to one side. Giant bowls of fire crackled to either side of it, the flames a beautiful, glittering black.

Vittoria snapped her fingers, and suddenly a werewolf appeared holding a lavender garment. The young woman looked to be in her midtwenties, and there was something familiar about the shade of her eyes and the shape of her face. She quickly averted her gaze and moved back. My twin motioned for me to step up onto the dais. "Put this on. Then lie on the altar with your arms relaxed at your sides and your legs straight out."

Relaxing wasn't something I thought I could achieve, but I gingerly took the item, which turned out to be a billowing gown, and quickly undressed and slipped it on.

It had two large swaths that tied over each shoulder and continued down the front. A silver rope tied it together at the waist, and two slits ran up to midthigh. The deep V of the front granted access to my spell-locked heart and had my mortal one beating furiously. I refused to think about how it would soon cease beating at all. A flash of calmness blew over me, almost as if propelled on a magical wind. All would be well. I glanced to the werewolf who'd brought the clothing and wondered if she'd somehow altered my mood. It was rare and covetable magic. The princes of Hell could influence sins, but to influence joy was something else entirely.

Letting that oddity go, I squared my shoulders and climbed onto the altar, lying as my twin had instructed. Vittoria stood over me, then surveyed the chamber where the lone shifter waited, standing guard, I realized.

"We're not to be disturbed." My sister glanced at me, her lavender eyes glowing as she called upon her power. "It will be over quickly."

Before I had time to give in to my rising panic, Vittoria's fingers lengthened and her claws punched through my chest. For a moment, I could hardly believe she'd done it.

Then I opened my mouth to scream, but nothing came out. My chest *burned*. Violently. It felt as if half a dozen knives had been set in a fire and then shoved into my body. That pain was so acute, so overwhelming, that I didn't feel anything else. The hold on my mind, my memories, the whole spell-lock cracked like an egg, and everything came flooding back.

My life.

My House.

My power. In my mind's eye I saw me and Wrath, making love and training and battling wits and wills. Another memory: my twin scheming with me in our throne room. I saw Sursea coming to us with her plan, her need for vengeance fueling my sin. Then I was in the garden and I saw the look on Wrath's face right before everything was torn away.

The scream I couldn't get out before ripped through me now, echoing in the temple. It was rage and torment given form. I heard shifters scatter from wherever they'd been hiding. And I screamed until the memories slowed.

Darkness swept in as quickly as the pain had, then I didn't feel or think of anything at all.

Once the pain receded and the darkness faded, I lay as still as a statue, listening. Several rooms away I heard the swish of a skirt, the soft tread of slippers. Hushed voices. Closer there was a sharp intake of breath as if someone had awoken suddenly.

I kept my eyes closed as I adjusted to my new range of hearing. My sharper senses. One thing stood out immediately. My pulse did not pound. I inhaled deeply and slowly exhaled.

The lack of a heartbeat wasn't as disorienting as I'd thought it would be. Though perhaps that was because I no longer felt fear the same way. I cracked an eye, surprised to see streaks of red and gold creeping in through the windows and under the door. Dawn had arrived. I must have been out longer than I'd thought.

I sat up and nearly launched myself across the room, my fully immortal body filled with incredible strength. I already knew no one was in the chamber with me, but I glanced around with new eyes. Vittoria had been right; it felt as if I'd been submerged below water and my head finally broke the surface. Colors were brighter, more intense. I could see individual threads on my gown. Dust motes glittered in a sliver of sunlight on the opposite end of the temple.

I felt full of energy, revitalized. I leapt onto the altar in one jump, then hurtled into the air, landing gracefully on the other side of the chamber. A strange, familiar feeling started in my center. In place of my heart, there was the steady thrumming of my power. It felt like coming home after being away for far too long.

*"Fiat lux."*

Roses and wildflowers burst into flame around the entire chamber. The fire roared with fury, sparking my own rage and igniting it. This power, this was what made me one of the Feared. There was no ending to it, only my desire to keep it locked away that kept it caged. I thought of Nonna Maria. I recalled her lies. The hurt. And the flowers burned impossibly brighter. My head cocked to the side as a familiar sound caught my attention.

I recognized my sister's footsteps before I turned to her. "Would you like to exact a little vengeance before I leave?"

Her lips slowly tugged upward. "It's good to have you back, Fury."

# NINETEEN

**Back in House** Wrath, I sensed a myriad of things at once. Servants bustling through the lower levels, demon soldiers running drills on some compound I'd yet to visit. A few angry members of the nobility arguing—their wrath sparking like little embers in my periphery.

What captured almost all my attention was my husband. His energy was like a raging inferno flanked by towers of ice. It was incredible. Like his *luccicare* I'd seen, his magic was a multitoned black with specks of gold. Glittering and dangerous. Like him.

Wrath was still at the Pit—I felt the pulse of his ferocious power from a distance away and would recognize it anywhere. There was a slight pull to him, but our reunion had to wait. Though, if I could sense his magic, I had little doubt he could also sense mine. I wouldn't have long before he came looking for his newly restored queen.

My focus was drawn to the Crone's tower next, where I knew Fauna was still working and I headed there at once. Time moved differently in hell dimensions, so I wasn't sure how long I'd been gone, but it couldn't have been that long or Wrath would have started searching for me. Doing my best not to startle my friend, I knocked gently—or so I'd thought—and the door crashed open. "Fauna?"

My friend jolted at the noise and twisted to face the door.

"Emilia! Thank the devil you're here, I found—" Fauna stood so abruptly her stool toppled over. She scanned my face—for presumably whatever familiar comfort she could find—and swallowed whatever she'd been about to say. "Your eyes..."

"I know." They were no longer warm brown. They were the rose-gold of my magic.

Her attention dropped to my chest. It didn't look any different. There was no scar, no trace of what my sister had removed. No evidence at all that I'd had a spell-lock. Though, given Fauna's demon senses, she probably didn't hear my mortal heart beating anymore.

Something like sadness crept into her features, though I swore I sensed horror. It had a prickly feeling attached to it, distracting me. If this was how Wrath sensed emotions, it was uncomfortable and would take some getting used to. I had forgotten what this was like. I'd need to retrain myself to focus on sensing feelings only when it suited me, or I'd go mad.

"Did they force this upon you?" she asked quietly.

My brow arched. Having my true form back was hardly a curse. Yet my friend sounded as if she were speaking with the dead. I attempted a smile that had her swallowing harder. I sighed.

"No. No one forced me to do anything. Except maybe the witches when they forced me to be a player in their games."

I moved into the room on silent feet, and the sensation I'd felt radiating from Fauna escalated. Fear. That's what my friend felt in my presence now.

My fingers trailed over the open grimoires. The paper felt rougher, the scent of ink stronger. "Did you know they locked me in true hell? The Shifting Isles. Clever name for a magical island that can shift time and place. Seemed only right for that to be the place I returned to my true self."

A beat of silence passed. Followed by another. Fauna took me in again, scrutinizing. I picked up notes of smoke on my clothing, in my hair. She did, too. Suspicion laced her voice. "Did you attack them?"

My lips curved. "I might have paid them a visit."

"His majesty will—"

"The move against my betrayers was justified. What did you find?"

"I..." Fauna followed my gaze to where it landed on the grimoire she'd been reading. Some of her earlier excitement slowly returned as she pointed to the page. "I think I found a way to break the curse."

"The one on Wrath?"

"Yes, but that's not all." Her smile didn't quite reach her eyes, but it was better than before. The fear was also abating a little, though it still lingered uncomfortably. "The Blade of Ruination is more than a hexed object itself—it can somehow *destroy* curses and hexes. I'm not exactly sure how it works, but I found something else that might explain more."

She grabbed another text and shoved it toward me. An intricate map of House Wrath that featured tunnels and temples and caverns hidden below like underground cities and towns.

"There is a place on these grounds called the Well of Memory," Fauna continued. "And I believe it is the key to finding out more about the Blade of Ruination." She pointed to a section of the map labeled GARDENS. "You must pay the goddess a tithe to enter the Well of Memory's chamber. It's unpleasant—the well must deem you worthy, and the memories it shows you are often nightmares others have purged. Or other things they wished to forget."

"Is that all?"

"It's not as easy as it sounds." Fauna bit her lip. "The well can trick you into thinking you are really *in* the memory it's showing you. Some are said to get stuck there for eternity, reliving the worst moments of memories that do not even belong to them."

It was not something I felt concerned over, but I knew spell-locked Emilia would. Fauna was doing remarkably well hiding her fear outwardly now, but I still sensed it simmering below the surface. My lack of fear didn't exactly frighten her, but it did make her uncomfortable. We couldn't afford to have any distractions with so much at stake—I needed to soothe over her worry so she could focus.

"How do you avoid that?" I asked.

Fauna's eyes narrowed, but she must have decided against inquiring if I was truly worried or appeasing her. She glanced down at the book in front of her.

"According to this text, if you focus on your question and don't lose sight of it, you'll be able to sift through memories until you find your answer. The memories are mostly imbued in clear quartz, hematite, amethyst, or lapis lazuli. You hold one crystal at a time while thinking of your question; supposedly it will attract the correct memory to you or vice versa."

I nodded, thinking of the question I needed the answer to the most. "You're certain this well will know the location of the Blade of Ruination if I ask it to show me where it is?"

"Theoretically, it should. Someone must know where it is, or at least know of someone who'd come into contact with it. Even if it's not directly spoken about, it might appear in a purged memory. It might not lead you to it directly, but it could give us a starting point." Fauna exhaled. "But I personally don't know anyone who's ever used the well successfully."

That caught my attention. "Not even the princes of Hell?"

"They cannot. No one knows why. His majesty certainly tried when the curse went into effect. He even allowed Envy to try to use it. Both attempts failed. They couldn't access any memories. Not from mortals, or demons, or any supernaturals."

How curious. "The well was here before the demon princes started their rule, correct?"

"Yes." Fauna nodded. "The goddess statue is new, but records indicate the well itself predates the formation of the Houses of Sin by quite some time. But..."

"It doesn't predate me."

"No, Lady Emilia. Aside from the Crone and the Sisters Seven, there aren't many beings that were here before you and your twin."

If my spell-lock were still in place, I'd be disturbed by the idea of my lengthy existence. Instead, I cast my newly freed memory back, tunneling into a vast cavern that spanned what seemed like eons. Recalling a time before the princes of Hell left me with an impression of boredom. Debauchery. Back before the devil took his throne, Vittoria and I had greeted souls.

And they did not enjoy our welcome party.

We were ruthless, wicked creatures. And we reveled in it.

I had a clear impression that was why our mother had tampered with memories to begin with, why she'd also created the veil between the mountains separating House Vengeance from the rest of the Seven Circles. Celestia didn't want anyone to recall the time before the demons ruled. When worse creatures reigned.

Wrath's power shifted suddenly, drawing me into the present; it blinked out from where he'd been and reappeared closer. More powerful. It burned like the heat of the sun. He was angry. Savagely so.

Great Divine above, his wrath made my fury sing like a battle hymn. His attention reached out, and I knew he was sensing my power and following it to its source. Outside the tower, footsteps thundered down the corridor. Fauna quickly offered her good-byes and dashed out the door. Her emotions spiking wildly. Our king was in a wretchedly foul mood.

And I had a good indication why.

I perched against the table, waiting for what promised to be quite a display of emotion. His arrival did not disappoint. Wrath wrenched the door off its hinges and tossed it away as if it weighed nothing. Golden eyes blazed with his sin as they settled on mine. If there was a quick flash of relief, it was immediately replaced by the hardness of anger.

"The door did nothing to deserve that," I said.

"You could have died."

I made a show of carefully looking myself over. "Envy was correct. Immortality won out."

"It was a risk."

"A calculated one." I smiled. This time it didn't provoke fear. Wrath's steady gaze never wavered from my face, his anger still burning brightly between us. "I know why you didn't wish for the spell-lock to be broken." He crossed his arms over his chest and cocked a brow. Alluring, arrogant demon. "I am able to control my fury. Your subjects have nothing to fear."

"Is that so?" Wrath shook his head. "The smell of smoke lingering on your clothes has nothing to do with vengeance? Somehow, I cannot picture you and your sister sitting around a fire, discussing times past like two civilized goddesses."

"A little act of vengeance was well deserved, and you know it." I gave him a hard stare, my power surging up to confront his before I gripped it tightly. "The witches ought to count their blessings I took only their restaurant and not their lives. They can rebuild. And they will think twice before crossing me again."

"You're right." Wrath sighed. "They'll think before directly attacking you. But that will not stop them from responding with fire of their own." He held my gaze, his own turning as icy as his tone. "Greed was called away from the Pit to his House. His spies spotted witches gathering in the mountains behind his circle. They're going to attack. Then they're going to blame you."

And that was the root of my husband's anger.

Greed would demand retribution from me as well as Vittoria and my prince would be forced to make a choice that would end in bloodshed. There would be no game Wrath and I could play to avoid that; more and more, Greed was becoming a problem. There was little doubt in my mind that he was responsible for the enchanted skull to cast suspicion on my twin. Whether he knew or suspected Vesta was alive didn't seem to matter. He wanted vengeance. And he'd use this as the perfect excuse to exact some.

My hands curled into fists at my sides. "Send a missive to House Greed requesting a visit immediately. We'll attack the witches before they strike. And this time, I will not be merciful. Let the witches and your brother see what I am capable of."

I spun on my heels and headed to my suite, my lavender gown billowing around me like a storm cloud. It was time to dress for war.

# TWENTY

**Sleet drummed icy** claws along the stone parapet of House Greed. We stood silently on the narrow pathway, gazes locked onto the tree line in the distance, ignoring the frigid water pelting our battle leathers. A guard spotted a flicker of light toward the northwest. It was impossible to know if it was meant to distract or if it had been an accident. I doubted the witches would be so careless, given how calculated they were, but stranger things had happened when emotions ran high. Which made me wonder...

I surveyed the quiet grounds, magic primed and ready. Even with the sleet coming down hard, no birds or animals stirred in the woods. It seemed as if the whole circle was holding its breath, waiting. I hadn't yet sensed any fear. Greed's lawn extended hundreds of meters in all directions, a clever way to remove any cover for unfriendly or unwelcome visitors. Like witches.

My hand flexed at my side. When thinking of witches, it was impossible to not wonder about Nonna. If she was with the witches here now, I would not hesitate to defend the demons. Even if that meant I had to battle her. I prayed it wouldn't come to that, but there was no longer any telling what my "grandmother" was capable of.

Wrath's arm brushed against mine, his warmth a contrast to the winter storm. Wind gusted along the castle wall, growling low. Dark clouds had gathered above House Wrath shortly after our plan had been made. The current weather was no doubt a result of my husband's tense mood. His first request for us to be admitted into this circle hadn't been met well. After the incident with the gaming hall, the Prince of Greed wasn't eager to have me in his residence again. The Duke of Devon had also campaigned against me, advising his prince to not allow a vengeful witch into their House of Sin again. He hadn't been informed that that vengeful witch was actually a goddess of the underworld and he ought to mind what he said.

A second, stern message had Greed grudgingly allowing me into his royal House, especially with the promise of aid. And a threat from Wrath's newly restored wife.

Fine hairs suddenly stood at attention along the back of my neck that had nothing to do with the icy wind. Demons wielding bows nocked their arrows, the sensation of their fear prickling over my skin like needles. Wrath didn't move, but I sensed his attention shift to the lawn beneath us. He felt what I did.

Greed signaled to a guard who peered over the edge. I stepped forward, that prickling feeling growing in intensity. And I realized it wasn't the guards' fear I was sensing. It was our enemies'. The witches were already here. My eyes narrowed at the seemingly empty lawn, then I noticed the tracks in the ice-coated grass. The broken blades had been trampled.

"Wait!" I cried out.

The guard didn't heed my warning. He leaned over the ledge, noticing what I had a second too late. Before anyone could act, blood burst from his eyes and he toppled over, crashing into the snow. Shouts rang out down the line, guards firing arrows into an enemy they couldn't see and, therefore, couldn't hit. If they continued like this, the witches would succeed.

And that was not something I'd allow to happen.

"Have them stand back," I yelled to Greed. "The witches are using magic."

"They are nothing but pathetic mortals. And we are using weapons." Greed signaled to the next line of guards.

Ignorant fool. He'd lead them into death.

Despite the miserable winter storm, my magic lit up the sky, plummeting like raging, vengeful stars shooting to earth. The rose-gold balls of fire hit with such speed they left craters in the ground. Screams rent the silence, the sound like animals being taken to slaughter.

I summoned more magic, more fire, watching emotionlessly as I rained fury down.

Whatever spell the witches had been using to render themselves invisible broke. Just as I imagined it would. Magic could only be battled with magic, and theirs was nothing but a mere dilution of what mine was. It was time to remind them of that.

*"Fiat lux."*

Hooded witches caught fire, their flesh burning and melting from their bones—the sickeningly sweet scent rising high. They fought back with impressive power of their own. They sent magic arrows careening through the air, striking demons with enough force to fell them. I could end this now, end *them* now, but forced myself to fight fairly. I wanted Wrath to know for certain that I could be trusted, even when emotions were running high.

A magic arrow sliced through my arm, drawing my attention to the witch who'd fired it. Nonna wrenched her hood back, her expression hard. Her look indicated that I had chosen to become her enemy the moment I removed my spell-lock.

I stared at her for a moment, allowing myself to fully digest that she had fired the shot. I could kill her right now. Mete out justice and vengeance for what she'd done to me and my sister. And yet…

"Run," I mouthed to her.

It was the one and only warning I'd give. And it was more than she deserved.

I didn't look in her direction again, was unsure if she listened. In the end, she had made her choice just as I had made mine.

Demons to the left and right dropped, and I didn't know if they were dead or badly injured. I kept firing my magic at the front line, doing my best to push the witches back to the woods, to frighten them away from House Greed. Soon they'd give up; their magic wasn't unlimited. We only had to keep them from doing any serious damage while they depleted their sources. A task that shouldn't be too hard to achieve.

I sensed Wrath's ice magic, and then I heard a hiss of pain. I jerked my attention to him, seeing a magical arrow that had cleanly pierced his shoulder.

"Are you all right?" I shouted over the sudden roar of sleet and wind.

He gritted his teeth and yanked the arrow out. "They coated them with dragon's bane."

Another flew through the air, aimed straight for his throat, and I plucked it from the sky, snapping it in my fist. Two more arrows with the burning agent soared toward Wrath.

Nonna must have told the witches to aim for him to either distract or punish me for choosing him. Rage, white-hot and all-consuming, ricocheted through me. My husband was being targeted and that was where all pretense of civility ended for me. To hell with our plan.

*"Enough."* My voice was barely more than a whisper, but it carried over the guards and witches. It was like the gusting wind of a hurricane, and the witches must have sensed the danger sweeping in. They stopped firing their magical arrows, grabbed one another's hands and began chanting. As if their magic could ever hope to outdo mine, especially now that I was truly mad.

I inhaled and drew in the power pulsing in my center, tapping into Source fully.

That well was never-ending. Infinite. With my spell-lock in place, my power had been skimming only the surface of what I was capable of. And the witches' anger, their fury over the reemergence of House Vengeance, the attack on Sea & Vine, and the fear I now felt coming from them in waves fueled me. I became every twisted tale they'd told. I embraced my true self.

I was now Fury in the flesh, and they would not forget what it meant to strike out at a goddess.

Stories would be told in their coven of this battle. Warnings whispered in hushed tones as they kept one eye on the sky, searching for an omen that they'd stoked my sin by even daring to speak of this day at all. Wrath would live, but none of them would.

I commanded more power, more fire, more fury as I turned my magic on the witches. There were two dozen. Other than Nonna,

I immediately recognized none, though I wasn't truly looking. It wouldn't matter if I knew them personally or not. They'd come to fight, to kill, and I'd reply in kind. This time I would not allow anyone to get in between me and Wrath.

They'd hurt him, and even though he'd heal, I'd had enough.

I summoned every ounce of the fury I commanded, every bit of rage at the lies and the manipulation and the betrayal. Years of being kept from my magic unleashed in an inferno wholly controlled by me. One by one, the bodies collapsed, the charred ashes blowing away on the gusting winds. I rained fire down like a vengeful god, long after the last witch fell, content with watching the whole circle burn.

Warm fingers curled around mine, dragging me into the here and now.

The first thing I noticed was the eerie silence. Fire no longer crackled. The winter storm had also quieted. I barely even heard the demons beside me breathing.

I looked at Wrath, his expression tight but proud. "They're dead, my lady. All of them."

Prickles erupted along my body again. I tore my gaze from my husband's and glanced around. All the guards were looking at me with fear openly etched onto their faces.

Well, not *all* the guards. Plenty of demons dropped their gazes entirely, refusing to look me in the eye at all. I looked down the row of guards and soldiers until my attention rested on their prince. Greed wasn't afraid, but I sensed a bit of trepidation as he inclined his head. His hand still rested on the pummel of his sword.

"House Greed thanks House Wrath for its assistance."

*Assistance.* I'd ended a battle before any true war could begin.

I looked at the uninjured guards—aside from the first guard who'd looked over the ledge, none had lost their lives. My fury hadn't receded enough, and between the needles of fear stabbing me and the annoyance of male arrogance, I unleashed a bit more hell.

"Why is House Greed continually being targeted? I find it odd that both the witches and werewolves decided to attack your circle. No matter what match my sister keeps striking, they come to you. Not House Wrath or Envy or Pride. You. What have you done to make so many enemies?"

Greed lifted a shoulder. "Perhaps they're after my wealth. Coins from one gaming hall alone could help fund a war." He offered a bland smile. "Please see yourselves to your guest suite. I'd be remiss if I didn't throw a celebratory ball to honor you both."

With that, Greed and his guards marched back into the castle. I thought about tossing a few fire buds at their heels, the idea of watching them hop into the castle slightly amusing, but refrained. Wrath was still watching me as if I might lose control and burn the realm to the ground.

"I told you," I said quietly, "you have nothing to fear from me."

"I know that." Wrath's gaze shifted to the grounds. "But do you?"

I glanced over the parapet, staring down at the smoldering lawn, the bodies of our enemies were nothing more than a smudge of ash now.

It should disturb me, holding enough power to obliterate two dozen witches without breaking a sweat. Nonna might be down there among the dead. And yet I felt nothing. Except perhaps satisfaction that I'd protected the one I love. Which made me understand why my husband had been cautious with setting the vengeance goddess in me free.

I turned my attention back to Wrath. "I'd like to bathe off the scent of smoke before we dress for tonight."

Unsurprisingly, Greed's ballroom was bronzed decadence. As was true in his gaming halls, everything felt rich, luxurious, the best his coin could buy. Rich colors, an abundance of fine metals, silks and velvets, and an overwhelming amount of art showcased in gorgeous frames. It was a room meant to show the prince's greed for material riches.

Wrath and I casually strolled around the expansive dance floor. He hadn't said much when we'd bathed then changed into our formal attire, his mood nearly impossible to read.

But I wasn't a fool. I understood seeing me in all my glory, allowing my fury to run rampant, was troubling. But he knew what our strategy was; he'd helped to come up with it before we left House Wrath. Unlike his brother and Greed's army, Wrath hadn't been taken by surprise this evening. He knew if I felt like either one of us were threatened, I would unleash my power without mercy. I vowed that no one would ever take us from each other again.

And I meant it.

Still, I couldn't help but wonder whether he'd regretted any part of our approach. If the general of war preferred to do battle in a more literal, hand-to-hand manner; my willingness to toss that civility aside and annihilate might have disturbed him.

Wrath had used his magic as an added weapon when we'd fought the wolves, but he'd used his dagger equally. A prickle of unease ran over me. It was impossible to tell if it was my mortal conscience resurfacing or if it was spikes of fear from nearby lords and ladies.

"Lady Emilia." A footman approached with glasses of sparkling wines in pale golds and pinks and plums to choose from. Gold flakes swirled within each glass, another form of greed. I chose a pale pink wine and sipped from it carefully. Wrath chose a plum-colored wine, and we continued our slow stroll around the ballroom.

Harder prickles ran along my arms with each group of lords and ladies we walked past. The bolder demons inclined their heads, muttering a polite, "Prince Wrath. Lady Emilia," before quickly finding somewhere else to be. Something unpleasant wedged itself under my ribs.

I didn't expect their thanks, but averted gazes and spikes of fear were a surprise. An unwelcome one. It was difficult to discern if their fear was directed entirely at me or if they were also wary of Wrath. The last time he was here, he did destroy a gaming hall with his legendary anger. Perhaps we were both targets of fear.

Though my husband had no difficulty drawing other males to his side. A few lords chatted politely about the battle that wasn't and took sips of their drinks, giving themselves a reason to rush off once Wrath reminded them how my fire magic saved them.

Wrath squeezed my hand gently. "Would you care to dance, my lady?"

"Yes."

My husband led us onto the dance floor; it was a lustrous bronze that reflected our images in a fuzzy, distorted manner. It matched how I felt internally: distorted and fuzzy. I was unused to trying to incorporate mortal emotions into my immortal sensibilities. It felt like two halves of me were trying to come together, but one half was oil and the other was water. No matter how hard I tried to blend them together, they remained separate, almost warring with each other.

Wrath held me indecently close as the musicians struck up a waltz, his hand sliding low enough on my back to cause a honeyed warmth to ignite in my veins. If he was attempting to distract me from the needles of unease crossing the room, it was almost working.

Until I set my attention on the Duke of Devon and felt the heat of his anger. He promptly turned to the male he'd been dancing with and said something that made the demon chuckle. At my expense, most likely. Though I refused to allow that to sting. I, too, would have been upset if I'd been caught in Wrath's sinful storm with my cock out and ended up pissing myself.

Couples that had been seemingly unaware of anyone aside from each other stiffened as we passed. This time, I heard the whispers. They spoke of the rise of the Feared. How the goddess of death was wanted for murder and how Fury had come to settle my sister's debts. It wasn't my wrathful husband they were scared of—it was me.

I rested my head against Wrath's shoulder and ignored the murmurs. They could talk and gossip all they liked; none of them knew me or what I felt. How I wanted to help them all by finding the Blade of Ruination and breaking the curse. Even then, I imagined nothing I did would ever be good enough for some. They'd always find cause to hate or fear me if that was the path they chose to wander. The murmurs turned more pointed, crueler.

I held my head high as we continued to dance around the room. Soon the crowded dance floor was almost empty, and the prickles that indicated fear had turned to stabbing. I clamped my jaw together and kept my expression neutral. Perhaps it was the nearly twenty years of being mortal and living as a human, but I no longer wished to inspire such fear.

Power was one thing—I would not apologize for the ability to defend myself and those I loved, but this? This was not at all what I wanted. A memory of my old life came floating back. Despite the fiery magic I summoned, I'd been cold on the inside, alone except for my twin.

I'd forgotten how isolating it had been, being feared. I hadn't known anything else, had nothing to compare it with. Now I knew the warmth of friendship. The joy of laughter and the comfort in... acceptance.

Wrath was respected for his power, not punished for it. Demons and even his brothers thought twice before crossing him, yet they looked at me like I was an executioner ready to incinerate them for any perceived slight.

It wasn't fair to be punished for the very same thing my husband was revered for. Though maybe from their perspective I was something that did inspire true fear. House Vengeance was not simply ruled by one sin like the other Houses. It could come for all, and that was something the demons feared.

"... she tricked him into marriage."

A couple shot me a nasty look, and I stiffened. That wasn't at all what had happened.

"Ignore them." Wrath's voice was as smooth as silk in my ear. "You didn't trick me into anything. And you were magnificent today. You stopped a battle before it could start a war. Your magic brought peace. It was a necessary and strategic move. Never doubt that."

"That doesn't seem to be the consensus shared by this court,"

I said quietly. "I thought you might be questioning our tactics, too."

"I trust you, my lady. And I trusted your judgment out there today." He swept us across the dance floor, his touch grounding me. "The witches would not have fought a fair battle. They would have used more magic and trickery. In this instance, I stand behind our choice to fight as we did. You used your magic as a weapon today. It did not use you, Emilia. It was a true victory, and I'm proud of what you accomplished. None of these courtiers would stand up and fight for their own court."

"I acted mostly for my own benefit," I confessed. "I didn't want Greed to demand another blood retribution. And when they targeted you, I *wanted* to kill them all."

Wrath brought his lips to my ear, and I felt him smile. "Even more appealing, my lady."

"Liar." I gripped his hand in mine as we moved across the dance floor, thankful. I knew what he said was right, and yet with the ballroom full of fearful demons, it made me feel otherwise.

Obliterating an enemy by setting them ablaze didn't feel heroic. It felt callous. Or that's what I *would* have felt before the spell-lock was removed. Everything was confusing now, wrong. I was a goddess who shouldn't feel so deeply, who should act without judgment, but I knew one fact to be true: just because I had the power to do so didn't mean I should.

What sort of precedence would that set for the subjects of the realm? We were all trapped in an endless cycle of wrong acts. Sursea using us. Vittoria and I tricking Wrath and Pride. The witches binding us. Me and Vittoria striking back at them. Their attacking House Greed. This unrest between all of us could go on for eternity if we didn't put an end to it. Someone needed to stand up and say enough. That might wasn't always right. Otherwise, the next powerful creature could emerge and do whatever they saw fit to anyone less powerful.

"A kiss for your thoughts?" Wrath asked. Smiling at the unexpected request, I lifted my face, allowing our lips to brush against each other. "Now tell me."

"I don't feel as I used to." My admission was whispered so only the demon prince could hear me. "I'm happy to have my full power back, my memories. But... inspiring such fear, it's not what I desire. I don't want to walk into a room and have it go silent. Watchful. I don't want to feel that level of fear directed my way. I'd forgotten how lonely I'd been before I met you. How cold it had made me, bringing fear and chaos with me in place of warmth and love."

Wrath was quiet for a moment. "What do you want?"

I thought about the prophecy, and while it might not have been solely about us, I felt one aspect of it acutely. *As above, so below.* Balance. Now that I was fairly confident Vesta was alive and hiding of her own accord, I had a new goal to focus on entirely.

"I want to right this wrong. I don't just want to break the curse, I want to give all of us a true chance at coexisting peacefully."

"Peace might not be possible."

"I know. But I want to at least do something right. There's been too much anger and resentment. I want to wake up and not worry about who might attack that day. Out of jealousy, or anger, or greed—I want to focus on the good. I want to surround myself with love. And that will never be possible if we're all cursed." I took a deep breath and exhaled. "I want to go to the Well of Memory. And I want to end this endless cycle tonight."

Wrath leaned forward and pressed a chaste kiss to my lips. "Hold on tight, my lady."

Without saying good-bye to his brother or any member of Greed's court, Wrath magicked us away in the middle of the dance floor, earning a few shouted curses we both ignored.

# TWENTY-ONE

**"You must pay** *the goddess a tithe to enter the Well of Memory's chamber."* I recited Fauna's earlier instruction as I studied the statue of the goddess and serpent in Wrath's gardens.

There were no features carved onto her face, but she had flowers in her hair, much like how I used to wear mine. Her curved blades looked sharp enough to draw blood, so I climbed up on the edge of the pool and pressed my fingertip on one. A single drop of blood welled up before the wound healed, leaving no indication it had just been injured. It was now odd to recall this immediate healing ability hadn't been the case just two evenings ago. The spell-lock had well and truly changed me. But I would not dwell on that now.

I surveyed the statue for any hint of a change from the blood offering. None occurred. It would have been far too convenient for the statue to magically come to life and reveal that the curved dagger in its fist was the missing Blade of Ruination. But it certainly would have been nice. Wrath had warned me before I left that the statue wasn't hiding the legendary blade to his knowledge. Part of me had believed my goddess blood would unlock some spell on the statue that even the demons hadn't known about. Alas, that wasn't the case.

I held my hand over the still water of the reflecting pool, watching as the solitary drop of blood fell into it. In theory, the blood drop should have dispersed once it joined the rest of the water, but there was magic at play. The single drop of blood expanded and grew. It cycled around the pool, spiraling tighter together as it wound its way toward the center.

Ruby-colored stairs formed within the spiral, disappearing into a yawning darkness that dropped below ground level. Just as Wrath had explained would happen. He couldn't come with me—this was something I needed to do on my own—but that hadn't stopped him from divulging everything he knew, like a general preparing a solider for battle.

I gathered my skirts with one hand and stepped onto the crimson stairs. I followed them without fear as I traveled underground. No water from the reflecting pool touched me; it parted with each step I took deeper into the earth. Once I'd fully submerged myself, leaving the cool winter night behind, I descended for a few minutes, the air turning crisper the farther down I went. The temperature didn't bother me as it once would have. It wasn't comfortable, but I did not experience any teeth-chattering or rising goose bumps along my flesh.

There was no light, only endless dark that seemed to get thicker, more pervasive with each meter I traveled. But, with my immortal body and senses, I could see almost as clearly as if it were a sunny afternoon near the shore. After a few minutes of moving at a brisk speed, the stairs abruptly ended. I stood on rocky soil and glanced around the small cavern.

A shaft of unnatural bluish light illuminated a well made of what appeared to be bricks of rose quartz that sat just off center from the base of the stairs. The Well of Memory. I moved closer, noting arcane symbols and Latin had been carved into some gemstones on its edge. I ran a finger over the indentations, feeling the power contained within the well hum against my skin.

I peered into the magical well; the water was crystal clear, showing off what had to be thousands of crystals all along its bottom. Each gemstone represented a memory or a nightmare. Something terrible enough that whoever had let the memory go would not miss it.

I wondered if Wrath had come to find a memory or to lose one. It wasn't important. The only thing that mattered now was finding out as much as possible about this blade that, according to Fauna's research, could end my husband's curse. I could not lose sight of that, or I had no hope of succeeding.

I climbed over the small wall and submerged myself in the water, ignoring the slight nip of coldness that seeped into my clothing. "Where is the Blade of Ruination?"

I closed my eyes and leaned my head against the well, allowing my mind to focus solely on the answer I was searching for. My fingers skimmed over several crystals before I paused on one that felt slightly warmer. Fauna hadn't mentioned anything like that, but maybe it was a positive sign that I'd attracted the correct memory. There was only one way to find out. My fingers closed around the crystal, and I drew the memory into me, taking it on as if it were mine.

*Fear clawed at the young wolf, tearing screams from its already torn-apart throat. It was just a pup, but it sensed the dark magic of the man. Demon. His cruel slash of a mouth pressed into a thin line when his coin-colored gaze drifted back to her. She'd heard him enter their home, heard the hushed words he'd spoken with her papa, and immediately shifted. Something her papa told her wasn't supposed to be possible. And a mistake she'd immediately regretted once the demon had scruffed her up by the neck and held her up.*

"This is your firstborn? The hybrid warrior?"

*His tone hinted at disbelief. The pup growled, baring her small canines.*

*Papa's eyes widened.* "Yes, your highness. Her very name means 'dedicated to Mars,' the god of war, as you—"

"I care nothing for mortal gods. She will be given a proper demon name once we're back in my court."

*The pup wriggled in the stranger's grip, panicked. She didn't know what court was and didn't wish to find out. Papa's throat bobbed; the wolf pup pleaded wordlessly for him to take her back, take her from this stranger's grip. Her mother, the woman who never loved her for some reason, had already gone to bed. If Papa didn't save her, no one would.*

"Your highness"—*Papa squared his shoulders, and hope surged in the young pup*—"perhaps there is something else I can give you to clear my debt. She is but a pup. Scraggly and unremarkable. Let me raise enough coin instead. Or perhaps... perhaps I will succeed in finding the Blade of Ruination."

"You haven't found the blade yet and likely never will." *The stranger held the pup up to his face again, inspecting her closely.* "She shifted, about twenty years early, according to your own history. That seems fairly remarkable to me. And what of her demon abilities? What sort of magic does she possess on that end?"

"I...I'm unsure, your highness."

*The demon narrowed his eyes.* "Lie to me again and I will remove that troublesome tongue."

"Please." *Papa's voice was barely a whisper, a broken plea spoken from a broken man. Even though she'd been warned not to, the wolf pup used a bit of her magic to soothe him.* "Please, your highness. Ask me for anything else. Please don't take my daughter."

"How does your wife feel, raising the by-blow of a demon you bedded?"

"She will grow to love the child. My daughter shouldn't pay the price for my sins. Please. Please strike another bargain."

*The demon's mouth pressed into a displeased line as her baby brother cried out from his crib.* "Has your son shifted early, too?"

*Papa glanced at the cradle, swallowing hard.* "No, your highness. He shows no signs of shifting early."

"Then our business concludes here. Hand over your daughter and stand down."

*The stranger jerked his chin, and a man with deer fur and liquid brown eyes stepped from the shadows. The pup whined as the monster—demon—reached out and took her. Her whines turned to shrieks as he shoved her into a sack and cinched it closed.*

*Through her earsplitting howls, she heard the stranger say,* "You were foolish enough to bargain with House Greed. I suggest you think about the consequences the next time you gamble something so valuable away."

Tears streamed down my face, and I gritted my teeth against the mournful howls I still heard as the young wolf had been taken from her family. I felt the sorrow, the despair, the terror she'd experienced, but there was nothing I could do to help that pup. I desperately searched for a clue from the memory to guide me to her, to seek her out once I'd accomplished my task here.

The father seemed almost familiar, but his features had been obscured by both the darkness of the room and the tears of the wolf pup. I was almost certain his accent had been from my version of the Shifting Isles, but there was nothing to indicate how long ago that memory had been purged. It could have been months, or decades. Perhaps even a hundred years. Still, I felt helpless. And I hated Greed a little more.

How he could have taken someone's child, no matter what they'd gambled...

"A hybrid child." The result of a wolf mating with a demon. Just as I suspected Vesta had been. If she still lived—as I believed she did—then this memory proved the court rumors the duke had shared were correct—Vesta had to have been unhappy.

If she recalled any time with her true family, being torn away from them... it would have been hell, living with her captor. Serving as his commander. I prayed that she had escaped him, that my sister had aided her in some way.

I wanted to tear out of this well and pay House Greed a visit to exact some vengeance for the wolf pup, but I had to focus solely on my question. A feat more difficult than I'd imagined, given the rage searing through my veins. "Where is the Blade of Ruination?"

I tossed the wolf pup's memory stone aside and wrapped my fingers around another, immediately getting sucked into a new memory...

*Sursea heard the king approach his throne room, his footsteps as loud as thunder. He was in a foul mood, and it was growing darker the closer he got to her. Good. It was time he paid attention to her request, took it seriously. All he had to do was demand Pride give up her daughter, forbid them from marrying. Surely he had the power to stop such an unholy union.*

*If he wanted Sursea out of this realm for good, this arrangement would suit them both. All she had to do was ignite his hatred until it matched her own. She'd considered bringing her notorious hexed blade if he refused, but she needed him alive. For now.*

*The devil flung open the double doors, and Sursea felt the heat of his glorious wings on full display. She didn't glance up, refusing to give him the satisfaction of staring at his wings like so many others had. She'd seen them before, when he'd banished the vampires to the southern court, bypassing the mountains that belonged to the goddesses as if they were cursed. His wings were silver-tipped white flame, lethal, beautiful. And his most prized weapons, according to her spies. There was nothing he cared for more.*

*A general of war would surely do a great many things to retain such a prize.*

*Refusing to look in his direction, she caressed the bare skin along her outer thighs. She knew he would not be aroused; her act was not meant to seduce as much as to infuriate.*

"Get out." *His voice was harsh, brutal. It irked her greatly, though it had been what she wanted.*

*Sursea's attention cut to his.* "Talking with you hasn't worked. Nor logic and reasoning. Now I have a rather tempting new offer for you." *Over the thin material of her gown, she slowly skimmed the peaks of her breasts. The demon didn't so much as glance down, but his namesake sin did chill the room.* "Take off your pants."

*He crossed his arms, his expression forbidding. A flicker of rage ignited in those gold eyes of his.* "Get out," *he repeated.* "Leave before I *force* you."

"Try." *In one inhumanly graceful movement, she swung herself into a standing position, her long silver dress gleaming like a sword carving through the heavens. It was time for their true battle to begin. He was riled up nicely, and there was one thing she knew—a temper could get the best of anyone, including the demon who ruled over wrath.* "Touch me, and I will destroy all you hold dear. Your majesty."

*Sursea's tone had turned mocking, meant to needle him further.*

*He laughed then, the sound as menacing as the dagger now pressed against her throat.*

"You seem to be mistaken," *he all but growled,* "there is nothing I hold dear. I want you out of this realm before nightfall. If you're not gone by then, I'll set my hellhounds loose. When they're finished, whatever's left will be tossed in the Lake of Fire."

*She'd been around princes of Hell long enough to know he was waiting to scent her fear. When he didn't sense any, he'd grow suspicious, and she needed to retain the upper hand.*

*She jerked forward and slashed her throat across the blade in one brutal motion. Blood spilled over her shimmering gown, splattered across the smooth marble floor, dirtied his cuffs. She knew* that *would be the final insult.*

*Unfazed by her new vicious necklace, she stepped away from him, her smile more wicked than the worst of the devil's brothers. She would know. With the exception of Pride, she'd tried to seduce them all to no avail. For a group of scheming, selfish demons, they certainly protected one another when matters of the heart were concerned. The wound stitched itself together under his cold, watchful gaze.*

"Are you certain about that? There isn't *anything* you yearn for?"

*When he didn't respond, her annoyance flared. She was tired of being denied such a simple request. They didn't trust witches any more than witches trusted demons. Having her daughter banished would be best for all. There was no possibility that they would want a witch to corule over one of their precious Houses.*

"Maybe the rumors are true, after all. You have no heart in that armored chest of yours." *She circled him, her skirts smearing a trail of blood across the once pristine floor.* "Perhaps we should carve you open, take a look."

*She allowed her attention to pause on the unusual silver and white wings of flame at his back, her grin turning feral. She'd allowed just enough time for his brow to crease. Then she struck. With one quick snap of her fingers, his mighty weapons turned the color of ash, then disappeared.*

*Sursea watched with satisfaction as panic seized him. A rare showing of emotion from a demon known for his cool temperament. He repeatedly tried—and failed—to summon the wings.*

"Here is a trick as nasty as the devil himself." *Her voice was both young and old as she spoke her spell into existence. He swore impressively.* "From this day forward, a curse will sweep through this land. You will forget all but your hate. Love, kindness, every good thing in your world will cease. One day that will change. When you know true happiness, I vow to take whatever you love, too."

*Sursea watched as he strained to summon his wings to no avail, hoping he'd want them desperately enough to do as she'd asked, especially with a curse on him now. All she wanted was to free her daughter from the philandering drunkard. To ensure her true happiness. And to keep her safe from this miserable realm. Sursea had stood by and watched her daughter's light dim for far too long. Pride only cared for himself, was incapable of dedicating himself to one lover. Something that would be fine if her daughter was of the same temperament.*

*Sursea clicked her tongue once, disappointed the king didn't release his inner monster to fight back, and started to turn away. Instead of chasing her, he spoke in a voice assassins used before they slit someone's throat in the night.* "You're wrong."

*Sursea paused, tossing a glance over a shoulder. Not many dared to call her wrong. Especially after refusing to grant her a favor. She was a powerful ally and an even worse enemy.* "Oh?"

"The devil may be nasty, but he doesn't perform tricks." *His smile was slow, taunting.* "He bargains." *Sursea watched him closely, feeling her magic stirring at the quiet threat he posed. The air between them was charged with hatred. He would kill her without thought if she didn't possess something he wanted desperately.* "Care to strike a deal?"

*Originally, she had wanted a deal. Seeing him now without his wings, though, it filled her with a dark sense of glee. She hated Pride. Hated the princes of Hell. And exacting a little bit of revenge felt more satisfying than she'd imagined. Still, it would be remiss of her to not hear him out. Her daughter's happiness was what truly mattered. She ran her attention over him.*

"Pretend I'm entertaining the idea of a bargain, one small opportunity for you to break the curse and earn your wings back. What are your terms?" *Sursea asked.*

"Six years, six months, and six days." *The king of demons' voice was low, dangerous. He'd not hesitated with his response, which indicated he'd thought it through before offering. Not that she expected anything less from the battle strategist. Before she could agree or inquire further, he added,* "Time will be measured in the Seven Circles. Not any other hell dimension. During that period, you will not set foot in mine or any of my brothers' Houses of Sin unless invited. If you do, then you risk a curse of your own. One I shall not reveal until it's too late."

*Sursea eyed the devil speculatively. The bargain was relatively simple enough, but she recognized the dark gleam in his eyes. Knew the deceptiveness it hinted at. Wrath was no fool. And neither was she. There was great risk by agreeing to it, but the potential for an even greater reward was too tempting to pass up.* "I want a guarantee that no one associated with you or your brothers will try to make an attempt on my life or cause me harm in any way. And if you cannot break the curse within that time, it shall *never* be undone. No magic, no trickery, no bargain will matter. For all eternity, you shall never have what you love most."

"When I do break it, and when I decide I no longer wish to have you taint this realm, you will be banished from the Seven Circles. And you must erase the memory of this conversation."

*Sursea considered all angles. It didn't so much matter if he won, as long as* she *got what she'd been after all along. Six years, six months, and six days ought to grant her enough time to see her plan through. Though in other realms it could be closer to twenty years. Regardless of how much time she needed to endure, if she never had the misfortune of dealing with princes of Hell again, it was a small price to pay for eternity.*

*She didn't need to remember this conversation in its entirety, she only needed to recall her goal of protecting her daughter. An idea was stirring. She'd heard rumors the Crone had been using magic to shape the memories of anyone who tried to cross a particular mountain range to the south. But her interference was only directed at one particular, enigmatic House of Sin that stood apart from all others. It wasn't ruled by demons, but something much worse. And it was the one stipulation the king of demons forgot to include in his bargain.*

*Perhaps it was time to pay House Vengeance a visit.*

"What of the Shifting Isles?" *she asked.* "They technically are their own dimension."

*The king seemed to consider this. She'd heard rumors that he disliked the isles but wanted confirmation.* "If you'd like to be banished there, in true Hell, be my guest."

"You know," *she made her tone sound bored,* "some believe six-six-six to be the sign of the beast. If I purge this memory, how am I to trust you won't break your word?"

"You know full well it symbolizes balance. Natural order. Don't feign ignorance, Sursea. I can scent your lies, and they reek of shit." *He called for a servant, then pulled a clear, smooth piece of quartz from inside his jacket pocket. Sursea did her best to not look surprised. The devil had come prepared to do battle. A moment later, that same servant reappeared with a contract and two blood quills. Unease trailed a finger along her spine as the king handed her the stone.* "Purge the memory and we'll sign the oath."

The memory abruptly ended, and I was thrust back into the here and now. My clothes were soaked through, the water frigid. Yet I was consumed with an inner fire that had the air glimmering from the sudden heat. I glanced at my hand, at the pulverized crystal in it. The memory hadn't stopped, *I'd* crushed it in my fist.

Six years, six months, and six days. Wrath never mentioned a clock counting down our time to break the curse. But he had wanted me to swear a blood oath to him, for six months. And then Anir had also mentioned his having six months left to regain his full power. Then, of course, there was Sursea's snide comment about time moving quickly in the throne room.

I swore, using every foul word and phrase I knew. Given Sursea's glee, we probably didn't have much time left.

I wanted to charge up to the castle and demand to know how long we had left, but that had to wait. I still hadn't found what I'd been looking for. And now, more than ever, I needed to discover where the Blade of Ruination was so I could break the curse before it was too late.

"Where is the Blade of Ruination?" I concentrated on my question, fueled it with *my* fury and my magic, and shoved my hand below water again. I grabbed a fistful of crystals, and each one that tried to suck me into a nightmare was crushed to nothingness. I had neither the time nor the patience to deal with anyone else's fear. I *was* fear. And I was capable of being a nightmare. The Well of Memory vibrated as if it trembled from the surge of my raw emotions. "Show me who last saw the Blade of Ruination. Now."

My fingers closed on a roughened crystal that drew blood. A hiss of pain escaped my lips right before I was dragged into the next memory.

As the scene sprang into place, I swallowed my surprise. It seemed the secrets the people in my life had been keeping hadn't been completely revealed.

Until now.

# TWENTY-TWO

**"Demons are not** capable of love. I've told you that countless times."

*Her mother's superior tone grated on Lucia. She'd been scheming for years to put an end to Lucia's relationship and didn't hide the fact she was thrilled by recent events. Lucia wished to curl into a ball on her side and weep, but she refused to prove her mother correct.*

*Mother had said the Prince of Pride was the worst rake of the seven princes of Hell. That he'd fallen into infatuation time and again, always leaving broken hearts in his wake. And it would be no different when his attention finally wandered from her, an immortal witch he had no business consorting with. And not simply* any *witch, as her mother often reminded her, but the eldest daughter of the First Witch, the all-powerful, sun goddess–descended Sursea.*

*For years her mother chided her over how Lucia ought to have taken more care to set a better example. To not be deemed a fool in front of other witches who looked to her for instruction on how to carry themselves around the denizens of the Seven Circles. Courting—and worse yet, marrying—a demon was the worst sort of example, especially one as notorious as Pride.*

*Lucia wasn't naive enough to think Pride would change, nor did she wish for him to do so for her benefit, but nothing prepared her for the pain of watching him fall under another's spell. His actions weren't done out of malice; Lucia believed that with each piece of* her *broken heart. She'd seen his kindness, knew his affection for her wasn't feigned. Her mother thought her a fool, but she'd heard the rumors well before she agreed to his courtship. Knew he might be infatuated today, but tomorrow was an unknown. He needed attention and adoration the way flowers needed sunshine and rain to bloom. She'd found his whims terribly exciting, never falling into predictability or routine. Being a guardian between realms, she'd had plenty of routine and hated the monotony of it.*

*When they'd first met, the charming prince had been taken with her name. Lucia was derived from* lux, *the Latin word for light. Pride, Lucifer, was the Morningstar. The light bringer. He'd called it star-crossed fate, claiming they were from two opposing sides meant to hate each other, but instead were unable to deny their fated love. Lucia didn't believe in fate, but she rather enjoyed bantering with him. His nose would crinkle in the most adorable way when she good-naturedly rankled him. For his part, Pride seemed to adore her for it.*

*It had all seemed wildly romantic at first. Capturing the attention of someone like that. Someone who she never should have spoken to, let alone fallen for. Pride had been correct on one account. Their love was forbidden. And like all things forbidden, it held greater appeal. A sense of danger hung over them whenever they sneaked off for one of their clandestine meetings. At any moment they might be discovered, might cause a scandal for witches and demons alike.*

*As a Star Witch, the first of her kind, Lucia was meant to guard the realm, to ensure the demon princes behaved. Her sole duty was to make sure they remained in the Seven Circles, playing their sin-fueled games with their wicked courts and left the mortals in peace. Then she met* him. *Like the morning star he was, Pride came blazing into her life, igniting her passions and waking her up from a mundane, duty-filled existence that paled in comparison.*

*Even when he'd asked for her hand, she knew it wasn't always going to be as it was then. He burned too brightly, too powerfully for his fires to ever be contained. Truth be told, she wouldn't ever want him to change. But she'd come to realize that* she *had. And that was the issue. Her discontentment began small as most troubles often do, a tiny seed that grew into something more over time. She wanted something Pride never could give or even be. At least, not with her. And that was the root of her heartache.*

*Pride had always remained true to himself; it was Lucia who hadn't been honest with herself or with him about her desires. He'd called her on her lies, begged her to tell him the truth, but she'd refused.*

*In fact, they'd argued that very night. Pride asked her again and again to confide in him, to tell him why she was upset. He vowed to do anything to make her happy. He promised to miss the feast, to stay by her side, to work through whatever was troubling her. But Lucia believed happiness couldn't come from another, it had to be found within first.*

*She knew Pride would do anything for her; he'd never speak to another in any romantic way. And eventually, he'd be as unhappy as she was now. No matter how much love there was between them, Lucia realized some people just weren't meant to be.*

*Tears burned behind her eyes, but she refused to let them fall. Her mother watched her closely, disapproval written all over her immortal face.*

"His first and only love is himself. That is the nature of his sin. Leaving was for the best, Lucia. In time you'll not only believe it, but feel it to be true."

"Of course it was."

*Mother spoke as if Lucia hadn't been the one to choose to walk away. It hurt, beyond anything she'd experienced before, but she'd done it. While Pride openly courted Nicoletta of House Vengeance at the feast tonight, Lucia had feigned a headache and remained at House Pride. Once her husband had finally given in to her demands and left, she grabbed the trunk she'd packed earlier and raced to the portal on their lands.*

*Mother had been staying on the Shifting Isles, so before she could convince herself it was a bad idea, Lucia pictured her mother's home—the charming cottage with a thatched roof that sat high on the bluffs in the isle's version of Ireland—and stepped into the portal.*

*Now, as she sat primly at the small dining room table, sipping a cup of herbal tea, she half-regretted her destination. Part of her wondered if her own pride was clouding her judgment.*

*Perhaps she* should *have found the courage to tell her husband every fear or worry of her heart. This doubt wasn't for long, she reminded herself as she gathered up her courage to ask what she'd come here for. Mother would hopefully give her anything to ensure she didn't return to the Seven Circles.*

"I want to forget." *Lucia held her mother's gaze.* "I know you have a spell from the Crone. I want it. And I want to be left alone until I'm ready to come back. *If* I'm ever ready."

*Her mother, to her credit, didn't so much as bat an eye.* "Where do you wish to go?"

*Lucia let out a breath, thankful there would be no fight or argument. She'd given much thought to where she'd love to be, where her heart could mend and she could live the sort of life she desired.* "Sicily."

*Mother's expression turned calculating. Lucia knew it meant she was privately scheming and didn't care. So long as Lucia got what she wanted, her mother could play out whatever game she wished. Mother stood and retrieved a small satchel from a hidden panel in the wall. She placed it in front of Lucia and tapped the buckle that held it together.* "This package contains all you need to forget. Not just your heartache, but whatever you wish to leave behind."

"And you just happened to have this lying around?"

"I've been prepared for this day since you first laid eyes on that demon and he sank his claws into your precious heart."

*Knowing the conversation would go nowhere, Lucia unlocked the leather strap and pulled the satchel open, surveying the strange assortment of items. A rough, rare piece of blue quartz from the Southern Hemisphere. Rolled-up parchment—with a spell for forgetting. And a dagger. One Lucia recognized at once.*

*It was legendary, an object hexed by her mother that could kill any creature, even a prince of Hell. The dagger was also rumored to break curses, but Lucia knew a secret about it that no one else did, save her mother. A secret that would either activate the blade or see it destroyed forever if done incorrectly.*

"The Blade of Ruination? What will I need this for?"

"Silly, child." *Her mother tsked.* "Protection. Do you think his pride will allow him to sit idly by as his wife makes a fool of him? Do you not think he'll seek revenge?"

"He would never harm me or wish me ill." *Lucia stared at her mother in horror.* "Do you truly think so little of him, even after all these years?"

"He might not cause you harm, Lucia, but I doubt he'll let his wife vanish without searching for her. Did you leave a letter of explanation? Does he know you're not coming back?"

*Lucia's eyes fluttered shut as shame pinked her cheeks. She'd tried to. She'd sat at her writing desk, ink pot ready, quill in hand, and couldn't find the right words. Any words. It had been cowardly. Cruel, even. But instead of saying the wrong thing or writing all of her wants and worries and fears out for him to ultimately reject her, she simply left.*

"One day he will find you." *Her mother's tone was as steely as her expression.* "He will remember all you do not. And I promise he will stop at nothing to win you back. His pride will see to that. Only you'll be at a disadvantage, having forgotten him. Do you think he'll be a devoted husband after that? You'll have shamed him, bruised his legendary ego openly in front of his whole court. In front of the whole realm. And you won't even remember."

*Lucia shook her head. She knew what her mother wasn't saying—she disapproved of Lucia taking a tonic to forget. It wasn't a smart battle tactic, and Mother considered witches and demons to constantly be at war. But the pain in Lucia's chest, the acute, all-consuming grief, was too great to overcome; she couldn't walk away from Pride if she remembered him.* "I'll take the dagger. Just see to it I never fall for another prince of Hell again."

*Mother's gaze turned hard, like the hell-forged steel in Lucia's hand.* "When I'm through with the demons, I'll make sure no witch ever falls for their lies. And they will hate us in return, so passionately they wouldn't deign to fall in love with a witch again. That I vow on my life's blood, daughter." *She whispered a summoning spell, and within moments another witch appeared. Lucia vaguely recognized her from one of the more powerful covens.* "Maria, I have an assignment for you. You're living in the Shifting Isles' version of Palermo, correct?"

*While Mother plotted with Maria, Lucia read over the spell. It was nothing more than an herbal tea blend, really. It would be easy to make. Even when she forgot why she was making it, she'd be able to pull the ingredients together. As she set the spell aside and picked up the roughened crystal, a steaming mug appeared before her. She glanced up, meeting the other witch's kind eyes.*

"Drink. It will help ease the pain, bambina."

*Lucia knew it was the first dose of the spelled tea. Knew that once she brought the porcelain to her lips, things would truly be over between her and Pride. Her mother didn't speak, but Lucia felt her attention shift to her, almost in challenge. Lucia picked up the cup, pausing before she took that fateful first sip that would signal both the end and a new beginning for her.*

"I want a new name. A new family. I want to forget everything except that I am a witch." *Lucia finally brought her focus to her mother's.* "And I do not wish to see you until I ask for you."

*There was a flash of what looked to be hurt in her mother's face, there and gone in an instant.* "Very well. Maria will monitor the situation from afar and will set you up with a family in a dark coven."

*The other witch nodded.* "You'll be well cared for."

"Good." *Lucia nodded back—a quick jerk of her chin, then gulped the tea down in one, scalding shot. It took a few moments, but the heavy pressure on her chest lessened. Her muscles loosened. The sadness and despair lightened. If there had been something troubling her a moment ago, Lucia couldn't recall what it was. Perhaps it had been a bad dream. She blinked at the crystal in her hand and the dagger on the table before her, her brow creasing.* "What are these for?"

*Maria gave her a sad smile.* "You must never show this dagger to anyone. Never speak of it. It's only to be used on the Wicked."

"The Wicked?" *Lucia's heart pounded furiously. If she didn't know any better, she'd think someone was manipulating her emotions. But that sort of power was supposed to be forbidden.* "Who are they?"

*An unfamiliar witch with strange starlight eyes slowly moved around the small wooden table. Power radiated off her, and Lucia fought a shudder.* "The Wicked are bloodthirsty creatures known as princes of Hell. They seek to destroy you. To destroy all witches."

"If you see one," *Maria added,* "you must hide. And if they come for you..."

*Lucia glanced down at the deadly-looking blade.* "I must protect myself." *She inhaled deeply, feeling the truth settle inside her. The Wicked. Her mortal enemies. She prayed to the goddess she'd never encounter one but was thankful for the dagger just in case. Lucia picked up the rare blue crystal.* "Is this a memory stone?"

*The witch with starlight eyes nodded.* "For your safety, you must purge your memories of this night now. I'll give you a sleeping draught, and when you awake, Maria will have taken you home."

"Am I in danger?" *Lucia asked the witch, hating the edge of fear in her voice.*

"Not anymore."

*As Lucia held the magic crystal and started feeding her memories of the night to it, the stone took something she couldn't recall if she wanted to lose or not. She drew her brows together again as the stone heated up, taking more and more of her thoughts from the last few hours.* "Who... what is my name?"

*Starlight eyes didn't seem to think her lack of memory in that area was a surprise, which indicated she had wanted it gone. At least, that's what the witch without a name thought.* "Your name is Claudia. You're from Palermo. You're a powerful witch with an affinity for dark magic and have been blessed with Sight. You are talented with a blade and aren't squeamish around the dead. And your family is waiting for your arrival."

*Claudia. She nodded; the name seemed to fit. Though the rest of the story didn't ring as true. Claudia noticed the witch hadn't said her family was waiting for her* return. *Only her arrival. Claudia didn't remember taking the sleeping draught, but her lids suddenly felt too heavy to keep open. She managed to ask one more question before sleep claimed her.* "Who are you?"

"A powerful ally to some. A nightmare to others."

*As Claudia drifted off to a troubled sleep, she prayed to never see the witch with strange eyes again.*

# TWENTY-THREE

**Back in the** Well of Memory, I stared at the roughened crystal in my palm. For the first time since I'd become immortal again, I swore I felt the phantom beating of a human heart I no longer possessed. I couldn't believe it. I'd found what I'd been searching for, but collecting the blade would not be easy. Claudia, my dearest friend, was the First Witch's daughter. Lucia. Pride's missing wife who was presumed dead, even by Wrath. And Claudia did not remember any of it.

Unlike me, she'd *chosen* to forget her prince. A decision that tore her apart, but she'd found the strength to do it. Because she'd felt it was best for her. *Blood and bones.* I didn't want to be the monster who made her recall her heartache, and I had no desire to lead any of the demon princes to my friend after she'd successfully disappeared. It was a miracle none of them had encountered her while they'd been on our version of the Shifting Isles.

Claudia clearly didn't want to be found, especially by her husband, and she'd moved on. She was happy, content with the new life she'd carved out for herself.

But my choices were limited. Claudia had the Blade of Ruination, the only weapon capable of severing the curse, and hidden in her mind was a secret about how to get the dagger to work without destroying it. I carefully replayed that part of her memory in my mind, desperate for any other way to get the information and leave my friend to the peace she'd found.

*The dagger was also rumored to break curses, but Lucia knew a secret about it that no one else did, save her mother. A secret that would either activate the blade or see it destroyed forever if done incorrectly.*

I had little doubt my friend would hand over the dagger if I asked for it, but for me to use it properly, Claudia needed her memory back. I wasn't sure if there was a limit to how many times one could purge a memory. If she took the memory of that night back now, she might never be rid of it again. In our realm it had been nearly two decades of forgetting, of moving on for her. And I saw no other avenue to take to avoid causing her pain. It was a terrible price to ask of someone else, and I'd do anything to pay the cost myself.

"Divine goddess above. There has to be..."

*Lucia knew a secret about it that no one else did, save her mother.*

"Blessed be the wicked."

My lips curved. The devil truly was in the details as humans liked to say. Wrath, the king of even the most minute of details, would be pleased his reputation preceded him. There was one other person who knew the blade's secret. One I did not mind hurting to get information from.

If anything, I was eager to offer revenge for my husband and my friend. I carefully placed the memory stone in my bodice and headed for the dungeon. It was time to thaw out Sursea and see what interesting things she had to say about the Blade of Ruination.

By blood and by pain, or of her own free will, she'd tell me what I wished to know.

Burning wildflowers floated above the frozen statue that was Sursea, the heat of my magic warming the otherwise frigid room. I sat on a stool a guard had brought in and watched impassively as ice melted and dripped onto the stone floor.

Thawing her was a tedious process that was taking longer than I'd anticipated, but it had to be done properly or she could revive "wrong," according to my husband.

I normally wouldn't care about any ill effects she'd suffer, but I needed her to tell me how to activate the blade, and I wouldn't risk any chance of losing that opportunity for petty vengeance. My sister would roll her eyes if she saw me now, but this was how I hoped our House of Sin would handle such matters once reestablished.

Wrath stepped into the small subterranean chamber and pressed his lips together at the sight of Sursea. His hatred for the witch was palpable. If she weren't immortal and if he didn't want his wings back, he'd have killed her long ago. The temperature dropped a few degrees, which would not do the thawing process any favors.

"Once she's thawed enough to speak, is there a certain amount of time I should aim to complete the interrogation by?" I asked, successfully dragging Wrath's attention away from the dark place he'd been descending to. The temperature returned to the normal chill that nipped at the air this far below ground.

"Take all the time you need. Once you're done questioning her, send for me. She's not to be left alone until she's frozen again."

I gave my husband a quick smile. When I told him what I needed, he didn't hesitate to make it happen. Even when I'd asked him not to be present or ask questions. Now that I could also sense emotions, I knew with certainty he'd not experienced even a moment of doubt or hesitation. "Thank you for trusting me."

"Try not to maim her too terribly." He kissed my forehead and headed for the door.

Anir skidded to a halt outside the dungeon and nodded at me before following Wrath from the room, their heads bent in hushed conversation. The other Houses of Sin were still on high alert after the failed attempt to attack House Greed. With the constant correspondence coming in and interruptions of emissaries and war room debates, I hadn't yet asked Wrath about how much time was left to break the curse. Not that I'd had more than two minutes with him since my return from the Well of Memory. I'd rushed here immediately following my request.

In case something went wrong with my questioning of Sursea, I didn't want to get his hopes up and tell him what I'd learned. But we needed to speak. Soon.

That is, if the stubborn witch thawed in this century. I swore she was taking her time, twisting the blade any chance she got. My fingers strummed against my forearms. Water slowly dribbled from the thick wall of ice surrounding Sursea. *Drip. Drip. Drip.*

I added one more burning flower to the flaming bouquet above her, then turned my attention back on Sursea's face, taking the time to truly look her over. The resemblance between her and Claudia wasn't overwhelming, but it was there once you knew to look for it. They had the same shape to their faces, and arch of their brows. Sursea's dark hair had waves and Claudia's had a bit more curl, but it was the same shade of luxurious brown.

With my own memories intact again, I knew I had never met Claudia when she was still Lucia and I was Fury. Seeing that revelation in the Well of Memory had been a shock.

I casted my mind back to the time before I was spell-locked, to remember what I could. From the beginning of our scheme, Vittoria and I never showed up to the same party while playing our role of "Nicoletta." She attended any meetings or parties with Pride, and I did the same with Wrath. Sursea insisted that we couldn't be caught until the time was right, as she wanted to ensure both princes had time to truly fall in love.

Through all the parties and events, I couldn't recall Claudia at any function *I'd* attended. Still, I dove deeper into my memories. I recalled that Vittoria and I would take turns ruling our House of Sin every other week to allow Pride and Wrath to question the whereabouts of our combined persona—Nicoletta—when we weren't with them. Of course, we'd told them the truth in part. We were returning to House Vengeance, a House they knew little about, thanks to our mother's magic and our secrecy.

I recalled how we took care of every detail, just as Sursea asked—we even timed our visits to the Houses, to convince the princes there was adequate time for "Nicoletta" to have visited the other prince during the time she wasn't with one, driving a wedge between brothers as it was revealed they were courting the same woman.

The only event that Vittoria and I both attended was the

fateful night that the First Witch asked us to make our pivotal move—the night of the Feast of the Wolf. That evening, on the one night when all seven princes gathered, her plan for vengeance was simple: Vittoria was expected to lure Wrath to "catch" her in the act of seducing Pride. When he walked in on the scandal, we'd expected him to let loose his fury and fight his brother. Pride would lose his wife and possibly his court if Wrath unleashed the might of his House. Thus securing the ultimate revenge against Pride for the First Witch.

While *I* had never encountered Claudia in all that time, Vittoria had to know who she truly was. My sister had been the one sent to seduce Pride after all. And yet my twin never mentioned it, never gave up our friend's secret. I wasn't sure if it was kindness on Vittoria's part or if she didn't want to alert the princes for her own reasons. If I was correct about my sister having feelings for Pride, she wouldn't want anyone to find out Claudia's secret. Maybe not even Claudia herself.

But when I considered my theory about Vesta—about my sister helping her to escape a court that made her so unhappy—I couldn't imagine my twin was as selfish or terrible as she'd like the realm to believe. She'd certainly done her fair share of dark deeds, like murdering the daughters of the witches who'd spell-locked us, but thus far that was the only true vengeance she'd sought.

She'd also murdered Antonio, but now I suspected he was close to revealing information regarding Vesta. It didn't excuse what she did, but it indicated she wasn't committing monstrous acts without calculation as she'd been all too happy to let me and the demon princes believe.

A chunk of ice cracked and slid off Sursea's face, drawing my attention to the present. The First Witch was now completely thawed from brow to chin. She slowly blinked until her lashes were free from ice and settled an impressive glare on me.

"Fury." She spit my true name at me. "You always were the one most like—"

Sursea's mouth snapped shut with an audible click. I smiled. "The most like Lucia?"

"I have no idea who you mean. I was going to say Wrath but didn't wish to taint my already foul mood by speaking his cursed name."

Instead of calling her on the obvious lie, I stood and moved around the block of ice that contained the rest of her frozen body. "Were you aware that Claudia and I were the best of friends while I was spell-locked? Vittoria, too. I could go to her right now, and she'd welcome me into her home. She wouldn't even think twice if Vittoria showed up, risen from the dead." Sursea's gaze glittered with anger, but she kept her troublesome mouth shut. "I want the Blade of Ruination. And I will do anything to get it. Even harm a dear friend by telling her a very intriguing story. Unless you decide to help me and your daughter."

Sursea's expression didn't shift, but I sensed her calculating mind whirring. "Helping you is not in my best interest."

"You achieved your ultimate goal and got what you wanted. Pride and Lucia are separated. Your vengeance against Wrath ends now. He's paid the price of your curse long enough. And so have I. And that was never part of *our* bargain."

"Wrath's curse was very clear. Once he knew true happiness and love, it would be removed and replaced by hate. You never should have allowed him into your heart. That is your issue."

"Are you certain about that?" I summoned a large orange blossom and held the burning flower in the palm of my hand. My head canted to one side, admiring the magical rose-gold flames. "I'm not sure it's wise to ignite my fury. Have a bit of respect for your gods."

I blew the flower in the First Witch's face and singed her brows off. She screamed as the flames hovered above her skin, close enough to feel the burn but not have her flesh melt. Yet. It was a show of the control I had over my magic, the precision with which I could wield the magical flame.

"I have neither the time nor the patience to prolong this meeting. If you do not tell me what I want to know, I'll set your entire head on fire. You'll scream and choke on the scent of your own burning flesh until your vocal cords no longer work. Then I'll visit Claudia and give her this." I pulled the memory stone from my bodice and held it up. The threat of being tortured hadn't caused the color to drain from the witch's face, but seeing the memory stone did. "How do I activate the blade to break the curse?"

A muscle in Sursea's jaw flickered. She still did not want the curse to be broken, even after she'd gotten what she'd wanted: her daughter free from Pride. That's how much she hated Wrath for not giving her what she'd asked for. It was petulant. A tantrum thrown by a spoiled, highborn immortal. I shook my head.

"Vengeance. It's an ugly pursuit that encompasses many sins. Careful," I whispered, leaning in close, "or your pride will be your downfall, Sursea. A bit ironic, all things considered. That you would succumb to the sin you hated most above all, just to punish Wrath for saying no to your whims. For respecting his brother and his wife's choice. You meddled and schemed. You chose hate when all you should have done was love your child unconditionally. Allow her to make her own choices. Become her own person."

Sursea heaved a breath out, her face contorted in rage. "My

daughter's blood—and only her blood—activates the blade. But she must willingly give it to you. Like all magic, it cannot be forced or taken or gotten through deceptive means." Something inside me that still felt human tightened in my chest. Sursea didn't miss the minute change, her lips pulled back into a sneer. "Regardless of my interference, Lucia does not deserve to be brought back into this world of sin. I hope you can live with your choice to ruin the happiness she's fought so hard to find."

Wrath escorted me back to his private chamber in silence, sensing my need to sort through my options. He paused outside his door and looked me over. "We haven't had many opportunities to discuss it, and now isn't the most ideal time, either, but I'd like for us to share a room. It can be either of our suites, or we can tear the wall down between them and turn it into one floor for our private living quarters. We'll add a small kitchen if you'd like."

For the first time in days my mind stopped spinning. I stared at my husband, who never ceased to amaze me with his consideration. His endless acts of love. I rolled up onto my toes and dragged his face close to mine. "Let's add the kitchen and tear the wall down. The idea of having this entire floor as our private living quarters where we can hide from the whole court is wildly appealing. And I disagree entirely. This was the perfect time to discuss it."

"Consider it done, my lady." Wrath kissed me gently, then opened the door. I followed him in and collapsed onto one of the oversized chairs set before the fireplace. The momentary elation passed, replaced by the seriousness of what had to be done next.

Wrath looked me over, his lips tugging into a frown. "Did you get the answers you needed?"

"Mostly." The flames danced in the fireplace, reminding me of excited puppy tails wagging. I turned my attention to my husband. "The bargain you made with Sursea was for six years, six months, and six days." Wrath dropped into the chair beside me, giving me an assessing look. Before he could ask any questions, I added, "How much time is left?"

He gazed at the fire, the flames gilding his face in warm light. "A day."

"A day." I hadn't thought we'd had much time left, but a day was ridiculous. Through a remarkable act of self-control, I pulled in my fury, keeping a clear head. "If we don't break the curse before tomorrow, it can't ever be broken."

"The Well of Memory worked for you." Wrath's tone didn't indicate how he felt about it. And his expression was even harder to read. He got up and poured a drink from the decanter he kept on a sideboard near the mantel. He turned to me and held the lavender liquid up. "This will ensure I don't lose you again. Curse or not, we'll get through it this time."

He sipped the tincture that prevented him from feeling love, and the rage I felt at our circumstances and the First Witch came flooding out.

"We will *not* get through it like that. I want your heart, Samael. I want your love without spells and tinctures keeping it locked away. Only having half of you is a curse, too. We both deserve more. We deserve true happiness. Happiness without chains or restrictions or strings attached to it. No matter the sins of our past, we do not deserve to be punished for eternity. Your only crime was helping your brother and his wife make their own choice. Now you must give up love? For what? A hateful witch's vengeance? I will not accept that. I cannot. You ought to give your heart to whomever you choose, whenever and however you choose to give it."

"That might never happen." Wrath's tone wasn't harsh or unkind. There was a glimmer of sadness in his eyes. "So decide now, before we complete our bond, if this—what we have right now—will be good enough for you. If I cannot love you, if I cannot offer you my heart in return, you need to decide if that's something you can live with. If you cannot..."

Wrath would walk away; he'd set me free even if it crushed him.

"That's why you haven't brought up completing our bond before."

He sighed and ran a hand through his hair. "I'd hoped to find a way to break the curse before we had to have this discussion."

Silence fell between us again.

The fire crackled, its excitement over our combined anger feeding the flames. I wasn't upset with Wrath. I understood why he'd crafted a secondary strategy in the event the curse remained intact. That showed his love even when he couldn't express it. But I was greedy. I wanted it all. All of him. The good parts and the bad and every piece and part in between.

Having him love me in half measures was a miserable fate for both of us.

I stood and crawled onto his lap, resting my head against his heart. "In the Well of Memory...I found a way to break the curse." Wrath stiffened beneath me. "I need to leave to accomplish it, and I need you to remain here."

He rubbed a hand up and down my spine. "You don't sound happy."

I sensed he wanted to ask more, but he'd already figured out I'd shared all I could. I nestled against him, taking the comfort he was offering and wrapping it around me like the sweetest sort of embrace. "I might have to hurt someone I care about. Someone that doesn't deserve an ounce of pain."

Wrath kissed the top of my head. "I'm sorry."

He didn't tell me to find another way, because there wasn't one. He didn't offer to stand in my place, because he knew I needed to be the one to do it. There were no words of comfort, because I had to do something I hated to free us.

Wrath carefully tilted my face up to his, his gaze penetrating enough to stare into my soul if I allowed him to. When he brought his lips to mine, he unleashed all the things that were pointless to say and communicated all our hopes and sorrow without words.

Before I knew what was happening, Wrath used his supernatural strength and speed to maneuver us onto the plush carpet. He lay beneath me, holding me above his face, and flashed a devilish grin that had my toes curling from its sinful intent. I might have been the one on top, gazing down into his seductive eyes, but he was in control now.

"What are you doing?" I asked. "We don't have time..."

"The world could end before we know it. And I have my own fantasies to live out, my lady. If you're willing to indulge?"

I understood his need for a connection. To feel something other than fear or our sins as we raced to a finish line we weren't sure was close by. I needed him, too. He might not be able to tell me he loved me, but he could certainly show me. I nodded. "I'm happy to oblige."

"Thank fuck." He lowered me so that my knees were on either side of his head, his thumbs rubbing lazy circles on my hips.

Wrath lifted my skirts and parted my lacy undergarments, slowly dragging a finger over the slickness waiting for him.

"Is this a new lesson in conquering or surrender?" I managed to ask as his finger dipped inside, then curled ever so gently. I swore as he repeated the motion with a second finger, stretching me. He withdrew his fingers, then pushed them back in, pumping slowly.

"You tell me, my lady."

"I—goddess *curse* me."

Wrath ripped my undergarments off, then brought his mouth to my body, licking hard and deep. I jerked forward, gripping the chair as each flick of his tongue threatened to topple me over. He pulled my hips forward, then pushed back, never once removing his mouth from me.

Holding my gaze, he repeated the action, and I knew what he was requesting without words. And who was I to deny him or myself the pleasure?

I rocked forward, and the demon rewarded me with a satisfied growl that vibrated over my most sensitive area. My cursed skirts fell over him, hiding him from view.

I slowly released the chair and ripped off the lower portion of the gown, earning an amused look from my husband. I braced one hand behind me on his thigh, and the other I tangled into his hair, pulling it until he was angled just right. With my gown out of the way, I could see him and his wicked gaze much better.

Unadulterated hunger crossed his features. "Tug it harder, my lady."

"Heathen."

"My dark angel." Wrath wrapped his arms around me and feasted as I set the pace. His tongue plundered, making my body clench around it until I thought I'd go mad from the feeling. I yanked his hair even harder and rocked against him, my head thrown back. Wrath plunged a finger in with his clever tongue and set a rhythm that had me seeing stars. I came with reckless abandon, moaning his true name as a shock of pleasure bolted through me. Before I'd fully come down, I broke apart again, calling his name like a plea or a curse. Only when my legs started trembling from the aftershocks did the demon press a chaste kiss to my inner thigh. The light caress set my blood on fire again.

What we shared wasn't nearly enough. But time was our enemy at the moment, and I'd already lost too much. My husband saw the indecision in my face, and I saw the yearning in his. We needed this. Even if it meant I had less time to get the blade, I'd make it work. I moved down his body and guided his thick length into me.

Wrath laced his hands with mine, and together we soon fell over that glorious edge, reminding ourselves what we were fighting so hard for. Love.

# TWENTY-FOUR

**Domenico snarled when** I summoned him. "Do I look like your personal carriage?"

"No. But you will look like a new fur rug if you don't stop complaining," I said sweetly.

"You're not as fun as your sister."

"Perhaps not to you. But I am as deadly, and unlike Vittoria, if I kill you, you won't come back. I can't do that demonic hand trick." I wriggled my fingers at him. "Let's move."

The werewolf made a disgusted noise that sounded suspiciously like choked laughter, then he sank his claws into my arms and stepped into the glittering portal. The gates were still locked from the outside, but traveling by shifter was actually best. Wrath couldn't *transvenio*, and even if he could, I didn't want him to know where I was going. He might suspect I was heading to my version of the Shifting Isles now, but I didn't want to confirm anything.

If Pride found out that Lucia lived, I had little doubt he would come for her. Seeing Lucia's memories offered only one side of their story, but as with most tales, I suspected there was much more. If Pride cared for her half as much as Wrath cared for me, then he'd tear the realm apart to make sure she was safe.

And if Wrath had been correct, if Pride had never truly fallen for anyone other than his wife—and it had all been a terrible misunderstanding based on their shared pride—I could only imagine how hard he'd fight to win her back.

When I'd first encountered Pride before the Feast of the Wolf, he'd been growing slumber root and patrolling his grounds with an army none of his brothers knew about. I'd been worried he'd been plotting against Wrath, but now I wondered if he'd been training his guards for other purposes. Perhaps he'd been preparing to fight for his missing wife since she first disappeared.

Nonna had gotten one thing correct about demon princes: they stopped at nothing to get what they desired, especially when their hearts were involved. And if the one they loved most of all was potentially in danger? Then they'd unleash hell to save them.

Grumbling to himself about goddesses, Domenico stepped into the alley near our childhood home, a temple in disguise, and peered down the quiet street. He lifted his head and inhaled, scenting the air for any mortal or supernatural being. "Clear."

My own senses told me that, but I was pleased for confirmation. His ability to scent was greater than mine. "Stay here. I'll return as soon as I can. We need to be in and out as quickly as possible."

Domenico folded his arms across his chest and stared down at me. I knew he'd been tall, but he seemed to have grown over the last few days. He was broader, his muscles more defined. It must be another werewolf trait. "If your sister asks, I'm not going to lie to her."

"Which is why you don't know where I'm going." I patted his chest, and he grimaced. "Make sure no demons followed us. Or witches."

"I don't like this."

"I know. Thank you for doing it anyway."

Displeasure was written all over his face, but he didn't argue. As a shifter, his emotions were easily readable. He didn't hide his feelings like the demons did. Wolves were too close to nature for courtly games.

After what we'd been through, I understood the appeal my sister might see in them. Unlike vampires, witches, and demon princes, it was almost refreshing to know exactly where you stood with a werewolf. It wasn't the time to ask, but I needed to see what his response was.

"You met Vesta, Greed's commander."

"Your point, goddess?"

"I heard a rumor that she might have been half werewolf. If that were true and she chose to run away, would you fight for her if that's what she wished? Even if Greed were to find out she lived."

His eyes glowed that pale purple, which indicated he was close to shifting. And he was also enraged. "I would tear the throat out of anyone who threatened my family. And I don't care about demons enough to aid them in any way, especially if one of their own decided to leave."

"Are all pack members considered family?"

Domenico lifted his face and breathed deeply. "Go. We're about to have company."

I hesitated for the span of one breath. A new theory was forming, but I couldn't lose my chance at breaking the curse to follow that thread. Soon there would be no clock ticking and I'd solve this mystery once and for all.

I hurried down the alley and darted into the night, sticking to the shadows and listening for any signs of pursuit. It was late enough that most lights were out in the houses I passed. No one walked the streets, save for one or two stragglers who'd been deep in their cups. Claudia would be in bed, but she'd rouse when I knocked at the door. Or tossed a pebble at her window.

I was just rounding the corner and wondering what I'd do if her aunt Carolina was awake when I saw her slip out of the house wearing a dark hood. Carolina headed straight for a woman lingering near the opposite end of the street, wearing a similar dark robe. After their loss at House Greed, their use of cloaks didn't surprise me.

I stopped dead in my tracks and pressed closer to the nearest building. Carolina paused, and the other woman glanced around, inadvertently giving the light from the moon an opportunity to reveal her features. Nonna Maria. I wasn't surprised to see her cavorting with a dark witch. Nonna had been the witch Sursea summoned in that memory Claudia purged. The one who'd escorted Claudia here and gave her a new family. My grandmother had been working closely with the First Witch all along, and that alone ought to make me hate her.

I was…not relieved, but content to see she'd made it out of the bloodbath that occurred at House Greed. She'd wronged many, but I didn't want her to die. Regardless of anything, she still felt like my grandmother and I believed the love she'd had for us had turned real. Nonna had been tender with us, had cared for us and been there on our darkest days.

I strained to hear her voice, but the two witches must have cast a spell or set up a ward to contain their whispers. No matter how hard I tried to hear them, no sound drifted my way. I hadn't had the capacity to feel anything about Nonna's involvement with Sursea while trapped in that memory, but it would have been another crushing blow if I'd remained mortal.

Nonna never liked that Vittoria, Claudia, and I were such close friends. She'd blamed it on the fact that Claudia's family practiced the dark arts, but now I knew the truth. They'd purposely tried to keep us apart because of who we all really were.

That, at least, I understood. Keeping House Vengeance away from Claudia after we'd helped Sursea's devious plan come to life would have been a kindness to her.

How naive we'd all been, scraping together time after work to drink wine on the beach and share our hopes and dreams. We'd all cried together as many times as we'd laughed. We'd shared our broken hearts and secret longings. The three of us were sisters not all by blood, but by choice. None of us knew something far more sinister had originally bound us together.

Nonna took one last look around before she and Carolina hurried off together. Part of me wanted to follow them, see where they were going, what they might be plotting, but there was no time to waste. I lingered in the shadows for a few more minutes, just to be certain they wouldn't double back and attempt something nefarious. Using my heightened senses, I listened hard and didn't hear anyone walking close by. Wherever the witches were heading, they'd truly gone.

Quickly, I stood on the stoop and brought my fist to the door. I pounded loud enough to wake Claudia, but not loud enough for any neighbors to overhear or be startled by it. A moment later, a candle flickered to life upstairs. I subtly glanced down the street again. I didn't sense any Umbra demons and only heard the muffled sounds of mortals breathing next door as they slept.

Another moment passed, and then the bolt slid out of place and the door creaked open. My friend stood there, mouth agape as she took me in. "Emilia! Stars above, you look...are your eyes a different color?" She shook her head and stepped aside. "Come in. Your nonna said you were missing. Are you all right? Where have you been? I've been so worried. I thought whatever had been killing those witches had gotten you, too, and they just didn't want to tell me."

I stepped into her home, and she'd just shut the door when we both wrapped our arms around each other in a fierce hug. With everything that had happened, with all I'd learned and how much I'd changed, I was relieved there was still one person who genuinely cared.

Even if things weren't exactly as they seemed, our connection had been real. Possibly the only real thing in an entire realm made up of fantasy. And even that might not last if she wanted her memory back.

"I wish I could tell you everything," I said, meaning every word. "But I can't stay long. And you can't tell anyone you saw me."

"What the devil is going on, Emilia? The coven rebanded, but they won't allow anyone aside from the council to attend meetings. I tried scrying, but it's as if they've put a block on my magic. I haven't even been able to dream."

I'd almost forgotten that Claudia had been blessed by the goddess of sight and premonitions; she'd have visions we couldn't always decipher.

Having her magic blocked was a fate I knew too well, and I hated that they'd clipped her magical wings. I wondered what else they might have taken from her, what powers might be lying dormant inside her she couldn't recall. Her mother was always scheming and plotting, and it seemed she was still playing a game.

"And do you know what is most unusual?" she asked, and I shook my head. "They were able to free old Sofia Santorini's mind from its curse. My aunt was heading over to her house now to see what she remembers, if anything."

I squeezed her gently, then stepped back. At least I now knew what Carolina and Nonna were up to. "Don't trust everything the witches say. They're not necessarily bad, but they have an agenda."

"The witches?" Claudia's brows knotted together. "You speak as if you aren't one of us."

I inhaled deeply and held my hand up, summoning a burning flower, and watched my friend's expression turn from confusion to wonder. She reached for the flower and yanked her hand back from the burn, searching my face.

"Goddess above. You can't be." Her voice dropped to a whisper. "How?"

"It's a very long, twisted tale."

She stared at me, then at the burning flower for another silent moment. Awe spread across her features, and she looked ready to explode from all her questions.

"Given your fire magic and the fact you're a goddess, I imagine so." She turned and motioned for me to join her. "Let's sit."

I did my best to not rush her, trying not to focus on the ticking clock in my mind, and followed her into the tiny kitchen. She pulled open the cabinet and went about pouring us drinks from her personal collection. I noticed the herbs drying for her tonic to forget and swallowed hard. She placed my drink in front of me, then raised her brows.

"Tell me. I need to know what's going on."

"The short version is the witches put a spell-lock on me and Vittoria, containing our magic and immortality, essentially making us mortal witches. That curse you mentioned? The one with the devil? It affected several other beings. Me and Vittoria included."

Claudia pressed her hip against the countertop and tossed back her drink. "My best friends are goddesses. It's a lot to digest. I feel as if I should bow or pray." A look of horror crossed her face. "Should I set up an altar? Stars above, Em. This is strange."

Despite every dark thing in my life, I laughed. A genuine, happy sound. Her questions hadn't been laden with sarcasm, only concern. "Please do not ever pray or bow. Most especially to Vittoria. You know how insufferable she can be."

Tears shimmered in her eyes.

"Vittoria is alive?"

The hope that crossed her features brought a tightness to my chest. I nodded. "Yes. Her death was the beginning of breaking the spell-lock. She'd figured out what happened from hearing the secrets a spell book whispered to her. She orchestrated her own 'murder' to free herself and plot our revenge." I didn't want to overwhelm my friend, so I quickly moved on. "There is a dagger called the Blade of Ruination. It's the only weapon with the ability to break curses."

"Emilia, no." Claudia sucked in a sharp breath. "Hexed items come with a steep price."

"I know." I watched her carefully. "Please. I need you to activate it for me. And tell me what I need to do to use it to break the curse. Time's running out. I have less than a day."

My friend shook her head. "I... can't. I would do anything for you, you know that, but please don't ask me to do this."

"Do you not remember how?"

She gave me a sad smile. "It's something my aunt has instilled in me since I first came to live with her. I just don't think you realize what the price will be. For you."

I exhaled. "I'm willing to pay anything. Just tell me what I need to do."

Indecision warred with what I sensed was her desire to help me.

"The blade expects an equal trade," she finally said. "If you wish to break a curse, it will want to use your power to do so. All of it." Claudia bent and pulled up a travertine floor tile, removing a cloth-wrapped dagger. "The one who's cursed needs to use it. Willingly."

Dread rolled through me. "How do you mean?"

"The cursed one needs to feed the blade your magic until it collects each drop."

I stared at the dagger in her hand. It looked like a regular dagger; the steel shined in the candlelight, and the hilt was made of a dulled onyx leather. For something so powerful, it was rather unremarkable. It didn't appear to be capable of anything as diabolical as killing a prince of Hell or breaking a curse. Which was why—aside from being hidden under my friend's floor—it likely went unfound for decades.

"The price is magic for magic," I reiterated. Claudia nodded. "When you said, 'feed the blade,' you meant I must be stabbed?"

"Yes."

"And only the one who's cursed can deliver the blow?"

"Yes. Breaking a curse is a complex process." Claudia heaved a great breath. "My blood activates it, but then the rest depends on following the rules precisely. The one who is to sacrifice must do so willingly. Then the one administering the blow must also be willing to do so."

Wrath would need to willingly deliver the attack, and I doubted my husband would be easily persuaded to do so. Then there was the one thing I wasn't focusing on just yet. The part where I needed to give up *all* my power. Forever. I'd only just gotten it back, and I felt whole for the first time in what felt like an eternity. Now the gods were mocking me, forcing me to relinquish it again. Of my own free will. Without hesitation or regret.

It was one more way the First Witch would take from me, and I hated it.

"There's one more catch," Claudia said. I was incapable of being surprised at this point. This hexed object was a hideous tool created by a vengeful witch, of course there was one more unpleasant string attached. Sursea didn't operate in an easy or giving manner. I mentally prepared myself. "Once I activate it with my blood, you have only one hour to complete the rest of the power exchange. The blade only allows one opportunity for any one curse to be broken."

"How would it know?"

"After I feed it my blood, you will do the same. Then your hour begins."

Which meant I had one hour to return to the Seven Circles, decide if I was truly willing to give up my power, convince my husband to stab me, and break the curse before this opportunity was forever lost to us. Unless... blood and bones. *No.* I refused to bring Claudia back with me.

"I could go with you," she said, reading my mind and the

worry that had probably been written on my face. "Wherever you've been. I could go to make sure you have a full hour."

Claudia's earnest expression held no deception. No ulterior motives. She was simply a good friend. A decent person. Someone who was willing to help a loved one in need.

And I would never put her in a place where she might expose her true identity to herself or those who'd been seeking her. I might have conspired against her before, but that was one mistake I'd never repeat again. If giving up my power could help undo even the slightest bit of pain I'd caused by working with the First Witch, there really was no choice left to make at all.

I would right these wrongs and pay the price.

I removed the memory stone from my bodice and laid it on the table before me. Claudia's attention moved to it, her face paling.

"This memory stone contains the reason why I'll never ask you to come with me. It belongs to you. It's something you chose to purge, to forget for eternity. I'm leaving it here, if ever you want answers." I wished I could offer her more, but it would have to do. I tugged a little leather pouch from my belt and placed the stone safely inside so Claudia could decide what she wished to do without touching it. "Someone I trust very dearly told me that once you know the truth, you can never go back to the time before. Choose wisely. There is no urgency for you, no judgment."

"Do you regret it?" Claudia asked, her voice quiet, a touch sad. "Discovering the truth?"

I thought about the heartache. The deception. The many betrayals. "Life would be simpler if I didn't know. Familiar, even. But no, I wouldn't go back, given the choice. That's a decision only you can make, though. If you're happy now, content, that's all that matters."

With her attention locked onto the memory stone, she whispered, "Sometimes I dream. Of a life I think I might have lived. A man I might have loved. But it always ends in a nightmare. With him ripping out my heart. Other times it's me who tears it from my own chest. Or sometimes even his." When she finally glanced up, her expression was one of gratitude, if not relief. "Thank you for the stone, for the choice. Are you ready to activate the blade?"

I wasn't, but I had to be. I nodded. "Thank you, Claudia. For always being the truest friend I've ever had."

Her grin was full of mischief. "I'm sure we'll have plenty of trouble to get into in the future. Now give me your palm, goddess. The most important hour of your existence is about to begin."

# TWENTY-FIVE

**Wrath stared at** the legendary dagger. He'd been impressed I'd retrieved the Blade of Ruination right up until I told him what we needed to do to break the curse. Now he looked as if I'd brought a viper into his private library and placed it on his lap. He drove the dagger into the top of the desk, the force of it causing the weapon to vibrate. "No."

"It is my choice to give up my magic. I cannot imagine a better reason to do so."

The demon crossed his arms, his expression turning darker than his increasingly stormy mood. "I respect that, but not stabbing my wife is *my* choice."

We stared at each other, neither one of us backing down. Any other time, any other instance, and I'd not argue. He had every right to make his decision without interference. This was bigger than him, though. Bigger than us. And we had to act, now.

"We are running out of time and options. Quite literally. We have less than an hour to complete the activation or this option is lost. Please. Do not fight me on this. It is our best opportunity to shatter this curse, and you know that."

"And if the witches are lying, what then? Do you really believe Sursea?" He stood from his oversized desk, jabbing a finger down at the blade he refused to touch. It was likely the only dagger the general of war wouldn't wield. And ironically the one he needed to the most. Sursea had played her game well. "They have proved they lie and manipulate time and again. Where is our guarantee that if I stab you and remove all your power, you won't die? How do we know if the blade requires your magic or if they simply wish to take it for their own? We don't have enough information, and I will not risk you or your magic being given to an enemy, especially when Sursea is involved."

I pressed my lips together. I could not tell him who'd given me the information or who'd helped me. "I trust my source. And you will need to trust me."

"Trusting you isn't the issue." Wrath paced away, his hands flexing at his sides. "Your source might also be trustworthy, but there is no guarantee that their information wasn't planted. They might not be aware it's false. If I knew who you got this from, I could investigate further."

I'd already considered that Claudia's memory might have been tampered with and decided to press ahead. I glanced at the clock near the mantel. I wasn't sure how long the process of removing my magic took and didn't want to continue arguing. I loved my husband, but I would never betray my friend a second time. Claudia had a right to choose if she wished to become involved with the princes of Hell again.

I also would not put Wrath in a position to keep this secret from his brother, either. If Pride discovered that Wrath knew his wife was alive and where she could be found, that wouldn't be something easily overlooked or forgiven. With good reason.

I held my hands out, pleading. "The blade might kill me, but it also might do exactly what you, your brothers, Sursea, and my source say it does: *break curses*. When I first summoned you, you said, 'One day you'll call me Death.' You had to have known this was a possibility. And it would not have stopped you then. Do not turn soft now, demon. Not when we need your sin the most."

Wrath's gaze was pure gold fire when it clashed against mine. "Stop."

"No." I sensed the simmering rise of his sin and I sauntered over to him, eyeing him from head to toe. "When I stabbed you I *hated* it. Hated that you'd made me do something so brutal. But it was necessary. I do not want to bring only vengeance and hate to the world. I want to right a terrible wrong. It's the right thing to do, and I know you care about true justice, fair justice. Even when it's hard or personal. And then, when you are able to love me fully, you'll be free to tell me." I rolled up onto my toes and brought my lips to his ear. "Then you'll take me right here. On your desk. And *show* me."

Wrath's jaw was clenched so tightly it was a wonder he didn't crack any teeth. He drew back and stared at me with a strange mixture of emotion playing across his face, as if simultaneously memorizing my features and also desperately searching for a way out of this. But, the mighty demon of war knew I was right.

"Do you have my *cornicello*?" I asked. "And Vittoria's?"

The temperature plummeted. "Do you think my wings will tempt me?" Wrath's voice was low and dangerous as he prowled around the room. "That I'd put you at risk to get them back?"

"No. But I want to make sure when the curse breaks, we've truly succeeded. If your wings are restored, there will be physical proof it's broken." My breath came out in little white clouds as the air turned colder. Frost coated the iron chandelier above us. "We are going to get through this, Samael." A new thought crossed my mind. My husband wanted an equal, so perhaps the loss of my magic was another burden he didn't wish to bear. "Will you be all right if I don't have magic?"

He cast an incredulous look my way. "You haven't had access to your full power for twenty years, according to the way time works on the Shifting Isles, and you could cast only minimal spells as a shadow witch. Aside from my anger that they'd done that to you, and you were unable to know the truth, that didn't matter to me in the least."

"But this will be different. I'll never have that much magic or power again. Is that something you're concerned about? For your court? I'm sure there are more like Lord Makaden who would stir the pot and gossip. Call you weak. Is choosing your heart something that will bring destruction to your House?"

His anger flared as he stalked back to me. "I don't give a high holy fuck about my court, my lady. Magic does not make you powerful. Your courage. Your heart. Your mind. Your very soul makes you a force to be reckoned with. My only concern is whether you will survive. I will take you without magic. Without godsdamn royal titles. Or care for anything other than your happiness. Once restored to my full power, I'll have enough magic for both of us. Trust in that."

If only he could share it. I reached for his hand, rubbing my thumb in calming circles over his skin. "We're running out of time. Where should I stand, by the desk, or is it easier if I sit?"

He shook his head. "I'll send for the Crone. There has to be a way around this."

"We don't know where she is." I squeezed his hand gently. "And if we wait any longer, we might never have this chance again. Please. Don't keep your heart from me out of fear."

I let go of his hand and moved to the desk, yanking the Blade of Ruination from where he'd stabbed it and held it out, hilt first. "Take this." Frost kissed the wood, coated the journals on each demon House. I ignored it. The temperature didn't warm, but Wrath finally came to my side and accepted the blade. It was too soon to feel relief, but the first hurdle had been crossed. "Get the amulets and put them on. Once you're ready, we'll begin."

Silently, Wrath removed a pouch from a secret compartment near the fireplace and dumped the contents into his palm. Silver and gold glinted in the firelight. Our amulets.

I felt nothing when I looked at them. No sense of nostalgia. No warm memories of blessing them each full moon with Vittoria while Nonna guided us. I saw them for what they were: objects that had caused my husband pain and torment for years. Objects that brought confusion to my memories and Vittoria's, forcing us to remain in the dark. It was time for them to return to where they belonged. Wrath looped them over his head, jaw locked as he came back to where I waited.

He stood before me, blade in fist, and stared down. His expression was as cold as the air now. My husband was donning that mask again, becoming the king his realm needed, even beyond his court. He was becoming the partner *I* needed.

We'd been through hell and back, quite literally, and this would set our world right. I held my own emotions in check, refusing to show one second of doubt. If he sensed any trepidation, he would damn us for eternity.

Wrath's attention finally dropped to my bodice. It was a simple, rose-gold gown with lavender, pale blue, and green flowers embroidered onto it. After I'd returned from Claudia, I'd quickly changed. I didn't want any trace of where I'd been remaining, and I hadn't put much thought into what I'd grabbed from the wardrobe.

Now I realized my mistake in wearing the pale pink instead of black. My husband would see me bleed as he twisted the dagger. Just as I'd watched his white shirt turn red when I'd stabbed him. It was not the sort of favor I wished to return.

With nimble fingers, I unlaced the front of my dress, pulling the top slightly apart—just enough to expose the bare skin over my heart. I held his gaze, pouring all the love and emotion I felt for him into it. I imagined how it felt to kiss him, how incredible it was to make love to him and feel him joined to me as if we were one.

Hate and fear and vengeance had torn us apart. And love would heal us.

Nonna Maria once told me to follow my heart, and even though she'd lied before—even though I no longer *had* a mortal heart—I felt the truth of that now. Love was the most powerful magic. No matter how many twists and bumps I'd encountered along the way, I'd finally found my home. And no one, no curse, no force in this realm or the next would take it away from me again.

"I love you."

Wrath couldn't say it back, but the iciness left his features. He brought his mouth down on mine, his kiss passionate and full of longing. He'd felt the emotions I'd fed to him, knew I wanted to do this with every fiber of my cursed soul. I kissed him as fiercely, as freely. His tongue demanded entry, and as my lips parted, I felt the sting of metal pushing into my chest. Wrath bit down on my lip, distracting me from the pain as the Blade of Ruination sank deeper.

"*Incipio.*" Wrath spoke the activation spell against my lips as I cried out, the sound swallowed as my husband kissed me again with desperate fervor. As if the connection of our lips and tongues would tether me to him. Would prevent me from fading into Death's realm.

As soon as Wrath activated the spell, my magic flared up, sensing a new master taking control. The Blade of Ruination. My power wanted no part of it; it did not wish to obey a new master. A raging inferno was being ripped from me, and it fought against the blade's pull, but I'd given my power freely, willingly. And it could not overcome the summoning.

I screamed as my body burned and the blade heated. The metal seared inside me, and I'd never known such intense torture as I did in that moment. Wrath's mouth moved across my jaw to my temple, his arms wrapped around me as if he could tear the pain away.

"Shh." He pressed a kiss to my temple. "It's all right. It'll be over soon."

I tried to focus on his featherlight kisses, tried to hold on to the little bit of light he offered. But it was no use. Pain rose up and crashed down, dragging me with it. This was worse than when Vittoria removed my mortal heart. There was no end and no sense of time as the blade continued to tear my magic from me.

Rose-gold fire exploded between us, the blade hungrily lapping up the flames before they could touch Wrath. I squeezed my eyes shut, teeth clenched, as the heat grew to unbearable temperatures. Sweat dotted my brow, dripped down my chest, sizzled against the blade.

Tears streamed down my face, dampening Wrath's fingers that still clenched tightly around the Blade of Ruination's hilt. My instinct to survive, to retain my power, made me want to fight back. It took effort I didn't know I possessed to lock my arms at my sides, to will my magic away. The tortuous magical transfer went on for several long minutes that felt like hours.

A hole in my center grew, and where power once welled up, it was slowly being replaced with nothing. My body grew weaker with each ounce of magic that left me, the instinct to fight draining from my tensed body. My screams slowed as my knees shook, and suddenly the dagger was yanked free. It clattered onto the floor as Wrath scooped me up and cradled me against his chest. His heart hammered a frantic beat, the rhythm keeping my own blood pounding.

I hadn't died, but it felt like some not-so-small part of me had. A sob wrenched free, and I couldn't tell if it was relief for what we'd done or grief at what I'd lost. Perhaps it was both. My eyes squeezed shut as if that would prevent the tears from continuing to fall.

Wrath held me tighter, rocking me for several long minutes, until the overwhelming sense of loss receded a bit. I didn't want him to regret our choice and struggled to pull myself together.

Heat continued to surround us, and I finally managed to crack open an eye. Beautiful burning wings of flame extended from behind Wrath. Silver-tipped and fierce. Another tear slid along my cheek. Not from sadness or grief this time, but from witnessing divine glory so close. Vittoria and I were goddesses from the underworld, but Wrath was true divinity, and I was overcome by the force of love that radiated around him.

That sense of great loss, that grief of giving up my magic, it didn't disappear, but I allowed that feeling of awe to cleanse my sadness. To remind me of all I'd gained. All *we'd* gained. The curse was truly broken. This part of our nightmare was over.

As above, so below. Together we'd achieved balance. We won. And yet...

"They're incredible," I whispered, blinking as the wings grew impossibly larger. I'd never seen anything as stunning and deadly in all my life. Even when we'd known each other before, Wrath had never shown me his wings. They were a weapon he'd kept hidden. "*You're* incredible."

Wrath held me tighter, his chin now resting on my head. Tension hadn't yet left his body—if anything, he was coiled tighter than before.

He also hadn't uttered a single word since we broke the curse.

A bead of sweat rolled from my hairline down my neck, and I shivered. Wrath shook slightly, burying his face in my hair, and I realized it wasn't sweat, but tears. I mustered enough energy to wrap my arms around him, holding him as he wept.

"We're all right," I croaked. "It's all right. It's over."

His mighty wings flapped, and within the flames of the inner feathers there were a thousand tiny gold flecks. My focus slid from the gold flecks to the silver tips. The colors of each of our amulets were aspects of his wings. I'd always wondered about that. Once, I'd thought it meant one was blessed by the sun goddess and the other by the moon goddess. How wrong I'd been.

Wrath inhaled once, then exhaled slowly. He pressed his lips to my forehead and placed me on my feet. I couldn't stop staring at the fiery wings. They reminded me of my magic, but there was not a sense of familiarity to them. This was his magic through and through, and yet I was drawn to them like a moth to a flame. I went to touch a feather but drew my hand back and gave Wrath a sheepish look. "I forgot fire will likely burn me now."

Sadness crashed into me again as I inadvertently sought my magic. A rift in my center split further at the emptiness that was there; it was the place where Source once curled up, waiting for me to tap into it. Now there was nothing. It felt as if I'd lost a limb—my body still reached for it, confused when it grasped nothing at all. I blinked until I was able to control any tears from falling. Despite my loss, I *was* happy I broke the curse. I wanted redemption for the role I'd played as a vengeance goddess. But even through the good, I still mourned my loss. Felt it acutely. I'd never again know what it was like to wield fire magic.

"Touch them." Wrath watched me closely, sensing my mood. "I am able to control my wings. And even if I wasn't, you're my wife. They will not burn you; they'll simply feel warm."

Tentatively I reached out, curling my fingers through the magical feathers of flame. Wrath was right—it didn't burn. It was similar to placing a hand in a warm patch of sunlight, soaking in the rays. Or running my fingers through the water of a summer sea.

This, at least, was like my magic. Comforting, yet capable of massive destruction. Even though the power wasn't mine, it felt like some small part of me carried on in him.

"The wings depicted in your throne room are ebony," I said. "I didn't expect to see these."

"I'd had the stained glass changed to what I'd last seen."

I thought of the scene I'd witnessed from Sursea's memory

stone—of how the wings had turned the color of ash when she'd drained away his magic. I was glad we'd won. That we'd defeated someone so driven by hate through the power of our love.

My lips tugged upward as I stroked another feather and the flames teasingly fluttered against my skin. I dragged another finger along the outer edge of his wing, and the same sensation rolled down my back. My attention shot to my husband, immediately noting the devious expression he wore.

"What was that?" I asked as heat slid down my spine, similar to a feather lightly caressing me. My skin tingled pleasantly for another few seconds where the magical feather had touched.

"I might have forgotten to mention an ability I'd lost when my fire magic was taken."

Another feather of honeyed heat meandered along my neck, gliding across my collarbone before descending to lovingly stroke the wound the Blade of Ruination caused.

The feather slowly spread outward, tracing circles along my breast. Any lingering hollowness or grief dissipated as the flicker of heat rolled across the tight bud, causing a new warmth to unfurl from my belly downward.

"Devil curse me." My fingers dug into Wrath's shoulders as that wicked bead of delight moved to my hips, then curled around my inner thighs.

"I'd rather not, my lady. I've had enough of curses." Wrath's chuckle was deep and sensual as that feather fluttered against my thigh and I swore under my breath. "Lust isn't the only one who can manifest desire. Only this isn't yours." He nipped at my earlobe before kissing the sting away. "It's *mine*."

What had begun as a gentle, featherlike feeling turned into a finger of heat. Wrath grinned as he walked us back toward a shelf of books, slowly pinning my arms above my head. His glorious wings spread wide, covering us in our own private, fiery blanket of white-hot passion.

He bent until his lips brushed my ear. "Would you like to see what sinful things I can do with them, my lady?"

# TWENTY-SIX

**Heat pulsed between** my thighs. Wrath's magic was as soft as velvet as it gently stroked me, waiting for an answer. Taking a dagger to the chest rapidly faded from my mind, thanks in part to the quick healing of my immortality and the exquisite caresses from my prince. Instead of dwelling on the loss of my magic, I focused on my husband and the wicked gleam in his eyes, the seductive privacy his curtain of wings provided, and all the things we could do right here.

My attention dropped to his full lips while I vividly imagined the interesting places we might make love, the positions. Losing my magic hurt deeply, but suddenly picturing Wrath and me joining high above our realm, among the moon and stars, took *some* of the sting away.

If I searched hard enough, I would still find magic in everyday things. And making love to the king of demons among the stars was hardly average. The curse was broken, and there were no limits to what we could achieve together. I eyed the manacles hanging from the ceiling in the alcove, and new, devious thoughts flooded in.

"I can't tell exactly what you're thinking, but I can sense what you're feeling now." He kissed up the column of my throat, and my eyes fluttered shut. Wrath knew exactly where to touch to drive me wild with need. "If you want me, say the words, my lady." He traced the bare flesh along my bodice, his caress a seduction of its own. "My queen." He dipped his head, and where his clever fingers had just touched, he now used his tongue. "My love."

His mouth closed over my breast, and my breath caught from his words and the way he drew on my flesh, sucking and teasing over my clothing.

"I want you, Samael."

I'd only just finished whispering my consent when Wrath's heated magic unleashed itself. That soft, decadent, featherlike stroking moved across my sex, teasing my flesh until I chased the sensation building inside me. Another feather of heat licked my breasts, replacing Wrath's mouth as my husband leisurely kissed me.

With my hands still pinned above my head and Wrath's tongue in my mouth, his magic caressed me everywhere at once. Pleasure rocketed through me, electrifying each nerve as the demon intensified his magic, feeding more of his power to those phantom fingers of ecstasy.

Wrath had called himself His Royal Highness of Undeniable Desire, and I'd thought I'd tasted that level of seduction before. But nothing, *nothing*, compared with this.

Not Lust's magic or Greed's. Gluttony's sinful party and witnessing couples lost in the throes of pure rapture—none of it held a candle to the magnitude of Wrath's... love.

It wasn't simply the magic he was using to enhance my pleasure, nor was it the immense power he had. It was the attention and care he used, the unending desire to please me, to satisfy the person he loved in every way imaginable, that heightened the experience. Wrath's desire to show his love for me far outweighed any baser wanting of my body. He wanted that, too, but it was my heart he yearned for above all else. My mind and my soul. Just as I wanted his.

Wrath's magic slipped inside me, the sensation a glorious mixture of hot kisses and deep thrusts that filled and stretched me, perfectly synchronized to each flick of his tongue against mine. All the while that magic heat lathed my breasts until they grew heavy with need. Wrath kissed me harder, grinding his hips against mine, his erection hitting all the right places. I writhed against him, searching for release.

"Wrath."

I didn't have to elaborate. In a thrilling motion, my husband banded an arm around me and flew us the short distance to his desk. With one wing, he cleared journals and pots of ink from the surface before laying me down on it. A beat later, his trousers were off, and he towered above me, looking like a brutally handsome god. The demon prince didn't rip off my gown like his expression hinted he wished to; he slid it up my body as he moved over me.

He drank in each inch of my skin as if it were all he needed in life. A flash of something unreadable crossed his features, but he crushed whatever doubt or worry he'd felt.

When he pressed the blunt head of his erection to my entrance and slowly pushed in, he brought his mouth close to mine and whispered, "I love you."

Tears pricked my eyes. I held him tightly, committing this

moment to memory. Even though he'd shown me he loved me, hearing it...it made the bad parts we'd endured somehow more bearable. The last time he'd said those fateful words, I'd immediately forgotten them.

"I love you." I cupped his face and kissed him chastely, savoring the bliss of the moment as we fully joined. Wrath pulled back, his gaze locked onto mine. For a moment, he didn't move. His fists were planted on either side of me, hard against the desk, his body just as tense.

He was bracing himself for the curse to exact its revenge once again. To wrench me away, except this time it would be for an eternity.

*Devil curse, Sursea.* I'd be damned if I would allow her to ruin this moment. I did not give up my magic to see the haunted look in his eyes, the flicker of uncertainty when he finally admitted how he felt and didn't dull his emotions with a tonic. Nor would I allow any doubts to surface each time he said those three cherished words.

I rocked my hips upward, drawing him to the present, and drawing him deeper inside me. We were here. Together. And nothing would change that. Unless we decided to murder each other, he was *mine.* And I was his. For eternity.

"Please say that again." I ran my hands up and down his arms, soothing, pleading. His wings flared out to either side like weapons, the heat making the air around us shimmer. Wrath, the king of demons, afraid of nothing—except losing me—hesitated. "I'm still here. We're all right."

He traced my features with his gaze. "I love you."

"I love you, too. Demon." I reached over and stroked a warm feather, marveling at the full body tingles I suddenly felt. I stopped playing with his wings and pulled him in for a long kiss. It took only a moment for him to respond, his mouth moving over mine hungrily. Thank the goddess his mind was finally on more pleasant things. "Now that that's settled, show me all your new tricks. I want you to take me on every surface and every damn wall in this chamber."

The last vestiges of stress left him and were quickly replaced by a roguish glint in his eyes. "Let's try half the surfaces for now, my love. Even with your immortal body, I doubt you can handle the full might of my... power."

Cocky prince of Hell. I thrusted upward, earning a surprised curse from the demon followed by a groan of pleasure as I repeated the motion. "Try me, demon."

"Remember, I warned you, wife."

The demon's wings glowed a brilliant silver as he brought them around us. The magical heat returned and moved down my body like warmed honey, sliding around where Wrath and I were already joined. The heat pulsed there for a minute, strumming my body until it hummed with need. Then my husband began waging the best sort of war on me—he slowly pulled out and thrusted in, the magical heat tingling so intensely I came before he'd even truly begun.

"Fuck," I swore. Repeatedly. The only words or coherent thought I was capable of.

Wrath's low chuckle, combined with his continued deep thrusts, had me writhing up from the desk, my back arched high as my body exploded from the sensation again and again.

"Pace yourself, my love," he said. "We haven't even left the desk yet."

"I hate you," I cried out, the sound proving I felt the very opposite as it quickly devolved to a moan of pleasure. "I hate you in the darkest of ways."

"You've told me that before." Wrath tugged my bodice apart and nuzzled against my heart before turning his attention to my heaving breasts. "Let's see how badly you hate me now."

My husband unleashed himself and his magic, and soon he didn't even need his wings to bring us both to soaring heights. We came together, murmuring the words that had been stolen from us, over and over until we flew higher and plummeted over the edge once, twice, then half a dozen times more.

# TWENTY-SEVEN

**Wrath squeezed every** drop of moisture from the linen cloth, dripping soapy water and bubbles down the front of my body. I leaned against his chest and closed my eyes, enjoying the first pure bit of relaxation we'd ever experienced.

After we'd accomplished making love on top of only *two* surfaces in his private library, much to the demon's vast amusement, he magicked us to his bathing chamber for a refreshing soak. His wings were tucked away, but I swore I still felt the phantom heat lingering around us.

Nestled between his powerful legs, my head resting in the crook of his shoulder while he leisurely dragged the linen over my body, I released the remaining tension I'd been carrying for the last few months. There were still matters to be dealt with—what to do with the First Witch, as well as clearing my sister's name. Proving that Vesta was alive and well and left of her own free will and that my twin had nothing to do with her "murder." And whatever trouble the Star Witches might still be plotting. I hoped that my show of magic was enough to keep them in the Shifting Isles for a while. And as for the vampires, after Wrath's brutal display, I believed they'd remain in their region and rethink any notion of war.

But for now, with the curse finally broken, we had a moment to simply breathe, to enjoy each other's company without anyone interfering or any clocks ticking down our time together. I'd like nothing more than to put off dealing with those final pieces for a month.

Sleep tugged at me, and I gave in to the alluring pull of dreams. It had been a long, exhausting haul. I'd gone from removing the threat of the witches as they invaded Greed's circle to attending a celebratory ball to the Well of Memory; from there I'd threatened Sursea, visited Claudia to retrieve the dagger, and broken the curse.

Resting never felt so good.

"We should send invitations out within the hour." Wrath's deep voice startled me awake. "For the coronation. We'll want to crown you by nightfall, if possible. With the curse broken, and your magic gone, it is a prime time for someone to attack."

And just like that, the serenity was gone. I twisted in his arms. "Remind me to not make the mistake of thinking a bath with you will *ever* be peaceful. First the Blade of Ruination speech, now this." I smiled as I shook my head. "It's a good thing I love you, or I'd wish to hold your head under water for a few seconds."

He kissed the tip of my nose. "At least you didn't say a few minutes. That shows progress, my lady."

"Perhaps I simply enjoy certain parts of you too much to give them up for good."

He splashed water at me. "I'll make sure those parts tend

to your needs daily, lest I find myself on the wrong end of your blade."

"Smart demon." I lovingly patted his cheek. Seriousness replaced the levity. "Who do you believe will attack? The witches?"

"Sursea is in captivity, but I doubt her location has remained a secret. The coven could be planning something as they rebanded. They already staged an attack on House Greed. Without the fear of your magic, they might strike here next."

"To free Sursea."

Wrath nodded, a grim expression on his face. "If they timed it perfectly, and somehow managed to slip past my defenses, they could break her free while we're at the coronation."

"It would be an ideal distraction. A good opportunity. But would they really try something again so soon after they'd lost so many?"

"I would think they'd be smart enough to leave well enough alone, especially after taking such a large blow to their forces, but one can never be too sure."

I studied my husband. "Even if it's unlikely, you're still planning on the attack happening."

"If presented with an enticing opportunity, most do not pass it up. Even if they believe it's a trap. There's always a chance it isn't. Or that they still have a higher rate for success."

"Which would be true. As we'd both be occupied."

"Not just occupied. The coronation will take place in the Sin Corridor, in front of each of my brothers."

It wasn't fear that made my stomach twist, but unease. "They could attack each House of Sin while all the princes are gone."

"Or they could focus on the Sin Corridor."

And if they managed to free Sursea, they wouldn't need to

worry about the numbers they lost. They were undoubtedly craving vengeance, and they could potentially destroy every demon prince and at least one goddess if they took a chance. I didn't like it, even with the combined power of the seven princes of Hell, it seemed too great a risk.

"Why not have the ceremony here?" I asked.

"The crowning of a prince or princess consort would take place in the House of Sin they'd rule over. But to be crowned queen, the ceremony must take place in the corridor. It shows you will rule fairly and justly over each House of Sin, should any prince request assistance. It hasn't happened; my brothers are more than capable of tending to their circles, but the law remains in place."

There was a slight twinkle of excitement in Wrath's gaze, reminding me of our fight with the werewolves. My husband was a delightful heathen. He wasn't nervous about a potential attack; he anticipated it. Outmaneuvering his enemies was a challenge, an opportunity to create a strategy and use his sin. And if I knew anything about my husband, he'd already had a plan in place.

"If they believe the First Witch is here, they'll strike. So you're going to move Sursea." I eyed him speculatively. "Instead of banishing her like you'd bargained for, you're going to send her to House Pride, aren't you?"

Admiration glinted in his eyes. "My brother was only too willing to oblige my request. Sursea never agreed to *when* she'd be banished. Only that she would be. After what she did to corrupt his marriage and steal his wife, he's been waiting for an opportunity like this."

The memory of Claudia when she was still Lucia flitted across my mind. I shifted to the other side of the tub to face the demon. "Does your brother still love her?"

"Lucia?" Wrath asked. I nodded. He pulled my leg onto his lap and began rubbing the soles of my feet, thinking. "Only he can answer that. I know he's never stopped searching for her. He believes she's alive somewhere. That perhaps her mother put a spell-lock on her, too." His attention dropped to my chest, where my mortal heart had been. "Now that you and Vittoria are restored, he's more determined than ever to find Lucia and see if his theory is correct."

"But did he ever love her, or was it his pride and ego that made him covet her? I imagine she would have been quite the conquest as the daughter of the First Witch. The one witch who was supposed to lead others to guard the realm and keep princes of Hell in line."

Wrath leaned back, his expression thoughtful. "My brother was and is still widely known for his dalliances. Mostly because it is an image he wants to project. He'd never once proposed to any of his lovers. Nor has he ever so much as spent more than one night with anyone since Lucia."

"You're certain he never slept with Vittoria?" I asked, thinking of our previous conversation.

Wrath's mouth lifted on one side. "Your sister is the only other being that matches him in a lot of ways, which was why her betrayal hit him so deeply. But I still don't believe they ever consummated that relationship. By then, he'd already been trying to work on issues in his marriage, but Lucia distanced herself. Personally? I think she loved him as much as he loved her, but they might have been too dissimilar for it to last. If things were different, if he'd met Vittoria first." He lifted a shoulder and dropped it. "I do know none of that matters until he finds out what happened to Lucia. Regardless of what anyone may think, Pride is loyal."

"If Lucia asked him to stop having dalliances, do you think he would have?"

Wrath considered that for a minute. "At that time, I believe he already had stopped. And if he hadn't, he would have done anything she asked of him. At his court, dalliances are not scandalous or looked down upon the same way they are in the mortal realm. If that was what made her unhappy, he likely wouldn't have even considered it a possibility. Not out of callousness, but ignorance."

I looked my prince over closely. "Is that how you feel about taking lovers?"

He gave me a slow, devilish grin. "No, my lady. I'm quite satisfied with my wife."

"Good answer, husband." I thought back to my friend's memory, how troubled she'd been by her decision to leave without writing a note. "You believe Lucia was murdered?"

"I never found a trace of her when I looked. And when the new murders began, I thought perhaps one of Pride's enemies had found her." He lifted a shoulder. "After finding you again, I believe she may be alive and well. Pride had searched for witches with the strongest bloodlines matching hers, the ones with the most goddess magic, but he hasn't located any direct descendants. He has a chamber dedicated to grimoires and witch history. He'd hoped if he'd found the right bloodline, he'd work backward until he found Lucia."

Wrath continued to massage my feet, and my mind drifted through the tangle of lies, deceptions, and schemes everyone had been involved with, both together and separately. No wonder it had been hard to unravel. When Vittoria had said the devil was looking for a bride, that had been true. Just as breaking the curse did, in a twisted way, involve the devil marrying within a certain time frame. In this realm Wrath had only six years, six months, and six days before all was lost, while nearly twenty years had passed on the Shifting Isles.

Our bond and my subsequent sacrifice because of it *did* break the curse. However, the murders of the witches unfortunately tangled with Pride's quest to find Lucia—he had been seeking women descended from Star Witches, in the hopes of finding his former wife.

Unbeknownst to him, Vittoria sought the Star Witches, too, but for her own gain—she hunted them down because their matriarchs had spell-locked us long ago.

And Wrath had investigated each of those murders to see who was killing anyone that was potentially related to Lucia. I recalled the night I summoned Pride—unlike when I'd summoned Wrath, Pride had been unable to appear.

Wrath's hand slid up to my calf and he squeezed gently. "What are you thinking now?"

"I finally understand why you were trying to stop the murders," I admitted. "The curse took your wings, but it locked Pride in the Seven Circles, correct?"

"Yes. When it went into effect, it took something from each prince. Pride lost his ability to travel outside our realm, hindering his attempt to locate Lucia."

Knowing what I did now about the night Pride's wife left, that had to be terrible. Rushing home after Wrath nearly destroyed his brothers, only to find his wife gone without a trace. Then to be locked in the Seven Circles without any way to search for her… it was another form of hell. Especially if he truly hadn't done the things Lucia believed he had. It was tragic for both of them.

"And your other brothers? What did they lose?"

Wrath shook his head. "They've never spoken to me about it."

"That's peculiar, isn't it?"

"Not really. To admit to losing something, even a small amount of power, would signal vulnerability. They would not risk their courts. I only knew what Pride lost because he understood how it felt when I lost you. He set his sin aside in the hopes if I found you, Lucia wouldn't be far behind."

Now that the curse was no longer an issue, I wished I could set everything right, but some choices weren't mine to make. Claudia had made her decision before the curse was activated. And while Vittoria and I had played a terrible game House Vengeance had been contracted for, my friend had realized she wasn't happy *before* our scheme. Cracks had appeared in her relationship long before her mother broke them apart. Sometimes loving someone was shown by letting them go, not clutching them closer. Though I couldn't help but wonder what the ending of their story might have been if they'd just talked.

"Are you all right?" Wrath pulled me across the tub and hoisted me onto his lap. "Is it the loss of your magic?"

"A little." I rubbed his shoulders, noting that, unlike me, he was no longer tense. "I also want to help your brothers. I hate that the mess is only partly cleaned. There's much left to do."

Wrath brushed his knuckles against my jaw. "You have helped them."

"I know breaking the curse has helped to some extent, but the rest is up to them, isn't it?"

"Standing back so someone can walk the rest of their path alone is often the most difficult part, especially when you care." Wrath leaned forward, pressing a tender kiss to my heart. When he looked at me again, his expression was contemplative. "Do you *want* to become queen?"

His question caught me off guard. I thought it over.

"I want to stand beside you. And while there are some unappealing aspects of ruling, shouldering the burden, becoming a united force, it's something I do want." I smiled sadly. "I may not wield the magic of Fury anymore, but I still rule over it. I am happy to join your House. It feels right."

Wrath didn't say anything for a moment; he simply studied me in that intense way that indicated he was seeing far more than I wished to share.

My attention dropped to that pale ink on his collarbone, *Acta non verba*. He might not believe I wanted to be queen, but perhaps I might show him otherwise. My lips curved. "Do we need to send the invitations this moment, or do we have a little more time?"

Wrath's gaze turned molten as he sensed my true question. He hardened beneath me, devious demon. "What did you have in mind, my lady?"

"As if you don't already know." I guided him into me, laughing as he cursed softly, and rode him until we both swore the old gods and new.

Coronation of Lady Emilia,
Goddess of Fury,
princess of House Wrath

*By Command of the King*

You are directed to attend
the ceremony of
Her Majesty Queen Emilia
this evening in the Sin Corridor.

*Do not be late.*

# TWENTY-EIGHT

**"I'll take over** from here." For a moment, Pride's mask of a proud, debauched royal slipped, revealing the calculating demon hidden underneath the courtly charm. Gone were most traces of his sin; the magic and ego were shed as easily as one removed a winter coat. The demon with us in this room had earned the scar that cut through his lip, and he seemed proud of it.

Anir stepped aside as requested but didn't leave his post beside Sursea. Wrath hadn't given the order, and Anir's loyalty to his king and court was unmatched. I stood next to my husband, watching Pride slowly take in the frigid cell where the First Witch was kept.

Before his arrival, Wrath had told me this was the first time the Prince of Pride had encountered his mother-in-law since his wife's disappearance. Now, the mood in the subterranean dungeon was tense—as if a match had been lit near an open container of kerosene, an inferno of death ready to ignite at any moment.

Pride's one request was for no one to speak of what occurred in this chamber tonight. His attention finally landed on Sursea and remained there, cold and fathomless.

Had she not still been frozen, he might have unleashed the monster I sensed prowling under his skin, scratching to get out. He had no audience, save for us and a handful of his closest guards. No courtiers to show off for. No lords or ladies to witness him indulging in a different sin. That was exactly why he'd requested silence from everyone in attendance here. Pride was going to give in to his anger, his wrath.

Pride rolled his shirtsleeves past his elbows and cocked his head to one side, his expression turning thunderous, savage, the longer he stared at the frozen witch. His hand flexed, ready to strike out if Sursea showed any signs of life. His jaw hardened as he flicked his attention to the guards still flanking the witch. They stared straight ahead, but their hands tightened on their weapons.

"Honestly, *you* called *me* here," Pride said, annoyed as he turned to Wrath. "Are you going to let me take the prisoner or must I kiss your ass and beg?"

Wrath held his brother's gaze for a long moment, then inclined his head. "Don't forget your ultimate goal. Sursea will do her best to force your hand, should you thaw her."

"Any other words of wisdom, dear brother?"

"Your pride fucked you royally before. Keep that in mind for whatever game you play next. Figure out what truly matters, and plan your attack accordingly."

Wrath jerked his chin, dismissing both his brother and the guards waiting in the shadows. Demons wearing the colors of House Pride stepped into the cell, sharp ice picks in hand. They'd come prepared to carry away the frozen statue that was our biggest enemy. Good. Having her out of our House and under someone else's care was a relief. If I never saw her again, it would be too soon. With any luck, they'd keep her frozen for eternity.

Wrath held his arm out to me before facing his brother. "You have two hours before the coronation begins. I don't suggest arriving late."

I stood before the massive floor-length mirror in my newly appointed dressing room, twisting to better admire the coronation gown the royal dressmaker had created. It was not simply a garment, but a masterpiece. Instead of paints and brushes, the dressmaker's medium was tulle, thin gold chains, faceted onyx beads, and sparkling diamonds. It was as heavy as armor, but there was a delicateness to it that leather and chain mail could not hope to possess.

My fingers trailed over the detailed work. In the design, bits of each House of Sin were represented, plus an ode to my affinity for flowers. It was the perfect marriage of the demons and me, signaling my unbiased rule over all seven courts. Eight if everything went according to plan. I glanced to the clock on the little side table, then to the arched window. Twilight was the normal state of this realm, but the sky had darkened. Night had fully arrived.

Fauna bustled into the room, tears glistening in her eyes when she saw me. She stopped short and pressed a hand to her mouth. "You look like the goddess you are, Lady Emilia."

I stopped fretting and pulled her in for a hug. "Thank you for coming."

"Of course, my lady." Fauna squeezed me once more before stepping back and dabbing at the corners of her eyes. "What did you need?"

I strode over to the small table covered in jewels—all options left for me to choose from for tonight—and pulled out the sealed letter I'd hidden there. "Will you deliver this to my sister?"

Fauna's attention flew to the wax seal. A downward dagger with burning flowers. The symbol of House Vengeance. A similar tattoo marked my husband's leg, his way of never forgetting the eighth House of Sin that had upended his world in more ways than one.

Instead of looking fearful as I'd been worrying over, Fauna's lips quirked up on one side. It was easy to forget she was part of this House for a reason. War and battle and inspiring anger didn't make her anxious in the least. She thrived on it. "Princes Envy, Greed, and Pride are going to have quite a surprise this evening."

I released a nervous laugh. "Wrath, too."

Fauna's grin widened. "You two are well matched, indeed. His majesty is lucky to have found you again. And that you were willing to put up with him for eternity."

"Fauna! Did you just mock your king?" I feigned shock. "If I didn't already like you, that would have sealed our friendship." A friendship that I realized I'd been failing spectacularly. "How are things progressing with Anir?"

She suddenly found the clock to be fascinating. "I really must be going if I'm to deliver this invitation and arrive to the coronation on time. His majesty clearly stated to not be late."

Curiosity gnawed at me, but I didn't press the issue. When we both had more time, I'd sit down and have a proper conversation with her and catch up. I hated that things had been so chaotic and that we hadn't had much time to simply enjoy each other's company. My friend looked like she needed to chat and sort through the emotions playing over her features. I vowed it would be one of my first personal orders of business as the new queen—making time for her.

"Thank you, Lady Fauna. I'll see you at the Sin Corridor soon."

Fauna dropped a small curtsy and hurried from the chamber, leaving me alone once more. I returned to the table full of precious stones and jewels, my attention snagging on a ring. Rose-gold vines with thorns made up the band and wove around a large lavender stone.

"I had that one made."

I stiffened at the unexpected sound of my husband's voice, turning to see him enter the chamber. My breath caught as I drank him in.

On his head sat a simple pale gold crown. He wore black accented in gold, as were the colors of his court, but he also had rose-gold flowers sewn onto one of his lapels. It gave the appearance of wearing a royal sash—complete with a serpent pin.

His trousers were fitted to his frame expertly, and if we didn't have some place to be, I'd wish to show him how much I appreciated how handsome he looked in his finery.

A grin spread across his face. "Later, my love. I promise, nothing will keep me from admiring every detail of your gown. And everything beneath it."

I gave him a coy smile. "There is nothing beneath it, my king."

"Emilia." He closed his eyes as if trying to banish the image and fight the urge to take me right there.

"Come on." I threaded my arm through his. "Some ornery demon proclaimed no one was to arrive late."

"I ought to murder that idiot."

"Please don't. I'm rather fond of him." I kissed his cheek.

Wrath and I somehow managed to keep from ravishing each other long enough to get to the front entrance, where a surprise was waiting. I dropped my husband's arm and grabbed my skirts, rushing over to the beautiful lavender mare. "Tanzie! Sweet baby."

I rubbed my horse's mane, admiring the flowers someone had threaded in. Tanzie loved being pampered and toed the ground as I cooed over her. I glanced over at my husband, who wore an openly amused look. "Gluttony had been certain you'd remember her, even with the spell-lock. You used to ride—"

"I used to sneak onto his grounds and ride her until he'd set baby ice dragons after us." I laughed at the memory. "I forgot how much I loved to annoy him."

"He missed you." Wrath whistled, then turned back to me. "He didn't care what your House had been contracted to do. Gluttony always placed the blame on Sursea, rightfully so."

"We could have denied her request."

"No, you couldn't have." Wrath shook his head. "You are a goddess of vengeance. Just as I am a prince of wrath."

Before we could argue the point, the ground shook. Again. Footsteps. Massive, thunderous footsteps rumbled close by. I tensed, my hand twitching toward the blade I'd hidden under my gown. From the snowbank to our right emerged one of Wrath's hellhounds. The three-headed dog ambled over to its master, tail wagging as Wrath scrubbed behind each of its ears.

I looked between my horse and his hound and shook my head. Of course my husband would show up to my coronation riding a giant hellhound. I could imagine the look of jealousy on Envy's face and had to stifle another chuckle.

"Are you ready, my queen?"

Anir and Fauna exited the castle, both dressed impeccably. Fauna gave me a subtle nod, letting me know the invitation—and request—had been delivered. I exhaled. With any luck, my sister would do exactly as I'd asked.

After Pride had taken Sursea and I'd had some time to myself, I'd thought a lot about my last conversation with Domenico. And my sister. I was almost entirely certain I'd finally fit all the pieces together surrounding the mystery of Vesta. Tonight, I'd share my discovery in front of each demon prince. Even if the witches didn't attack, there was sure to still be *some* excitement aside from the coronation.

I looked to my husband, allowing his presence to soothe me. "I am ready."

I accepted Wrath's help up onto my horse—the gown was beautiful but didn't allow me to swing my legs up. A detail I'd speak to the dressmaker about for future garments.

Two ebony hell horses trotted over to Anir and Fauna, and once they were settled and Wrath climbed onto his hound, we slowly marched toward the Sin Corridor. When we reached the base of it and started up the sharp incline, I felt the not-so-subtle prodding of each sin.

The trek through the mountain, then up the snow-covered pass, went by surprisingly quickly, though trepidation wound through me with each step the horses and hound took. A lot depended on whether my sister showed up. I was nervous to see if my theory was correct. And if it was, how Greed would react to me revealing the role he'd played.

Wrath shot a look of concern my way a few times but would hopefully believe my nerves were solely for being crowned in front of his brothers. He had enough on his mind with any potential witch attacks, and I didn't want to distract him from his own mission.

Hopefully, all would go according to plan.

Our procession reached the top of an incline, and I immediately recognized the goddess tree, though it had shifted locations as Envy had claimed it would. I sensed the Sisters Seven lingering nearby. Celestia also hadn't come to collect her spell book yet, and I silently prayed she didn't choose this moment to want it back. Things would be tense enough if my sister showed up and followed my instructions.

"My lady?" Wrath nudged his hound close to Tanzie, who snuffed the hell beast.

"I'm ready."

Wrath eyed me speculatively but didn't press. His suspicion flickered over me and I flashed him a look I hoped comforted him. The six princes were already in attendance, waiting stoically for our arrival. Wrath helped me dismount, and the moment my feet touched the ground, the princes lined up, three to each side, forming an aisle for us to walk through.

Someone had created a small dais just large enough for Wrath and me to stand on. Behind it, in the distance, were the gates of hell, towering like two pillars of fear. My attention roved over the snow-covered ground. Aside from our gathering, there were no fresh tracks. No signs that the witches or anyone else might be lurking. I took that as one positive sign.

I also didn't see my—

A thunderous crack rent the air, followed by a snarl. I spun around, relief shooting through me. My twin stepped out from a portal, looking like a queen in her own right. Vittoria flashed an annoyed look at the werewolf entering the realm by her side.

"Domenico, mind your manners. If you ruin my sister's evening, my hand will find its way into your chest."

Wrath slanted a look in my direction but didn't say anything. Pride and Greed, however, both exploded. "What is she doing here?"

I expelled a breath. I wasn't even crowned queen yet and I already had to crush an inter-court squabble. "She is the goddess of death, your soon-to-be queen's sister. And the sole ruler of the newly reinstated House Vengeance."

"She is a murderer," Greed spat.

"A title we all share," I tossed back at him.

Pride's gaze raked over my twin. Hatred flared in those strange eyes, but I could have sworn I saw something else in them, too. Something that suspiciously looked like hurt. He held his hands up and stepped back. "Just keep her away from me."

Greed had his House dagger out, blade angled in my sister's direction. "Thank you for this gift, brother. As already decreed, I am within my rights to collect my blood retribution."

"Greed," Wrath warned. "Don't move."

I pushed my way through the princes and looked at Domenico. "Where is your sister?"

It had already been silent, but I swore all sound ceased. Even the wind. Domenico's jaw locked. "I want an oath from your prince that she will walk out of here if she so chooses."

I inclined my head and looked to Wrath. "Will you grant his request?"

My husband searched my face before turning his focus on the werewolf. Wrath was putting an enormous amount of trust in me. An action that would not go unnoticed by the other princes. "Your sister will not be taken by any House of Sin against her will."

Vittoria reached for Domenico's arm, and he allowed her to hold on. Pride didn't miss the action. And neither did Greed. He stepped forward and pointed his House dagger at Wrath. "You granted me a blood retribution. I am well within my rights to attack."

"You were granted a blood retribution for the murder of your commander," I said, my voice cold. "A murder that never occurred. Therefore, you are owed nothing. Put your dagger away. Now."

Greed's attention whipped between me and Wrath. "Vesta is dead. You saw her remains."

"Vesta is pack," I said. "You made a bargain with her family because you coveted an alliance with the wolves. You wanted her magic. Her power. Your greed got in the way of seeing how unhappy she was. How much she longed to reunite with her family."

I remembered the young wolf in the Well of Memory, the terror of being ripped from her family as a cub. The howls, the fear—it had been a true nightmare. Then there was way the wolf pup had sent a flicker of soothing energy to her papa, which made me think of the unfamiliar werewolf in the Shifting Isles, the one who'd brought my clothing before Vittoria removed my spell-lock. That wolf had altered emotions, too. Had soothed me when I was most afraid.

"Tell me everything you learned." Wrath nodded in encouragement, and I launched into the sordid tale, laying all the clues out there for Greed and his brothers.

It took some time to piece it all together, but the man whose face I couldn't see in the Well of Memory had *sounded* familiar, and after I'd ruminated over the memory in my mind, I placed his voice—Domenico's father. The young boy in the crib had been

Domenico, Vesta's half brother. After that, everything made more sense than Vesta's "murder" ever did.

While initially searching in Sicily for my sister's murderer, I found Domenico Senior in Greed's gaming den, intoxicated and gambling. That felt like a lifetime ago, but I could easily recall the pain in his eyes. His gambling seemed to be more about punishment than pleasure.

His sadness couldn't have simply been because his son shifted for the first time. But if Domenico Junior's shifting brought up memories of his firstborn, Marcella, then his descent into drinking and gambling made sense. Domenico Senior had been punishing himself for the pup he'd gambled away. He never forgave himself, and he'd sought out Greed's gambling den, probably in the hopes of seeing her. Or maybe stealing her back. But Greed had kept her busy as his commander, had kept her far away from the Shifting Isles and her pack.

Until my sister arrived, wanting an alliance with him and the wolves.

I'd wager anything that the body Greed found in his House that contained blood similar to Vesta's had been Domenico Senior. He was dead due to "pack business," just as Domenico had stated—freeing his daughter. They must have been attacked in their attempted escape, and sacrifice was an action any parent would take for their child.

"I don't know what else transpired between Greed and Domenico's pack," I said, "but I suspect there's much more to the story. But somehow, when Vesta and Domenico were in those initial meetings for the alliance Vittoria sought, they recognized each other."

Wrath stepped up beside me, his focus hard on the werewolf. "Is this true, alpha?"

"It is." Domenico looked ready to tear out everyone's throat. "And it's *our* business."

I looked at my sister. "Please. Tell Marcella it's all right to show herself."

Vittoria's attention moved to Domenico, and she gave him a tight nod. He winked in and out of existence, reappearing with another wolf. Vesta. Marcella. She was tall and lithe, but there was a deadly sort of look in her eyes that had been missing the night I'd had my spell-lock removed. There was a threat to her safety here, and she looked ready to battle if it came to it.

Standing beside Domenico, it was impossible to deny they were related. Marcella's attention darted around the small gathering before landing on Greed. "One day, you'll pay for what you did to my family."

The Prince of Greed glared at his commander. "I gave you a home. A title. A position of power. You had no right to make a fool of me."

"You kidnapped me. Do not confuse the matter by justifying anything that came after." She looked to Vittoria. "With respect, I'd like to leave, my lady."

Vittoria cocked her head, raising her hand as Greed stepped forward. "I wouldn't do that, your highness. Marcella has made her choice. You will respect it."

I moved to stand beside my twin and Marcella. "As there was no murder, I request that the blood retribution against Vittoria be deemed null and void."

"Very well." Wrath gave his brother a disgusted look. "In

light of this information, Vittoria Nicoletta is no longer an enemy of the Seven Circles. No blood retribution is in effect. And if anyone"—his attention was only on Greed—"*anyone,* decides to attack her, or the wolves, or Marcella, if any act of vengeance is brought about, they will be personally dealt with by me. Now, if all the extraneous bullshit is over, I'd like to crown my queen."

Greed's hand tightened on the dagger he didn't put away but had lowered. There was a tense beat that passed that had me holding my breath. Finally, he shoved his blade back into its sheath. "Very well."

I released a quiet breath, thankful we wouldn't have to fight. Though the dark glimmer of rage burning in Greed's eyes made me wonder if this was truly over. Or if he was simply standing down for the moment, already scheming his next move.

Vittoria flashed Greed a taunting smile before sidling up beside Envy. Both princes quietly seethed but didn't cause a scene. Thank the Divine above, we might get through this coronation without any bloodshed. Marcella quickly said her thanks to us, then she and Domenico left for the Shadow Realm, proving my theory about her being unable to travel there alone correct. A moment later Domenico returned to stand beside my twin.

With that finally settled, Wrath and I moved to the dais and faced each other.

My husband removed the crown from his head and held it up, showing it to the small crowd gathered behind us. "As a symbol of our shared rule, I offer my crown to my queen."

With a show of power that made me want to kiss him senseless, Wrath broke the crown in half using nothing but his bare hands. Goddess above he was alluring.

His mouth curved for a fraction of a second before he held the broken crown to me, nodding encouragement as my fingers closed over the shattered gold.

"With these two halves, we combine our strength. Unifying our hearts, souls, and power for the betterment of our realm." Wrath placed his half of the crown on his head. "Emilia, goddess of fury, coruler of House Vengeance, kneel, my love."

With my gaze locked onto his, I slowly went to my knees, not bothering to hide my smile as I recalled the last time I'd been in this position. The power I'd felt then, the control.

Wrath must have recalled the same thing, the cool royal mask slipped. He raked his attention over me, allowing the Sin Corridor to bolster his desire. I noted the slight bulge in his trousers a second before someone wolf-whistled in the crowd.

I twisted in time to see Envy kick Lust in the shin. I brought my attention back to my king, my love, my salvation. My equal. To hear him call me his love, to openly share our hearts and souls, I'd walk through Hell again and again.

Wrath's gaze burned with desire and pride. "Place your half of the crown on your head and rise—in front of all witnesses here—as the Queen of the Seven Circles, princess of House Wrath, and the goddess of the underworld and Shadow Realm."

I placed the crown on my head and stood. Wrath looked to the crowd. "Brothers, Vittoria, it is time for the blessing from each court of our realm."

Everyone yanked their House daggers out and pricked their fingers, shedding a drop of blood onto the snow-covered ground. My sister went last, her focus only on me as she allowed her blood to bead up and fall. Blood we'd always been warned against spilling.

Her lips moved silently, and I drew in a tense breath. I released it once I'd read what she was mouthing. *"I love you."*

I'd mouthed it back, then the ground rumbled below us. Magic threads in the colors of each demon House along with my sister's lavender whipped around me and Wrath, coiling tighter and tighter as the threads rushed around our bodies, circling our heads.

In a flash of glittering power, each of our broken crowns became whole. I reached up, brushing my fingers over the cool metal. My crown fit perfectly. Shouts rose from our family members, signaling the end of the coronation. I could scarcely believe it. I was truly queen.

"Your majesty." Wrath lifted my hand to his mouth and pressed a kiss to my knuckles.

Gluttony stepped forward and clapped his brother on the shoulder, then kissed each of my cheeks. "Welcome to the family, Queen Emilia. I hope you're ready for a feast to end them all."

A young demon woman with pale frosty-blue hair rolled her eyes as she moved through the princes. It was the reporter I'd first seen at the Feast of the Wolf. I hadn't noticed her before, perhaps she'd arrived during the murder-that-wasn't reveal. She shot Gluttony a saccharine look.

"Prince Gluttony is correct about one thing—his feast will make guests wish he'd end them all."

Gluttony's easygoing smile vanished. "My dear, if my parties had the ability to kill, I'd personally deliver your invite."

"That was as clever as your idea to lace wine with slumber root, promptly knocking all your guests out. At least that time it wasn't sheer boredom that put them to sleep." She gave him a cutting smile before dropping into a curtsy. "Once Your Majesties are settled into your coruling, I'd love to interview you both. Demons of each court are curious about the curse and if they need to worry about its return. They'd also like to know if love truly has the power to overcome all."

"Trust me, demons are not just asking about the curse's return. They live in fear some superior reporter with a penchant for snobbery will ruin their good time." Gluttony shooed her away, promptly earning a fierce glare. His smile was genuine when he turned back to us. "The coronation celebration is being held at House Lust. We've decided to combine our efforts."

Wrath shook his head and expelled a good-natured sigh. "We'll see you there."

Gluttony rubbed his hands together, a devious expression falling into place. "You know? That viper gave me a great idea—I think I'll offer her a glass of wine laced with slumber root and kick her and her assistant out. Then we'll see who thinks I'm unclever. At least we won't have to worry about your coronation party hitting the gossip columns."

"It's touching to see your concern for our privacy," Wrath deadpanned.

"Yes, well"—Gluttony flicked invisible lint off his lapel—"if she caught you two like Lust did, I doubt she'd be as discreet."

"Lust!" I searched for that miserable demon, but he'd already left the Sin Corridor. And here I'd mistakenly believed he hadn't told anyone about the boat incident in House Greed. Or perhaps the kitchens of House Wrath. Gossiping demon princes. Gluttony chuckled, and I rolled my eyes. "Go on, laugh. You've all done and seen worse. I'm sure *I'll* see worse tonight."

"Only if we're all very lucky." With a wink, Gluttony spun around and cupped his hands around his mouth, shouting over the low murmuring of conversations. "May I have everyone's attention—we meet at House Lust within the hour!"

"Wait," Wrath said, his low voice carrying over the small gathering. "There's one more matter to attend to." I gave him a questioning look. "Would you like to swear a blood oath and officially become the coruler of House Wrath?"

I glanced to my sister, who offered me a small smile and nod. Vittoria would be all right ruling our House on her own. Excitement surged inside me as I faced my husband again, removing the dagger I'd hidden under my gown.

"Yes. I'm ready to become the Princess of Wrath. Officially."

# TWENTY-NINE

**"You taste divine."** I closed my lips over the blunt end and sucked as much as I could into my mouth. I was trying to maintain *some* semblance of dignity, but devil curse me, it was *so* good. I drew back, my prize still in hand, and admired my work. "I want to lick each inch of you."

"So do I," Wrath murmured from the doorway.

I dropped the spoonful of cannoli filling I'd whipped together and burst out laughing when I noticed where his attention was. The fiend was *definitely* talking about his favorite dessert, not his wife. My bright laughter earned a wide grin from my husband as he fully entered the kitchens. We had just under an hour until we needed to be at Lust's, and according to Wrath and Envy, it was fashionable for the couple of honor to show up a little late.

We decided to come home, and while Wrath tended to the hellhounds, I came to the kitchens to make a treat for our victory. We solved the "murder" of Vesta, cleared my sister's name, and broke the curse. I couldn't be happier.

"Gluttony sent five demons to fetch us. If we don't show up to the party soon, he's threatened to come here. With everyone. And he swore he'd personally escort the columnist."

Wrath's expression hinted that he'd happily choose to fight a horde of werewolves again rather than host a party and invite all his debauched brothers to our House of Sin. I handed him the bowl of sweetened ricotta. "You have time to at least steal a little taste."

"You're right. I do." He set the bowl aside and pulled me in for a kiss. I melted against him, fully indulging in the sweet embrace. Much faster than either one of us would prefer, he drew back, his gaze dark with a carnal need that matched my own. "Much as it pains me to not lay you down and lick every inch of you this instant, we should leave."

His voice was deep, velvety. It hinted at all sorts of fantasies and desires. Ones I'd gladly welcome as reality.

I glanced longingly at the countertop, recalling the last time we'd been interrupted, then stepped out from his arms, putting distance between us. "It would certainly be unacceptable for the king and queen of sin and vice to be extremely late."

Wrath tracked me across the kitchen, his attention never leaving mine as he slowly pressed me against the table and reached down, curling his fingers around the hem of my gown and swiftly dragging it upward. He parted my legs to stand between them.

"I said we *should* leave, my lady. I never said we were going to." Wrath's clever fingers discovered I hadn't lied about my undergarments, and his attention zeroed in on that secret spot that yearned for him. He rubbed the slickness of my arousal until I whimpered from growing need. "At least not yet."

My king knelt before me, his gaze dark and wicked as he made good on his promise to lick every inch of me.

The Prince of Lust might rule over all forms of pleasure, but the exterior portion of his House of Sin was dedicated to the one he was most famous for: lust. Our carriage had only just stopped outside the circular drive when it was made clear which prince ruled this court.

Marble statues of couples engaged in passionate encounters lined the grand staircase leading to a set of oversized wooden doors. My attention traveled to a frieze of an orgy placed above the entrance, the phrase ENTER ALL carved onto it.

I smiled a little at the double meaning. Subtlety was an art form Lust refused to learn.

Wrath and I were ushered in and promptly announced to the court. We strode into the grand ballroom where lords and ladies all bowed low—one of the first and last times a rival demon court would do so when their own ruling prince was in attendance.

"Rise," Wrath said. "Tonight we celebrate Her Majesty Queen Emilia. Thank you to my brother, the Prince of Lust, for graciously hosting."

A string quartet struck up a tune, and revelers returned to their merriment.

The ballroom was unlike the crude showing of lust outside; this chamber was tasteful sensuality on every level. From the deep plum shade of the brocade wallpaper to the velvet and silk fabrics meant to bring tactile pleasure, it was easy to identify every aspect of his sin's influence. Overstuffed pillows were piled in the corners, welcoming lords and ladies of this circle to lie back and recline. To indulge in simple pleasures like food, wine, and conversation.

Of course, it wouldn't be a House of Sin and debauchery if there weren't more literal displays of lust happening.

Couples paired off both privately and publicly, submitting to physical pleasure. Swings hung from the ceiling, and more adventurous demons rode each other above the dancers swirling across the checkered limestone and marble floor below.

I hadn't visited this circle before the spell-lock, so it was all new.

Unlike the overindulgence on display at Gluttony's, Lust's ballroom and all the demons of his court exuded that same sort of sensuality that was pervasive in this room.

From the artwork Lust had chosen to the clothing and seductive glances, fluttering of lashes and...the hunt. Members of this court thrilled at the dance of seduction, almost as much as they enjoyed the actual pleasure. Ladies wore sheer gowns that offered a hint of nakedness. Lords' clothing was made of the same material—all of it designed to inspire lust, desire.

We moved through the room of politely chattering demons, taking in the full splendor of the party. One section was curtained off, and I peered through it. Here was the more daring section. Lords and ladies wore nothing but masks while they danced.

A male couple embraced each other, lost in each other's gazes. Around the outer portion of this closed-off chamber, mattresses lined the floor. Couples moved from the dance floor to the beds, continuing their seductions.

"If you'd like a mask, your majesty, that can easily be arranged." Lust grinned as I dropped the curtain back. "A password is also required to indicate consent. Would either of you like it?"

Wrath took a sip of the drink he'd snagged earlier and said

casually, "I would like to be home with my queen instead of tolerating your paltry jabs."

"Oh, I see." Lust's voice turned mocking. "You're angry because you'd like to be home jabbing your wife."

"Perhaps your idea that anyone would enjoy 'jabbing' is why you're unattached, brother."

I spotted Envy across the crowd, and he raised a glass in my direction. Help came in the most unexpected places sometimes, but I didn't care. "If you'll both excuse me."

I rushed away, leaving the brothers arguing, and swiped a glass of demonberry wine. I clinked my glass against Envy's. "Thank you for saving me from that fight."

"I figured they were having another adolescent argument involving their cocks."

"You're not wrong."

At that he grinned. "I rarely am."

"Humble, too."

"I'm a prince. Royals don't bother with something as pedestrian as humility."

I chuckled, the sound bringing another grin to the prince's lips. It was hard to believe—after everything we'd been through—that we could stand here, willingly, smiling together.

"Careful, you don't want to show too much emotion or someone might think you actually like your queen."

"I wouldn't go out of my way to stab you," he said. "So that's progress."

Now it was my turn to smile. "And I wouldn't go out of my way to incinerate you."

"Obviously you cannot wield fire magic anymore, but I appreciate the sentiment." His brows raised. "Are we... friends?"

Envy looked and sounded aghast, but somehow I felt my answer mattered. More than he'd let on. I gave him a disgusted look, not feeling disgusted at all. "It would appear so."

"How tragic."

"Indeed. I'm rather put off by it," I lied.

Envy's scowl didn't quite match the new glimmer in his eyes. It wasn't happiness—whatever dark thing he'd gone through, he hadn't healed from that—but it looked suspiciously close to contentment. It was there and gone, and I might have read it wrong, but for his sake, I hoped I was mistaken. Each of Wrath's brothers, my sister, and all our friends deserved to find their own happiness, however that looked to them.

A hush fell over the crowd as the doors swung open.

"Vittoria, goddess of death, princess of House Vengeance."

The court announcer's voice rang out, and for one short beat, the music halted.

Vittoria entered the ballroom looking the feared goddess she was. Her black gown was sheer everywhere except for carefully placed gemstones and appliques.

All eyes turned to her and lingered. She looked stunning—with her dark hair tumbling down her back in soft curls, her lips painted a brilliant red, and the confidence of a woman who owned who she was and didn't give two damns what anyone thought.

My lips twisted up. House Vengeance would certainly face some difficulties as it reestablished itself, but if anyone could handle adversity and thrive, it was my sister.

"Your majesty." Envy bent over my hand and pressed his lips to my knuckles before straightening. "I suppose it will be beneficial to have the Queen of the Seven Circles' favor."

I surveyed him closely. "That sounds ominous."

"Oh, look. You have another guest to attend to." Envy shoved Pride in front of him and flashed his dimples. "Enjoy your celebration, Lady Emilia."

Envy finished his wine and fled the ballroom, narrowly missing an encounter with Vittoria. Pride folded his arms across his chest, watching my sister accept a dance from a rather dashing demon. Pride's expression was carefully blank, but he called for another glass of sparkling wine, well before he'd finished the one he currently held.

"I hope you know what you're doing," he said, his attention still on my twin. "Nicoletta"—his teeth gritted together as he corrected himself—"*Vittoria* loves stirring up trouble."

"You seem to enjoy a good challenge. Enough to be unable to turn it down."

Pride wrenched his attention from my sister and focused on me. "Your sister and I share many commonalities. Or at least the person she pretended to be shared my interests. I do not know who she truly is, nor does it matter anymore. Nicoletta was never real. My wife was. And I fucked that up. Royally, as my brother so kindly pointed out earlier. I should have tried harder to understand her. We both knew our ways were different. It was our responsibility to attempt to bridge the divide of our upbringing and cultures."

I chose my next words carefully. "Do you think, aside from loving each other, that you and Lucia were well matched?"

Pride's gaze flickered over my shoulder. I knew, without looking, he was watching Vittoria again. Whether in hatred or something else, I didn't dare to inquire.

He shook his head and downed the rest of his wine. "Forgive me, your majesty. This evening is about you, and I've somehow gone and made it about me again. If you'll excuse me. I'm not very good company." As Envy had done, Pride bent over my hand and kissed it. "Treat my brother well."

He straightened and bowed, then strode over to the table towering high with wine. Apparently, he wouldn't be feigning intoxication this evening. Sadness crept in, but there was nothing I could do. Vittoria and Pride and Lucia needed to sort out their feelings. And be honest about them. If Lucia even wished to involve herself again.

Sloth inched his way over, looking every bit as handsome as his brothers, though he seemed ready to curl up in the corner and read a book I was fairly certain he'd smuggled into his jacket pocket. Lust would tease him endlessly if he saw it.

"Prince Sloth." I greeted him warmly. "Thank you for attending."

A slow smile tugged at his lips. "One doesn't ignore a demand from Wrath. But I am happy to have shown my support. Regardless of the past, I know you'll make a fair and just queen. None of my brothers may say it, but we all appreciate the sacrifice you made, breaking the curse."

The reminder of my loss of magic only stung marginally this time.

"Thank you. Truly." I clutched his hands in mine. "What are your plans now that the curse is broken?"

He glanced around the crowded room, pausing on where Gluttony and the columnist stood a foot apart, not speaking. "My plan is to not plan anything. To take one day at a time. This is the Seven Circles, and things change swiftly here. I like to watch what happens after the puzzle is pieced together. What happens after that last chapter? That is the part of the story I'm always most intrigued by. Who rises up next, a hero or villain? There are certainly many more tales that have yet to be told." He bowed and kissed my hand. "Your majesty."

Once he left on that curious yet ominous note, I was introduced to several high-ranking demons from House Lust. Between meeting lords and ladies, dukes and duchesses, I managed to catch sight of Fauna. She turned to Anir, and I'd have paid good coin to know what she'd said to make his brows hit his hairline.

Anir quickly set his wine aside and escorted her toward the curtained-off room. *Good for you, my friend.* I grinned. The mortal was detail-oriented enough to be Wrath's second-in-command, highly trained in battle and war, but he had missed the subtle art of seduction. Fools, the lot of them. I was proud Fauna had taken charge, going after what she wanted. I hoped tonight was the start of something wonderful for both of them.

Something I hadn't felt in what seemed like eons filled me with warmth. *Happiness.* Nonna and the Star Witches might still be plotting against us in some way, that would likely never change, and the vampires might rise up one day. But for now, Sursea was out of my life. My sister had her House of Sin back, Wrath and I were finally together, and my memories were my own again. Giving up my magic had been worth all the good that came from it.

My sinfully debonair husband stepped up beside me and brought his lips to my ear. "Would you like to go somewhere more private, my love?"

A flash of the last time we'd been at a party crossed my mind. We'd sneaked away to an empty room to make love. This time, I didn't simply recall fragments. I remembered in vivid detail how that night had gone.

Wrath's eyes twinkled as I took him by the hand and flashed a devious smile of my own. "I know just the place, my king."

# THIRTY

**House Vengeance was** a gothic castle nestled between soaring, snowcapped mountains to the south, keeping it hidden from the seven demon courts in the north.

As my sister had shown me on that magical map, its remote location and magical veil of memory loss helped keep it an enigma from the demon princes and their subjects. Only an invitation, which Vittoria and I had never extended, would grant the princes passage to the realm ruled by the goddesses of vengeance. The realm where the Maiden, Mother, and Crone were rumored to reside.

With my memories now intact, I recalled that it had been a lonely existence. One we filled by reveling in our title of the Feared.

The morning after the coronation party, I stood on the terrace of House Vengeance's castle facing the eastern gardens, icy wind whipping my unbound hair as I looked out at the familiar landscape. This had been my home for centuries. The seat of my power. This was where the great goddesses of death and fury played their vengeance games.

And now, not only had I returned as a goddess without magic, but I was also the coruler of a rival House of Sin. I might have lost my magic, but I'd certainly gained a heart, a soul. Things that now mattered more than cold, impersonal vengeance. Once upon a time, it had felt like justice. And maybe in our world, full of sin and vice, it had been. Now, having lived among mortals, I saw how wrong I'd been. There was more to life than vengeance and retribution. If we went after everyone who ever hurt or wronged us, we'd never appreciate the good in our lives.

Knowing what I did now, experiencing how it felt to focus on the good in life, to feel genuine peace, I'd never return to who I was before. My life might be long, but I still wanted to savor each bit of brightness that came my way.

"You're quiet," Vittoria said, joining me. "It's been quiet without you."

I glanced down at the wolves fighting on the snow-covered lawn. Domenico was training newly shifted werewolves, and like the damned demons, he'd forsaken his shirt despite the brutal temperature. "It looks like you'll adjust well enough."

Vittoria watched the alpha work through a series of kicks and punches, her expression purposely emotionless. "They can't stay. The pack needs to be on the Shifting Isles with the rest of their families. They need to ensure that the Star Witches maintain balance and only guard the prison. It's time they left this realm alone."

"You could go with them."

"I fought hard for us to get back here, to our rightful home." Vittoria looked me over. "House Vengeance is where I belong. Where I'll stay." A small smile ghosted across her features. "Plus, I need to be close by in case my sister needs me. Your king might not sanction the messier parts of ruling. Which is why you'll have me."

She wriggled her fingers, and I shook my head. "Goddess help the demons."

"And the witches." Vittoria glanced back down at the wolves. "Thank you for finding the evidence I needed to clear my name. And for trusting in me even when I didn't make it easy."

"It would have happened much sooner if you'd just told me the truth."

"It wasn't my secret to share. Plus, I wasn't sure if Vesta—Marcella—was pack at first, but I knew Domenico was hiding something. During that first meeting, when I'd persuaded him to accompany me to secure an alliance with Greed, he'd stiffened the moment they were in the room together. There were only the four of us that night, and it hadn't been me or Greed he'd responded to. I suspected Domenico had hatched a plan and carried it out, based on the timing of Vesta's 'murder' and the arrival of Marcella to the pack, but I didn't want to draw attention to him."

"You didn't recognize her?"

"Initially, she cast a convincing glamour. That, mixed with her ability to change the emotions of those around her, kept me from questioning her for a little while. Once I figured out the truth and she stopped hiding her identity, it wasn't my place to force her to return. Besides, I wouldn't betray Domenico. Even if that meant keeping the truth from you."

For a goddess who was supposed to only be out for vengeance, my sister took the blame when she easily could have given Domenico to Greed. "Do you like him, the shifter?"

"It doesn't really matter if I do." She lifted a shoulder. "He'll live longer than most, but he's not immortal. One day, many moons from now, he'll realize that he's changing and I am not. Domenico needs to be with someone who will grow old with him. And I need to be with someone I can aggravate for eternity. That is, if I choose a partner rather than simply enjoy myself on my own terms."

"Does that special someone rule over the sin of envy or pride?"

Vittoria snorted. "Envy wishes he could hold my attention for eternity. I might be curious about rumors I've heard regarding his sexual talents, but that would be a passing fancy." Her eyes sparkled as I squeezed my eyes shut, not wanting to think of Envy's *talents*. "I've heard his—"

"Please, I do not want to hear any rumors about Envy. I've already heard about the portrait painted above his bed, the one where it shows how well-endowed he is."

"Devil be damned." Vittoria tossed her head back and laughed. It was the first time she'd sounded like her old, mortal self, and it gave me hope for the future. "I thought he was kidding about that painting. I should have taken him up on his offer to use his bedchamber."

I noticed she hadn't said anything about Pride, but I didn't point that out. It was a wound that clearly hadn't scabbed over. Even if he didn't desire her in any romantic way, I suspected Vittoria did feel differently. Something else I'd been curious about resurfaced. "When you got your goddess magic back, did you recognize Lucia?"

Almost imperceptivity, my sister tensed. "Did you tell her?"

"No. I did give her the memory stone back, though. She ought to be the one to decide her future."

Silence spread between us, broken only by the faint echoes of the training going on below. Instead of metal swords clashing, the sound of claws scratching stone and flesh drifted up. When my sister still didn't say anything, I continued on.

"If you did form an attachment with Pride, and if Lucia truly doesn't want to be with him, you ought to sit down and tell him the truth. Without games or lies."

"I do not wish to be his wife."

"No one said you did," I said. "What *do* you want? Now that you've got our House back."

My sister thought it over for a quiet moment, her attention never leaving the alpha training below. "I want to focus on rebuilding our House. I wish to settle our court and earn back our subjects' trust. And I do not want to answer any more questions about that wretched prince. Thinking of Pride makes me want to tear out hearts and stomp on them." We both cracked a grin at her outburst, but I didn't press the issue. "What about you, dear sister? What in the name of everything good and sinister possessed you to give up your magic?"

"It was either that or the curse would remain intact forever."

"No," Vittoria said, a rare bout of anger lacing her voice, "killing Sursea was a viable option. One your prince should have mentioned."

"She's immortal."

"And *I* am the goddess of death. Even your powerful husband succumbed to Death's poison. Until Mother interfered with her tonic." Vittoria's lips twisted in a cruel smirk. "Anyway, our mother is the Crone. Do you truly believe she couldn't have assisted us in murdering a single witch, even one blessed with immortality?"

"Her niece," I reminded my sister. "Celestia would not have killed family."

"You forget our mother has an issue with pride, herself. She would never allow someone to destroy her favorite creations. Us, this realm, we all live in the world she made. It's larger than just you and me." Vittoria's lavender eyes flashed. "And you gave up your power for him."

I was surprised she'd felt that way, but it was far from the truth. I gave myself a few beats to gather my thoughts, to make her understand why my choice empowered *me*.

I dropped my attention back to the wolves. They were now fully shifted and running through their drills. "I chose to end a curse that would have kept me caged for eternity. I gave up my power for freedom, to right a wrong I'd helped to create, intentional or not. I did not give up my magic for one demon. Though following my heart was the right path, at least for me. When I considered the paths open to me, I could live without magic, but I couldn't imagine giving up everything else I loved to hold on to it. I chose the path that offered me the life I want to live."

My sister shook her head but didn't continue arguing. It was all right for her to feel differently, to choose a different path. I didn't have to agree with all her choices, and she didn't have to agree with each of mine, either. That didn't mean we didn't still love and respect each other fiercely. We were twins, but we were our own goddesses.

"I chose happiness over fear," I finally said. "And I'd choose it again without any regrets."

Vittoria expelled a long breath, the cold air creating little clouds in front of her. "Then I am truly happy for you, Emilia." She turned mischievous eyes on me. "And if you need anything, anything at all, you'll always have me."

# THIRTY-ONE

**Wrath's wings of** flame burned brightly against the twilight sky. We stood facing each other in the gardens of House Wrath near the statue that—I'd suspected, and finally had confirmed—represented a feared goddess Wrath had never allowed himself to forget. Our left hands were clasped together, palm to palm, our matching *SEMPER TVVS* tattoos lined up as if to remind us we'd given our hearts to each other forever.

The king of demons wore a suit of black, though he'd fastened an orange blossom to his lapel, a nod to the flowers I'd once again threaded into my unbound hair.

My pearl-colored gown was sleeveless, a beautiful silk edged with the most delicate lace, but the frosty cold never touched my skin. A fine perk of having a husband with such unusual wings. It felt as if a fireplace traveled with us, even during a storm.

Thankfully, the snow had stopped for our bonding ceremony, though dark clouds gathered overhead, a warning that the calm would not last.

Anir and Fauna stepped forward as our witnesses to the old gods, each holding one end of a vine with thorns. It was more twine than inflexible vine as they slowly wove it through our hands, then up around our wrists, tying us together, both literally and symbolically.

Once the knots were tested and tightened, our friends moved back. Fauna's eyes misted, and Anir blinked furiously. The two sentimental fools had my own eyes tearing up.

Wrath waited to speak until my gaze met his. "When I first saw you again, I hated you."

I burst out laughing and shook my head. "Ever the romantic one, dear husband. Just like the heroes in my favorite romance novels, you know precisely how to win the object of your affection over."

"Now you know why he's a demon of action, not words, Em," Anir called out.

The demon's lips twitched. "I hated you because in that moment, I remembered. Just as the witch said I would. For the first time in years, my memories of you came flooding back. Instead of recognition or relief, I sensed your fear, then your fury, and I'd realized the curse hadn't been broken. That there was only a slight crack. I hated you because you'd become one of the very creatures who'd torn us apart. You'd adopted their ways. You despised me; I felt it each time you were near. I vowed to leave you to your own choices, to stand aside while you sorted through your own path, even if that meant you'd choose to be a Star Witch."

A darkness crossed my husband's features.

"When I'd met that human boy in the monastery, Antonio, I was prepared to leave you forever. But then you'd said my true name, and I wondered. Perhaps you did remember, somewhere deep inside. Perhaps there was something the curse hadn't corrupted." His expression shifted again as if this admission cost him. "I told you to never call me Samael again, not because you'd said my name, but because I did not want your witch family to use it against us. If they knew we'd found each other again, against all odds, I hated to think what they might do to tear us apart."

"I'd wondered about that."

"The curse kept me from saying certain things, as you know. Which ultimately gave us an opportunity to get to know each other all over again. We were both different in some ways. I wasn't sure if we'd still fit as we used to. But little by little, you slipped inside."

I smiled at that. "Once, when I'd found myself in your mind after the Viperidae attack, I felt your fear. I had the impression I was like a splinter, burrowing under your skin."

"It did feel that way." Wrath's deep chuckle was unexpected and warm. "I'd wanted vengeance against Sursea, and I wanted my wings back more than anything." His magnificent wings flapped to punctuate the point. "Somewhere along the way, I started to want something else more. You. I didn't simply want your body. I wanted your heart. Your mind. I wanted a partner. A confidante. Someone to walk through hell with, and someone who could also show me heaven. Someone unafraid to challenge me, who called me on my shit. I wanted my equal. Fury."

My attention shifted to the fiery wings that seemed to have grown in flame and in heat when he said my true name. "I'm still Fury, just with a little less fire."

A secret smile touched his lips. "When a bond is fully accepted by both parties, we will share all things in life. I accept our bond. I give my heart, my soul, my power to thee."

The vine on Wrath's hand sank into his skin, the magic flashing like a star streaking across the universe. All I had to do was utter those same words, then we'd be bonded for eternity. This time it would be a choice made by each of us. No magic involved.

"I fell in love with you slowly, though I'd always found you frustratingly attractive." Anir and Fauna both snickered at my admission. "Something I'm sure you sensed. When I'd come here and discovered the Sin Corridor and the subtle magic of this world, a glimmer of excitement flared to life inside me. I hadn't been ready to admit it to myself, let alone to you, but I'd been grateful for a chance to finally act on feelings I'd been desperate to ignore." I inhaled deeply. "It might have been cowardly, but I needed time to sort everything out. You never rushed me. Or tried to force my hand. I'd been falling for you, but I knew it was something special after I'd stabbed you."

"Ever the romantic one, my love." Wrath deadpanned, using my words from earlier.

"It was the first time we'd set boundaries. And it was important to me. I wanted to see how you'd react, if you'd ever repeat that action. You didn't. Even when you had more information, even when you could see potential curves in the road I couldn't, you never once overstepped again. You respected that boundary, respected an established rule between us, and I knew I would have a true partner, should I choose a relationship with you. Not an imperfect one, but someone who'd own his shit and not attempt to make up for it, but to put setting it right from there on out into actions. To show me I could trust you moving forward."

"You both need to work on your declarations of love," Anir said, not unkindly. Fauna elbowed him in the side, and he promptly closed his mouth.

"I love you, Samael. The good parts, the bad, and all the parts in between. Each messy piece—" Wrath raised a brow at the mention of "messy," and I rolled my eyes. "I choose you today, tomorrow, and every day thereafter. I accept our bond. I give my heart, my soul, my power to thee."

The vines on my hand flashed as brightly as they had for Wrath and settled under my skin. We both now bore one more tattoo—the vines with thorns would forever show we were tied together, more than just husband and wife. We were bonded soul to soul. Because we chose to be.

Wrath drew me close and kissed me deeply, then smiled against my lips. "Do you recall when I said we'd share *everything*?"

"I do." My eyes narrowed as his grin widened. "What scheme are you working on now?"

He whispered something in an ancient tongue, one I couldn't speak but knew was angelic. Once he'd finished his speech, he leaned in and whispered, "As above, so below. We are now truly balanced in all ways. My ice to your fire."

"But I no longer—"

Wrath's wings flared brilliantly, the fire burning hot enough to make the air around us shimmer from the heat. The gold and silver flecks in his wings pulsed, and I watched silently as they flickered in and out like stars. It was beautiful and—

In a flash, the fire and the color drained from his wings. It looked as if someone had upturned a bottle of ink and ebony liquid slowly dripped down the feathers, replacing the fire with darkness. While the fire faded, I noticed something else, something oddly familiar that began as a small flutter in my center. The very place where my magic had once dwelled.

"What..." I clutched my stomach as the flutter grew.

One more flash of power, a streak of lightning crossing a stormy sky, and the fire of Wrath's wings were completely snuffed out. My knees buckled as the power rushed into me, filled me. My husband held me tightly until the last bit of his power settled into me.

Tears I hadn't known were falling dampened his lapel. In my center, where Source had lived, I felt magic. I drew back, staring at his wings. Where they were once white and silver flames, they were now a glittering black. They looked like his *luccicare.*

"What have you done?" I asked, my voice a mere whisper.

Wrath kissed the top of my head. "What's mine is yours, my love. I told you I had enough magic for both of us." And he'd given half of it to me. The tears came harder, and he kissed each of them away. "Call upon your power, Fury."

I wiped my tears away and tested that new, churning well of magic. *"Fiat lux."*

Burning flowers burst into the sky above us, larger and more powerful than ever. I'd expected the magic to be silver and gold and white. But it was still my rose-gold. The magic might have come from my husband, but it truly was *mine.*

"Thank you," I whispered. Wrath wrapped me in his arms, staring up at the flowers burning across the sky. They were like our own personal stars. "Thank you for giving up your wings for me."

Wrath's wings shot out to either side, flapping hard enough to kick up snow. "I didn't give anything up. I have my wings. I have my wife. And I have some very interesting ideas about our new bedroom design. I'd like to test them out first, though."

"We'll take that as our cue to leave," Anir said. "Congratulations to you both."

He kissed each of my cheeks and clapped his king on the back before Wrath hooked an arm around him and hugged him properly. Fauna dipped into a curtsy, but I pulled her in for a tight hug instead, too. She held me back fiercely. "We must speak soon, my lady."

"Are you free tomorrow?" I asked. Fauna nodded. "Let's meet then. I want to know *everything* that happened at the coronation ball."

Fauna's eyes twinkled. "I'll have tea and brandy cake ready."

Once our friends left the garden, I faced Wrath again. He was a devious, scheming demon. And I couldn't imagine loving him more. "Does your bedroom design involve ways to utilize those wings?"

A wicked gleam entered his gaze. "Not exactly. But we can add that to our list of requirements."

"What other items are on your list?"

He held his hand out. "How about I show you, my lady?"

The instant I placed my hand in his, Wrath magicked us to his private library. I surveyed the empty room. A fire crackled pleasantly; the candles on the chandelier had been almost all blown out, adding a soft, sensual feeling to the private room. At first, I wasn't sure why he'd chosen this chamber, then my attention snagged on the alcove where a pair of manacles hung. Heat pooled low in my belly as anticipation swirled through me. He couldn't mean . . .

Wrath moved behind me, lightly running his hands down my arms, then slowly dragging them back up again. Each stroke felt like magic and had my body craving more. "Do you remember when you asked if I'd be willing to tie you up?"

Goddess curse me, I did. "Yes. You were about to freeze us both to death. I had to find *some* way to distract you."

He pressed a kiss to the back of my neck, the sensation causing the peaks of my breasts to ache, needing his touch. "It wasn't your request that caught my attention, but the arousal I sensed." His hands slowly worked my bodice down. "Much like what I'm sensing now."

His thumb stroked over the little nub of my breast. I reached back, threaded my hand in his hair as he bent forward to kiss along my neck, my shoulder. I arched against him, feeling the proof of his own arousal hard against my backside. Wicked demon.

"Be careful what you wish for, wife. Your husband might be depraved enough to deliver."

I turned in the circle of his arms and wet my lips, drawing his hunter's gaze right where I wanted it. "I should hope so. I'd hate for things to get boring or predictable between us."

Wrath chuckled darkly, his expression promising to torture me in the best of ways for that sassy comment. "That mouth..." His attention fell to my lips like he had some very wicked ideas for it indeed. "Will ensure things remain interesting. For a very long time."

He cast a ward around his personal library, then turned his fierce, hungry focus on me again. No one would hear my screams of pleasure. Or his moans. Because I swore to myself I'd have him shouting loud enough to reach every House of Sin.

My immortal heart went from thumping to galloping in my chest as he backed me into the alcove. The heat that started gently spread like wildfire through my body. His lips curved with the hint of a sardonic smile. "You twisted, dark angel. I haven't even touched you, and you're more aroused than ever."

I dropped my attention to the strained material of his trousers. "Seems to be a problem we share, husband."

"We are lucky, indeed." Wrath admired me for a beat, his attention moving across my face, before dropping to take in my bare breasts. He dipped his head and sucked a bud into his mouth, flicking his tongue until I writhed against him. "I'm going to give you everything you desire."

"Dangerous proclamation." I wanted to spend hours submitting to every devious, debauched thing I craved from my husband.

"How dangerous would you like me to be?" He trailed a finger between my breasts, following a line down my middle. Goddess-cursed demon, he stopped right below my belly button.

"Do your worst, your majesty. I'm ready for every twisted, dark thing you can dream up."

With a flick of his wrist, my gown disappeared. Wrath's clothing followed next. His raw masculine sensuality sent a searing ripple of heat through me as he looked me over again; this time there was strategy in his gaze. Like he'd taken this particular challenge personally.

"One thing I can promise you." Wrath stepped forward and clasped a manacle around one of my wrists. He bent to whisper in my ear, his breath sending pleasant goose bumps along my body as he slowly took my other wrist in hand. "I can be very, *very* wicked, my love."

Of that I had little doubt.

I allowed my gaze to drift over the pale tattoo written along his collarbone. *Acta non verba.* It was the perfect reminder that now was the time for action, not words. I rattled my chains, enjoying the way his gaze snagged on my body right before he hoisted my leg up.

A smile teased the edges of my lips. "It's high time you *showed* me, demon."

Wrath's ebony wings shot out to either side. He looked like sin incarnate, and as his magic enveloped me, I thanked the goddess he was mine.

# ACKNOWLEDGMENTS

This entire trilogy was launched, written, and concluded during a global pandemic, yet it still found its home in the world because of YOU. Thank you, dear reader, for loving these characters and this sin-fueled world so much. I absolutely adore the Seven Circles and am so grateful you followed Wrath and Emilia on this treacherous journey through the underworld. Thank you a thousand, million times over for your support and for championing these books. I'm so happy they were able to take you away from the chaotic state of the world for a few hours.

Many thanks to my publishing team for turning my dreams into a reality. Barbara Poelle, agent, friend, and goddess extraordinaire, thank you for the many hats you wear and for all that you do behind the scenes. The whole crew at Irene Goodman Agency. Heather Baror-Shapiro for getting these books translated into more languages than I could ever dream possible. To Sean Berard at Grandview.

My champions at Little, Brown Books for Young Readers, a giant thank-you to my editor Alexandra Hightower who worked around the clock with me to get this into readers' hands, despite complications with the supply chain and an extremely tight schedule. Her notes made this book exactly what I'd hoped it could be and more. Cheers to amazing teamwork, Alex! Alvina Ling, Cassie Malmo, Savannah Kennelly, Stefanie Hoffman, Emilie Polster,

Victoria Stapleton, Marisa Finkelstein, Tracy Koontz, Tracy Shaw, Virginia Lawther, Danielle Cantarella, Shawn Foster, Claire Gamble, Karen Torres, Barbara Blasucci, Carol Meadows, Janelle DeLuise, Siena Koncsol, and my publishers Megan Tingley and Jackie Engel. Thank you for so much in-house support and excitement!

My UK Team at Hodder & Stoughton—Molly Powell, Kate Keehan, Laura Bartholomew, Natasha Qureshi, Callie Robertson, Sarah Clay, Iman Khabl: you are all such treasures to work with. I hope I added enough spice. ☺

To my family, it's hard to believe this is the seventh time I've gotten to write out acknowledgments. I love you all more than words can express. As always, special shout-out to my sister Kelli and her boutique (Dogwood Lane Boutique) for all of the inspiration. (And retail therapy.)

Booksellers, librarians, indies, book boxes and every book business both large and small in between, thank you for your unending support. BookTok—I adore you! Special shout-out to Ayman Chaudhary (@Aymansbooks) and Pauline (@thebooksiveloved) for their amazing videos and early support of this series.

Stephanie Garber, Isabel Ibañez, Samira Ahmed—you are all rock star authors and, most importantly, incredible humans. Anissa de Gomery—your friendship brightens my days! I'm so happy to call each of you dear friends. Thank you for all of the texts and calls and love. Through deadlines and pandemics and regular life, you are the best.

Thank you for reading all the way to the end. I cannot wait to see what wicked adventure comes next…xoxo.

# ABOUT THE AUTHOR

**Kerri Maniscalco** grew up in a semi-haunted house outside New York City, where her fascination with gothic settings began. In her spare time, she reads steamy romance novels, cooks all kinds of food with her family and friends, and drinks entirely too much tea while discussing life's finer points with her cats. She is the author of two #1 *New York Times* bestselling series, the Stalking Jack the Ripper quartet and the Kingdom of the Wicked series. She's always excited to share snippets of her projects on Instagram @KerriManiscalco. For news and updates, she invites you to check out kerrimaniscalco.com.

# *Investigate*

the deadly world of

*#1 New York Times* bestselling author

# KERRI MANISCALCO

BOBI014

# The Seven Circles

Violent Winds

House Lust

The Gates of Hell

Sin Corridor

The Lake of Fir

House Wrath

The Black River

KINGDOM OI